BLACK RAIN
FALLING

ALSO BY JACOB ROSS

Song for Simone and Other Stories

A Way to Catch the Dust and Other Stories

Pynter Bender

The Bone Readers

Tell No-One About This

Behind the Masquerade, the Story of Notting Hill Carnival
(with Kwesi Owusu)

Voice, Memory, Ashes: Lest We Forget
(co-edited with Joan Anim-Addo)

Ridin' n Risin: Short Stories by New Black Writers

Turf (co-edited with Andrea Enisuoh)

Closure: Contemporary Black British Short Stories

The Peepal Tree Book of Contemporary Caribbean Short Stories
(Jeremy Poynting, Jacob Ross)

JACOB ROSS

BLACK RAIN FALLING

sphere

SPHERE

First published in Great Britain in 2020 by Sphere

1 3 5 7 9 10 8 6 4 2

A CIP catalogue record for this book
is available from the British Library.

Hardback ISBN 978-0-7515-7444-9
C-format ISBN 978-0-7515-7443-2

Typeset in Bembo by M Rules
Printed and bound in Great Britain by
Clays Ltd, Elcograf S.p.A.

Papers used by Sphere are from well-managed forests
and other responsible sources.

Sphere
An imprint of
Little, Brown Book Group
Carmelite House
50 Victoria Embankment
London EC4Y 0DZ

An Hachette UK Company
www.hachette.co.uk

www.littlebrown.co.uk

To Adrian 'Straight Nose' Bierzynski
for your tragedy and your genius

ACKNOWLEDGEMENTS

With gratitude to Ed Wood, Sphere Editor, without whose feedback on structure and procedure this book would not have been as fully realised as it is.

I'm beholden to Jeremy Poynting for his wonderfully perceptive feedback and for nudging me down this path.

And to my friend Dave Martin, whose unerring eye for contradictions and structure made a major difference in the refinement of this book.

You can't put the past behind you.
It's buried in you.

Claudia Rankine

1

One thing I learned from my two years fighting crime in Camaho – sometimes, to uphold the law, you need to break the fuckin rules.

Five days after I arrested a police officer for drink-driving and much worse, Miss Stanislaus, my partner in San Andrews CID, shot down Juba Hurst – the man who raped her as a child. The trouble I started was nothing compared to hers. And there was no way I was going to let her face the consequences on her own. That's me, Michael Digger Digson. It is the way I'm wired.

I'd spent all Sunday in the north of the island with my friend, Caran, who headed a semi-military unit of four: three fellas and a woman named Toya Furore – Caran's lieutenant. We called them the Bush Rangers. They had the gun skills and bush-craft of soldiers, the arresting powers of the police and the deductive skills of detectives.

Detective Superintendent Chilman, our old boss, had handpicked Caran and his crew to patrol the gloomy interior of the island. Fit, fast and armed, they'd stay out in the mountains for weeks if they had to, turfing out ganja growers, bush-meat hunters, murderers and the occasional jail-breaker who ran for the mists and high forests of Camaho. Caran's Bush Rangers could navigate the island in their sleep. They were legends in the north of the island.

As usual I'd spent the first hour with Caran puzzling over what Detective Superintendent Chilman had done to us. The old fella, we decided, was a bagful of contradictions: he'd resigned from the Force a couple of years ago, but still came in to San Andrews CID to run our lives. He was a full-time drunk with a brain that had no room for bullshit and a tongue that stung like a syringe. The old fella had spent thirty years in the Police Force and he despised his colleagues because they were so useless at tackling crime. In fact, the old fella believed they were the cause of the crime sometimes. Like that young Canadian tourist who was walking her dog on one of the isolated beaches on the western coast and got accosted and murdered by a youngfella that the police had arrested only a couple of hours earlier for assault. The superintendent who'd ordered the killer's immediate release was a relative.

Chilman decided he'd had enough. He couldn't change the Police Force, but he could create his own team 'by any and all means necessary'. That meant breaking every recruitment rule.

He picked me up off the streets in San Andrews. I was nineteen, I'd just left school with no job – despite my qualifications – and no prospect of one. A street killing changed my luck. My crime was simply being there. Chilman spotted me on the sidewalk busy doing nothing. He arrested me and brought me to his office. Join the new CID unit he was forming or face time in jail, he said. And I knew he was not joking.

He picked up Chief Officer Malan on Grand Beach with a shopping bag of marijuana, peddling the stuff to tourists. Fourteen years in prison and an unlimited fine or full employment with perks and prospects was Chilman's offer to Malan Greaves. And there was Spiderface, arrested with a bale of ganja in his boat. Spiderface gave the coast guard so much hell before they caught him that Chilman was impressed enough to reward him with gainful employment.

He must've said something different to Miss Stanislaus, his daughter. 'Best brains on the island,' he told us when he dumped the woman on the Department. Pet and Lisa – trainee admins in another department – were invited to lunch and never went back to their old jobs.

'Fuckin blackmail,' I'd shot at the old fella once, in a fit of irritation.

'Talent spotting,' he'd retorted. 'Look at y'all record, Digson! One thousand police officers serving the island, sixteen stations throughout the parishes, and San Andrews CID got the best crime-busting record in Camaho two years running. No wonder the whole damn Police Force want to mash us up. Including the Justice Minister!'

I'd left Caran's little house feeling good with the food Mary, his wife, had fed me. I was shaking my head and chuckling at his stories about the mysteries of Camaho's forests: boiling springs that gushed from crevices in the rocks, voices he swore they heard on the wind up there in the mountains, the shadowy creatures they often glimpsed, and Princess Orchids that fed on the sap of forest trees and killed them. At the end of it he'd nudged me with an elbow. 'Beautiful t'ings, Digger. Beautiful t'ings does kill.'

He'd directed his chin at his wife and grinned at her. Mary burst out laughing and tossed her kitchen towel in his face.

It was dusk by the time I came off the murderous mountain road of Grand Etang onto River Road, which would take me into San Andrews town. A line of vehicles stretched ahead of me as far as the old iron bridge that hung over the sea. Blaring horns and shouting a few yards ahead.

I pulled up on the side of the road, left my car and followed the noise. A man was pinned up against a Nissan minibus by a mob. The windscreen was a spiderweb of punched-in glass. The vehicle was skewed across the road with its engine running. About three yards ahead, a group of chattering teenagers were comparing phone footage of what looked like the mangled remains of a body. A slim-boned, detached arm with five copper bracelets told me it was a woman. About twenty-five, I guessed. The rest of the woman, I was told, was scattered along the stretch of road.

I walked into the crowd, raised my ID and ordered them to disperse. They shuffled back a couple of feet, with agitated voices.

I knew the fella. He was a constable from San Andrews Police Central, locked down to a desk job because of a prosthetic leg. There was a story floating in the Force about his wife and a lover she flaunted in his face.

Someone had already called the ambulance. No one phoned the police.

I called Recovery – a three-man unit that Detective Superintendent Chilman had created for situations such as these – fellas who would think nothing of eating their dinner with their plates sitting on a cadaver. They used to be gravediggers.

'DC Digson here. This one is a scrape-up job. Four hours' worth of work.'

I gave them the coordinates and turned to the officer. He was stinking of alcohol. 'So what happen?'

People must have read my lips.

'He knock down the woman, drivin' drunk. He murder her. The woman got two lil children and . . . fucker drag she all de way from—'

I raised a cautioning hand at the speaker – a youngfella with his hair pulled out in tufts like a fluffy porcupine. His voice was lava-hot and raking.

'You, Digshun, frum Shandrooz She-Eye-Dee, nuh so? I didn see 'er. I could'uv swear was, was a dog I hit, man.'

'So, you run over a dog, and you keep driving?'

'Naah, fella, I—'

'Don't fuckin "fella" me! Address me by my rank and name. You stinking drunk and you driving! You should be first to know is a criminal offence.'

I turned to face the crowd. 'Who witnessed this?'

Four youths stepped forward with lit-up smart phones.

I took the handsets and stuffed them in my pocket. 'Collect them tomorrow from San Andrews CID.' I ignored their protests. 'Anybody actually saw the accident?'

A man raised his hand – short, oily face, big eyes. I took his details.

I turned back to the officer. 'If you dunno it yet, I arresting y'arse. I want jail for you. I want the maximum for you.'

'O Gorsh, Digshun. I'z a officer too.'

'That makes it worse!' I handcuffed him and dragged him into my car.

By the time I got to San Andrews Central station, I was close to throwing up. My car stank of the officer. He'd clearly pissed himself and was a mumbling wreck on the back seat.

I dragged him out and carried him inside. I demanded the keys from the duty officer – a bug-eyed youngfella with a loose mouth, who dropped his gaze on the crumpled man then fixed my face. He looked confused, moved his lips as if he were about to say something, but then changed his mind. He followed me to the cell. I opened it, dumped Buso inside, then locked him in.

'I'm DC Digson – people call me Digger,' I told him. 'San Andrews CID.'

'Missa Digger, you sure—'

'I more than sure. This officer just killed a woman. He said he mistook her for a dog. Look at him – drunk no arse and driving.' I pocketed the keys.

The young man pointed at my pocket. I ignored him, pulled out my notebook and spent a few minutes writing. I tore out the page and held it out to him. 'What's your name?'

'Kent, Sir.'

'You new here, right?' He nodded and took the page.

'Make sure the Superintendent gets this,' I said.

'The, erm, keys, Missa Digger ...' He was chewing his lower lip and throwing glances in the direction of the cells. A low hum came from down the corridor. A gargled hymn from Buso – 'Rock of Ages' ...

'I keeping the keys,' I said and strode out of the building.

2

I was up at seven, a cup of hot cocoa in my hand, looking down from my veranda at the houses in Old Hope village spread across the hillside on which we lived. Directly ahead were the foothills, pulling my gaze all the way up to the Mardi Gras mountains – purple-dark in the early light. Last night's accident was sitting on my mind.

At nine o'clock exactly I received a call from Staff Superintendent Gill of San Andrews Central Police Station. He demanded the keys to the cells in the building. Didn't I know that a police officer never arrested another officer in public no matter what they did? And they certainly didn't lock them up overnight and take away the keys. Where did I get my training? Who the hell did I think I was?

'Detective Constable Digson, Sir! San Andrews CID!' I retorted. 'Two years serving, and I'm asking you to read the report I left with your duty officer before you start to insult me.'

'That's no excuse,' he snapped. 'I want the keys. When you bringing it in?'

'When I ready,' I replied and hung up.

I left my house at 11am, the jail keys in my pocket. I could smell the ocean from my place in Old Hope – the long cane valley that ran all the way down to the sea. Already the hills crackled with a strange high heat. All month it had been like this: dry, dusty, sapping; the air filled with the lament of suffering livestock that were hugging the shadows of the trees and hills. I could see the brown flooring of the forest receding all the way to the hilltops. With all that dryness a pusson felt afraid to strike a match, and I worried at the sight of smoke.

I took the long road to the office in San Andrews.

Chief Officer Malan called. I didn't pick up.

Five minutes later, Office Admin, Pet, texted me: *wh r u?* I didn't reply.

The chief officer phoned again. I ignored him. Then Miss Stanislaus's number popped up. 'G'morning, Miss Stanislaus. How you?'

I imagined her at her desk in one of her glorious lily-patterned Monday-morning dresses, the window light on her hands and face, the phone poised delicately against an ear.

'Count five,' she said. It was her way of telling me she wanted to talk in private. Now, I could tell by the background noises that she'd stepped out of the office and was in the concrete courtyard.

'Missa Digger, you askin for trouble?' she said.

'Nuh.'

'Why you lock up de policefella?'

'He killed a woman last night, Miss Stanislaus. Drunk driving, and he's not getting away with it just because he's an officer.'

'I didn know,' she said.

'That's because it is not on the news. San Andrews Central will bury it as usual.'

'You plannin to fight them?'

'That's for the family of the victim to do. Ask Pet to get a lawyer who's prepared to take the case on a no-win, no-fee

8

basis – pro bono, they call that. I'll give Pet the details when I get in.'

'Send it now.' Miss Stanislaus's tone had changed.

I pulled up the car, consulted my notes and sent the details through my phone.

The whole department was there when I walked in, clearly waiting for me. DS Chilman sat near the door, his elbows on his knees, his mouth twisted in a tight worried knot. The two office admins, Pet and Lisa, were side by side, their desks facing the door. Chief Officer Malan had wheeled his chair out of his office. He sat straight-backed in a pressed blue shirt following my movements with steady, vicious eyes. An officer in uniform was on a chair next to him.

Miss Stanislaus, in a beautiful sea-green dress, looked relaxed at her desk, her gaze directed through the window at the marketplace below. For a moment, she rested those big brown eyes on my face and then turned back to the window.

'What take you so long?' Malan grated.

I lifted my shoulders and dropped them, pulled a chair and sat down. 'What's the upset?'

The chief officer exploded. 'How you mean what's the upset! That's the best you kin do? You lock up an officer, take the key an' walk! And you asking, what the upset is?'

'What makes Officer Buso different from any other person out there in Camaho?'

'Digger, you can't go arresting officers, jusso. Y'all doing the same blasted job!'

'Malan, you shouting. Chill! You didn answer my question. Answer it.'

He shot to his feet, pushed out a hand. 'Gimme de keys!'

'Nuh! Not yet. And get outta my face, Malan!'

DS Chilman cleared his throat – a wet, threatening sound.

Malan retreated. Miss Stanislaus turned from the window to take us in with an irritated, sidewise look.

'Answer my question,' I said.

'Where y'ever hear about police arresting police? Is de same Force. You want to start a civil war?'

A flush of anger ran through me. 'A police officer stinking drunk and driving run into a woman on the roadside. Woman went to buy some milk for her two children. The youngest child is two years old. The other one is six. Officer lost control of the vehicle and hit her. He so drunk he say he thought it was a dog. Didn stop for half a mile. Recovery had to scrape her off the road. Put yourself in my place, Malan. What you would've done?'

'Why you didn take him aside?'

'For what?'

'Nuff of this!' Miss Stanislaus's voice cut through. She pulled her handbag, plucked a tissue and began to fan her face.

'I still say he deserve different treatment!'

'Not from me,' I said.

DS Chilman came to his feet. 'Okay, Digson! So you upset! You not happy, what you got in mind?'

'Like I say, the woman got two children left behind. Ain got no law in Camaho that exempt police. I prepared to make a statement on that woman's behalf in court.'

'It not going to go to court,' Malan said.

Pet shook her head, then looked at Lisa with a wide-eyed, appalled expression. Pet hadn't lost her cool yet, but I had no doubt that she was getting there.

Miss Stanislaus swung around to face Malan. 'Scuse me, Missa Malan, you wrong! It got to go to court and if it don' want to go to court, I going make it go to court.'

They locked eyes, a tight-lipped unflinching stare from Miss Stanislaus. Malan's was dark-eyed and clenched. He could barely disguise his hostility towards Miss Stanislaus. He'd never recovered from her first day at the office when he tried to humiliate her. I'd never seen anything like the fury in those big brown eyes when she cut him down: told him about his womanising ways, the young wife he hid from the world and the child he'd anchored her at home with – all in a coupla minutes and without ever meeting him before. It shocked his arse to realise so much of his private life was in full view to a person who knew what to look for. It shocked me too. Made disciples of Pet and Lisa.

Chilman spread his palm in front of me, the rum-yellow eyes on mine. I pulled out the keys and dropped them in his hand.

He passed the keys to the officer from San Andrews Central.

In silence, we watched the young policeman leave.

DS Chilman gestured at the door. I followed him to the courtyard. He ran a hand over his salt-and-pepper head then looked into my face. 'Common sense tell me to advise you to let this go. But I know you – you like a dog with a bad case of lockjaw. When you get your teeth into somefing, you won't let go, not even if I make it an order. When you arrest Officer Buso, it was a snake that you pick up in your hand. He's friends with the same kinda policeman who kill your mother. We still got a few left in the Force. And now they see what you done to Buso,' he coughed into his hand, 'they'll be wondering if is them next. They going to have their eyes on you, Digson. Mebbe is time for people to know who your father is.'

'Nuh!'

'Okay.' He pushed a dry-stick finger under my nose. 'Then start wearing your blaastid piece. From now! That's an order.' He hitched up his trousers and headed for his car.

I stared down on the wide curve of the Carenage, cluttered

with inter-island cargo boats. There were days when I could barely look down there. It was where, in '99, a posse of renegade police officers, led by a man named Boko, murdered my mother and disappeared her body.

I heard Miss Stanislaus's crisp footsteps behind me, then I smelled her lime-lavender-nutmeg perfume. She placed herself beside me, her sea-green dress complemented perfectly by matching shoes and handbag, her hair pulled back in a glossy bun. She had a hand inside her handbag, which could just as readily emerge with a tissue or that little Ruger revolver she loved. She called the gun Miss Betsy.

'Missa Digger, how come you didn greet me when you come in?'

'Sorry, Miss Stanislaus. How you?'

'Too late,' she sniffed. 'What botherin you?'

Chief Officer Malan came out the office, jumped into his jeep and slammed the door. He gunned the engine, the vehicle shot out onto the road. I followed the yelp of his tyres as he took the corner further down the hill.

'Let's take some breeze,' she said.

'Something on your mind?' I said.

She did not answer.

'What's going on, Miss Stanislaus?'

I thought it might be her daughter, Daphne – a thirteen-year-old mini version of Miss Stanislaus. They were the only two people whose voices I sometimes confused. They had the same bright gun-barrel stare, the same love of vivid colours, and a delicacy in their movements that hid the steel inside them.

I glanced at my watch: 1pm. 'Let's go eat something,' I said.

I took her to Kathy's Kitchen, one of those eating places in San Andrews town that you have to know existed in order to find it. No signs on the door, no menu. The woman served one meal a day and it was whatever she fancied cooking. It was always working people's food. We walked into a small front room with a single fluorescent light. Floor carpeted with linoleum, five plastic tables – a pair of matching chairs pushed against each one. We sat before a bowl of calaloo soup with photos of Miss Kathy's family staring down at us, dead-eyed and unsmiling.

'Tell me,' I said.

She threw me a quick glance. Miss Stanislaus had those eyes you couldn't help noticing. Bright, translucent brown, with a luminosity that seemed to come from inside. There were times when I thought I saw hints of that glint in her father's, Chilman's, too.

'Still not sleeping?' I said.

'I awright, Missa Digger. Somefing I want to show you.' She lifted her bag from her lap, rested it on the table. Miss Stanislaus eased out a newspaper cutting and slid it towards me.

The article was three days old. I remembered it. One Lena Maine from Kara Island, aged thirty-two, had walked into the sea and drowned.

'Is Juba Hurst cause it,' she said.

My heart sank.

She'd pushed the bowl of soup aside, was almost mumbling the words. 'I been on the phone to people back home becuz it didn make no sense to me. Kara Islan woman know trouble from the time she born, and if she can't fight trouble, other woman help her. She don't kill 'erself. Look at the day it happen!'

I shook my head.

'Saturday, not so? Juba Hurst come back from Vincen Islan every Sunday. Miss Lena kill 'erself the day befo becuz she can't take it no more from him.'

'Evidence, Miss Stanislaus …'

'Is what Dada, her gran'mother, tell me on the phone and I got no reason to doubt them. She say Juba come to her gran'daughter every Sunday night stinking like a grave. Lena don't want im near her. People hear she bawlin like a cow and they dunno how to save her. Becuz if she don' let im have his way, he say he kill her and her chil'ren—'

'Miss Stanislaus,' I said, 'is ten years plus since Juba Hurst assault you, erm, sexually—'

'I not talkin about that! You not listenin to me! Months I been sayin this to San Andrews CID – my own department dat I work in.' She halted on that and shook her head, her face tight with outrage and disbelief. 'I tellin y'all dat somefing bad happenin on Kara Islan and we got to tackle it. Right now, Missa Digger, Juba rule Kara Islan. Coupla years ago, he take over all my great-uncle, Koku, land. To make matters worse, nobody can't find my great-uncle since Juba take his property. And nobody can't go near that place 'ceptin some ole wimmen who don give a damn no more. Last three months, they been burnin down his place soon as he go off to Vincen Islan becuz they say is bad fings he dealin in.'

I looked at her dabbing at the side of her mouth, her other hand restless in her lap. My mind switched to Juba Hurst – suspected murderer and enforcer. Eight cases of serious assault against minors with intent to commit buggery, four attempted murders, fifteen threats to kill, twelve unlawful woundings, nine indecent assaults on a female, two reported cases of detention of a woman against her will – every one of those cases had been retracted a day or two before it went to court. I had my ears and eyes tuned in on that fella. The problem was, he lived on Kara Island and from what I heard, the few police over there were terrified of him. Without proof of some new crime to pin on Juba Hurst, we could not move.

The only jail time Juba did was for the abduction and rape of a fourteen-year-old schoolgirl on Kara Island. That schoolgirl was Miss Stanislaus. Happened a week after Chilman walked away from Miss Stanislaus and her mother and moved to Camaho. First daughter, and Chilman didn look back, not even when Juba left her with a child I saw her struggling to love.

I picked up Miss Stanislaus's daughter Daphne from late-evening netball practice in San Andrews on Fridays and dropped her off at their little painted gate. A couple of weeks ago she remained in the car, her schoolbag on her knees. Daphne looked at the gate and then raised wide, entreating eyes at me. 'Missa Digger, I can come stay with you – mebbe for a while?'

'Not possible, Daph. Miss Stanislaus won't allow it and I can't either. What's the problem?'

'She don' like me no more, Missa Digger. She won't even talk to me, not even to—'

Daphne broke down.

I tapped out a text message to Miss Stanislaus: *Daphne don't want to come in. I taking her to Miss Iona house or mine. U got 2 mins 2 dcide.*

My phone vibrated. Miss Stanislaus, soft-voiced, exhausted, was at the other end. 'Send her in, Missa Digger. Fanks.'

I touched Miss Stanislaus's arm. She pulled away, her eyes hot and fierce on mine. Then something in her crumbled and her voice dropped almost to a murmur. 'I want y'all to believe me, Missa Digger. I – I dunno what to say to make you believe me.'

She sat staring past my head for a while, then drew breath. 'Problem is, Missa Digger, now Miss Lena gone – Juba Hurst goin throw himself on some other woman, not so? He going find them wimmen who been burnin down his place and is *what* he won't do to them. Gimme a reason why I should sit down here in Camaho and allow that to happen to my fam'ly.'

'I didn know Lena was family,' I said.

She threw me a sideways glare. 'On Kara Islan, Missa Digger, everybody is fam'ly.'

She got up, dragged her bag towards her and strode out.

3

I parked at the side of the road and walked up the concrete path to my house. My body craved sleep; my limbs were heavy with it. I'd sat through most of the night in the office scrolling through scores of Googled pages, my mind full of Miss Stanislaus. I'd stopped at PTSD and was seized with a kind of terror when I took in what it said. Rape survivors have a harder time overcoming it than combat veterans.

And there was not always an end date.

They'd listed sleeplessness, depressive disorders and denial. Suicidal thoughts were there too, irritation and self-loathing, even anger. It crossed my mind that they hadn't met a case like Miss Stanislaus. If they had, they would have added another: revenge. Not only that – in her case, they would have placed it top of the list. It was clear to me that Miss Stanislaus was not the kinda woman to forget an outrage against her body however long ago it was. She'd brought the rage with her when Chilman dumped her on San Andrews CID. All that indignation! Sometimes I saw her struggling to hold it back. There were days when she shrank at the slightest touch, grew dangerous and moody when news of a sexual assault reached our department.

I pushed those thoughts out of my head and played a game with myself. I pretended to be a private investigator entering my own house.

*

I climb three concrete steps, pull the bolt of the glass-fronted door and switch on the ceiling lights. I tiptoe past four Morris chairs and a sofa in the front room. Shelves line every wall, stacked with books that cover every aspect of the human body before and after death. Books on human bones cover the kitchen worktop. The thickest has a pencil in it: *Osteometry: The Mathematics of the Human Form.*

Two fridges. I pull open the door of the smaller one. Its shelves are crammed with bottled chemicals, the frozen larvae and pupae of arthropods and blowflies at every stage of their development. Old 35mm film canisters stuffed with soil samples, burrs and blades of grass. Human tissue in phials of formalin.

A music player sits in the far corner with stacks of CDs crowding it, mainly jazz, some Lovers' Rock, a pile of Bump n Grind with Lycra-clad Jamaican rude-gals cocking fully loaded, G-stringed backsides at the camera. Downright provocative.

A spare room on my right with a skeletal iron bed jammed against the wall. A battalion of vintage-labelled rum bottles on the floor.

There is a furnished bedroom at the far end of the house. An ancient mahogany bed takes up more than half the space, with a single slatted wooden window about five feet above it. All the other windows in the house are glass. Hurricane house, obviously, built circa 1955, stripped of its Guyana wood, extended and strengthened with concrete, steel and Temple stone.

Expensive condoms of the super-sensitive variety on the side table. No evidence of cohabitation.

Conclusions so far: male occupant aged twenty-three or thereabouts, obsessed with death and human body parts. Possibly cannibalistic. Visiting relationship, if any. An unhealthy interest in rum cocktails and disgusting music.

I leave the wall of the living room for last. There are three photos. The first is of an old Indian woman sitting on wooden steps, the door behind her propped open by a length of wood. She is staring at the camera with the cocked chin of a warrior. The second is of a young Afro-Indian woman in her mid-twenties with a glorious head of untamed hair and a smile white and wide as a beach. I wonder what happened to that woman. A little boy is leaning against her thigh. His eyes are wide, his mouth half open.

The last is a framed newspaper photograph, pasted on a sheet of Bristol board. A tallish, not-too-bad-looking fella is standing beside a full-fleshed woman with big brown eyes – pretty like hell in her tie-dyed ocean-blue dress. A swarm of red and yellow coral fish populate the lovely garment. She stands like royalty beside the not-too-bad-lookin' fella, an aquamarine handbag dangling from her elbow.

The caption reads: Michael 'Digger' Digson (left) and DC Kathleen Stanislaus (right) of San Andrews CID. The duo that cracked the Nathan case.

I concentrate on Miss Stanislaus's eyes. Now, I see something there I didn't notice before: a deep-down hurt, a simmering outrage. A sadness that makes me want to cry.

4

Friday, great columns of cloud were gathering over the eastern hills, dulling the day and releasing the occasional measly scattering of rain that only raised the humidity.

I took the airport road to work, driving through Coburn Valley – the gateway to the Drylands and the tourist south. I had a craving for raw cane juice and it was the only place to get it.

The seller had his own little mobile mill designed and built by himself. I'd handed him the money and turned back to my car when I felt eyes on me. I looked up quickly. A San Andrews Central Police jeep had stopped in the middle of the early-morning traffic. Vehicles edged past it, their drivers casting nervous glances in their rear-view mirrors. Three officers trying to stare me down. It was about Buso, of course, the drunken officer I'd locked up for running over a woman. I knew all three, their names usually got mentioned in the same breath. Skelo – because the bones of his skull were so pronounced. Machete – murderous, they said, when he lost his temper, which by all accounts he often did. Machete had his arms wrapped against the driver's wheel, his chest pushed forward, his head angled at me. Staring. The officer in the front passenger seat I knew as Switch. He controlled the two.

Switch was an older version of Malan – perhaps forty, with a reputation to maintain. A grim-faced human with a mouth and eyes designed for intimidation. The kind of officer that would think nothing of smashing a fella's face through a pane of glass or demanding sex from a woman in exchange for not arresting her. The subspecies you found in every police force in the world. The type that murdered my mother. I raised my chin and stepped onto the sidewalk.

Switch must have seen the rush of hatred on my face. He directed a gob of spit in my direction, said something to the driver and the engine came to life.

'I'd do it again,' I shouted. 'Any fuckin time!'

Their engine revved, the vehicle shot off. And just like that, my morning was soured.

At the office, I greeted Miss Stanislaus. She didn't answer me. Her face remained directed at the window. I pulled a chair and sat in front of her. She left her desk and walked off to the bathroom.

Pet and Lisa were looking at me as if I'd done the woman something criminal.

Malan strolled past, glanced at my face and chuckled.

I went back to my filing and kept my head down, but much as I tried to pretend otherwise, I felt dismissed.

Miss Stanislaus and I argued all the time, especially in the heat of a difficult case. We looked forward to it, knowing that at some point a spark would fly and ignite an idea that would lead us to a breakthrough. This felt different.

I went down to the marketplace and bought her lunch, returned to the office, laid the cartons in front of her and watched the woman eat my food with pleasure. She still wouldn't talk to me.

I sucked my teeth, grabbed my bag and strode out of the office with Pet's chuckles trailing after me.

5

Saturday was beginning to feel chilled out.

I was looking forward to a laid-back night with Dessie Manille at The Blue Crab – a late-night drinking hole with its own little beach facing Whale Island. I was thinking of jazzy steelpan music and dressed-up rum cocktails, fussed over by a bartender who knew how I liked my mixes.

Close to morning, Dessie and I would drive down to Grand Beach, shed our clothes on the sand and throw ourselves into the sea. What happened between us with the water above our shoulders was nobody's business but our own.

Woman waiting, she'd texted.

Man ready, I'd replied. I shrugged on my shirt, my eyes on the time.

My cellphone buzzed. I placed it against my ear, deepened my voice. 'Patience, woman, I coming.'

'Mind my arse, Digson! Is Chilman here! I want you in the office right now.'

'The—'

'Y'hear me first time.'

'I can't, Sir. I got an, erm, encounter in a few minutes.'

'Tell me about it when you get here.'

'Is past midnight!'

'Same time here too. Come right now.'

I could hear the old man breathing down the phone. He didn't sound drunk but that was always a matter of degrees.

'You not telling me what the problem is, Sir.'

'You not giving me a chance, Digson.' I waited through the pause, imagined Chilman licking those leather-purse lips of his.

'Kathleen disappear,' he said.

'Miss Stanislaus! Disappear, you say?' Even as I spoke, I felt the sinking sensation in my guts.

'I can't find the woman. She left her girlchild on her own. Daphne call' me, upset. Say she frighten. But my granddaughter refuse to tell me where her mother gone. Digson! I got a good idea what she about to do.'

His voice retreated down his throat and then he hung up.

I didn't have the courage to call Dessie and cancel. I sent her a text message.

I had more than a good idea of what Miss Stanislaus was about to do. In Kathy's Kitchen she'd told me. I hadn't wanted to believe her.

I grabbed my keys and stepped out into the night. A fingernail of a moon hung over Old Hope valley.

I stood for a while eyeing my little Toyota, polished to a shine by two youngfellas I'd paid to do the job earlier in the evening. I spooled through a string of dirty names for Chilman in my head, hurried into the vehicle and kept my foot on the accelerator.

I'd broken out in a sweat by the time I reached the Western Main Road, my radio turned down low, the rumble of my tyres layering the dread that had crept into my head.

The office was lit up. Chilman's beat-up Datsun sat in the middle of the concrete courtyard. He was at my desk, his head cocked towards the ceiling.

He took in my new Adidas NMD trainers, then the rest of me. 'You rescheduled the encounter?'

I slid a glance at his hands – my only way of reading him. His thumb was making circles around his index as if testing the texture of the air. Disturbance. Deep.

Chilman pushed aside the sheet of paper he'd placed under his elbow. 'Where's your piece?'

'I left home soonz you called me.'

His dry-bone hand convulsed. 'Poor excuse is no excuse, Digson. Not wearing your gun going to kill you one day.'

'What's up, Sir?'

'You know what's up.' He was rubbing his face and shaking his head. 'However justified my daughter feel, it is still goin to be murder. And that's the end of all my hard work.' His gesture took in the office.

'You telling me what I know, Sir. She might've gone some-where else, though.'

'Like where?' He rested those evil eyes on me. 'You left your brain at home too? You two work together, how come you didn see it coming?'

I swallowed back the irritation. 'Mebbe I did. What about you, Sir?'

I held his gaze, doing nothing to hide what I was thinking.

Where the hell wuz you when Juba Hurst dragged your daughter off the road and plant his seed in her? And in all these years, what you done about it? So why you so fuckin surprised she gone off now to shoot down the fella who damaged her?

'All I asking is why you so sure is Kara Island she gone to, Sir.'

Chilman dismissed my question with a flick of his hand. He slid the sheet of paper towards me. 'You not the only fella I call up tonight. I speak to Officer Mibo on Kara Island.'

'What Officer Mibo say?' I visualised a tall officer, twig-thin with a shy, pleasant voice. I'd never known Mibo to make an arrest. As Chilman put it, Kara Island didn't work that way. People were punished and rewarded as the islanders saw fit and there was nothing Camaho law could do about it. Mibo was meant to police the marijuana trade between Vincen Island and Kara Island. That meant doing nothing until one of their young men became too ambitious and ventured into the waters of the French islands of Martinique and Guadeloupe. When they got caught, Mibo called Chilman for help and advice on how to rescue their 'citizen'. Chilman passed the paperwork to me.

'Mibo confirm that Juba Hurst work on one of them inter-island cargo boats name *Retribution*.' A chuckle rattled out of him. 'Boat come in every Sunday and Thursday from Vincen Island. It drop anchor any time between eight and nine in the morning, depending on the tide.'

'You tell Mibo what the issue is?'

'Why?'

I tried to imagine Officer Mibo attempting to stop Miss Stanislaus from doing anything, and promptly understood Chilman's cynicism.

DS Chilman tapped the paper. 'According to what lil Daphne *didn* say, I got reason to believe she left this evening with the last ferryboat. The *Osprey*.'

I turned to face him. '*Osprey* leave Kara Island nine thirty in the evening. Ain got no other ferry after that. That mean she's spending Sunday night on Kara Island? What about Daphne?'

'Daphne say she going to be awright. Is all she say.' Chilman's thumb made a fast circle against his index. 'Digson, I bet all the money I don't have that tomorrow morning, Katheen going to be on the jetty, waiting for that boat to dock. I don't give a damn how well you two get on. I

25

don't care less if she's my own daughter. Like I say, if she kill dat fella, is murder plain and simple, with enough witnesses on that jetty to fill up ten court house. I ordering you to arrest 'er and bring 'er back. At least people will see we done somefing about it.'

'And then?' I said.

'What you think?'

'I not thinking now, Sir. Is answers I asking for.'

He jabbed a finger at the paper. 'You got work to do. Fastest way to get there is by that lil mosquito they call a plane. Problem is, it leave seven forty-five morning-time. It take twenty-five minutes to get there. That mean you reach—'

'Ten past eight,' I said. I looked him in the eyes. 'Airport to jetty is just under a mile. Might be too late.'

DS Chilman looked as if he wanted to cry. The old fella stood up and dragged open Malan's drawer. He reached inside it, withdrew a pair of plasticuffs and tossed them at me. They struck me on the chest and fell to the floor. 'Bring her back in them if you have to.' The gesture seemed to exhaust him. He pushed himself off the chair and shuffled to the door. 'Sorry to call you out like this, youngfella. But, s'far as I kin see, you the only man on dis fuckin island could lay a hand on my daughter and get away with it. Is why I got to send you. Go catch some sleep.'

My watch said 3.52am. 'I leave from here,' I told him. 'Night almost done.'

'And your piece?'

'I'll take the Glock from the storeroom.'

He grumbled and jangled his keys.

With my back to him, I heard the brush of his skin on the door handle. 'Call me,' he said. It sounded like a threat.

Chilman closed the door so softly I barely heard the lock engage.

26

I waited until the old Datsun grated to a start, watched it shudder out of the concrete courtyard onto the road, loud enough to wake the parish dead.

I took up the cuffs, stuffed them in my pocket then strode over to Miss Stanislaus's desk. I ran a hand through every drawer. Chilman would have done this, but I felt I knew his daughter better than him.

A packet of unopened tissues, a nail file still in its packaging, two neatly ordered piles of multicoloured rubber bands and paper clips, five pencils, their tips honed down to needle-points. The very faint odour of Miss Stanislaus's perfume.

Working alongside Miss Stanislaus, I'd learned one important thing from her: people's actions were driven by what they most wanted to protect or destroy. This polite, soft-voiced woman with a preference for bright handbags, pretty hats and dresses would be no different.

I went over to the small storeroom at the back of Malan's office, stepped over the black tin trunk in which we kept the Department's M24 Sniper Weapon System rifle along with a couple of F2000 patrol shooters. I brought down seven boxes from the top shelf. They contained shells for Miss Stanislaus's Ruger LCR. I handed them out to staff the way a doctor dispensed opiates. I recorded everything.

The five cartons of .38 Special +P bullets were exactly as I'd left them, but the hollow point Spear Gold Specials had been broken into. Four rounds missing, along with a couple of moon-clip speed-loaders.

I remembered explaining to Miss Stanislaus the difference between a full-metal-jacket bullet and a hollow point, and why Malan should never have ordered the hollow points. 'A standard bullet will drill a hole through you,' I said. 'A hollow point will make porridge of your insides.'

I spent twenty minutes pulling aside the cartons and boxes on the shelf until I had to accept that the Glock was missing.

I retrieved two rounds of standard bullets for Miss Stanislaus's Ruger, filled up a couple of speed-loaders, repacked the shelf and returned to my desk. The office clock said 4.57.

My thoughts turned to Daphne. I wasn't surprised that Chilman couldn't get a word out of his granddaughter. Lil Miss Daphne Stanislaus would just as readily kill for her mother as die for her. When she was away or working late, Miss Stanislaus left her child with Iona – one of her Fire Baptist friends. I wondered why she didn't this time. Still, I had no doubt that Daphne would be sitting up this time-a-morning, her cellphone in her hand, waiting to hear from her mother. Daphne never lied, she got that from Miss Stanislaus too.

I tapped out a message: *Digger here, Daph. Where's Mam?*
No reply.
U there?
My phone vibrated, *Yh.*
Want 2 talk?
No.
She tell u where she gone?
Yh.
Kara Island?
No reply.
She tell u why she gone?
No.
You kno how to use it?
?
The gun.
?
The gun. Black, small. 43 Austria 9x19 marked on left side.

It took a while before she answered.

Yh.

U sure?

Yh.

U at Iona house 2morow?

Yh.

NOBODY 2 kno u got d gun EVER! K?

K.

Take care.

U2.

I pocketed my phone; felt a headache coming on.

6

I left the office at 7.15am. It would take me less than twenty minutes to get to the airport – ten minutes before boarding. San Andrews town was now heaving with traffic. I took the West Coast Road to Salt Point. On my right the Atlantic was almost black with the threat of rain. It began hammering down when I got to the airport. Through the wire fence, I spotted the five-seater Cessna at the far corner of the runway.

I parked in the tiny square of concrete marked out for the police, raised my ID at one of the fellas in Immigration who looked asleep on his feet.

He rolled his eyes in the direction of the aircraft. 'Weather no good, Digger. Careful you don't fall out.'

I didn't mind flying, but not in a tin-can pretending to be a plane, with a pair of propellers that made me think of the battery-operated fans tourists held up to their faces to cool themselves. The American owners called it the Island Shuttle. Kara Islanders who preferred the truth to marketing hype, nicknamed it the Flyin Turtle.

The aircraft shuddered north, dipping like a drunken insect. I sat behind the pilot, my nose a couple of inches from his ear, my seat belt pulled tight against my stomach, my shoulders so tense, they ached. A couple hundred feet below, the sea had gone white in the driving rain.

Twenty minutes later, Kara Island loomed ahead, its approach pockmarked by dripping rock-islands we called the Family.

A teacher told us once that these were the most dangerous waters in the world, forget the Bay of Biscay and the Irminger Sea.

With wind speeds reaching one hundred miles per hour on an ordinary day, rip tides ran like rivers just under the surface, provoked by a dozing twin-headed volcano that Kara Islanders named Kick em Jenny and Kick em Jack. And to add an extra bit of spite to the danger down there, a plate of granite someone had named Devil Tooth lay beneath the boiling waters. Every now and then it made the news by splitting the hull of a careless boat. They never found survivors.

Someone had come up with a word for all that violence below us: Blackwater.

With the squall behind, the air-insect I sat in entered another climate: bald sandstone hills, more grass than trees, everything below me biscuit-dry. The little plane battled with the updrafts as it took unsteady aim at the narrow strip of asphalt less than fifty yards from the ocean.

From up here, Garveyhale, the tiny town, looked like a stack of seashells with the ocean chewing at its edges. The long wooden jetty shot out from its centre like a fossilised proboscis. It was crawling with people.

The cause of the commotion was no doubt the fat-bellied schooner about two hundred yards or so out in the water, belching a column of black smoke. My watch said 8.25.

The wheels of the plane hopscotched on the tarmac for a minute, then juddered to a halt. I'd already unbuckled and was crouched in my seat. I muttered 'Thanks, Man' in the pilot's ear as he released the trapdoor and I squeezed out.

I hit the asphalt running, upped my pace on the narrow

coastal road, with nothing between me and the ocean but a hedge of wilting manchineel. The morning had already begun to heat up. Rivulets of sweat ran down my throat. Even from this distance I could hear the engine of the big steel boat drumming the air.

Between gaps in the trees, I caught glimpses of the rusting hull already beginning its ponderous sidling towards the jetty.

The crowd of milling bodies came up in the distance. I lengthened my stride.

The boat had finished docking when I got there gasping, my shirt plastered against my skin. It looked as if all of Kara Island had turned out. People were prodding sacks, inspecting sealed containers winched down to them by three seamen, so muscular they looked corrugated in the hot morning light.

I swept the crowd from front to back, then more slowly in the spiral pattern I'd picked up in my forensics course in England. I felt my shoulders relax. I pulled out my phone to call Chilman and inform him that we'd got it wrong.

But then I sensed a change in the crowd. The voices around me quietened. Now I could hear the slap of water against the hull of the boat. I followed people's gazes and saw why. An apparition – the biggest human I'd ever seen – emerged from somewhere in the hold of the boat.

He stood on the deck looking down on us, a huge gaff in his hand. Deep-set eyes buried in the broad slab of his face.

Juba Hurst!

I'd met him once before, a couple of years ago, on that same jetty. I'd travelled to Kara Island to unravel the mystery of Miss Stanislaus who, almost as soon as Chilman had thrust the woman on San Andrews CID, was accused of laying low a child-abusing preacher named Bello, who turned out to be a close friend of the Justice Minister.

Looking up at Juba, the big head turning as if it sat on

32

ball bearings, my mind returned to a night of chafing seas when I stood at the end of that same jetty with his hulking body in front of me. He would not let me go past him until I explained what I was doing there. I realised I'd come too close to something he was protecting in one of the boats in the bay. A crewman in a nearby schooner had heard my raised voice. He'd looked out and seen the big man facing me with the weapon in his hand and had alerted the others. I had no doubt that they'd saved my life.

Juba took his time coming down the gangway, his canvas boots vibrating the green-heart planks of the jetty, the big hook in his hand so polished it looked like glass. I moved back with the crowd, feeling the same dread I'd experienced the first time I met him – that I was in the presence of something not quite human, a creature from my grandmother's story-world of fire-rolling demons and blood-guzzling loup garou that she used to frighten me with as a child.

And he stank. The smell of rotting fish and rancid diesel oil came off him like a spreading shadow. It was all I could do to keep myself from retching.

And this, I thought, was the man that had laid his hands on Miss Stanislaus – just fourteen then – and forced a child on her. No fuckin wonder she wanted him dead.

I backed away, my mind on making the call I promised Chilman.

From the edge of my vision I caught a movement, a little eddy of heads and shoulders. I swung round and there she was, her hair tied back with a grey square of cloth, the morning sun glossing that smooth round face of hers, her chin raised, lips pouted as if she were kissing the air, trickles of sweat running down her neck. She was in a loose man's shirt, its sleeves rolled up and buttoned at the elbow, her right hand just above the mouth of her handbag.

33

I lowered my shoulders, began pushing my way past limbs and torsos towards Miss Stanislaus. A snakepit of hisses and cuss-words assaulted my ears as I elbowed my way through. I surfaced a couple of bodies behind her, then began edging forward.

And now it was as if the whole tide of bodies around us receded and left Miss Stanislaus facing Juba Hurst. She dipped into the small handbag with that same daintiness I was accustomed to by now. Juba spotted her and halted, his face so shadowed by the hard morning light I could barely pick out his features. I was less than a foot behind her when she raised the gun.

Perhaps something in me wanted to see whether she would really bring down a man in cold blood in the presence of all these people. Maybe it was because I too wanted this fella dead. Dunno!

I followed the rise of the gun barrel, her levelling it, the small pause before she slipped her index inside the trigger guard, the tensing of the tendons against her skin, then I shot my hand up under hers and snapped the muzzle skyward. The pistol barked. I heard gasps and squawks, then the fast shuffle of feet, followed by a stampede. I pulled her back hard against my chest, wrestling the pistol from her grip. A sharp, distressed sound came out of her. Her left elbow slammed into my gut. I gasped and pushed myself backward, but she'd already rammed her shoulders into me, her heels digging into the toes of my shoe. I swung her around to face me, heard my own voice grating. 'Miss Stanislaus, what the fuck yuh think yuh doing! Eh?'

I was counting on my language to snap her out of it. It did. She froze, her mouth partly open, her eyes bright with disbelief.

I made a show of unlocking the cylinder and tilting the

cartridges into my hand. I was about to pocket the gun when she made a lunge for it, her eyes somewhere beyond my shoulders. I swung around and saw Juba bearing down on us, the big steel hook angled stiffly from his side. He was almost upon us by the time I retrieved a packed loader, slammed it into the pistol and raised the gun at his head.

He braked, backed away a few steps. A sound rumbled out of the man as he dropped his gaze on Miss Stanislaus. She returned his stare – calm, unreadable – her mouth moving around words that didn't go past her lips. With his eyes still on her, the big body erupted, and in a single sideways movement, Juba was on the concrete walkway that ran along the beach front. Miss Stanislaus followed the rolling shoulders up the road, her eyes as attentive as a cat's.

At the bend in the road, Juba stopped, his back to us. The big head swivelled round, the silver hook tapping the tree trunk of his right leg. I could hear the slap of the steel against his flesh. He rumbled something. I cocked my ear.

'What he say?' Miss Stanislaus said.

'You don't want to know,' I said. I changed my mind and told her. 'He say next time he catch you, he, erm . . . '

'He?'

'Cripple you.'

She blinked and muttered, 'He done do that already.'

With Juba gone, a hive of murmurings rose up around us. I raised my badge above my head. 'Okay, people. Party done. Go home.'

An elderly woman, dark and gnarled like the bark of a seagrape tree, raised a shaking finger at my face. 'Why you stop her? Eh? What you know about Kara Islan bizness? Eh? Is God send her to get rid of the dog, and God going punish your Camaho-man arse for stopping her.' She sent a cloud of spittle in my direction, then turned her back on me.

35

Miss Stanislaus was throwing up sand with her heels in a fast walk down the beach. I hurried after her, my whole body tense with the words of the old witch who spat at me. I caught up with her in the shade of a whitewood tree at the other end of the beach.

We sat on an upturned crate, our bodies angled so that we had a good view of the road along which Juba disappeared.

Twenty-footers cluttered the foreshore, their insides piled high with fishing tackle. A couple of sleek, low-profile crafts bobbed quietly among them, their transoms reinforced to withstand the thrust of oversized engines. Sprint boats – the ganja runners' choice for fast dashes between Kara Island and Vincen Island.

From time to time, we made a raid to give the Justice Minister something to boast about on the news, but we didn't break the trade because, in Chilman's words, Kara-Islan-Man wouldn have no Gee-Dee-Pee. Tell Donald Trumpet, haul his arse, with all his talk bout 'War on Herbs'.

'War on drugs,' I'd corrected.

He'd turned rum-shot eyes on me. 'So! You siding with him? Illegal is anything that Donald Trumpet can't find no way to tax. How come you dunno that yet?'

'Missa Digger, you didn have to throw no obstreme words at me.'

'Miss Stanislaus, I want to understand why the smartest woman I know leave her one girlchild alone and go off to do the stupidest thing any police officer could do. You cross twenty miles of water with a loaded gun to kill a fella in broad daylight. You think youd've got away with it?'

'What make you fink I want to get away with it, Missa Digger?'

'Is murder, plain an simple, Miss Stanislaus.'

'Is murder here too, Missa Digger.' She dropped a hand

36

over her heart. 'Somefing get kill' inside you. Man do what he do to woman, he go to jail. He come out an' he ferget it. De woman he done that to can't walk decent in the worl till she build back what he take from 'er. She got to born again. Not all woman could do that. And like I tell you, it wasn that that bring me here.'

I unloaded the Ruger, stacked the gun with standard shells and handed back the weapon. She dropped it in her bag, the butt facing upwards as usual for a quick draw. I held out my palm. She rummaged in her pocket and dropped a packed speed-loader along with a handful of snub-nosed bullets in my hand.

'The gun you left with Daphne, soonz I get back, I want it. Okay?'

'You—' She stopped short, pulled a tissue from her bag and flung it in my face. 'You mus' never hold onto me and drag me back like that, y'unnerstan?'

'Dragging you back like that or dragging you to jail, which you prefer?'

I pulled out the plasticuffs and tossed them at her feet.

'I wan' to walk,' she said.

'Not on your own, you not!'

I followed her all the way up to the highest point on the island.

We stood shoulder to shoulder on Top Hill looking down on the wooden jetty, now empty. Against the dazzling morning glare, the boat Juba had arrived on was perched like an overfed cockroach. Further out was Goat Island, facing Devil Tooth. Just after that stood the curving chain of rock-islands dotting the stretch of boiling sea that Kara Islanders called Blackwater. Down there, the Atlantic had sliced through one end of the land and created a channel. A shortcut to the chain of islands further north and North America.

The departing *Osprey* was taking the treacherous turn just before Goat Island, the engines of the big white catamaran creating its own whirlpool behind it.

Scatterings of houses along the coastline. Patches of green here and there. Kara Island had no natural source of water. Rain avoided the place – all twelve square miles of it. Yet these people thrived.

'Where you staying?' I said.

'I got people here,' she said. 'You goin meet them after here.'

She'd spoken with her back half-turned. A different kind of calm came off Miss Stanislaus – almost as if she'd left the raging part of herself on the jetty. She pointed at the storming sea below then slid me a sideways glance. 'Missa Digger, what you know about the two Wimmen of the Waters?'

'A lot, Miss Stanislaus. My granny was—'

'What she tell you?'

'Olokun and Yemaya. Olokun is the god-woman of the Dark Waters. She rule the bottom of the ocean, yunno. The only one who know what happen to all them African who never reach this side of the Atlantic. Everything go down to her in the end. My granny used to say that whiteman religion got it wrong. Hell is not full ov fire, hell is full ov water.'

Miss Stanislaus smiled. 'You talk pretty, Missa Digger. Is so you sweet-talk Miss Dressy?'

'Dessie, Miss Stanislaus, not Dressy. Wait till I tell you bout Yemaya. She rule the surface. She's the storm-bringer, the life-giver and life-taker. She's a man-chastiser too! Ain't got a single fella in Camaho who not afraid ov her – except me, of course. Is that temper she got. Lord Gord! Spare us! And,' I winked at her, 'she don't take no shi – er – nonsense from nobody.'

Miss Stanislaus was tinkling with laughter. 'Missa Digger, you too stupid!'

'Which one of them you follow, Miss Stanislaus?'

'Both,' she said.

'Makes sense,' I said. 'Scuse me, I got to call your father. You talk to Daphne yet?'

She said yes with her eyes.

DS Chilman picked up promptly. 'Digson, what time it is?'

'Right now I not looking at my watch, Sir. I talking to you.'

'Why you got me waiting so . . . so, bu–laasted long?'

Stinkin' drunk, I thought, or almost there. 'Why you bawling me out this time-a-morning, Sir? I done the job.'

That shut him up for a second. 'You stop 'er? You handcuff 'er like I order?'

'Nuh!'

'Handcuff 'er, Digson. Bring her on the, erm, plane or boat, or – how you bringing her back?'

'I can't do that, Sir.'

'Can't! What she done to you?'

'Sorry, Sir, I not doing it.'

'Digson, she got to know is cuuuu–riminal behaviour.'

'She know that already. I not doing it.'

He went into a sputtering riff about rude'n'stubborn jack-ass. 'Digson, you'z a damn failure! I should've got Malan to do it.'

'Then you'd have two dead fellas up here and you'd have to arrest your daughter yourself. Sorry, Sir, I got to go. Urgent matters.' I switched off.

Chilman rang back twice. I ignored his calls.

'Drunk?' She sniffed.

'From guilt,' I said. 'When you going start behaving with him like a daughter?'

'After you start behaving with yours like a son, Missa Digger.'

She turned to me, her brows pulled together. 'You move so quick – unloadin an loadin Miss Betsy like dat.' She snapped her fingers. 'How come?'

'Usain Bolt. Ever hear bout him?'

'What bout im?'

'He got what I got. A lot of it.'

'Wozzat?'

'Switching muscles, Miss Stanislaus. Make you quick, yunno. My time in school, I break every sprinting record.'

She raised a finger. 'Dat remind me, Missa Digger.' Miss Stanislaus took the Ruger from her bag. 'I never show you how me and Miss Betsy get on, not so? I want you to throw her at me any ole how.'

She handed me the gun. I emptied the cylinder, closed it and tossed it at her. She caught it easily. I sent it looping, spinning, underarm and overarm. I tried every bowling trick I knew. Miss Stanislaus caught the weapon every time, and by some trick of her left hand had the muzzle pointing at my chest.

I suppressed a flush of envy. 'Where you learn that?'

'Knittin muscle,' she said. 'And I not even showin off.'

7

Miss Stanislaus's 'people' were two elderly women, one of whom had spat at me. I looked into a fine-boned face, skin taut and dark like polished ebony. Cotton white hair peeped out from under a purple headwrap. She held a small machete in her hand.

'Dada,' Miss Stanislaus said. She pointed at me. 'Missa Digger.'

Sharp disapproving eyes scoured my face then slid off it.

The other woman was dressed like Dada – a loose paisley-patterned cotton dress that reached a couple of inches above her feet. She said her name was Benna. Skin the colour of burnt cinnamon, with a way of looking that seemed as if she were staring from a great distance. Unusual eyes – pale and with that glass-like translucency. I sensed that I was in the presence of a woman who was not unlike my grandmother: fearless, full of mystery and reserve.

Benna had a hand around a long black stick. From time to time she tapped her leg with the rounded tip.

Close up, I realised their age could be anything between seventy and eighty, and that was more by the foam-white hair peeking from their headwraps. They had the bearing and the firmness of body of women half their age. But then, centenarians were no big deal on Kara Island.

Miss Stanislaus stood quietly in their presence, her arms

down her sides. The old women had caressed her face and called her 'daughter'.

'My house,' Dada said.

We followed a curving road till we came to a pair of stunted Bermuda fan palms, then walked into a yard surrounded by a low hibiscus fence. A blue house, with a small veranda crowded with spider plants, sat in the middle of the space.

There was a rusting machete stuck in the soil beside the first rung of steps leading into the house.

They sat me in the veranda and disappeared inside.

I walked out into the yard, taking in the brown rounded hills that overlooked everything. I heard footsteps behind me, then Dada's voice, sibilant and accusing, 'Why you come and spoil it? Why you stop Kathleen? If I was her, I wouldn have nothing to do with you after that. You know what Juba done to her?'

I opened my mouth to answer. The woman silenced me with a flick of her wrist. 'You know the trouble Juba been causin us? You know what he done to my gran'daughter? What the hell you know bout us?'

'If I didn spoil it, she'd've been in jail tomorrow and awaiting trial for murder. And lemme ask you this: every case y'all bring against Juba Hurst y'all drop it last-minute. Why?'

The old woman did not answer. She seemed more interested in the movements of my mouth than in my words.

Benna came out and joined her. 'What's she to you, Missa Digger?'

I opened my palms and stared at her. 'Who?'

'Kathleen.'

'She's an officer; I'm an officer. I—'

'You lying to yourself.' She tapped her staff and shook her head. 'We talk bout Juba now?'

'Is all everybody want to talk about since I got here,' I muttered.

'Juba been doing something over there by the sea,' Benna said. 'He used to bring over boys from Vincen Island to work with him. He had a camp o' somefing on the piece of land he take over a coupla years ago from Missa Koku. Missa Koku bring up Kathleen, yunno that?'

Juba, she said, had funny-looking boats that had been coming and going until few months ago. They wouldn't have given a damn if he didn't start turning Kara Island's children into thieves and liars.

According to her, Kara Island children never used to threaten their own parents with murder before. Whatever Juba been feeding them changed them.

'The whole of Kara Island gone and change and every man here turn useless with fright. And look what Juba done to Dada' granddaughter Lena, and nobody couldn stop im!'

She fixed me with cool, defiant eyes. 'Somebody *had* to take the fight to Juba Hurst, not so? And who better than us?'

She said that whenever Juba left for Vincen Island, they filled bottles with kerosene, went to that place he set up by the sea and emptied his demijohns. They drove nails into his containers and set the place alight. They'd been doing it for the past three months.

'And what Juba goin do to us?' The old woman threw me a look. 'Kill us, Missa Digger – that's all. But yunno, death is nothing. Death is an embrace for those ov us who prepare for it. Besides, we done live this life – or most ov it. So!'

Did they know exactly what Juba was doing? I asked.

They didn't care, they said, though they'd heard that it was drugs.

'Y'all show me the place tomorrow?' I said.

'You give back Kathleen 'er gun?' Dada wanted to know.

I told her, yes.

'You got yours too?'

'Nuh,' I said.

'Just one should do, not so?' Benna might have been enquiring about the effectiveness of a kitchen knife or spoon.

'I just want to see the camp,' I said. 'We not looking for Juba.'

Benna tapped her rod and looked very disappointed.

'Where's Miss Stanislaus?' I said.

'Restin,' Dada said. 'She tired.' The woman placed a hand over her heart.

They fed me fried sweet potato wedges and spiced fishcake. Miss Stanislaus came and sat beside me. The day had suddenly quietened. The sound of the sea became more present in my consciousness. The last of the evening sun threw a yellow glow on everything. I looked at my watch: 6.45. I wondered where the time went and suddenly felt exhausted.

The women mentioned a small guest house further inland. They'd already called the couple who ran it and told them to expect me.

'I meet you here tomorrow,' I told Miss Stanislaus. 'First ferry.'

'I comin with you,' she said.

The women gave us a small bag stuffed with lambi roti and waved us off.

Dada even smiled.

Kara Island became a ship at night – all twelve square miles of it – anchored in some of the worst waters in the Antilles.

I sat on the edge of the bed in Sea View Guest House suffering from the hammering out there. It felt as if the ocean had invaded my head. And there was that smell of rotting fish and rancid diesel oil that seemed to seep through the crevices of the building and wrap itself around me.

I heard a tap on my door. 'Missa Digger, you decent?'

I got up and pulled on my tracksuit.

Miss Stanislaus was in the corridor in black slacks, a pair of canvas shoes and a loose-fitting, beaded T-shirt. She looked as if she were going for a jog. 'Missa Digger, you want to take some breeze?'

I glanced at my watch: 3.57. 'This time-a-morning?'

'I know you wasn sleepin. Didn hear no snorin.'

'I don't snore,' I said. 'Best to wait it out. Ferry leave eight thirty.'

'First quarter moon,' she said. 'A pusson want to walk.' Miss Stanislaus sounded desperate.

'Gimme a minute.' I slipped on my sneakers, grabbed my torch and pulled the door closed behind me.

A clear sky and a hard wind coming off the sea and grabbing at our clothing, though the thundering of the ocean was less amplified out here.

We walked the main road towards the town and then branched off it, Miss Stanislaus in front, her head switching this way then that, as if she were reacquainting herself with the island. Some houses were no longer there, she said, and there were quite a few – big concrete constructions that looked ghostly in the moonlight – that hadn't been there before.

A long stone building was the school she went to. She took me past it, her walk purposeful, her footsteps quicker. She headed for a patch of limestone rocks and razor grass, stopped at a tangle of old sea-island cotton trees, their trunks choked with tufts of cus-cus grass and sun-parched weeds. Miss Stanislaus pointed at the tangle of vegetation. 'Right there, Missa Digger, is where I got Daphne.'

45

And then gently, very gently, she rested a hand on my upper arm and led me back onto the main road.

'You think you'll ever come back here to live?' I said.

'I feel the pull sometimes, Missa Digger, when my fam'ly blood is callin me, but yunno—' She turned up her face at the moon. 'Juba all over dis islan, Missa Digger – you been smellin im too, not so? Benna say they even smell im in deir sleep. And if you dunno it yet, he been outside de guest house waitin'n'watchin.' She stopped short, pointed a finger at her chest. 'So, Juba Hurst in here – and Juba Hurst out there, too. You don' fink I have to clear him out?'

Miss Stanislaus released my arm, dropped it stiffly on her bag, sniffing the air. 'And s'pose I tell you, Missa Digger, that I smell im comin? S'pose I tell you I got to finish it right now becuz I don' have no choice?' She threw me a sudden urgent look. 'Use your speed.'

I felt the prickling of the hairs on my neck and arms, my nerves flaring as I too picked up the scent of Juba Hurst.

Then I saw him – a giant upright shadow at the beginning of the bend in the road. Behind us, the long dust track to the airport; on our left, the wall of manchineel and the sea. Our only chance of retreat was the tangle of grass and stones from which we'd just emerged.

I felt my heartbeat quicken, my mouth go dry. 'Jeezas,' I muttered. 'She fuckin plan this!'

With fast heavy movements, the giant shape began bearing down on us. Miss Stanislaus pulled away, her voice rising to a shriek. 'Use your speed, Missa Digger.' I heard the rapid pad-padding of her retreating feet, then I could no longer hear her.

I spun on my heels, thrusting forward in a crouching zig-zag dance away from Juba; was about to hit my stride when something struck me between my shoulders, hollowed out my head and my legs gave way. I hit the asphalt hard.

When I rolled onto my back Juba was standing over me.

'Catch you.' His voice seemed to rumble out of a tunnel. He was holding the big steel gaff in his right hand, the metal hook winking back the moonlight.

'I goin gut you like a fish.' A slow roll of the massive shoulders, a deep-chested intake of his breath and the big man lunged. I threw myself sideways. The metal struck the road and sparked. I leapt to my feet, began backing away, my eyes on the half-raised weapon, my nostrils flared, and all I could hear in that moment was Chilman's snickering condemnation unspooling in my head. Not wearing your gun going kill you one day . . .

Another belly-rumble came from Juba. 'Lemme see you dodge dis one.'

He switched the weapon to his left hand, the curve of the big hook brushing his knee, his right arm spread wide. I shuffled backwards, dizzy with the stink of him, my instinct dropping my hand to my waist for the belt that wasn't there.

Something hot and sudden flushed my head and I felt the snarl rising from my gut. 'Fuck you. You smell like a pit latrine. C'mon, you fucker. Kill me!'

Crouched low, I followed the arc of the rising weapon, bracing myself to leap sideways.

On the peak of Juba's swing, the night crackled and splintered.

The big man straightened up, his arm still raised. From behind me came the quick soft shuffle of footsteps. And there she was, Miss Stanislaus, barefoot and rigid in the moonlight, her Ruger levelled like the finger of God on the swaying man.

The second shot convulsed him. The third seemed to pin him there against the night. The steel hook left his hand and struck the road – its clatter flat and sharp. Miss Stanislaus's

47

Ruger barked again, and the pause between each shot was terrible because Juba wouldn't fall.

I counted all five shots, visualised the placement of each bullet by the recoil of the big man's body. And yet he didn't fall.

I watched Miss Stanislaus reload, her eyes not on the weapon but on Juba's face. The next shot brought him to his knees. And it struck me then that she was killing Juba and wanted him to know it.

She shot him again, and he sank onto his haunches, the big face turned up to her. All I could see were the whites of his eyes.

'Finish it,' I snapped. 'Finish it right now!'

My voice seemed to rouse her from that taut, wide-eyed trance. She straightened up and the night crackled with the quick succession of bullets.

And then silence, disturbed only by the suck and surge of the waves between the mangroves.

Miss Stanislaus lowered herself on to the road and buried her face in her hands, sobbing with great soundless heaves of her shoulders.

I eased her to her feet, held her for a long time, my chin in her hair, the early-morning chill creeping under my shirt and settling on my skin.

None of this felt real: the sudden preternatural stillness of this foreday morning, the mass of flesh lying on the road bathed in moonlight. Not a movement anywhere, and stars so close a pusson could reach up and stir them with a hand.

Miss Stanislaus's voice broke through my thoughts. 'Missa Digger, you awright?'

I shook my head and stared at her, her face gone smooth in the moonlight and that glow in her big brown eyes. I was reminded suddenly of Caran's story about Princess Orchids.

Miss Stanislaus stepped back. Now she wouldn't look at me. 'Missa Digger, you think I wicked, not so?'

'S'not what I thinking now, Miss Stanislaus.' And I wasn't, my mind had shifted forward to the days ahead, the impossibility of any of this making sense to DS Chilman. And that would be just to start with.

There was a disturbance in the air. What sounded like murmurings. I closed my eyes and listened, and recognised the shuffle of feet on dust. When I looked up I saw them: shadows emerging in the morning half-light, bare-chested men in shorts, women in fluttering nightdresses. Hardly a word between them, just the occasional mumble that ended with 'Juba'. A few raised their hands in our direction. Five women approached us. I picked out Dada and Benna among them. They gathered around Miss Stanislaus and began leading her away. It was then that I noticed Miss Stanislaus's shivering. She must have said something to them because Benna turned her head, raised her stick and pointed ahead. I followed close behind, drifting to the side of the road when we passed the dead man.

'They'll clear dat up,' Benna said without looking down.

At Dada's house, they took Miss Stanislaus into a room at the back. I heard the sound of running water, caught the smell of cerasee, chado beni, nutmeg, and other odours for which I had no name. These smells dredged up a wave of childhood memories. They brought to mind my grandmother, who had mothered me, muttering in a closed room with other women that she'd gathered around her. I remembered the secrecy of their ritual cleansing – women, preparing one of their own for the trouble to come.

DS Chilman remained silent on the phone. Once or twice he coughed and cleared his throat. At the end of my report, he said, 'Blame me, Digson.' Then he cut off.

It was the first time I'd heard him take responsibility for anything he did or did not do in relation to Miss Stanislaus. I'd always thought it was what explained his drunkenness – dulling his guilt from abandoning a young girlchild who, judging from the depth of her resentment, had probably loved him to distraction. I dunno!

Miss Stanislaus would take no gift from him, would not look her father in the eyes, pretended not to hear him whenever he addressed her. She spoke to him through me. I'd never heard her say his name and he did the same. Yet she would not tolerate a put-down of her father by Malan in his absence.

I understood that. My father hadn't been all that different from Chilman. To let go of that resentment required something stronger than forgiveness. To pretend it didn't matter was to deny what I had become because of my father's rejection.

8

A blustering early Monday morning in Kara Island. Benna and her women friends walked us to the jetty. A whipping wind had them grabbing at unruly skirts and dresses. In the near distance, Blackwater looked like a giant boiling cauldron.

Before I boarded the ferry, Benna placed herself beside me. She smelled of the herbs they'd bathed Miss Stanislaus in earlier. 'We countin on you to hold 'er up – proud girl, yunno. She'll never make you know she need some holdin up. Specially now.'

Benna rested sly, enquiring eyes on my face, her cheeks spread in a wide gap-toothed smile. 'She say, never mind that pretty baby-face ov yours, you stubborn like a Kara Islan ram goat. That true?' Benna was looking at me as if she really wanted to know.

I opened my palms and shrugged.

'Y'all headin back to trouble, not so?'

'Big trouble,' I said.

'We here and . . . ' She raised her stick and pointed it south, in the direction of Camaho. 'We over there with y'all too.'

They were still on the jetty when the big catamaran swung into Blackwater.

Miss Stanislaus slept all the way, her head against my shoulder. From time to time she woke with a start and muttered, 'Sorry, Missa Digger,' before dropping off again.

I watched as Camaho took shape on the horizon, the scattering of villages along the coast as the ferry drew nearer, the mountains above them all – purple and forbidding – and I felt a tug of regret that Miss Stanislaus and I had over-nighted on Kara Island.

The *Osprey* slid into the Carenage at 10.12am. Outside, on the sidewalk, Miss Stanislaus brought her hands together and raised them. 'You handcuffin me?'

'Nobody handcuffing you, Miss Stanislaus. Nobody touching you! You unnerstan? I want you to stay away from work for a coupla days. That alright?'

She nodded. We took a minibus to the airport to pick up my car.

Somefing get kill' inside you ... Miss Stanislaus's words had made a small nest in my head. I dropped her off and retrieved the Glock from Daphne. The child came out running, stood looking up into her mother's face, her arms straight down her sides. I couldn't bear to watch the adoration and vulnerability in Daphne's eyes. Miss Stanislaus reached out and touched her daughter's cheek, then pulled the child against her and she too began crying. I felt awkward watching Miss Stanislaus trying to wipe the child's wet cheeks with her bare hand and Daphne burrowing her face into her. And it was clear to me that something between these two had been lifted. I left them on the veranda, aware that I'd avoided talking to Miss Stanislaus about the trouble I saw coming.

It was still early afternoon. I told Chilman I was coming to see him.

I drove through indecisive weather – rain one minute, bright sunshine the next – to DS Chilman's drinking hole, a rickety single-room rumshop that looked more like a shed. It seemed to have been built for his convenience because it was no more than fifty yards from his house, which looked straight out to sea from its perch on a low granite cliff.

He'd asked Miriam, the woman who ran the place, to put us in the 'backroom' – a tight space separated from the rest of the shop by a plastic curtain full of holes. Two upended crates served as seats. We rested our elbows on what looked like a cross between a table and a bench.

Chilman looked old, with none of the cantankerous energy I loved and hated him for. For the first time I had a sense of his fragility and with it came a sinking feeling in my gut.

'Y'awright, Sir?'

'Talk,' he said.

I ran through the incident with Juba again.

'Anybody else see what happen?'

I shook my head.

'You say Juba hit you?'

I curled a hand behind my back.

Chilman got up, walked around me and rolled up my T-shirt. He prodded my shoulder blade, then released the fabric when I winced.

'You got Kathleen to take a picture?'

I nodded.

'Digson,' he said, passing a vigorous hand across his head, 'we deep in shit, and I got to tell you I don't see no way out of it. Apart from that lil bruise you got on your back, you can't prove a thing. Kathleen' history with Juba Hurst mean she got a very strong motive. She left 'er girlchild on her own, travel twenty miles by boat, armed with a police gun to kill him. She didn get through first time, becuz you stop her, so she spend another night to make sure.'

'I was there, Sir, I—'

'Tell that to a hearing, Digson, or a jury, and they'll laugh at you.'

53

'The fella attacked us. I saw everything.'

'Tell that to a jury too! They'll laugh you outta court. Everybody know that you and Kathleen together like bim-and-bam. Everybody expect a cover-up story from you and you not going to get no support from the Force, especially the fellas in Central, because you arrested one of them a few days ago. They going to make sure it turn back and bite y'arse. My problem is Officer Mibo.'

I frowned at him. 'I know Mibo. Spoke to him coupla times.'

'You speak to Mibo, but you dunno Mibo. You will note that you didn see him when y'all wuz there. Mibo is a snake and a greedy coward! I call him soonz you put down the phone and ask him if he prepare to support y'all. Mibo inform me that he done send in his report about the murder. You notice the word? Murder! He not telling me who he send it to. Is not to the Commissioner of police, like he should've done, and is none of the superintendents in Camaho either. Because I check.'

'Justice Minister,' I said.

'That's my guess.' Chilman licked his lips, glared at me as if I'd done him something. 'That Justice Minister jackass won't do the work people elect him to do. He won't keep his hands off police bizness. He will sell his mother and his children for a vote. He keep picking on police – wait till police turn on him.'

'Why Mibo got that attitude?'

'Mibo is Juba' family – second cousin, I think. He got a big house and cars that his salary can't afford. Juba gone, so Mibo' bowl of gravy empty now. No more backhanders for passing a blind eye to all of Juba' dealings.'

'We didn't mention Malan,' I said.

He went sullen and deep-eyed, then tilted his head at

54

the roof, his eyes roving along it. 'Ever read the *Royal Reader*, Digson?'

'Nuh.'

'Then your education not complete!' He showed me a row of yellow teeth. 'Is the schoolbook English-people try to corrupt we mind with, Digson, but it got one good story in it. Ever hear about de Englishfella and the tiger?'

'Tell me.'

'Englishfella bring up a tiger from since it was a puppy, yunno?'

'Cub—'

'Eh?'

'Go ahead, Sir.'

'Tiger-puppy grow up and behave just like the dog Missa Englishman bring it up to be. Englishfella love that animal like his own child. One day he siddown comfortable reading while he petting the tiger. Digson! I bet you never know that tiger got tongue like sandpaper! Anyway, tiger lick so hard, it bruise the whitefella hand. The hand start to bleed, lil bit at first. Then a lot more. Guess what happen?'

Chilman rapped the table with a knuckle. Miriam pulled the blind and pushed in her head. 'Miri, gimme a quarter bottle. A Malta for the youngfella.'

I shook my head. 'Let's finish this bizness first, Sir. Else I going.'

Miriam soured her face, sucked her teeth and pulled the curtain closed.

'You not going nowhere, Digson! Miri, bring the drink. That's the reward I get for teaching him every blaastid thing he know!'

Miriam stretched a hand through the slit in the curtain with a tiny glass and a quarter bottle of spirits.

I lifted my bag, rose and headed for the door.

Chilman launched himself after me. He caught up on the threshold. He was smacking his lips, his eyes feverish and blinking. 'I don't have to drink it till we done the conversation, Digson.'

'I need to talk to the Commissioner—'

'Your father.'

'At the end of the day he's—'

'Your father.'

'Jeezas Christ! I trying to have a conversation here!'

'Digson, he can't get Kathleen off. I talk to him already.'

'I not asking him to get her off. I asking him to do his job.'

Chilman cocked his head. Frowned. 'You going pick a fight with him?'

'Whatever it takes – what happened in the story?'

'I not the one who decide to run off!'

I'd turned to leave when he prodded me on the shoulder. 'You got to see the tiger-puppy.'

'What you talking bout, Sir?'

'Malan Greaves.' He cleared his throat, spat and hurried back inside.

9

I drove back to San Andrews with DS Chilman's words throbbing in my head – *I don't see no way out of it . . . you got to see the tiger-puppy . . .*

Malan Greaves didn't just want Miss Stanislaus out of San Andrews CID, he would have preferred if she didn't exist. 'She the kind ov female that man dream about an' wake up in a sweat about,' he told me once. I knew he meant it.

A couple of years ago, Malan had almost succeeded in getting Miss Stanislaus arrested for the killing of Deacon Bello, the paedophile preacher. He'd even bypassed the Commissioner of Police and taken the case straight to the Minister of Justice who happened to be the preacher's 'spiritual advisor'.

From then, I'd watched the poison between them ferment. In the office, Miss Stanislaus would not step aside to give way to him. She'd stopped him bringing his women to the office by greeting each one with a pleasant bright-eyed smile, then turning that smile on Malan. How were his wife and girlchile doing? she would ask. When last did he go home to check on them? Was this lovely lady his wife's family?

I would watch the Chief Officer go sick with rage.

These days, if Malan approached Miss Stanislaus too abruptly, or came too close, her hand would drop to her handbag and I saw the effect that had on Malan. I'd even tried to talk her out of the hand-to-bag gesture. 'Is a threat,' I said.

'Is self-protectin that I self-protectin, Missa Digger,' she retorted. 'You fink I dunno that he want me dead?'

Besides, did I know that Malan didn like wimmen? S'matter of fact, he didn even like his wife. 'He want to own-and-control every Camaho woman, Missa Digger. Is why he try to plant imself inside all ov dem. That's what make im feel he's man. In odder wuds,' she'd sniffed and brought a tissue to her lips, 'Missa Malan sick. And is not just him, is most ov y'all.'

Well, look what she just gone and done! She'd given to Malan what he wanted on a tray!

As soon as I got home, I shrugged off my shirt and texted Pet. *Buzz me, wn u kn.*

I stepped out onto my little veranda and lifted my head at the Mardi Gras mountains. When I was a child my grand-mother taught me to read the weather by what was happening on those high blue peaks. Thick mists rolling all the way down and smothering the foothills promised heavy rain.

Down below, in the cleft of the valley, I could hear the little river swollen by the water it had gathered in the moun-tains. I closed my eyes and imagined its raging journey towards the sea.

It was close to midnight when Pet called. She greeted me with a yawn. 'Digger, what you want?'

She was silent while I briefed her.

My words ignited something in her. 'Malan going to call a meeting tomorrow, Digger – soonz he get the news. You call him yet?'

'Nuh.'

'I going to ask Lisa to stay home becuz she will write

whatever Malan tell her to write. I want to take the notes. Make sure you come with a case against him.'

'Pet, I ain got no—'

'Digger, you give up too easy! Is two years you been workin with Malan. How much thousands-a-time he break the law to suit imself? Make a case, Digger. Throw it in his face when he talk about dismissing Miss Stanislaus at the meeting – because that is what he going to try to do – ask the dog, how come he never fire imself for doing worse things. Like that man he make take jail, becuz he want stress-free time with the fella woman, or the youngfella he shoot in his foot last month because the boy give im backchat. You got a lot worse things on Malan. Make the case, I write it down, and I goin to make fuckin sure the Commissioner and the Justice Minister get a full record of the meeting. And I will inform Malan of my intention. Let him get me fired too!'

'Pet, you amazin ...'

'Say that to my face, Digger. Call me when you done.' She cut off.

I didn't call her back. I phoned Malan and told him I wanted to talk.

'Digger, I at De Flare, come down, nuh.' Not the usual badman voice and attitude. Malan sounded almost friendly. 'And bring your woman.'

Why not? Been a coupla weeks since I last saw Dessie. I composed a long text message, full of apology and honest explanation about why I stood her up the last time. I laid my phone on the table face up and stared at the screen.

It took Dessie a while to respond – a long while. I submitted to the punishment.

Uh-huh, she responded finally. Nothing more.

Dessie and I – we'd been together and apart for two years. I'd laid with no other woman and Dessie said she had no other interest elsewhere. After her marriage failed she returned to her parents' place and visited me when she felt like it. Once or twice, to keep her happy, I turned up with her at their cocktail or beach parties, dressed up the way she prescribed. I hung around the edges of her crowd, a drink in my hand, and with what I hoped was a pleasant face. I was happy to be her staked-out territory which she defended with a quiet smiling aggression that got the message over to whichever female drifted in my direction and attempted to engage me for longer than a minute.

Luther Caine, the man she'd married, was never far away, even when he was absent – a big-boned, red-skinned fella who I referred to privately as 'the mulatto'. Her friends would call his name by accident sometimes then bring a quick hand to their mouths, their eyes swivelling towards me.

'Cruel' was the label I had for Luther Caine – one of those people who used their relationships to plumb the depths of their own depravity. To see how far they could push another human to self-destruct. It seemed to me that Luther Caine's special interest in Dessie was trying to make her kill herself. He almost achieved it – twice – by convincing the only daughter of the wealthiest family on Camaho that not only was she useless, she was better off dead. He'd brought her to the point where she actually believed him. To save her, I had to call her parents.

Her father Raymond 'Coldfish' Manille's punishment was as swift as it was brutal. He took away Luther Caine's bank manager job and had the post given to Dessie. He had him banned from every one of their private clubs and social gatherings on the island. Now, from what Dessie told me, Luther Caine gave water skiing lessons to tourists on Grand Beach.

In 2 hrs? Dessie texted.

n e time, I replied.

10

I didn't mind The Flare, but I hated getting to it. You drove down an almost vertical incline to a bridge that straddled an inlet which flowed in from the sea. High chalk cliffs rose up on either side. Soil crackled under-wheel. My nostrils itched at the man-smell of crabs, manchineel and sun-blasted rocks. I could never get down to The Flare without my nerves flaring with the awareness that I was driving through a place of buried disasters.

Camahoans called it The Furnace, after the US invaded the island in '83. The local militia was holed up there. It was the first place the F16 fighter planes dropped their radioactive bombs. More than thirty years on, clusters of cancer still riddled the villages perched on the hills above it. I'd read somewhere of an October night of rain, a couple days before Reagan sent in his Rapid Deployment Force, when fellas in the government had an argument over ideas. They settled it by lining up eight of their colleagues against a wall and shooting them. Eight bodies, bullet-riddled beyond recognition, then brought down here by a crazed militiaman who'd made a furnace in a rock-hollow above the sea, bulldozed their remains, then burnt what remained of them.

A whitefella, who did the same job that I did now, identified the only female among them from a flared hip bone. The grooves on the inside surface of her pubic bones told him she'd been a mother. A voice on the phone ordered the white-fella to stop the investigation. Couple days later, the hollow was scooped out and covered up, the bones disappeared almost as if they'd never been there. Hardly any difference from what happened to my mother ten years ago. One day, I decided, I would continue that whitefella's work.

I pulled myself out of my thoughts as The Flare came up – a pool of brightness against the black backdrop of the ocean. I wondered if the Swiss couple who owned the place, and the Camahoan middle-class males who flocked to it with their young working-class mistresses, had any idea of what they were sitting and drinking on.

My phone dinged. *Woman cum soon. 1 hr. :)*

Man arrive, I replied. *Take ur time.*

I parked and stepped out of my car. Directly ahead, a wide wooden platform, dotted with rough-hewn tables, a cocktail bar running the length of one side, candles sputtering in tiny coconut shells. The pillars of the whole establishment were planted in the shallows of a white-sand beach with waves seething under the floorboards.

Malan had his elbow on the wooden rails, his back against the ocean, his head turned down at a woman. He spotted me and curled a finger in my direction.

The woman gave me a bright, full-mouthed smile. Almost as tall as Malan in her heels. White culottes, fine silver bracelets that winked in the candlelight. Yellow-skinned and smooth like a ripe Ceylon mango. Night-black hair, close-cropped, and eyes that seemed not so much to look at you as to embrace you. Pretty nuh raas, like the Jamaicans say.

Malan flicked a wrist at me. 'Dat's Digger.'

The woman dropped a hand in mine. 'Sarona,' she said. Low, throaty voice that carried. 'Malan said you both detectives?'

Malan's eyes were switching between our faces. 'Get us a drink, Digger.' He pulled out his purse, peeled off a hundred-dollar bill. 'Buy yourself one too.'

I held his gaze. 'What you want, Malan?'

'The usual.' He turned to Sarona with raised brows. She laid a silver-ringed hand on his shoulder. 'Something local? Not too strong?'

I cocked a thumb and headed for the bar.

I ordered a lager, then took the bartender through the steps of making a proper Camaho cocktail. I waved Malan over. He spread his palms, frowning. I waved again and waited.

He came over – sweetman swagger, saga-boy step. Not bad, I thought.

'I didn't know you like this kinda place, Malan. You upgrade?'

He tensed, the black eyes narrowing down to pinpricks. 'Digger, I invite you here—'

'To make the new woman know who's bossing who – I know.' I stuffed his change into his shirt pocket. 'Pick up the drinks. Who's she?'

He shook his head and smiled. 'Sweet! Where's the gauldin?'

'Dessie running late. I ask you a question, Malan.'

He reached for the drinks, threw me a wink. 'Laas week, yunno. Woman step in my drinkin place cross de Carenage. I pay for de drink she order. And then, yunno. Man make a move.' He threw a glance over his shoulder. 'High class an' nice arse. An' ...' He raised a finger at my face. I slapped the hand away.

'You better watch yuh mouth,' he said.

Through the hum of voices, the clink and scrape of glass and cutlery, in the near distance I picked up the shout of a woman, pitched high and desperate.

I lifted a hand. 'Y'hear that?'

63

'Hear what?' He'd gone alert, his eyes searching my face.

I pointed beyond the railings at the beach, pushed myself off the counter and began weaving through the tables.

I walked out on the low-cut lawn that sloped down to the beach. Fifty yards or so ahead at the northern end of the bay, I picked out three shapes barely distinguishable in the spill of light from the restaurant. Two males and a female.

The woman's back was pressed against the bare chest of the shorter of the two men. He'd pinned down both of her hands with his. She was kicking and bucking to break free while the taller of the two – in a knee-length wetsuit – was scooping up handfuls of sand and plastering her face and neck. Both men, mahogany-coloured and muscular. They were chuckling and muttering amongst themselves. Tourists.

'She don't like it. Let her go.'

Shortman pushed the woman forward hard. She floundered, regained balance and scooted to the side. He turned to face me, smiling. Thick as a pig, heavy brows, hands like sledge-hammers. The skin of his lower face pulled back in a tight gold-toothed grin. The taller man stood back, his arms folded.

I pulled out my ID and held it up.

Shortman's grin widened. He shook his head and brought up his fists, his shoulders hunched, feinting punches in my direction. I slipped off my belt, rolled the heavy leather around my wrist, my grip on the tail. 'You take another step, I bring you down,' I said.

I let the belt hang loose.

I saw the big punch coming before he threw it – the adjustment of his feet on the sand, the tensing of his back muscles. I swung away from the fist, convulsed my arm. The heavy steel buckle snapped at his ankle, struck bone. He keeled over and hit the water flailing. He struggled to his feet and fell over again. Not a sound came from him.

'Yuh want to dead?'

Malan's voice behind me – soft and caressing. I hadn't heard him arrive.

The Chief Officer was on the bank a little way above me. I realised that Wetsuit had manoeuvred himself behind me with what looked like a fisherman's knife in his hands.

'Come an dead.' Malan stood straight-backed but relaxed, his big Sig Sauer flat in his palm. I'd heard that invitation four times before – throaty and seductive, yet dripping with malice. And it was always when Malan was about to kill.

If Wetsuit didn't see what was coming, the shorter man did. He'd pulled himself out of the water, taking his weight on one leg. Fast words spewed from him, some of which I didn't recognise. He was making urgent circles with his hands at the dinghy bobbing a few yards beyond the foreshore. Wetsuit turned, threw one last glance at Malan before dropping an arm across Shortman's shoulders.

They splashed towards the small rubber boat, climbed into it and kicked the engine into life.

'You didn say thanks,' Malan said. 'I jus save y'arse, Digger.' He made a point of slipping the gun back under his shirt. Now there was no sign of it. 'People tired telling you to wear your fuckin piece. But nuh,' he glared at the belt in my hand, 'you behavin like you in a movie with dat fuckin ting. Flim star does dead stupid too, yunno.'

'If you did shoot that fella, you would've spoilt the evening with your new woman,' I told him. 'And for the other people up there too. That's what you wanted?'

'So, I the one to tell you thanks? I not tellin you thanks. What dat lil bitch up to now?'

The young woman was still on the beach, hugging herself and rocking slightly – a light-skinned Camahoan, whip-slim, in yellow halter-back. Jeans as tight as Lycra. Braids pulled up in a high nest on her head. I beckoned her over. She shook her head, turned and waded out into the water towards the boat. She seated herself on the prow, her back towards us.

'Fuckin whore,' Malan mumbled.

I slipped on my belt. 'Mebbe she got no choice, Malan. From what I figure, she got a young child – her stomach still distended from the pregnancy. I guessing – that's all.'

A quick flash of Malan's teeth and that sideways look of his. 'You even talk like De Woman.'

'Miss Stanislaus would've done better – probably get the woman to stay away from those two fellas. Malan, I got a coupla things to raise concerning Miss Stanislaus.'

'I not talkin bout she right now, Digger. My free time is my time, y'unnerstan? But tomorrow, we handle it.'

'Meaning?'

'Armed officer without probable cause gone off and kill the fella who done time already for playin wid her. Dat's bringin de Department into, erm, is disrepute you call it? Anyway, is askin for trouble.'

'Is rape we talking bout, Malan, not playin.' I realised I'd raised my voice. I stepped away from him. 'You say Juba done time. Well, s'far as I see, Miss Stanislaus still doing time. She been doing time since she fourteen. You got a wife and girl-child, put yourself—'

'Digger!' He showed me his palms, then pressed a finger against his lips. He threw a quick glance up at the veranda and dropped his voice. 'You pushin it right now.'

What came from Malan was more breath than words now. 'I got bizness dealing with right now so watch yuh mouth. What I sayin is De Woman went about it wrong. She dig a hole for 'erself and I going make sure she stay in it. I going make sure she never get a police job again. I want 'er father to go with 'er too. I not making no mistake dis time. I calling a meeting with staff tomorrow first thing so I kin inform her ov my intentions. Then I goin demand a hearing. After that . . . ' He slid his eyes at me and grinned.

'You doubt her, you doubt me too,' I said.

'Let's suppose I make meself believe you. How come De Woman always savin y'arse? How come everybody got to save y'arse? If I didn come down here tonight you'd ha been dead too, not so?' He threw me an evil stare. 'Who de hell you think you is? Anyway, I not backing de bitch—'

'Don't call her no bitch!' I felt the growl rising to my throat. 'You call her them kinda names again, I go up to that balcony and make Sarona know the kinda fella she dealing with.'

He stepped back, showed me his palms. 'Lissen, fella, I know De Woman is your weakness. Dunno what you gettin out of it because is obvious she 'fraid ov man. All I sayin is De Woman stupid! You train 'er but you didn teach 'er no sense. If she did want to take down de fella, she had to set him up de right way. She had to do what I do, y'unnerstan? Put de fella in a position so he make de first move, and is clear to everybody dat she in de right. Den she take him down. Dat's self-defence. Dat's actin within de auspices ov de law! We not no American or Jamaican gangster cop. Camaho police oblige to do it legal.'

He was still for a while, looking out at the water. 'My advice is to stay clear of De Woman from now. If you stick with 'er, you get pulled down too. You bet me?' He'd swivelled his eyes in my direction, his whole body a threat.

He'd become no-nonsense and precise. 'She got the motive, she got no witness apart from you, and people expect you to lie for De Woman. Case close!'

I shook my head and smiled. 'Don't raise your hopes too high, Malan. I know what happened. I was there.'

'Show me de evidence.'

'I working on it. Give it time.'

'Time is what y'all ain got! By de end of de week, she gone.'

I could hear the waves sucking against the pillars. People were against the railing, looking down at us. Sarona stood out amongst them like a lily in a garden of weeds.

Malan glanced up at the crowded balcony. 'Digger, I decide you owe me. Next week, you take over my night duty. I not wastin my night-time in no office.'

I nodded. 'You sure you didn set up dis whole thing to impress the woman?'

A chuckle-hiss came from him. 'You jokin, right? I gone, night wastin!'

'I getting out of here,' I said.

'What happen, your bourgeois woman change 'er mind?'

I didn't answer him.

When we got back, people were out on the grass with glasses in their hands and questions on their faces. I skirted the crowd and headed for my car. Malan stood in their midst showing his teeth and gesturing. Sarona's face was turned up to him as if she were about to receive the sacrament.

I stood on the bank above The Flare looking out to sea. In the near distance, Kalivini Island, once a sacred burial ground for the people who discovered Columbus on their shores, now floodlit and forbidding, owned by a Frenchman with bodyguards who carried guns.

I glanced at my watch, then at the sky, pockmarked with stars, becoming suddenly aware of myself in this dry, ghost-ridden valley, walled in by bomb-struck limestone. I felt like an insect trapped in a dust bowl.

I messaged Dessie: *Still @ home?*

Leavin now.

4get it. Place dead.

An emoticon with a seriously distressed face popped up.

I texted back. *Still 1 2 meet?*

No reply.

I cleared the hill and swung the car for home – in my mind, the image of Chief Officer Malan with the Sig Sauer lying flat in his palm, his death-whisper to the tourist-fella with the fishknife, . . .*come an dead* . . .

That was Malan forgetting himself, forgetting about the woman he so obviously wanted to impress, just for the thrill of a kill.

After all this time working with the fella, I still feared that side of him.

I texted Dessie, *?*

F-off, she replied.

11

I took up Caran's invitation to come to one of his 'blockos'.
It was the first I would attend.

Once every two months, he organised a cook-up for his
area. His 'area' was the scattered clusters of houses that sat
at the foot of Saint Catherine Mountain whose western side
sloped gradually down to the sea. A narrow road, cut pre-
cariously into the hillface, ran through it. That place of cool
mountain air and thick-headed vegetation grew the nutmeg
and mace, saffron and cloves, bay leaf, ginger, turmeric and
cocoa that Camahoans claimed were the very best in the
world. Me, I wanted to believe every word!

Problem was, that same soil grew the best marijuana on the
island and explained the ruthlessness of Caran's Bush Rangers
in driving the growers out. He'd told us in no uncertain
terms, 'This land feed everybody. It send chil'ren to school. I
not going to watch people here starve because some fellas in
San Andrews want to get high.'

From early morning, he said, adults from the outer set-
tlements brought mountain yams, salted meat along with
a carnival of vegetables − dasheen, tania, sweet potatoes,
eddoes − and heaped them in the middle of the playground
a few yards behind his house. Children scoured the foothills
and returned with piles of firewood. Then they filled oil
drums with spring water while teenagers laid out battalions

of cooking pots on stones. When they were done, the adults took over and did the cooking.

I'd taken up Spiderface's offer to get me there by boat. We left San Andrews in the afternoon at two and followed the coastline northward: mountains rising up from the very shore, covered in blue–green vegetation, their valleys sunken in deep shadow.

The cooking was almost done, the air about me dripping with the smell of steamed provisions and salted meat, when I arrived. I'd turned up in time to witness two small miracles: an ancient East Indian man teaching a gathering of youths how to pulp a broken unshelled coconut with nothing but the saw-toothed edge of a bent machete. A very old woman sat on a downturned pan beside him, converting the poisonous flesh of manioc into healthy food, while urging the young men to introduce the milky fluid into their bloodstream and kill themselves.

Mary, Caran's wife, stood behind him, her arms draped around his shoulders. I hugged them both and waved at the others in his Rangers team. They'd formed a little cluster at the entrance to the playground. The fellas waved back. The woman, Toya, barely nodded.

Mary drifted off to join a group of women. From time to time she tilted her head at Caran or flashed him a look. He would nod as if in agreement or chuckle and raise his brows. A couple of times a big grin spread across his cheeks. Their way of loving always lifted me. Some invisible thing flowed between those two. It came off them like an aura.

'Digger, how's De Queen?'

'Miss Stanislaus not bad, Caran.'

'I hear about the trouble that happenin to her. You think y'all kin manage this one?'

He was probably thinking about the last 'trouble' we had with Deacon Bello.

'We'll have to,' I said.

'How Dregs dealing with it?'

'Malan wants Miss Stanislaus not just out, but down.'

'We can't let that happen,' Caran said. 'Let's go get some food.'

I followed him to a row of makeshift tables. People were spread out on the grass feeding themselves. Others began trickling in, some emerging from the spice plantations surrounding us. Most came off the main road and raised a shout or an arm in greeting: East Indians – sometimes four generations deep, mixed-blooded Afro-Indians and the red-skinned offspring of ancient Scotsmen. All the bloodlines of Camaho converging here on this one little patch of ground called Mont Sur Mer. All heading straight for the food.

'Real people,' Caran said. 'My kinda people. I ask you to come becuz you need to chill out before things get really hot for you and De Queen.'

He was distracted by a few teenagers who'd brought out what looked like a giant ghetto blaster and placed it in the middle of the field. They ran a few wires to it and attached an additional pair of speakers.

'What's going on?' I said.

'You'll see later,' he chuckled.

I dropped onto the grass and must have dozed off. Caran was tapping me on the leg. I sat up, realising I must have slept a couple of hours because the sun was already yellowing the ocean in the near distance. A young woman ambled over to the ghetto blaster and slotted a USB stick somewhere at the front of the machine. The air about us pulsed and shivered with rich almost subsonic bass.

'Watch that,' Caran said, grinning. A flock of youths crowded the machine and began contorting around each other, every inch of their bodies riding on the bassline. And it

was a thrilling thing to see the children copying their movements for a while, then getting the hang of it and bringing
their own vibes to the dance.

'That's just the warm-up,' Caran said. 'Now watch.'

The elders had risen to their feet. Great-grandmothers in
their usual headwraps, gnarled old men – not one of them
with an upright spine – converged on the music with the
slow intent of tortoises. They kicked off their footwear and
began stepping on the bassline until something inside them
lit up. They shifted gear, became different people altogether,
dipping and turning with rapid complex footwork, raising
waves of applause from the gathering. I felt the hairs stir
on my arms.

'Jeezus!' I said.

A burst of laughter came from Caran. 'You come to live
here, Digger, and you dance like that when you eighty.'

Spiderface was suddenly struck by whatever it was in the
music that animated these old folks. He flitted among them
like a delighted cricket and didn't seem to give a damn about
the laughter that he generated.

Caran nudged me in the rib. 'Digger, you see why I love
dis place?'

'I see,' I said and meant it.

Even here, in the middle of all this fun, he and his team
had not lost their alertness. From time to time they would lift
their heads, breaking their conversation to scour the perim-
eter of the playground.

I felt Caran's eyes.

'What?' I said.

'Digger, I know is rough times for you and De Queen
right now. I want y'all to know that me,' he dropped a finger
on his chest then extended the same hand in the direction of
his unit, 'Carlo, Roy and Toya – we at your and De Queen'

disposal. It don't have to be official. We kin come as friends. Just make the call.'

I nodded and looked away.

The dancing was over, the music from the ghetto blaster shutdown, the fading evening light replaced by blazing kerosene torches planted around the field. Down below, the ocean had become an inky darkness. Some young boys were on the outer edges of the field tossing a ball around. The air throbbed with the voices of older folks, talking about the times they'd lived.

Mary walked up and high-fived her husband, a mischievous gap-toothed grin aimed at me. 'How yuh doing, husband number two?'

I made the sign of the cross, raised my arms in mock defence and backed away.

Caran cracked up. 'Smart fella! You know what's not good for you.'

I pointed at the sea below. 'Got to go, we ain got no headlamps. I turned back to Caran and Mary, told them thanks with my eyes. They both nodded at the same time.

12

I stepped out of my house and stood for a moment looking down Old Hope valley towards the sea. The world around me was still dripping with last night's rain. I'd barely slept. My mind kept drifting back to my childhood and the old woman who'd brought me up. My grandmother – a thin-boned, cinnamon-eyed Afro-Indian, fierce like a hive of hornets when she got stirred up. I'd seen her stand up to men ten times her size with nothing but a rusty machete in one hand and the heavy leather belt she'd taught me to use as a weapon in the other. My grandmother, resolute, inflexible – upholding the single commandment she taught me to live by: don't go askin for no trouble, but when trouble come askin for you, don't just stand your ground, go out there and meet it halfway.

I was carrying those words in my head when I took to the road and headed for the Commissioner's house in Morne Bijoux.

I anticipated that Malan's first move would be to file his report to the Justice Minister, demanding the immediate dismissal of Miss Stanislaus on the grounds of gross misconduct. His temper made him predictable. He'd be acting on the resentment he carried for DS Chilman, who'd resigned but never really left the job to him, and for Miss Stanislaus because the woman stirred him up in ways I could not always fathom.

Miss Stanislaus would be out of a job, and it would be impossible to have the Commissioner reverse the Justice Minister's decision once it was done.

I'd decided to meet the trouble halfway.

I was on the road before the sun broke over the hills and was parked by the Commissioner's gate at five. I didn't know what time his house woke up, and I didn't want to intrude. Besides, it wasn't family business.

My two sisters were the first to come out. They were dressed for the private school they went to on the outskirts of San Andrews.

They spotted me and raced down the steps. I was out of the vehicle by the time Nevis and Lucia swung open the gates and raced across the road: Lucia – a gangling, clean-skinned seventeen-year-old, brows arched like the Commissioner's, a mouth like mine; and Nevis, fourteen – soft-voiced and reserved, with black, probing Amerindian eyes. Lucia and Nevis didn't hug, they squeezed with all their strength, their eyes on my face to see whether I would wince, or probably die from asphyxiation.

'What brings thee hither ere this foreday morning?' Lucia said.

'Shakespeare gone to your head?' I grinned. 'I here to see y'all father.'

'Michael, you got to stop this! He's inside.' Her eyes lit up with curiosity. 'Things happening?'

'Things always happening.' I walked them back to the house. Their mother was in the doorway. For most of my life, I'd convinced myself that this red-boned Dominican woman hated me. In all my years of knowing her, she'd never said a word to me. She'd ignored my greetings as a child when my grandmother, in times of desperation, sent me to the man she told me was my father, for money. The silence between us had become a habit that was hard to break and, perhaps to spare herself the awkwardness, The Wife retreated inside.

My sisters followed her in. I heard the Commissioner's rumble, then the scrape of sandals on the floor. He came to the door dressed in shorts and one of those short-sleeve shirts that always seemed a size too large for him. He rested puzzled eyes on my face. 'You all right, Michael?'

'I awright. Need to have a conversation, Sir, that's all.'

'Important?'

I nodded.

I submitted to his gaze – being taken in, in a way I experienced with nobody else. An old fella appraising the product of his loins.

Lucia and Nevis came out; each hugged him from behind and pressed a cheek against the side of his neck. I watched him closely. He avoided my gaze.

'Parting is such sweet sorrow, Michael.' Lucia showed me a row of perfect teeth, held up a hand and flopped her wrist at me.

'You just told me a lot about your teacher, young lady: she got to be in her sixties, white, probably English, and she been living in Camaho a long time.'

Her hand shot to her mouth. 'You know Mrs Martineau?'

'Through you, yes. I bet she never heard about a fella name' Walcott.'

Lucia's mother hurried her into the car.

The Commissioner brought out a bottle of Malta, opened it and filled a glass. He gestured at it, then at me. He pulled a chair and sat. 'Tell me, Michael.'

I told him about the shooting.

'Chilly already told me about it. What's her name – Kathleen – she doesn't look like a violent woman.'

'She's not a violent woman.'

'How d'you call what she did, then?'

'Self-defence, Sir.'

He shifted in his seat. 'I can't ignore it, if that's—'

'I not asking you to ignore it. I asking you to jump ahead of the Justice Minister and take on the disciplinary procedure yourself. Else the MJ will go on the radio and announce that he's fired her so you'll be forced to rubberstamp it.'

'And you think I won't?' He sounded irritated.

I often wondered how he took this daily undermining of his job by the Justice Minister who described himself not just as 'the voice of law and order' on the island, but the one who hired and fired.

It seemed to me too that the Justice Minister had always been hostile to San Andrews CID. He'd objected to the way we were brought into the Police Force by Chilman and in our very first year on the job we'd embarrassed him in public. Like Chilman kept reminding us, the MJ was probably biding his time – waiting for us to do something indefensible so he could make his move. Malan knew that too.

The Commissioner cleared his throat and shook me out of my thoughts. 'So what you asking for, precisely?'

'I'd like you to put Miss Stanislaus on Restricted Duties and call the hearing in six weeks' time – that's the legal maximum. She'll still get her salary, and it will give me time.'

'For what?'

'Is clear to me my testimony won't count, however true it is. I asking for time to find something to pin on Juba Hurst, to show people the sonuvabitch he was and why h'was better off dead. We never followed up the allegations against him for murder, rape, extortion – whatever. I want time to get the ammunition to fight y'all.' I realised I'd broken out in a sweat and my voice had risen. The idea I had earlier of a quiet, reasoned discussion with the Commissioner was completely gone now.

'Y'all?' he queried.

'Who else?' I said.

'Michael, I take offence—' He stopped short; was staring at me quietly. 'She means a lot to you – Chilly' daughter. What about Dessima? I heard—'

'I here to discuss a policing matter, Sir. If I had my piece, I would've killed Juba Hurst myself. I got no evidence to show that Miss Stanislaus acted in self-defence and in my defence. I want a chance to correct that. Is why I asking for time.'

'How far you prepared to go with this?'

'As far as I can go, Sir.'

'Even if it means losing your job?' He was searching my face.

'Yessir.'

He stared into the distance for a while. 'You two getting a reputation in the Force. You aware of that? I happen to know that most of the superintendents on the island have a lot of respect for what Chilly's unit is doing and they'll stand with him. Some of the rank and file – they've begun to resent you two, especially since that incident with Officer Buso. What I'm saying, Michael, is – so far I've respected your wish to keep your connection with me quiet. But if I have to make it known that you're my son to protect you, I will do it without asking you.'

'Won't be necessary.'

He stood up. 'Let me think about it. You off to work now?'

'Yessir.'

'Be careful.'

I didn't ask him what he meant by that.

13

On the way to work, I switched on the radio and tuned into the government broadcasting station. The news broke at twenty past eight.

Unconfirmed reports are reaching us of a fatal shooting on Kara Island involving two police officers and a local man. Stay tuned, we'll keep you updated as more details come in.

Twenty minutes later, a voice from Kara Island was on air. The caller said his name was Richard. The shooting was not no accident, he said, it was a murder. He happened to know that one of the officers involved – the woman in San Andrews CID – had a lotta bad blood between sheself and the man she killed. The morning before, she tried to shoot the man in question and one of her friends who was also from San Andrews CID just managed to stop her. Mebbe that was for show, becuz it was daytime and everybody on the island would've witnessed the killing. And if it wasn't for show, how come the same officer was there when she shoot down Juba Hurst and he didn't do nothing to prevent it?

Despite his attempt to sound different, I recognised the voice as Officer Mibo's. It was with a growing sense of dread that I walked into the office.

Malan greeted me with lifted brows and a steady stare. 'I got a feeling you been working overtime, Digger. Dat don't change the price of cocoa. She still going.'

The air was taut with the electricity of the Chief Officer's anger. Pet was making her keyboard rattle. She was the fastest typist I knew, depending on her mood. Lisa was pecking away at something on her computer, her eyes on a handwritten sheet of paper at her elbow, in Malan's handwriting.

He tossed me a printout of an email from the office of the Commissioner, notifying the Department of his decision to put Miss Stanislaus on Restricted Duties pending a hearing in six weeks.

'I know how to get a better verdict.' Malan nodded at Lisa. The laser printer in his office woke and spat out a couple of sheets. Malan crossed the room and retrieved them, slotted them in a folder and stepped back out his door. 'Today I show you something, Digger.'

'Wozzat?'

'I way ahead of you.'

'We'll see,' I said.

Malan didn't return to the office. Instead, he had the letter from the Justice Minister's office biked over to us.

When Pet opened it, her face went dead. 'He's shutting us down,' she said. 'He's shutting down San Andrews CID. Digger, that legal?' She handed me the letter.

I scanned it then passed it back. I kept my voice as level as I could. 'He's disbanding the Department: you and Lisa going to Port Authority Customs, Malan and me to San Andrews Central. And like you see, he didn't mention Miss Stanislaus.'

'Why, Digger? What we done?'

I got up, went to the sink and washed my face. I realised my hands were shaking. The mirror presented me with a hollow-cheeked fella with the night-black, sleep-deprived East Indian eyes and the eyelashes of my grandmother.

When I returned to my desk, Pet's voice had shifted gear. She was talking to Lisa.

'You not letting me see it?'

Lisa wouldn't look at Pet, whose eyes were fierce on her face. These two were tight as two pegs in an orange – Pet being especially protective of her when Malan, in one of his nasty moods, was giving his PA hell. Right now I sensed that their friendship was on the verge of a meltdown.

Lisa was shaking her head, her eyes on her keyboard.

'Malan instruct you not to show us the report he make you type for Justice Minister?'

Lisa said nothing.

'Then you got a choice, not so? You got to decide who' side you on, because is people living y'all playing with right now. And Miss Stanislaus' future. I asking you one last time to show us the report he make you type to the Justice Minister, else I want nothing to do with you from now on, y'unnerstan?'

Lisa printed it out on the office printer.

Pet picked up the pages. 'Was Malan' idea to break us up, not the Justice Minister,' she said. 'Thought so!' She curled her lips at Lisa. 'If you can't control it, kill it. That's what he been thinking ever since. And you love im up so much, you keep it to yourself. Don't fink I dunno about y'all off-and-on bizness, Lisa Bubb. I know from time.' She pulled her bag. 'Digger, you come with me? I got DS Chilman waiting.'

I hadn't seen when Pet called Chilman. I suspected that she'd been anticipating this, or perhaps she already knew what Malan was up to but had been testing Lisa.

We headed for the hill above St Mary's Convent – a well-ordered girls' school run by local nuns, which produced the top academics on the island. Most would migrate to the United States and excel there. Their love for Camaho would become stronger as the desire to return grew weaker. I didn't blame them – we were run by fools who were terrified of intelligence.

There was a cafe up there – a quiet little place on the hill, over which an ancient flamboyant tree arched like a giant awning. Pet seemed to know everyone she met on the road. Women drivers poked out their heads, waved and shouted her name. Fellas tapped their horns and called her Miss P. She took it all in her stride, and I felt myself looking at her with new admiration. 'Pet, you could be Justice Minister tomorrow. Everybody'll vote for you, including me.'

'Digger, I love my job. I work hard to be good at it, and now I good at it, Malan Greaves want to send me someplace where I'z a nobody. As if I'z some kinda plastic plate dat he done lick and decide to throw away. Like dat!' She snapped a finger. Pet halted, looked me in the face. 'I not goin to let it happen easy so. If I fall, I make him fall too – before me!'

14

DS Chilman was in the sitting area outside Pretty Pus. From up here San Andrews town receded downhill in waves of red corrugated roofs towards the Carenage and Esplanade. In the far distance, past the white smudge that was Grand Beach, the international airport – named after a murdered Prime Minister – on the edge of the sea. Chilman looked like a crumpled leather bag on the white plastic chair.

He took Pet's hand, guided her to her seat and dropped the other hand on my shoulder. The old man was quiet and dreamy-eyed, his mouth compressed. I felt better in his presence. He ordered us soft drinks and a glass of water for himself.

We told him everything. Not once did he interrupt, and when we finished he laid his arms across his stomach and leaned back. 'Y'all thinking wrong. San Andrews CID not done.' Chilman took out his purse, extracted a hundred-dollar bill and spread it on the table. 'How much this is?'

'Hundred.' Pet shrugged.

'Is not!' He pulled out his pocket notepad. Tore a sheet and laid it beside the money. 'This worth about the same. What's the difference, Digson?'

I didn't answer. I nodded.

'Correct! This is a hundred dollars because everybody agree that is a hundred. Is both paper. Same with San Andrews

CID. The Department finish becuz y'all agree it finish. A building is a building. Y'all got phone, y'all not dead, y'all got the same skills and y'all still employed as police. Only difference is where they choose to put y'all.' He lifted a finger. 'In the meantime, I going be trying to fix the damage that Red Pig do.' Chilman said the MJ's nickname with relish.

'Malan—' Pet said.

Chilman stopped her with a look. 'Put a goat on a cliff, Miss Pet; give it enough rope and it sure to hang itself. Right now, Malan Greaves on a cliff. Y'all dunno this yet, but I happen to learn that he getting a promotion. Justice Minister negotiating a position for him in Central: Chief of Patrol, San Andrews South.' He leaned back, folded his hands across his stomach and bared his teeth. 'What Malan just done is what he do to all the women he use up. When he finish with them, he don' want them to find a life of their own after him. He try to mash them up – make them useless. Digson, get us another drink.'

I rose, went to the bar and ordered the drinks.

A dense row of potted yucca plants separated the counter from the sitting area. The conversation between Pet and the old man was a low rumbling affair. I cocked my ear when Chilman said my name. 'Y'was in love with that youngfella from the first day he join the Department. I think he know it. Two years gone, Miss Pet, and he never done nothing about it – how long you intend to keep your pretty shoes hangin up?' His voice was warm and gentle – almost like a father to a daughter.

I decided to tune them out.

The old DS sat up when I returned. Pet looked distracted.

'Digson, if you kin help it I don't want you to treat Malan no different. That's what he going to expect and he done prepare himself for it. Give him rope. Please!' Chilman threw me a disdainful look. 'Digson, I ever tell you about the Englishfella and the tiger- puppy?'

'The first part, Sir. And you playing the arse with the rest.'

A chuckle gurgled out of him. 'Okay, well the Englishfella call the servant.'

He reached for his water and brought it to his lips, his eyes bright with playful malice. 'Right! On with the business of today.'

'Okay, so you playing hard-to-get, I could deal with that! On with the business, Sir.'

Chilman's face grew tight with concentration. 'I'll tell y'all what I been thinkin. None of this involvement by the Justice Minister making sense to y'all because y'all not seeing it the right way. In Camaho' law, a Commissioner call the shots for good reason. He stand between politics and the law. In other words,' the old man said, 'when an order come from up there,' he pointed at the sky, 'the Comissioner' job is to block that order if it mash-up your rights to life and safety, and tell "up there" why is criminal to give that order. But, yunno, in Camaho, the rightful name for minister is overseer. In other words, we still on the plantation.'

He pushed himself to his feet. Pet rose with him. 'Miss Pet, you going to be awright in Customs till I get you out. You, Digson, you know as well as me that San Andrews Central is a snake nest. The officers in Central want you dead. My advice,' he splayed a hand and showed me his fingers, 'don't take on no night duty or go anywhere on your own when you on duty. Stay where other people kin see you, at all times. Whatever office they give you, arrange the room to suit yourself and siddown with the back of your chair against a wall and the door in your line of sight. Wear your piece at all times, y'hear me? Wear your piece!'

Pet dropped a hand on Chilman's arms and pecked him on the cheek.

Chilman winked at me. 'Digson, where's mine?'

'Nuh!'

'When they moving y'all out?'

Pet's eyes were switching between our faces.

'Next week, Monday.'

'So y'all got six days. We didn't talk about Kathleen. Digson, I see you got her on Restricted Duties so you got the time you say you need to clear her. I hoping it pay off. My advice – carry on with the job as if nothing happen.'

The old fella pushed past and nudged me with an elbow. 'Digson, you'z a rascal!'

'Quite!' I said, mimicking his voice.

We watched him hobble up the steps.

'Digger, he luv you,' Pet said. 'From, erm, the time you join San Andrews CID.'

'He got strong feelings for you too, Pet. He'll do anything for you.'

'I know,' she said.

15

I was probably the only policeman on the island who didn't mind the quiet and isolation of night duty. With my nose against the glass of our office window, I stared out at the ocean, speckled with the lights of ships and fishing boats. From the esplanade below, the floodlit jetty shot out like a giant gangplank into the ocean. Miss Stanislaus would still be up, I thought, probably fretting against the restrictions that the Commissioner had imposed on her.

Malan had, of course, left me to break the news to her and to hand her the letter. She'd taken it from my hand and read it without expression. Camaho's version of Restricted Duties was torture. The officer was sent home but always had to be on call and was given jobs to humiliate them. They cleaned out the station's holding cells, opened and closed doors for dignitaries who were quick to insult and put an officer in their place. I'd asked the Commissioner to have Miss Stanislaus answer only to him – not just to save her from the indignities she was sure to meet, but to protect those dignitaries from one or indeed several of her devastating put-downs. It also meant that until the hearing happened, I could call on her.

Malan had wanted to 'disarm' Miss Stanislaus himself. And by disarm, he meant rub her face in it. She was to come into the office and hand over 'de Department property'.

I'd told him to hell with what he wanted. I would get the gun from her.

Miss Stanislaus had said it was very nice of me to offer, think you, but she would bring it in herself.

She called mid-morning the next day to say she was on the way. I chose to keep that information to myself. The resentment in the office was palpable, the tension between us brittle. Pet would not look at Malan and she ignored Lisa so completely it was as if Malan's PA wasn't there. Lisa kept on trying.

I sat cross-legged in my chair waiting for Miss Stanislaus to turn up.

She arrived in a billowing white dress, shoes so pristine you were afraid to look for fear of soiling them. A big handbag hung from her shoulder. She offered us a bright democratic smile, strolled over to her desk and dropped the bag on it.

'The gun,' Malan said. He held out his hand while remaining seated.

Miss Stanislaus pretended she didn't hear him. She took out a long fluted vase and placed it in the centre of her desk. A giant round-headed ixora flower came out next – blood-red, and so perfectly preserved I thought it was artificial. She dropped the flower in the vase. The light from the window struck the glass and made bright patterns on the wall. Pet got up and fetched a cup of water and half-filled it.

Then Miss Stanislaus retrieved the gun. She did something with her hand and the cylinder dropped open. Another movement and the shells tumbled into her palm. She settled the bullets in a small nest around the vase, fished out what looked like a shallow flower-patterned saucer from her bag and laid the weapon in it. She narrowed her eyes as if she were making some sort of calculation. Then she spun the saucer with a fluid movement that travelled all the way down her arm to her wrist. Miss Stanislaus turned her back on the Ruger, and us. The saucer was still spinning when she walked out of the door, a tissue fanning her face.

The saucer slowed down and stopped after a final lazy turn.

I thought I noticed something new on Malan's face – his mouth partly open, his shoulders pulled back hard against the chair, his eyes on the revolver as it came to a stop with its muzzle pointing directly at him. Fear, I realised. The real thing.

I gave Malan the sweetest smile that I could muster before settling back in my chair. I felt like running after Miss Stanislaus and asking for an encore.

That was two days ago.

Now, my mind drifted to the present. It was Thursday – three days to go before they kicked us out of this little box on the hill and dumped us among people we did not know. The memory of those three officers parked in the middle of Grand Beach Road, their faces stiff with malice, had never left my head. The thought of being amongst them in San Andrews Central made my heart flip over.

I checked my watch: 4.47am. Thirteen minutes to go before I headed home to my bed.

The phone rang. I picked up, reaching for my pad to note the time. Heavy breathing in my ear. A babble of voices in the background. The sound of running engines. An accident, probably.

'San Andrews CID. DC Digson here.'

'Sah, I was driving down the road good-good . . .'

'What's your name, Sir?'

'Peter Crayton, Sah, but people call me Mokoman. I drive the bus name *Reliance*. I was coming down the road good-good, and when I reach Beau Séjour, I see someting by de road.'

'What you see?'

'Someting by de road, Sah. I was jus startin me day work, mindin me own business, yunno, but dat thing stop me. I say to meself, "Moko boy, that don't look good!" So I come outta the bus—'

'What made you come out of the bus, Mister Peter?'

'Something on de side of de road that look like a man, Sah. So, I say to meself—'

'And what it was?'

'A man, Sah! What else? A real man lyin down on his face. The fella lay down wiv his head sideways ... like ... like this ... '

'We on the phone, Mister Peter, I can't see what you doing. You been drinking?'

'Drinkin! Drinkin, you say? Naaah, Sah! That fella don't look like he been drinkin ... '

'How the fella look?'

'Laard Gaard, Missa Officer. You ask me how he look?'

'Yes!'

'Dead, Sah – that's how he look. Dead like a crapaud. You have to come and see for yourself.'

'You sure?'

'I more than sure, Sah. I—'

'You got people around you – right?'

'Everybody here, except y'all, Sah.'

'Okay. Tell everybody to stay away from the body – if it is a body you find ... '

'How you mean if is a body I find. I lookin at the fella right now.'

'Nobody is to go near it or touch it or try to move it – not even family. Y'unnerstan? This is a police matter now.'

'Yessah. I was driving me bus, good-good an—'

'Mister Peter, you'll be kind enough to stop off at West San Andrews Police station and give a statement?'

91

'But I jus done tell you everyting! I'z a busy man. What I have to—'

'I wasn't asking. That's what you got to do.'

'Yessah, but if I did know y'was going to make me do that, I wouldn've call' you.'

'I appreciate it. Go make the report now.'

Peter sucked his teeth so hard I brushed my ear to check it wasn't wet with spittle.

I phoned San Andrews West, passed the details to the duty officer and asked them to get there right away and secure the scene.

Miss Stanislaus was subdued when she joined me in the car.

A still, cool morning – the roadside grass glinting with dew.

'I, erm, I not s'posed to stay home?' she said.

'Not if the Commissioner didn't tell you that, Miss Stanislaus. You still working, you still got a salary.'

'Until?' she said.

'Until, we get you off.'

'S'pose we never get me off, Missa Digger?'

'Miss Stanislaus, I used to get beat up in school by fellas twice my size. Everyday I come home bleeding. Yunno why? Because I do what my granny tell me. You don' just siddown and take no blows from nobody, you keep movin. You keep hitting back. Is what I live by.'

She raised her chin at the road. 'Let's keep movin den.'

16

Beau Séjour was seven miles up the western coast – fifty houses or so overlooking the Western Main. Across from the road, a clutch of mangroves and seagrape trees fenced a grey-sand beach.

Five youngfellas were peering into a burnt-out jeep, its insides a mess of wires and roasted foam. The front of the vehicle was buried in a deep trough of muddy water near the entrance to the bay. The naked rim of one rear wheel was a couple of feet off the ground, like a dog with a hind leg raised.

We elbowed our way through a crowd so tightly pressed together it took all six of the officers already there to clear the way. Silence fell on the gathering when we arrived. All eyes turned to Miss Stanislaus, though the woman was dressed very soberly by her standards: a white frilly bodice with blue trimmings and a navy-blue skirt patterned with yellow canna lilies. The skirt flared off her hips like a Bel Air dancer's. The sky-blue handbag matched her shoes and frills.

By the time we got to the high grass verge where the body lay, I'd heard the name Lazar Wilkinson a dozen times. We'd picked him up a few times for affray. Two years ago, the law had given him four months for aggravated assault. When Lazar Wilkinson came out of jail, he went straight to ferrying marijuana between Vincen Island and Camaho with one of those go-fast boats that littered the waters of the coastal villages these days.

Detective Superintendent Chilman had no time for us when we raised the trafficking with him. 'If y'all want to make arrest, then arrest the fuckin government who give away all we fishing rights to Koreaman and Chinaman that come with factory ship to suck up all we fish. And what we get for it?' I could see him now, shaking his half-drunk, salt-and-pepper head and wrapping his mouth around a hot cuss-word. 'A lil bit of concrete on the public road that get wash away soon as a drizzle fall! So who's the criminal? Eh? Leave them fellas alone.'

Someone had thrown a sheet of canvas over the upper half of the body. They said his mother did it, and it had taken twelve men (I deducted nine) to remove her, kicking and cussing, from the scene.

I turned to the officer in charge. 'Liam, y'all couldn't cordon off the place and move people away?'

He shrugged. 'Best we could do, Digger, apart from arrestin everybody.'

I chided myself for asking. Crime scene procedure had no relevance here.

I told the officers to make a barrier with their bodies between the crowd and us. I lifted the canvas and saw why Lazar Wilkinson's mother had hidden his upper body. A deep vertical slit ran down the length of his throat, his tongue pulled a couple of inches through it. A necktie killing.

I closed my eyes and drew breath. Times like these, it came home to me how much I disliked this job.

Miss Stanislaus folded her skirt around her legs and lowered herself beside me. For a moment, she seemed distracted by the boats anchored close to shore. 'Missa Digger, y'awright?'

'We got a job to do,' I said. 'Let's do it.'

94

Lazar Wilkinson's T-shirt was buttoned up unevenly. Shiny basketball shorts, twisted almost back to front. No shoes and not a speck of dirt on his feet. I took photos, unbuttoned the shirt and ran my eyes along his exposed chest. I took more photos and directed my LED light at the eyes. Miss Stanislaus curled a finger under the waistband of the dead fella's shorts. Ain got nothing in the world, I thought, that this woman wouldn't bring a lil bit of style to. She must have seen my smile; looked at me as if I'd caught her in some guilty act. I slotted a close-up attachment to my cellphone lens and took some pictures of the fingers and feet. Then I brought my face down to the bruised flesh that went all the way round Lazar Wilkinson's neck.

'Strangulation − cord or wire − most likely fishing line pulled from behind with force.' I pointed at the junction between the lower jaw and throat. 'See how deep the cut is there? In fact, they break the hyoid bone. They kill the fella twice, Miss Stanislaus. They strangle him, then they cut his throat.'

Miss Stanislaus raised her head at the gathering on the roadside.

'This don't look like no Camaho killing either,' I said.

'Is what?'

'Look to me like a punishment and a warning. Trinidad had problems with that kind of killing about five years ago − always drugs related − the heavy stuff that wicked people kill for. Happened here once in my first year in the Department. We never found the killer.'

I ran a toothpick under Lazar's nails and deposited what stuck to it into a sachet. Then we began the slow, meticulous search of the area around the body. I took photographs, made notes, explained everything I did to Miss Stanislaus. She would file it all in that enormous memory of hers until we sat together to process the information.

When I pulled back and glanced at my watch, four hours had passed. The sun had begun to sting and now there were twice as many people gathered on the road. News of the killing had, no doubt, drawn them from along the coast – people gone still-eyed and subdued once they'd been told the nature of this killing.

I was weak in the knees and dripping by the time we rose to our feet.

Miss Stanislaus treated her hands to a few daubs of hand-sanitising gel then offered me the bottle. I shook my head.

'Missa Digger, I think they kill im on the beach. Laza Wilkins under-garments wet and rain didn fall last night. Besides he got sand down there.'

'Down?'

She pretended she didn't hear me.

I lowered myself and ran a hand under the waistband of Lazar's shorts, then passed a finger across my tongue. I ignored the grunts of disgust from the officers above me.

'You right,' I said.

She stood for a while, scouring the bay with her eyes, then fancy-walked towards the beach. I hoisted my murder bag onto my shoulders and followed her.

The morning high tide had receded, taking with it whatever marks that might have been made on the sand overnight. It had left a clutter of driftwood and seaweed behind.

Miss Stanislaus pointed at a trough at the base of a low-hanging seagrape tree. The hollow was wide enough to fit a small boat. It was padded with straw.

'Love nest,' I said.

'How you know?'

'I'm not, erm, unaware of the nocturnal culture of Camaho, Miss Stanislaus. Part of the job, yunno.' I avoided her eyes.

She pulled away the straw revealing a bed of sand.

We spent another hour there, sifting the sand around the hollow, combing the crushed grass and gouged earth on the bank above the beach. I pointed at the dug-up earth. 'Look like he put up a big fight.'

'Why they take his shoes?' she said.

'Hard to clean. They didn want us to know it happened on the beach. Like you, I wondering why.'

'Mebbe they think we stupid, Missa Digger.'

We moved over to the burnt-out jeep. I eased my way as far down the muddy embankment as it felt safe to go and pushed my head inside. The front seats, now bare metalwork, were far forward and aligned, the foot-well flooded with ditch water.

I straightened up and scanned the crowd, pausing on the faces gathered in the road. Then I raised a hand at the officer in charge. 'He's all yours, Liam. I want y'all to leave this vehicle here overnight. Nobody to go near it, y'unnerstand? Treat it like your wife − in fact, treat it better.' I turned to Miss Stanislaus. 'We back here tonight.'

'Why?'

'I'll tell you later.'

I'd parked near the little red bridge that led into the village. I sat in the car staring at the 200-yard stretch of road at the end of which the gathering crowd hung with an intent, mute curiosity.

'Missa Digger, what botherin you?'

'They come from every part of Camaho to feed on this. Give it a coupla months and is like it never happen.'

'I sorry,' she said.

'About?'

'Your modder.'

'I wasn't talking about my mother.'

'You was, Missa Digger. So, we build the story now?'

I told her once that there were two stories to every murder: the one that happened at the crime scene and the bigger one which led to it – the machinations of the murderer and their motive. She'd never forgotten that.

'Miss Stanislaus, I think we looking for two people at least. It take no less than two fellas to roll that jeep from the side of the road into the drain. One of them is very strong. Probably the murderer. I used to see Lazar Wilkinson almost every week driving through San Andrews in that Subaru jeep of his. He's fit and full ov muscles. I figure the person who killed him got to be a lot stronger than Lazar because a fella fighting for his life will find the strength he never knew he had. Lazar put up a good fight. We know that by the way the place dug up.'

'Why you want to come back here tonight?'

'Becuz it will be dark, and this killing happened in the dark. All the signs point to them killing Lazar Wilkinson a couple of hours before the driver found him, which was around 4.47 in the morning. You kin judge that by the degree of clouding of the eyes. Like I say, I believe is a punishment and a warning. Question is: who the warning for? And why?'

When I pulled up at Miss Stanislaus's gate she rummaged in her bag and withdrew a brown paper bag. 'A lil bit ov cornky. Mek sure you wash your hand befo you eat it. Shouldn matter anyway, specially since you been lickin sand off dead-people body.'

A chuckle bubbled out of her. I glared at her, which triggered another burst from the woman.

Once outside the car, she poked in her head. 'Missa Digger, we got to talk to Laza Wilkins' modder.'

'What you thinking?'

'I thinkin Beau Séjour people say the woman kick an' cuss

98

but they never say she bawl. Mebbe she know who kill she son or mebbe she know why.'

I saw the old excitement in her eyes, could almost hear that brain of hers slipping into gear. And I felt a flush of relief that this awful case had arrived – something for us to chew on and fight over in the coming days, to ease the passage of time until the hearing happened.

17

Lazar Wilkinson's murder set the island buzzing: back-to-back coverage on television, all-day radio phone-ins with lay preachers and Evangelists pointing to the murder as proof of the presence of Beelzebub, the Demon Prince Himself, taking residence in the wicked hearts of Camahoans. For some, it was evidence of the Second Coming. They backed it up with quotes from the Book of Revelations. They invented verses and said they came word for word from the Bible. A small-time politician from the opposition said it was a message from The Higher Powers that Camahoans had a duty to vote them in with a landslide. Dreamers and soothsayers had seen it coming years before, and this, they said, was only the beginning.

Always, they talked more about the nature of the killing than the murder itself, except the drunk who garbled something over the phone that ended with, 'Y'all is a bunch of jackass'.

I nodded in agreement. I was hoping they would keep him on for the rest of the day, but the radioman cut him off.

I switched off the radio, mixed myself a Camaho cocktail – three measures of Bacardi, one Cinzano, one fresh orange – juiced – and a dusting of cinnamon. I fed my CD player Bob Marley's 'Guiltiness' and joined him in cussing all them blaastid downpressers who, without a shadow of a doubt, were going to eat the bread of sorrow, especially Red Pig, the Justice Minister.

Malan called me close to evening, his voice thick with sleep. 'Digger, what I hearing?'

'Dunno, Malan Greaves, tell me what you hearing.'

'Is all over the news about de killing in Beau Séjour. You check it out?'

'Who check out what? We ain got a CID no more. You forget you fucked it up?'

'Lissen, man, it wasn—'

'Wasn what? Your idea? You want to lie for me now? I read your report to the Justice Minister. Tell me one thing before I put down the phone on you: why? Gimme the real reason.'

Malan went quiet for a while. 'Put yourself in my shoe, Digger—'

'Nuh, I don't want to do that. Especially that!'

'Digger, I tryin to have a conversation with you.' Malan sounded plaintive. 'I work five years in that department. Chilman was s'posed to hand over the runnings of the place to me after he retire, but de dog won't let go. He resign but he won't leave me to do my job. He give himself new title – Consultant Without Borders or some shit like dat. Dat's not no post; dat is provocation! Why people goin offer you a job, give you a title and not give you a chance to do de job! Eh? He insult and undermine me everywhere I turn. He override every decision I make. Then he employ dat woman to mind my bizness and challenge everything I say. And yunno, I let him do it becuz I dunno how to fight him back. So, what you expect me to do?'

'Leave the job. Resign! Go back to Grand Beach and sell your marijuana like you used to before Chilman gave you a job. Not mash-up a whole department and spoil every-body' life.'

'Digger, you cussin me and I taking dis from you becuz we work togedder. Else—'

'Else what? You'd come here and shoot me in my house, not so?'

'Okay, Digger.' He'd dropped his voice. 'I going to call you when you cool off.'

'You didn mention the promotion, Malan. Chief of Patrol.'

He went silent, and then switched off.

I left home at 10.30 for Beau Séjour, the site of Lazar Wilkinson's murder. Miss Stanislaus was waiting for me on the grass verge outside her gate. I'd called her before I left and asked her to dress differently. She'd done something with her hair that made her look much younger. She'd put on a dark denim shirt and a loose-fitting pair of slacks that were elasticated at the feet, and to compensate for the shocking lack of colour on her part, rainbow-coloured canvas shoes. No handbag.

'Where's your protection, Missa Digger?' She dropped sceptical eyes on my belt. 'Becuz Malan take mine.'

I reached into my glove compartment, took out the Glock and held it out to her. She looked at the gun, then at my face; kept her hands folded in her lap.

'I figure you in trouble already and it can't get worse. And I thinking about you on your own in that house with Daphne, yunno. Anyway, if you get caught with it, the trouble is mine. Is I give it to you. Besides . . .'

'Besides?'

'I figure you been feeling naked without Miss Betsy.'

'Dunno what you gettin at, Missa Digger.'

'Depends on how you hearing me, Miss Stanislaus.'

'Missa Digger, I been thinkin – I been thinkin that a woman was involve' with Missa Laza Wilkins. You want to know how I know?'

'I listening.'

'The two front seat of the car that burn – they don make no sense.'

'I not following you, Miss Stanislaus.'

'Think about it, Missa Digger.' She smacked her lips and sat back. I visualised the burnt-out car, the two front seats perfectly aligned, pushed up against the dashboard. Straightaway I saw what Miss Stanislaus was getting at and I was appalled at my carelessness and Malan's stupidity for wanting to get rid of this woman.

I'd seen Lazar Wilkinson driving that vehicle many times. He drove with the seat pushed back for legroom, adjusted for a man six feet tall – like me or Malan.

Besides, both seats were too far forward for anyone to sit comfortably. It also meant that whoever killed Lazar Wilkinson had never seen him driving, or—

'Mebbe they was in a hurry,' Miss Stanislaus interrupted my thoughts. She did that sometimes and it always unsettled me.

Why would anybody want to adjust the seats of a car they'd torched unless it was so obviously out of place in the first case that ... I glanced at Miss Stanislaus. 'So what you saying is that the seats might've been flat down and somebody straighten them up before burning the jeep?'

'Uh-huh.'

'And you thinkin flat-down seats mean bed, and bed mean woman for a womaniser like Lazar—'

'Could've been a fella—'

'Nuh! Ain got no Camaho fella who'll want to be found dead lying in a car by the roadside with another fella, especially in the night.'

'Missa Digger, it look to me as if they didn't want nobody to think a woman was involve'. Is why they bring Missa Laza Wilkins back to the roadside, take 'way his shoes and even wash his two foot, and then burn the jeep. What I guessin, Missa Digger, is Miss Lady start him off in the car, then interrupt his bizness.'

'Their bizness, Miss Stanislaus.'

'Den she make im take 'er to the beach.'

'Why?'

'For decency, Missa Digger – woman got a lotta that. Fellas ain got none. She must've tell him she wasn comfortable by the road, she prefer somewhere private. In other words, she reduce him to de beach.'

'Seduce, Miss Stanislaus. She seduced him.'

'Same difference, Missa Digger – he dead, not so? So is reduce she reduce im.'

I swung the car onto the road and grinned at her. 'Yes, Mam. If you say so, is so.'

A pleasant Camaho night. A high wind was coming off the sea and cooling down the island. Miss Stanislaus dropped a small parcel in my lap. I smelled potato pone.

'Missa Digger, I been thinkin dat everything I say make sense 'ceptin the part where the woman tell Missa Laza Wilkins to take 'er to the beach. I wonderin if he won't get vex and tell 'er, no. He not going to force imself on 'er? I mean, right dere in de jeep, like how y'all—'

'Miss Stanislaus, not all fellas do that.'

'They don't?' She went quiet for a while. 'Well, that mean she different from all Missa Laza Wilkins' other little wimmen. She have to be a woman he got the heats for.'

'Hots, not heats.'

'Same difference, Missa Digger. Mebbe it was the firs time?

Mebbe she strong-mind enough to make im do what she want him to do?' She cocked her head at me. 'Missa Digger, you don think we need more wimmen like that in Camaho?'

I could hear the mischief in Miss Stanislaus's voice. 'All of that is guesswork so far, Miss Stanislaus.'

'I know, Missa Digger. But is good guesswuk!'

18

I dropped Miss Stanislaus on the bridge that began the stretch
of road into Beau Séjour. I drove straight through the village,
rounded a couple of corners and parked under a tree that
overhung the road.

What I didn't tell Miss Stanislaus when she asked me
why I wanted to return around this time was that I believed
Camahoans are a people of the night. We become our true
selves in the dark.

I'd seen self-righteous politicians, god-fearing wives, fire-
and-brimstone preachers and high-flying lawyers in places
and positions that would appal the dead. Come night-time,
right was no longer what the law books dictated. Right was
whatever a person could get away with. All the things that
would not pass their lips by day became the meat of conversation in the dark.

I'd wanted Lazar's burnt-out jeep to remain there because
it would draw the curious, and hopefully bring out those
who – assured by the cover of darkness – knew something
about his murder. Even a criminal might want to see the
effect of his handiwork on others.

The place was jumping with people. Coalpots threw off the
smell of roasted corn, barbecued pork and chicken. Women
moved around their fires like fat, industrious ghosts. News
of the killing had drawn folks out from as far as the inland

villages. A couple more murders around the island and the local economy would be booming. No need to tempt foreigners with sin, sex and serfdom.

Miss Stanislaus had gone ahead of me. It took a while before I spotted her at the fringe of the crowd, and that was a good thing.

I kept an eye out for young boys.

I had only to find my way to a food-stall. Growing boys were always hungry, drawn to food – or the smell of it – like bombo flies to a corpse. I slipped through a group of them and asked for a mix of roasted corn, barbecued pork, curried goat and chicken. I placed myself just outside the small circle. Sure enough their chuckles and gossip dried up. I felt their eyes on my hand.

I gave it a couple of minutes, soured my face and turned to them. 'Food smell so good. But I buy too much. Y'all want to help me?'

They went through the motions of polite refusal before they grabbed it off me. I was worried that they would move off and find some quiet place to eat.

'I heard a fella got kill round here?' I said.

A babble of grumbled assent. One offered to show me the spot.

'I'll look later. I heard he was a saga boy? Lotsa girlfren? Mebbe one of the girlfriends done it – jealous, yunno?'

They didn't think so. Merle, Lazar's baby-mother, was too softy-softy and she 'fraid of him. Linda hardly ever came down to the road. Paula had another fella and she was making baby for him. The new one he got, well she jus nice.

'The new one from round here?' I said.

'Nuh. We never see her before. Is only week-before-last she come. Best gyul Lazar ever had. She real nice.'

'Not nice like mine,' I laughed.

Four pairs of very interested eyes settled on my face. 'What yours look like?'

'*Tik*, yunno! Hair puff-up nice. Big brown eyes. Not tall but smooth like a star-apple. And smart.'

They paused over their food.

'Lazar' new woman was kinda tall. You say yours solid? Well, Lazar' own slim. Not thin, though. She got braids too and she pants does fit her tight. She does laugh real nice! And – and she brown-skin.'

The boy said the last words as if that – above everything else – confirmed the sweetness of the woman. He was the shortest of the four with bald patches on his scalp. He ate noisily, holding the food just under his chin and dipping his head to bite. A long scar, still healing, ran from his shoulder to his elbow.

'What's your name?' I said.

'Eric,' he mumbled.

'What happen to you there, Eric?' I pointed at his arm. The boy jumped as if I'd struck him. He raised round, startled eyes at me.

'He fall, always fallin. We call him Tumbledown.' The tallest nudged him with an elbow.

'They call you Tumbledown too?' I pointed at the black scar that ran from his calf to his ankle.

'Nuh, is them rock across dere.' He swung an arm at the beach. 'I went looking for whelks, and ... yunno ...' Shifting eyes. Big teeth in a loose mouth. 'Lazar gone now. You want to take over the new girlfren?'

'I'll have to see her first,' I said. They laughed and turned to chatting among themselves.

Eric had gone quiet, his hand poised above the Styrofoam container, taking in every word that passed between his friends. From time to time he'd raise his head, and his eyes would flit across my face, then past my shoulders, his head switching abruptly towards the occasional upswell of voices and laughter. He must have sensed me observing him. Eric swivelled his eyes at me. I offered him a smile. He held my gaze a while, his lips twitching slightly. Then he turned his attention to his friends. This youngfella reminded me of a boy I'd known at school who saw everything, heard everything and never forgot. We'd nicknamed him Radar.

Now I had no doubt that Miss Stanislaus was right. A woman was tied up in all of this. And this youngfella had just given me a picture of her.

'Okay, show me where they kill the fella,' I said.

It was then that I spotted the youth a little way behind us. Tall, and so slim he looked streamlined. A perfectly round head. Good-looking. It was the stillness with which he stood, his head angled in our direction, that caught my attention. I pretended not to notice him.

I followed the boys along the edge of the crowd. In my peripheral vision, I observed the tall youth threading his way through the press of bodies.

I took out my phone. The boys were interested in the make and model, then immediately lost interest when they saw that it was an 'ole-time ting' from last year.

'Gimme a minute,' I said.

I messaged Miss Stanislaus: *c u by d car. 20mins. Keys on top back tyre, right side.*

K, she texted back. That made me smile.

'I got to go now, fellas, girlfriend want me urgent.'

They looked disappointed. I stuffed a five-dollar note in Eric's hand. 'More food if y'all want. I gone!'

I swung round to face the youth and made a deliberate move towards him. He started, began fighting his way through the crowd. I pulled out my LED torch and switched it on.

He lunged out of the crush ahead of me, his body erupting in a sprint down the stretch of road leading to the bridge.

I kept the beam on his back.

He was fast – fast and light – the flash of his canvas shoes a white rhythmic blur ahead of me. They barely made a whisper on the road. Even as I pounded after him I admired his stride and coordination. Halfway along I began gaining on the youth. I was sure he heard me closing in, but the young-fella did not look back. Then came the jagged workings of his shoulders as he began to burn out. It was then that he threw himself into the roadside bushes. I followed the thrashing until it stopped. And there he was, in a small clearing, walled in by high tufts of elephant grass, crouched and panting.

I directed the light at his face. He brought up a defensive arm and swung his head sideways.

I reached down and took hold of a handful of his shirt. 'Why you running?'

He gulped, shook his head. I gave him a couple of minutes to catch his breath.

'You part of what happen to Lazar Wilkinson?'

He shook his head – a limp, exhausted movement.

'Then why you running? This killing is over drugs, not so?'

He heaved his shoulders and looked away.

'Listen, youngfella, if you don't know it yet, the only thing that stand between you and jail is me. I been watching you watch me and I want to know why.'

He was shivering with fear. I lowered myself in front of him.

'What's your name.'

A murmur came out of him.

'Didn hear that.'

'Jah-Ray.'

'You joking! You turn Rastaman God? I want your real name.'

'Jana Ray.'

'Try again.'

'Jonathon Rayburn.'

'Thanks! What you know about the killing, Jana Ray?'

'Nothing. When I come out this morning, first thing I hear is Lazar dead. I-I . . . ' He passed the back of his hand across his face and looked away.

'You upset. Why?'

'I like Lazar. He help me out. I get lil money from him for food and things.'

'What things?'

'Clothes, things like dat.'

'What he pay you for?'

'I help pack de bricks.'

'Bricks of?'

'I never see inside dem.'

'What's in the bricks, Jah–Ray?'

'Weed, I fink.'

'Think or know?'

He didn't answer.

'Anybody beside Lazar running you?'

'Nuh.'

'You lie! Don't lie for me. Lazar dead, so is not Lazar you going be reporting to tonight. Who running you besides Lazar?'

'I got a message to check what going on when police come.'

'From who?'

'Number didn show up.'

'So how you going to give report if you don't have a number?'

'They say a fella goin check me. They didn say who, and they didn say when.'

'How they got your number?'

'Lazar had my number. He got everybody' number. He must've given it to dem.'

'Who is "dem"?'

He lowered his head. His chest was still heaving from the run.

I shook him hard. 'Who is "dem"?'

'Dunno. Is Kara Island people Lazar deal with.'

'How you know is Kara Island people?'

'Coupla words he say.'

'How often they make the ganja run?'

'Ain got no special time. Is always night.'

'From here?'

'S'far as I know.'

'To where?'

'Down south – Trinidad.'

That checked out with what I knew about the trade. The fellas in the coast guard called it the HSJ – the hop, skip and jump: a short hop from Vincen Island to Kara Island, the skip over to Camaho to refurbish and refuel then the big jump south to Trinidad in one of those go-fast boats they called a cigarette.

'So! Everybody round here running drugs?'

He shook his head. 'Is not drugs, is weed.'

'What you call weed then?'

It was the first time he looked me in the eye. 'Things hard, people have to live.'

'You sound like my boss. Why they kill Lazar?'

'Mebbe somefing he done or didn do? I dunno.'

'What he done?'

Jana Ray shook his head. 'I tell you already, I dunno.'

I dimmed the torch and sat in front of him. 'Something round here change, Jah-Ray. Not so?' I was remembering Miss Stanislaus's words on Kara Island.

He raised his head as if he were listening to the night. He nodded. 'Is different.'

'Since when?'

'Now. This time.'

'Different how?

'Different packaging. Didn look like no Vincen Island packing.'

'In what way?'

'Just different. Heavier, better packing. Everyting.'

'And what they done with it?'

'It went San Andrews direction. Lil truck. Dunno.'

'Lazar organise it?'

He hesitated, then nodded.

'You don't look sure. Lazar and who?'

'Only Lazar.' That darting look again.

'When was that?'

He bunched his brows, made small movements with his lips. 'Last Tuesday, five days befo, befo—'

'Before they killed him,' I cut in. I gave him the grimmest look that I could muster. 'What you know about the woman?'

'I dunno nothing bout no woman.' He sounded irritated. 'Is only the lil fellas I hear talkin to you about woman.'

I ran my torch down the length of him. Faded grey T-shirt, a couple of holes in it but clean; loose trousers, mismatched buttons clumsily sewn on at the front. The broken zip that the buttons had replaced were showing. A pair of canvas shoes, threadbare at the toes. I brought the light back to his face. 'You still in school, not so?'

He nodded. 'Sixth form.'

'If I arrest and charge you for your involvement in this business, is the end of school for you. Which school?'

'San Andrews Secondary.'

'What House you in?'

113

He mumbled, 'Hume.'

'My House,' I said. 'You sprint for Hume?'

He shook his head.

'Well, run for Hume House. Record for the two hundred metres still mine. If you train lil bit, you'll break it. Why you doing this? They got something on you?'

'Lazar see things tough with me. He give me lil job sometimes.'

'Is the only way you make your money?'

Again the hesitation.

'Go on, I listening.'

'I sell a lil weed sometimes.'

'Where you get the weed?'

'Wherever. Place full of weed. I sell mostly in school.'

'Listen, fella, get out of this right now. You see what happened to Lazar? Same or worse going to happen to you.'

I stood up and gestured for him to stand. Jana Ray sprang to his feet, stood there facing me, hands dangling at his sides.

'You live on your own, not so?'

He nodded.

'Right now, Jana Ray, I dunno if I believe you because I want to. But I letting you go. I could lose my job for this, y'unnerstan? I got a lot more questions for you, so tell me where you live.'

I took his coordinates, left him there and stepped out onto the road.

Miss Stanislaus was sitting on the back seat, the gun in her lap. She joined me at the front.

'You take long, Missa Digger. What you find?'

'Sorry, Miss Stanislaus. You right! Lazar Wilkinson had a new girlfriend. I even have a good idea of what she looks like.'

I found myself shaking my head, searching for words.

'Funny thing is, Miss Stanislaus, I actually met a woman at The Flare who fit them lil fellas' description: slim, tallish, brown-skin, braids, tight-fitting jeans ... She was with two foreign fellas. We almost had an accident.'

I told her about my encounter at The Flare with the two men and the young woman that they had been distressing.

She listened with her hands on the Glock in her lap, her eyes fixed somewhere beyond the windscreen. 'So, Missa Digger, you sayin you might ha' meet the people who kill Missa Laza Wilkins?'

'Dunno what I saying, Miss Stanislaus. It don't make sense – too much of a coincidence.'

'What coincident about it? Lemme tell you what you jus tell me, Missa Digger. You meet a woman with two fellas who you say you see maltreatin her. One man might've stab you an kill you if Missa Malan didn come in time.'

'Well ... '

'Is so or is not so?'

'More or less.'

'Which part ov what I say you don like? That Malan save you?'

I said nothing.

'You jus done tell me about two foreign man who didn have no problem killin you. You tell me it had to be more than one fella to push Laza Wilkins' jeep down in the drain. Not so?'

'Uh-huh.'

'And then you tell me the woman in The Flare look egg-zackly like the one the lil fella describe?'

'Uh-huh.'

'So, why is coincident?'

I lifted my shoulders and dropped them.

Miss Stanislaus swivelled bright chastising eyes at me.

'Besides, you not the one who tell me if somefing walk like a duck an talk like a duck, then is a duck?'

'Miss Stanislaus! What mood you in tonight?'

'I not in no mood, Missa Digger. De woman with the whitefellas – you say you believe she from Camaho?'

'Uh-huh.'

'You fink she in trouble, Missa Digger?'

'Look to me like sh'was – how I should put it? A, er, lady of the night.'

'Dat's a flower, Missa Digger.'

'She no flower, Miss Stanislaus.'

'Den what she is?'

'Well, I kin tell you what Malan called her.'

'What?'

'A whore.'

'Okay.' She sniffed. 'An how you call 'er, Missa Digger?'

'A survivor, Miss Stanislaus. Like the rest of us. I also butt up on a youngfella name Jana Ray.'

'What about im?'

On the way back, I told her about the youth and what I learned from him.

'An' you didn arres' im?'

'Nuh. I seeing him again.'

'You sure?'

'I sure.'

'Malan would've arres' im. And he would've been right.'

'I not Malan.'

'I would've arres' im too and you not me either. He the only lead we got.'

'Mebbe I wrong, Miss Stanislaus, but is how I feel.'

We said nothing more. At her gate she sat in the car a while, then turned to face me. 'So, Missa Digger, is three people we got to find – one woman, two foreign fellas ...'

She sat back, her words directed straight ahead. 'You fink we goin have time to finish de case befo – befo—'

'Before what, Miss Stanislaus? You and I know you shoot Juba to protect both of us. And with your help, I going find a way to straighten this. Not even you kin stop me.'

She tapped her bag and stepped out of the car, then poked her head in through the window. 'Missa Digger, sometimes your feelins make you stupid. Mebbe is why I like you so much. Most times.'

I waited till the patter of her footsteps stopped. Then came the thud of her front door.

'Thank you!' I muttered and pushed off.

19

I sat on the railing of my veranda, my feet over the edge. I thought of the faces of the roadside crowd in Beau Séjour, caught up in that silence I learned to recognise from my early days in San Andrews CID while searching for the policeman who murdered my mother. By the time I tracked him down, Alzheimer's disease had stolen his memory.

I told myself that Camahoans are like living graveyards. We bury our dead inside ourselves, then we try to keep them alive in there. Maybe that's what people meant by being haunted. I dunno.

Earlier in the evening, I'd gone through all the allegations against Juba Hurst – his drug runnings which, like Chilman said, meant nothing. Accusing a Kara Island man of smuggling was like blaming water for being wet. It was, in the old man's view, the only way that the twelve square miles of sun-scorched rock on which he and Miss Stanislaus were born remained afloat in those awful waters north of Camaho. I ruled that out. The reported assaults against women and minors were the last thing I would turn to. There were the murders, or rather allegations, that had come through to us from time to time – no more than rumours. They could all be untrue.

I reviewed my conversation with Miss Stanislaus at Kathy's Kitchen when she'd left the table and walked off on me. She believed that Juba might have disappeared her great-uncle when he took over the old man's land. I should have listened. Things might have turned out differently. I'd never known Miss Stanislaus's convictions to be wrong.

Tonight, death sat heavily on my mind. Every murder case did this to me. I could not erase the image of Lazar Wilkinson lying with a slit throat on the roadside. And the memory of my mother was strong in me. She was a heaviness in my chest, a coldness in my groin. I was held hostage by the image of a woman, so shot-up by police in the Rape Riots of '99 that they didn't dare deliver what was left of her to my grand-mother. Instead they disappeared her.

My mind threw up fragments of a voice, the trace-memory of my childhood name, 'Sugar Boy', a hand at the nape of my neck, her breath on my face. I couldn't sleep until I put her back to rest.

I got in my car, drove to the far north of the island to the high place above the ocean they called Iron Pot. There, a finger of rock pushed out into the boiling Atlantic. It was the exact width of my car.

An hour later, I turned into the dirt road that took me through an old wind-whipped coconut plantation.

I took the sharp uphill rise at a steady 20mph. My head was filled with the thundering ocean as the car levelled out, slipped into second gear. I closed my eyes and stepped on the accelerator. I counted to eight then swung hard left. I counted to four, then braked, and I was on the narrow finger of rock with nothing on either side of me but the long fall to the waters below and the glittering heave of the ocean just ahead. I sat there soaked in my own sweat, conscious of the rise and fall of my chest and the throbbing in my blood. I remained until something in me quietened and readjusted. Then I returned home to rest.

*

When I got back, there were lights on in my house. Dessie knew where to find my spare key.

She put aside her phone when I walked in.

'Been calling you,' she said.

'Been out,' I said.

She uncoiled herself from the sofa, draped her arms around my neck and offered me a close-up of that face that never failed to turn heads. She'd made a mane of her hair, held together just over her shoulder by a band. She was wearing a light grey dress, soft to the touch, a pair of Clarks shoes – the preferred brand of the Camaho rich. She looked drowsy in the light.

'You been messing me about, Digger,' she said. 'I keep telling you I don't like it.'

'Is the job, Dessie. I sorry.'

'A time might come when apologising won't be enough.'

'Sorry again. You want a drink?'

'Something weak,' she said. 'But not now.'

I washed my hands, stripped myself and walked into the shower. Dessie trailed after me, leaned a shoulder against the door, observing me. It was the way we sometimes began our lovemaking – a slow, indirect journey to each other's bodies. She would dry me, we would touch then pull away. I would follow her out onto the veranda with my drink, sit and watch the moon make its cold indifferent arc over the valley, liking the discomfort of the early-morning chill because it roused our appetite for warmth.

'Digger, what's happening with you?'

I told her about the murder of Lazar Wilkinson.

'These things happen here?' She spoke in whispered shock.

Dessie and her people could live the rest of their lives with the island falling apart and they would only notice if the trouble touched their profits. When it got too hot they left for Washington or New York.

'I want to go in,' she said.

She did something with her hand behind her and the dress slipped to the floor in a soft grey heap.

It had taken me months to learn Dessie's preferred way of making love – the pleasure and the patience that went with it, the ritual and the waiting. I wondered if it was a reaction to her marriage to Luther Caine.

'Luther didn't use to lay with me,' she told me once. 'He used to take me. And if I wasn't in some kind of pain he wasn't satisfied. Sex wasn't something we did, it was something he inflicted. I didn't feel whole afterwards.'

Sometimes I felt his presence between us. In her silence, especially after sex, I sensed his shadow there. Sometimes she called me by his name. I never brought it to her attention.

She was up before me. I heard the shower going. Dessie came out dressed in one of my shirts.

I showered, slipped on a pair of shorts and a string vest with a marijuana leaf emblazoned on the front and back. She watched me watching her.

'Is the way you look at me that does it, Digger. You come in the bank sometimes and Jesus!' She rolled her eyes. That made me laugh.

She drifted around the living room looking at the pictures on the wall, passed a hand across my school trophies and stretched a finger at the picture of the child leaning against the woman. 'You get the looks from her,' she said. She turned around to face me. 'You never talk about your father, Digger.'

I'd never told Dessie who my father was.

'Breakfast?' I said.

For Dessie, I prepared food their servants ate – the food I grew up on: a cup of boiled Camaho cocoa, steamed green bananas and sweet potatoes, soused salt-fish blessed with coconut oil, tomatoes, chives, garlic and green pepper that I picked from my little garden behind the house. She ate with her fingers because she knew I loved watching her feed herself that way.

She came behind me and wrapped her hand around my stomach. Her chin nestled in the hollow of my neck, moved with me like a dancer would, with her breath against my ear.

'Digger, when you coming to meet my people?'

She'd been pressing me for months.

'Why?'

'My father says he wants to meet you.'

'What you told him about me?'

'I want him to find out for himself. You're doing this for me – for us.'

'Let's eat, Dessie.'

We sat on the steps, the plate on our knees. 'Dessie, you need somebody to run lil errands at the bank for y'all: photocopying, sweeping up, polishing up y'all marble floor and counter – that sort of thing? I know a youngfella perfect for the job.'

'Not sure, Digger.' She'd put on her bank-manager's face. 'We do need people sometimes. They don't always stay. How old?'

'Eighteen – nineteen, sixth form.'

She slid a glance at me. 'You come to lunch, I find a slot for your friend. Deal?'

'Get him the job first. Like tomorrow? Is urgent. Please?'

'You promise?'

'I promise.'

20

Monday morning, at nine o'clock I received a voice message that I was to report to work at San Andrews Central. It came from the MJ's secretary.

I was on the way there when Chilman phoned and said he couldn't get into the office – they'd changed the lock, but rather than let the Justice Minister have the place he, Chilman, would burn the damn thing down. It gladdened my heart to hear the fight in the old man's voice.

San Andrews Central sat in the middle of four streets, one on each side of it. A grey two-storey building with a wide forecourt, low-roofed rooms, strip-lit with cold, greenish fluorescent tubes. The market square began almost beneath the east-facing windows.

The place was a hive of offices. Through the walls, I picked up the grunts and coughs of middle-aged men. Four secretaries sat at their desks in the far right corner of the room – all with harassed faces, answering calls or deciphering pages of badly written reports. We knew them as a tight, secretive bunch who collected other people's 'sins', including those of officers. They thought nothing of using them as currency to have the excesses of their family and offspring overlooked.

Staff Superintendent Gill dragged a chair and table just outside the common area. I felt like an exhibit with all those eyes on me. Heads and shoulders were leaning into each other, muttering words: *youngfella ... soft-man ... trag ...* I took exception to 'trag', especially. It was short for toe rags – Chilman's toe rags. I pretended I didn't hear them.

I was flipping through a *Forensics Today* magazine and making notes when I sensed a presence over me. I raised my head. It was Switch, the man who'd stopped in the middle of Grand Beach Road with his friends and tried to stare me down. I'd never seen such malice in the eyes of another human before. And it was odd because I felt completely unflustered. I returned his gaze.

I thought I heard Malan's voice somewhere in the building, then I was sure. He strolled out of one of the offices at the far end of the corridor and lengthened his stride when he saw me.

'What go on, Switch?' Malan's voice was relaxed. His eyes weren't.

Switch shifted his gaze to Malan. Something in Malan's stance had changed. He'd hooked a thumb in his belt, his shoulders pulled back slightly. I had the impression of two bad-dogs sniffing each other out.

Switch nodded, held out a hand to Malan. Malan took it.

'You want to come for a drink later?' Switch said.

'I easy.' Malan shrugged.

He hung out with them for the rest of the day. By the evening, the stiffness between them was no longer there.

I was about to pack up at the end of the day. Malan was at the door with the men. Sidelong glances from the one I knew as Machete. He was bone thin, smaller than the rest with an oddly shaped head. His lips never stayed still. He wore steel-toecap boots, designed to strike bone and break it – the type extrajudicial henchmen used to wear in my mother's time. The wickedness came off him like smoke.

Malan turned back, muttered something and raised his

chin at the toilets at the back. He told them he'd meet them outside.

He was barely a minute there. When he returned, he halted at my desk. His words were hot and hissing with annoyance. 'Digger, walk with your fuckin gun.'

He threw his weight against the swing doors and was gone.

I was about to follow him when I heard my name. Staff Superintendent Gill was at his office door curling a finger at me.

'Is like everybody on my case today,' I mumbled.

A wide black desk took up most of the office space. Everything neatly arranged and in its place. It was the tidiest desk I'd ever seen. A full set of *Encyclopaedia Britannica* on a shelf above his head. A big red volume entitled *The Tragedies of Shakespeare* on the left corner of his desk.

Staff Superintendent Gill was broad at the shoulders, thick-fingered. A single gold band peeped through the flesh of his fourth finger, now impossible to take off.

Clear eyes in a very dark face.

He dropped into his chair and gestured at the one facing his desk.

'I didn't get time to tell you welcome,' he said. 'And sorry about my unfortunate use of language the last time we spoke about you locking up Officer Buso. You not enjoying it here, not so?'

'Nuh.'

He nodded. 'You younger than I thought. You look older in the pictures. The woman who partner with you, she's the same?'

'Miss Stanislaus and me same age,' I said.

'I been following the cases you and Chilman' daughter been handling. Is good work. I want to be honest with you. You look like a decent youngfella, not cut out for this place—'

'I not as soft as I look, Sir.'

'Regardless! What I want to say is I got no use for you. I not going to have you on night duty. I not going to send you on no patrol with the others. After what you done to Buso, a lot of the officers here got a problem with it.'

'In other words, they have it in for me?'

He shifted in his chair, picked up a stapler and replaced it on the desk. He nudged it into the exact position it was in before. 'You don't have to waste your time here in Central. You don't even have to come in. You'll get your salary as normal. Treat it like a holiday till I work out something for you.'

'We working on the Lazar Wilkinson case right now, Sir, and what you saying sounds like Restricted Duties to me. Sorry, I have to decline.'

The man actually chuckled. 'You don't do enforcement – Malan Greaves fit in easily with the others. Chilman' daughter – I sorry to hear about the trouble she in – she sounds to me like a real enforcer. You, I dunno what you do.'

'I just told you, Sir.'

'What exactly, youngfella?'

'Forensics,' I said. 'And a lil bit of enforcement too, as and when necessary.'

'Tell me about the forensics part.'

'The body is a book, Sir. Criminal forensics teaches you how to read it.'

He twisted his mouth and showed me his palms.

'Like I could tell that you sustained damage somewhere on your right side – probably a coupla ribs under your shoulder. It shows by the way you move your upper body, and how you sitting now, and the fact that the heel of your left shoe is more worn down than your right shoe. In other words, you favour your left side and you not left handed. Mebbe accident or bad fall? Also you would've been much younger when it happened.'

'Why you say much younger?'

'You had to be much younger to recover this well.'

'Twenty-eight,' he said.

'What happened?'

'Gunshot. Another officer. Over a woman.'

'What happened to the woman?'

'She married me.' He pulled open his desk drawer, took out an envelope and held it out. 'I – er – I could've held this back. I decided not to. Police Constable Buso will be appearing in court next week Friday. Sorry, my secretary opened it. Is accepted practice here.'

I scanned the letter – a request from A. J. Whitney & Son, attorneys at law, to serve as witness in the Buso vs Camella Whyte case.

'You going?' he said.

'I going,' I said.

'The judge is a woman. Things changing,' he said.

I rose from the chair and pocketed the letter.

The superintendent extended his hand. I took it. 'Go safe,' he said. 'You been issued with a gun?'

I pretended I didn't hear him.

21

I stepped off the *Osprey* at 9.47am. and stood for a while on the jetty on Kara Island watching a yacht with what looked like four panicking crewmen battling the tides around Blackwater. The seafront was quiet. Muted voices stirred the air. Four dogs brawling over something they'd just pulled out from the roadside drain.

I'd given myself enough time to meet Miss Stanislaus's people and leave them with a job. I also wanted to see Chief Officer Mibo. If my trip went as planned, I'd be back in Camaho by early afternoon.

I didn't tell Miss Stanislaus I was returning to Kara Island. I'd called her and reminded her to keep the Glock a secret.

'Is not like Miss Betsy,' she said. 'I got to practise a lot with it, Missa Digger, becuz it behave like a fella.'

'Try a bigger saucer,' I laughed. But Miss Stanislaus refused to be provoked. 'Missa Digger, we got a case to chase an' you not takin it serious.'

'I busy working on yours. Which you prefer?'

'Both,' she'd said. 'And you promise you take me see Missa Laza Wilkins' mother later.'

She wished me a good day and hung up. Miss Stanislaus sounded up-beat, even happy, but I wasn't fooled. It was her way of stifling the awful anxiety of waiting for a verdict. It had happened to me before and I remembered what that felt like.

Dada did not seem at all surprised to see me but she wasn't welcoming. I asked her what they'd done with Juba.

'The usual,' she replied and would say no more. It was as if she was meeting me for the first time, and I resented her attitude.

'How's Kathleen?'

'She's alright,' I said. 'She had a great-uncle who is no longer with us?'

'Koku. Yes.'

'Miss Stanislaus said something not right about the way he disappear, jusso?'

'She send you?' Dada said.

'You could say so,' I said.

'Is either so or is not so. She send you?'

'Nuh. I—'

'If Kathleen didn send you, we got no bizness with you.' She hadn't moved and yet it felt as if she'd turned her back on me.

'Miss Stanislaus got reasons to believe that Juba Hurst, the man who pushed your granddaughter to kill herself, is behind whatever happened to her great-uncle. Two years come and gone and y'all didn't have the decency to let her know her uncle dead or disappear. I happen to know what that feels like. In here.' I tapped my chest. 'Besides, she up for murder, yunno that?'

Her expression shifted and then her face closed up again.

'I want something to pin against Juba. If he got anything to do with that old fella disappearing and I can prove it, I'll have a case to argue on Miss Stanislaus' behalf. Just because you not interested don't mean I'm giving up. G'd morning to you.' I turned to leave.

'Hold on,' she said. She tilted her face at the sky and made a keening sound. I heard another somewhere in the near

129

distance, then another. Voices approached. Benna and two women walked into the yard. They threw quick glances at my face.

'Woman, you upset him!' Benna said. Dada seemed to wilt in Benna's presence. 'If you hate man so much, how come you have chil'ren with them? Not one but five!' She turned to me. 'Missa Digger, I glad to see you. What bizness you want with us today?'

I repeated what I'd said to Dada. Added, 'And because Miss Stanislaus convinced, I feel convinced too.'

Benna fixed me with those pale eyes, as if my words had alerted her to something. 'Is so close Kathleen let you get to her?'

I shook my head but Benna said nothing more.

I wanted to leave them with a job, I said. I could only afford a couple of hours on Kara Island. To explain what I wanted done, would they take me to their cemetery?

The way I figured it, I said, if Juba had anything to do with the old man's death, he wouldn't have disposed of him in the sea. Certainly not around Kara Island. He would have had to take him out to the sucking tides of Blackwater – most likely at night. I couldn't imagine Juba doing that.

Benna nodded in agreement. Juba was a sailorman, she said, but everybody knew he hated water touching him. She wrinkled her nose. S'matter ov fact, he couldn't steer a boat to save his life.

They settled their headwraps and asked me to follow them. They formed a tight group ahead of me, their conversation riddled with disbelief and exclamations.

These elders would be carrying in their heads the family tree of every person on Kara Island, and their connections to each other. They still named their children in the language their people brought with them across the Atlantic a few

130

centuries ago. Could tell the nations they'd belonged to and prove it with their dances and songs. They still held on to fragments of their old languages, cherished their bloodlines, built tombstones for ancestors that were more expensive than the homes they lived in. For one of their own to kill an old man and dispose of him without a trace was not just an act of wickedness, it was evil, pure and simple. Perhaps that was why they didn't tell Miss Stanislaus. They probably couldn't find the words for such a thing. All this I'd learned from listening to Miss Stanislaus and observing her.

I followed the women up a hill that sloped down to the sea. The grass and shrubs and tombstones were so groomed, the place felt almost cheerful. I'd asked them to show me a plot no less than one and a half years old and no more than three. The grave had to be unadorned.

Dada cocked her chin for a second as if listening to voices inside her head. 'Kwesi Jo,' she said, beckoning as if she were about to introduce a neighbour.

Once there, I pointed out the difference between a new and a subsided 'resting place'. I showed them what disturbed soil might look like after a couple of years. Then I took them along the path that we'd just walked up, and pointed out the kinds of plants that would first colonise a disturbed plot of soil. If that patch had lots of plants like those and looked different from the other vegetation around it, I said, they should make a note of the location and call me.

Benna repaid me by naming every weed I showed them, explaining what illness each was good for.

'How you call that?' the old woman said.

'Ruderal plants,' I said.

She shook her head. 'I mean dis kinda knowin you got.'

'Forensics,' I said.

'What he say?' Dada enquired.

131

'Furrin-sick!' she said.

I choked back a chuckle.

'What you grinnin at, youngfella?'

'Somebody just came to mind – that's all. I want to ask a favour, please. Miss Stanislaus not s'pose to know I been here. Just in case, yunno?'

They nodded like a chorus.

'I need to find Mibo,' I said.

A chuckle escaped Dada.

'What?' I said.

'Prob'ly gone fishin,' Dada said.

'He was around the night Juba got killed?'

Benna shook her head, 'Out on de reef divin lambi.'

'You sure?'

'I sure, he sell me some the same day. He even ask me how it happm? I tell im I wasn dere.' Benna swung her stick in front of her. 'S'far as I kin see, Mibo is more fisherman dan police. Night and day, he out in the water. He the best boatman we got. Pity he so damn greedy.' Benna chuckled again. It was all she was prepared to say.

I left them at the corner where Juba had appeared the night Miss Stanislaus took him down. I remembered the strangeness of that foreday morning, with Juba spread out on the road and the sight of a whole village emerging like shadows in the dawn.

The station was a concrete cubicle with a backroom added to it. A woman in a blue T-shirt, stamped *Don't stop de Carnival*, sat at the front desk, her fingers spread wide, admiring her blood-red nails.

'G'morning, is DC Digson, here,' I said. 'I looking for Officer Mibo.' I opened the door that led to the space and stood with my shoulder against it.

She blinked, ran dark appraising eyes up and down my body, then looked me in the face.

'Officer who?'

'Mibo! He around?'

She shook her head – those heavily mascaraed eyes took me in again. She became suddenly alert. 'You the officer name Digger, not so? Y'all the ones that—' She stopped short.

'Shoot down Juba, is what you want to say? In self-defence? Is why I here to see Officer Mibo. What's your name?'

'Shirley. I'z Admin. Officer Mibo lef about one hour ago. He chasing a case.'

'Where?'

Shirley gestured past my head. 'Other side ov the islan.'

'Look me in my face and tell me that, Miss Shirley.'

She lowered her head.

'I take it that you know his personal cell phone number?' I pointed at the notepad at her elbow and pushed the biro on the desk towards her.

'Hold on.' She retreated to the back room. I heard the clack of a receiver being lifted, a series of rapid taps. I shouldered the door and entered the tiny room. The woman's head shot up. She recradled the handset. Her shoulders had gone rigid – her expression hostile.

'What you don't want me to hear, Miss Shirley?' I said. 'Is clear to me you two got something going on. Tell me I lie.' I looked her in the face. She looked away.

'I got the work phone number but he's not been answering. What's his personal cellphone number?'

'Is private,' she said. 'I not s'pose to—'

'Tell Officer Mibo I want to talk to him urgent. Is important. I want him to admit that his statement about me and Miss Stanislaus was hearsay. Tell him if he don't contact me, I'll come back. He got my number, but I giving it again, so he don't claim he lost it.' I strode over to the front desk, took a sheet of paper and scribbled my cell number. I tossed the sheet on the desk.

I left her at the entrance, her arms folded tight against her chest. I felt the woman's eyes on my back.

22

I picked up Dessie at the high white gates of her parents' house. I loved watching her appear at the top of the winding concrete road that led up to their old plantation house, its white walls just visible among the royal palms and cedar trees that stood over the building.

She dangled a canvas bag in one hand, wore brown soft leather shoes and a simply cut light blue shoulder-strapped dress that shivered around her shape with every step.

'What you looking at?' she said.

'Possibilities,' I said and smiled as she dropped herself on the seat and nudged me with an elbow.

We took the long road to the beach, up through the Morne Bijoux Hills lined with the gabled mansions of old families who believed they still owned the island. Dessie knew every one of them. Those long arms of hers were always out the window, waving at people suspended in multicoloured hammocks or stretched out like hospital patients in chaise lounges on oversized verandas.

When we got to Coburn Valley we switched roles, with me shouting out to old fellas on donkeys, children with bundles of firewood on their heads or shirtless youths leaning against anything that would support their poor-arse, cool-vibes poses.

Grand Beach was overrun with children and harassed hotel

staff serving overdressed cocktails – hibiscus flowers and all – to tourists roasting oiled bodies under a spiteful sun.

Dessie rolled her eyes and sucked her teeth.

'Is Sunday,' I reminded her. 'And we got a tourist liner out there.' I raised my chin at the fat white boat sitting like a slug on the water in the distance, just outside San Andrews Harbour.

'No privacy here.' She broke out in a chuckle, dropped an arm across my shoulder and placed her full weight on me.

'We got some of what you want down the other end. C'mon, water wasting.'

We strolled the half-mile down to the northern end of the beach. The sand was darker there, the water rougher. A place the local children loved because they could launch themselves naked into the shallows from the giant granite rock that sprouted from the water.

The tourists never went beyond the white sand, not even the occasional dog that pranced around their legs.

We dropped ourselves on the sand.

A couple hundred yards beyond the shallows, two speed boats were cleaving the water back and forth, with skiers strung behind them. Dessie couldn't keep her eyes off the faster boat. She would drop her head, begin digging the sand with her fingers then look up abruptly.

'What's the matter?' I said. She had her arms around her knees now, which she'd pulled up to her chin, her chest pressed against them. Had it not been for the heat of the day, I would have thought she was feeling cold.

'Talk to me,' I said.

'I don't want to be here, Digger. Let's go.' She rose, took up the towel she'd been sitting on, shook it and folded it quickly, then stuffed it in her bag. 'C'mon, Digger!' She grabbed my hand.

'Hold on, Dessie! Tell me what going on with you!' Then I saw the distress on her face and relented.

We were halfway along the beach and just about to head towards the car when one of the speedboats swerved towards the beach, its engine growling. It cut off abruptly. I turned when I heard the heavy splash of water and followed the pale shape of the swimmer underwater until it emerged: a big head crowned with tight black curls, a broad pale face, a bristle of dark brown hairs on the man's chest and arms. Dessie's husband – Luther Caine.

Luther's eyes were on her – grey-green, steady – his mouth clamped down like a pot lid.

'Come on!' Dessie grabbed my wrist.

'Get in the car.' I shook off her grip, tossed the keys at her and turned around to face the man. Luther's eyes remained on Dessie. He looked as if he'd been wrestling sharks: two red welts streaked down his left shoulder and arm. Purpling skin just under his ear. He raised his right hand. A youngfella came sprinting over the sand towards him. Luther Caine swung an arm at the boat and the youth plunged into the water, climbed aboard and sat with his hand on the steering.

Luther Caine turned abruptly and strode along the edges of the water, the muscles writhing beneath the skin of his back and legs. It was as if he hadn't seen me – as if I wasn't there.

Back in the car with Dessie, I sat with my head pressed against the headrest. I rolled my head towards her. 'Next time, Dessie, you don't run from Luther – you unnerstand? Because every time you run, it is a win for him.'

'Your face, Digger! When you turned round to look at him. Jesus! You promise me one thing, Digger: you'll never look at me like that.'

'Like?'

She gave me an odd searching look, then frowned.

'Like – like you were ready to kill, Digger. Like – Jesus! I've never seen that side of you before.'

'Why Luther still wants to control you, Dessie?'

She shrugged, folded her arms around her shoulders. 'He thinks I know all about his fuckin shady dealings. You're a policeman and I'm with you, so!'

'Tell me about his dealings.'

She shook herself and straightened up. 'I don't want to talk about Luther any more. I hate that man.'

Dessie looked deflated, somehow reduced. I'd seen Malan intimidating women he'd been with just by turning his gaze on them. I'd seen them grow fidgety and uncertain in his presence, especially when they were with another man. But it was never as bad as the effect that Luther seemed to have on Dessie.

'Belt up, Dessie. I taking you on a rum-shop-run,' I said.

It was my way of trying to salvage what was a spoilt Sunday afternoon. I wanted to make Dessie feel good about herself again. I did that sometimes – take her on a trip along the East Coast Road of the island, which was lined with drinking holes, always filled with men slapping dice or arguing over games of rummy. Stepping into those rickety joints with Dessie nourished something in her. Charred old men, in their half-drunk stupor, would stare at this bottle-smooth, fine-boned creature as if she were an apparition and the more drunk they were, the more rapturous their gazes. She would bless them with her smile while I coughed up the money to buy bottles of drink – an excuse for entering the rumshop in the first case.

By the time I got back, the boot of my little Datsun was sagging with Camaho lager and Malta that I had no use for.

In bed, Dessie looked into my face. 'I didn't think you loved me that much, Digger.'

'What you talking bout, Dessie?'

'Luther, the beach . . .'

'That's what you call love?'

'It will do,' she chuckled.

'Tell me about Luther's shady dealings.'

'I can't,' she said, rolled away and turned her back towards me.

23

Lazar Wilkinson's mother was a dark-skinned wood-knot of a woman. Dora Wilkinson sniffed at Miss Stanislaus's words of condolence, barely looking at us. From time to time she threw darting, underhand glances in our direction with eyes the colour and sheen of soursop seeds. Miss Stanislaus kept fluttering her tissue and patting her forehead, distracted, it seemed, by a crippling sadness for the woman's loss.

I wasn't fooled. Miss Stanislaus's eyes were taking in the kitchen, the new concrete pillars, the pictures of Mary and Joseph and Jesus of the Bleeding Heart on the wall facing the half-opened doorway.

'Your loving son – he use to live with you?' Miss Stanislaus said.

The woman fanned her face and nodded.

'All the time?'

'Sometimes Lazar spend a night or two with one of his little wimmen, but his home is right here.'

'What work he do?' Miss Stanislaus's tissue went still.

Miss Dora twisted her mouth, lifted her shoulders and dropped them. 'As far as I concern Lazar is a good boy. He never rude to me and he help me out.'

Miss Stanislaus blinked at her and smiled. 'Yes, I sure you feel so. What work he do?'

'Work is work. I don't bother about that.'

'An the work that you don't bother about, what work it is?'

The woman cleared her throat. 'I never ask him and he never tell me, Miss Lady. All I know is nobody got no right to do that to my boy.'

'I agree,' Miss Stanislaus said. 'Sorry to upset you more. Missa Digger and me going right now.'

Back on the public road, Miss Stanislaus stuffed her tissue up her sleeve. 'Missa Digger, make sure you bring me back to see that woman ... in ... lemme see ... two weeks' time ... mebbe less.'

'You onto something?'

'Is only a feeling I got right now. That's all.'

I dropped her off in San Andrews market square and went off to do some shopping before returning to Beau Séjour.

I left my vehicle by the little bridge that marked the entrance to Beau Séjour village and turned into a stony path off the main road. I followed it past half-dead mango trees and wilting hibiscus hedges all the way up to a small house near the top of the hill.

The residences I passed were at various stages of improvement. Wooden walls were being replaced with concrete breeze blocks. There were unpainted verandas here and there and doorways decorated with fluttering, multicoloured strip curtains.

Jana Ray's two-room shack stood some way above them, its unpainted board walls blackened by seasons of sun and rain. A high bamboo clump curved over the tiny building like a second roof.

A small garden at the front, with limp okra plants and a couple of tomato vines held up by sticks of bamboo dug into the soil.

As if in defiance of all that barrenness, a banana tree

141

flourished – its silver-green leaves broad and ponderous with health.

I followed the slabs of stone dug into the earth to the rear of the house.

A length of electric wire bellied down from the eaves, anchored at the other end by a nail driven into the bark of an ant-blighted grapefruit tree. A pair of shorts and a T-shirt hung from it. All that remained of the steps was a dangerous-looking wood-stake in the earth.

I unwound the strip of cloth that held the door closed and shouldered it open. I stood at the doorway and surveyed the front room: a large lunar calendar with a poster of Bob Marley above it. To the left of that a black-and-white photo of a pensive-looking Malcolm X.

A small dresser built from an assortment of board cuttings on which sat two spoons, a kitchen knife, an enamel cup, two plates – washed and laid one on top of the other; five fingers of green bananas, a half-empty paper bag of flour, a beer bottle filled with cooking oil. A tin of condensed milk sat like a small island in a plastic bowl of water. The surface was thick with drowning ants trying to get at the sweetness.

Books lay stacked on the floor: school texts in one corner, a heap of big hardbacks in another. In the floor space between them, a neat array of Louis L'Amour Westerns, a couple of novels by Earl Lovelace, an assortment of Marvel comics, a book of poetry by one Vladimir Lucien, a Caribbean romance by Nailah Imoja, the folk poetry of Paul Keens-Douglas and Louise Bennett.

I dropped the two bags I'd brought with me beside the school books and sat on the floor. I paged through the big books – every one of them with a school library stamp in it. I laid them back exactly as I'd found them.

I dropped the shopping bags I'd brought at the entrance of

what I assumed was the bedroom, dug into my pocket and slipped two hundred-dollar notes between the pages of the heaviest book.

I tore a page from my pad and scribbled:

Stay in school – that's thanks enough.
  Hope they fit.
  Digger

  PS: Look up Histology . . .

I'd gone to the big Syrian store in San Andrews and spent a good two hours arguing and joking with the owner over prices. I left his counter with four cotton shirts, a stack of shorts and underwear, two pairs of patent leather shoes, a pair of decent trainers and enough T-shirts to last Jana Ray a year. I'd sweet-talked the Syrian into throwing in the toiletries for free by peppering everything I said with Insha 'a' Allah. I'd stepped out into the sizzling afternoon with two large shopping bags, very pleased with myself.

I pulled Jana Ray's door behind me, retied it and headed back to the road.

24

Miss Stanislaus was in a fever to get on with the investigation of Lazar Wilkinson's murder. There were moments when her urgency turned to panic, though she tried to hide it. It was all I could do to assure her that we still had another fifteen days – enough time to get a breakthrough before the hearing.

I told her that the woman we were looking for – the one I'd seen on the beach at The Flare with the two suspected men – was probably from one of the villages on the coast. 'Why so?' she asked.

'Is the way she walked into the water to climb onto the lil dinghy, and how she sat on the prow of the boat. Like it was no big deal. She's accustomed to boats and the sea.'

Miss Stanislaus frowned. 'That's all?'

'It take practice and experience to sit on the prow of a rocking boat in rough water without holding on, not so? I can't imagine a pusson who not from the seaside riding a boat so comfortable.'

'Mebbe,' Miss Stanislaus said.

'Is all we got to go on,' I said.

I'd gone into San Andrews Central and sent out a description of the young woman and the two men I'd seen her with, to every police station on the island, including Kara Island. No sightings, they said. And that was puzzling because even the bushes of Camaho had eyes and ears.

Miss Stanislaus decided that we should take to the rough roads of the island in search of the woman.

The first few villages we stopped at treated us with the disdain they probably reserved for foreigners – San Andrews folks being in that category too. Sometimes the hostility came off them like a heatwave.

We were entering Grenville Town when Miss Stanislaus ordered me to stop the car. 'Missa Digger, we been doin the whole thing wrong. We been talkin to the wrong people.' She got out, went into a shop and returned with a bulging paper bag.

'What you got in there?'

She opened the mouth of the bag and showed me. Sweets – all sorts, mostly lollipops.

I shook my head and frowned.

'Just watch!' She sat back, staring calmly ahead.

From then, we had to make our escape from the children who crowded us, offering whatever they thought we wanted to hear just to earn some sweets.

At Menere village, we learned that Missa Geoffrey had one baby with his sister; that Miss Panadool had two boy-friends – one who visited her on Tuesday and Friday nights, and another who came home once-a-year becuz he was bustin his arse on a touris' boat overseas.

Requin was full of late-night 'sexin' on the beach. 'An dem believe we dunno.'

The old Anglican priest in Bacolet had poisoned the mangoes that grew behind the church and drank aaaall the holy wine. He beat up his wife when he got drunk. And the Merican man in the big concrete house overlooking Prickly Bay got locked out by his wife every time he came home late or drunk. 'She one o' we,' they explained.

Once or twice an adult barged through the bunch and

shooed them off. They would scatter like a flock of routed chickens, then converge on us again. I could have stayed and listened to them all day.

We found the young woman's place halfway down the eastern coast – a small village without a name, perched on a rock above a beach bordered by a forest of manchineel and mangroves. The air was fresh and clean, the sea so clear it was transparent.

'I think she got a baby,' I'd told the children. They pointed out a narrow limestone track that wound like a limp thread towards a two-roomed board house with frayed curtains billowing through the windows. A sun-scorched vegetable garden at the front was almost taken over by patches of cactus and mint grass.

A woman was stooping over a basin of washing. Slim, dark-skinned, head tied with a blue wrap, bands of coloured cloth around one wrist, a plaited cotton cord holding her dress against her hips – Fire Baptist.

The transformation in Miss Stanislaus was immediate. Her face softened, her voice thickened with love. 'Sister,' she said and curtsied. I was sure they'd never met before but the woman seemed to recognise Miss Stanislaus by that call. I'd never ceased to wonder at the bond between the women of my grandmother's religion.

Conversation was a gentle affair between them: lowered voices, touches on the shoulder, fluttering fingers, the occasional lifting of widespread palms.

The woman brought out a baby and placed it in my arms. Boychild – firm and plump as a well-kneaded dumpling. About ten months old. Completely at ease in my arms.

I rocked the baby while they talked, my mind drifting back to a girlfriend I used to have called Lonnie, who – to shield herself from Malan – had offered to have my child.

146

We were on the Atlantic side of the island, the water in the distance kyanite blue. A raging procession of breakers destroyed themselves on the barrier reef that stood between the ocean and the bay.

The woman came out and took the child from me. 'How you, Missa Digger? I'z Philo.' She had quick brown eyes. About thirty-five, I thought. 'I remember your granny from Convention Time. Mother Sheila Digson, not so?'

'Is so,' I said. 'Miss Philo, you got a picture of your daughter?'

'Uh-huh,' she said, and without hesitation returned to the house with the child.

She came back with a small stack of photos and handed them to me. One was of a baby, head weighed down with ribbons. A couple were of a prepubescent girl, her hair in two long plaits, standing unsmiling at the end of a grinning line of children her age. All in school uniform. The last two were as I remembered the woman at The Flare. She was holding the baby in her arms and staring directly at the camera – no smile, no pose – just a lean, straight-backed Camahoan woman presenting herself to the world as she was.

Miss Stanislaus approached with an outstretched hand. 'You got your wallet, Missa Digger?'

I handed it to her along with the photos. 'Leave ten dollars. Give her the rest.'

'All of it? I done give her what I got.'

'All of it,' I said.

When Miss Stanislaus returned, she laid a hand on my arm. 'You know what I been thinkin, Missa Digger?'

'Tell me.'

'How much people we got on Camaho?'

147

'About a hundred thousand.'

'Eggzackly.' She sniffed. 'Camaho too small to have poor people.'

'What that got to do with the case we chasing now?'

'Everything, Missa Digger. Believe me.'

Back on the road, Miss Stanislaus pointed at a sprawling plantation house on the hill above the village, crowded by ancient mahogany and royal palm trees.

'Baby father,' she said. 'Lawyer name Joe Carter. Miss Tamara work for him five months. He pregnant her with baby. When wife find out, she fire the girl. Now they don't want to know.'

'Reminds me of a story,' I said. 'Ever hear about Olive Senior?'

'This not no story, Missa Digger, this is Camaho life. It got to stop.'

'Mebbe Miss Olive was thinking the same thing when she write that story. Okay, so what we find?'

The girl's name was Tamara, daughter of a hotelier in San Andrews' tourist south. He escaped the island when Tamara was an infant. She was a good girl, the mother said, strong-minded. Tried to burn down the house of the lawyer who'd left her with the child and stoned his car a couple of times, until he sent the police to arrest her. They ended up warning her, but from then, Tamara couldn't find a job anywhere in the parish.

Tamara took to sleeping in the day and leaving home at night, returning in the early hours of the morning. Began staying out for days at a time, but always sent home money for the upkeep of the child through one of the bus drivers.

The past coupla weeks, Miss Philo heard nothing from her daughter. She was worried. People from the parish sometimes caught glimpses of the young woman in a San Andrews

148

restaurant or night club. Whenever they did, they always brought the news to her.

'She might've skipped the island,' I said.

'Nuh.'

'Why you so sure?'

'She hate the father, Missa Digger, but she love the baby. Is obvious. To do what she doing to feed her child – that's love.'

Miss Stanislaus asked me to repeat everything I'd said about my meeting with the young woman at The Flare, including a description of the two men.

'Them two foreign fellas still got her, Missa Digger. I sure of that.' She turned worried eyes on me. 'You think she in trouble?'

'I *know* she in trouble. She got a murder to explain. I'll put out a lookout notice again. I'll notify Caran too, just in case.'

My phone buzzed. 'Digger!'

'Whozat?'

'Is me, Malan. You find de prostitute yet?'

'Still searching.'

'Digger, I decide you need a break. We going to Dog Island on Saturday. You want to come?'

'Not sure about that.'

'Digger, I really want you to come.'

'Why Dog Island?'

'I show you when you come. Besides, Sarona want to meet you proper. You coming?'

'What time?'

'Afternoon, about one. Bring your woman.'

'Uh-huh.'

'You sure you comin?'

'Yep.'

'Don' forget, yunno!'

'Nuh. See yuh.'

'What he want from you?' Miss Stanislaus muttered. She looked sullen, resentful. I didn't blame her.

'That's what I going to find out.'

'Careful, Missa Digger.'

'Uh-huh.'

25

I dropped off Miss Stanislaus and came home to find Jana
Ray sitting on my step, a cloth bag beside him and a blue
bum-bag at his feet.

I barely recognised the youngfella. He'd groomed his hair
with a designer pattern at the sides. A sky-blue, long-sleeved
shirt, grey trousers and perfectly laced-up Convos. He wore a
fluorescent-green plastic Casio watch on his right hand. The
youngfella looked stunning.

'You start trespassing now?' I said.

His face lit up with a grin. 'I bring you something.'

Without my torch in his face, Jana Ray looked relaxed and
self-possessed.

'I don't remember giving you my address.'

He reached into his blue bum-bag and pulled out
a cellphone – the cheap two-sim Chinese type. 'The
Camaho Chronicle got a big article on you and, erm, Miss,
erm, DC Stan—'

'Stanislaus. That was a while back.'

He looked around him then up at the Mardi Gras mountains. 'Small place.'

'Still bigger than where you from.'

'We ain got no mountain blocking the sea.' He grinned.
He pulled the cloth bag towards him and tipped it over. A
beautiful assortment of Camaho's rarest fruits tumbled out

onto the step: gru-gru nuts, star-apples, sapodillas and mami sipote from the mountains; water lemons, white-fleshed guavas and short lengths of crayfish cane that thrived around the streams of the interior; custard apples, seagrapes and red plums from the southern Drylands.

'How long this take you?' I said.

'Coupla days. You like them?'

'More than like them. I figure you don't take nothing from nobody without paying back – that right?'

He lowered his head, smiling.

'Well, thanks for thanking me. I like that. I telling you what I going do now. I going invite you inside. We going to eat something, then I going to do my job: interrogate you.'

I opened the door and let him in. 'I don't want no lie from you, else no amount of super-fruits going save you. I want names, things that Lazar said that you remember. Basically, I want to empty your head of all the information connected with this case, some of which you might not even know you know.'

I pointed at a chair and poured him a drink. 'You eighteen. In Camaho law, that make you an adult. Miss Stanislaus told me I should've arrested you. Fact is, I didn't, but nothing preventing me from doing that right now, or some time in the future. That clear?'

I watched his body tense. Now there was the same uncertainty and vulnerability about him that I saw when I'd pulled him up the first time. 'First, you tell me a lil bit about yourself.'

He told me of a mother who drank too much, grieving over a father he'd only heard about. She ignored the doctor's warning about her drinking. An epileptic fit killed her. He had an uncle who owned a shop a couple of miles from where he lived. As far as his uncle was concerned, he didn't exist.

He'd been sending himself to school and with the little jobs that Lazar Wilkinson gave him, was managing alright. University – that was all he thought about. University was a must because . . . he pointed at his head. 'I have plans, Missa Digger. Gimme a couple more years and I off to university. You want to bet?'

No, I didn't, I replied. Was he sure there was no new woman with Lazar recently?

Lazar was a dog, he said. He had lotsa women. He, Jana Ray, was never into that kinda living.

I asked him how come.

'Is wasteful, Missa Digger. Wasteful is not good. S'far as I see, a woman is an, erm, ecosystem. You interfere with one part, another part get affected. That's what Lazar and them fellas don't unnerstan.'

'And what a man is?'

'Ecosystem too.' He lowered his eyes and smiled. 'I think we less diverse.'

'You actually think like that?'

'Uh-huh.'

'Miss Stanislaus going to like you! You got any idea why they killed Lazar?'

'Lazar had dealings with people from all over. From high up and from low down. Could've been any one of them.'

'Where is all over?'

'Vincen Island, Kara Island . . . I even hear them say Europe.'

'Europe!'

'Is what I hear.'

'You not giving me names.'

'I don know no names.'

'You mention Kara Island. Ever heard about a fella named Juba Hurst?'

'I fink Shadowman from there.'

'Who's Shadowman?'

'What?'

'You just said, Shadowman – who's Shadowman?'

A change had come over him – his mouth gone loose, his arms hugging himself. Small tremors in his shoulders.

'You think this Shadowman fella kill Lazar?'

'What?' He shook his head and looked away.

'Who kill him, Jana Ray?'

'I tellin you I dunno.' His voice had risen a couple of pitches.

'And I tellin you, you got a good idea. Who you think kill Lazar Wilkinson, then?'

'Like I tell you, it could be—'

'Anybody! That's what you keep saying. Well, it can't be anybody. Somebody had a reason to get rid of him. I believe you know.'

'Missa Digger, all I want to do is go to school. Finish what I set out to do. I don't want no part in this no more.'

'Part of what no more?'

'Big things happenin, is why dey kill Lazar. Mebbe he got greedy, mebbe he didn want no part of it either.'

'No part of what, Jonathon Rayburn. Of what!'

Jana Ray had become a fidgeting wreck. He'd broken out in a sweat. I handed him a drink, stepped back and watched him gulp down the soursop juice. He rested the empty glass on the floor. Fear, I thought. No, not fear. Terror.

'You want another drink?'

He shook his head.

'I'll get you one anyway. Listen to me, youngfella, you think I rough? Well, we have a policeman I work with who will get whatever he wants to hear from you, and the price you'll pay is a coupla broken bones for taking up his time. So count yourself lucky. You like music?'

He shrugged.

'Ever hear bout John Coltrane? Nuh? One day I'll tell you about Coltrane.' I fed 'A Love Supreme' into my player. He looked absorbed, his forehead clenched. All ears.

'I like the patterns,' he said, then rose abruptly and strode over to my bookshelf. He reached up a long arm and began fingering the book spines. He pulled down a text, ran a hand along the covers. Now Jana Ray looked different: serious, focused, mature – someone who understood and valued books.

'Phytochemistry – I can borrow this?' He turned the front cover towards me.

'Not that one.'

'Which one then?'

'None.'

He dropped the book on the kitchen worktop. 'I got a question on plant chemistry for my exams. What use you got for it anyway?'

'Is my book, youngfella. I bought it. You into poisoning people with plants?'

'You didn tell me bout yourself.'

I gave him a quick rundown about my grandmother who brought me up, my murdered mother, the hole her absence left in me and the craving I sometimes felt for something close to family.

He nodded at that, his face grave and distant at the same time. I also told him how I got my job in San Andrews CID. 'Basically, Chilman cornered me and forced me to join the CID unit he was forming. Straight blackmail – no other word for it!'

155

Jana Ray found that funny. I still didn't see the joke.

'He pick y'all up off de street for true?'

'Is the way he enjoy putting it to us. And like you, I sent myself to school. My father didn want to know.'

'You know your father?'

I nodded.

'What's he like, Missa Digger?'

'Is only now he want to know me.'

'Because you doin all right?'

'Because I turn out to be the kinda fella he would like to call his son. Mebbe if I was shorter, darker – a thief – he wouldn want to know.'

It was late evening when he glanced at his watch and said he was ready to leave.

I offered to take him home. He would only let me drop him off at Cross Gap Junction, from where he said he would get a bus or walk.

He halted at the door. 'I could borrow the book? I know Phytochem is not just about poisoning.'

'I had a lot of trouble getting it . . .'

'I'll take care of it. Swear on my life.'

'You got to take care of it, Star Boy. You have no choice. Come, I drop you off.'

At Cross Gap Junction, a thought popped into my head. 'What you doing Saturday?'

He shrugged.

'Y'ever been to Dog Island?'

'I hear bout it.'

'We got a lime there. You'll meet my girlfriend too – she manages the Co-op Bank. I ask her to set up a lil job for you.'

'Don wan' no job, Missa Digger. Thanks but I awright.'

'You don want no job!'

'I kin still come with you, though.' He made it sound like he was doing me a favour.

'Okay, Saturday I come pick you up.'

I watched him walk away, upright, fast-footed, the white shoes flashing in the late-evening gloom. Jana Ray – man-boy, slippery as a river eel. Miss Stanislaus was right. I should have arrested him.

Perhaps.

26

Friday morning, I woke with a headache. All night my mind had been a hive of questions:

What really lay behind the awful killing of Lazar Wilkinson? Why would anyone want to strangle a man then cut his throat and leave him on display by the side of a public road? If it was a warning to others, why did it have to be in such a horrible way?

At first, finding Jana Ray felt like the beginnings of a breakthrough – my chance to get some useful answers from a young man who worked for Lazar Wilkinson, but my brief interrogation had reduced the youth to a state of babbling terror. It was clear to me that soon I would have to push Jana Ray to face whatever seemed to cripple him. Have him put it into words so that Miss Stanislaus and I could get to the root of it. And root it out!

Odd that Jana Ray never saw the woman that the little boys in Beau Séjour had spotted with Lazar Wilkinson. And why the hell would a young Camaho woman conspire with two foreign men to murder a Camahoan male she knew, in such a gruesome manner? That made little sense to me.

My thoughts shifted to Juba's death at the hands of Miss Stanislaus and the fast-approaching hearing. I visualised Miss Stanislaus and I facing a couple of superintendents, the Commissioner of Police and of course the Minister of Justice.

I imagined myself pointing to the killing of Lazar Wilkinson, one of our *citizens* and explaining the *critical importance* of finding and apprehending the coupla foreigners who I suspected were involved in the *nastiest* killing Camaho had ever seen. I couldn't *imagine* doing the job without the help-and-support of Miss Stanislaus. Besides, didn't they realise that a Camaho woman – *a young baby mother* – was probably held *hostage* by said suspects? The more I rehearsed the argument in my head the less convinced I became of their effectiveness on a bunch of stone-faced, overfed Old Bulls, including my fuckin father, the Commissioner.

And let's say I managed to pin some kinda murder on Juba. Would a character assassination of the fella be enough to get Miss Stanislaus off? Because that was all it was – a character assassination – something to convince a tribunal of fuckin Geezers of what Juba Hurst was capable of. I would still have no evidence to show that Miss Stanislaus had acted in her and my defence. Still, as far as I could see, pinning a murder on Juba would be my strongest argument – probably my only real chance of getting the hearing to drop the case against Miss Stanislaus. Hopefully.

I thought of the search I'd left Benna and her team to do for me and my heart flipped over.

It was not just finding Koku Stanislaus that mattered now. It was finding him in time – that was if Miss Stanislaus was right in her suspicion that Juba Hurst had killed her great-uncle.

I pushed the thoughts out of my head and got ready for the Buso case in court.

The court house was a big room in one of the government buildings overlooking the roundabout in Canteen. When I arrived, the concrete yard outside was packed with people – most of them teenage males clutching sheets of paper in their hands. They all looked lost.

Staff Superintendent Gill was right: the presiding judge was a woman – a broad-faced Barbadian with a locked-down mouth, formidable in size and demeanour. She tolerated none of the dramatic antics of the defence lawyer; told him she considered pointing his finger in a witness's face tantamount to assault; and furthermore, suggesting the victim was a whore was libellous, inappropriate and in contempt of *her* court.

Officer Buso's defence fell back on glowing character references from colleagues he worked with. The prosecution called his wife to the stand and she left us with the picture of a short-tempered man, brutal with his children, who slapped her around at the slightest provocation. Buso's wife announced to the court that she was starting divorce proceedings against him.

I was last to take the stand. I delivered my statement to a hushed court room.

At the end of it, Buso did not get a jail sentence. He ended up with a 15,000-dollar fine and an order to pay for the care of the woman's children, including their education, until they were fourteen. The money, the judge told him, would be deducted from source. Her hammer came down, and that, for me, was better than nothing at all.

There were faces pressed against the window of San Andrews Central when I drove into the station courtyard. It was clear to me that they'd already heard the verdict.

Superintendent Gill looked surprised to see me. Malan leaned against the cooler at the far end of the corridor, a plastic cup against his lips. His eyes travelled down the length of my body, then up to my face, checking no doubt whether I'd taken his advice and walked with my weapon. I flashed him a glare, pulled my chair and sat at my desk.

I'd taken Chilman's advice, placing my back against the wall so that every approach was within my line of vision. Switch emerged from one of the back rooms, Machete trailing after him. Skelo hung behind, stopping at the cooler to exchange words with Malan. I expected the usual hate stares from them, or a murder-threat printed on their faces. They ignored me, shouldered the door and left.

I was listing the things I needed to remember if I were to make headway with Miss Stanislaus's hearing when the men returned. Skelo walked past me and met Machete at the door. Machete was holding up a cup in his hand and deliberately blocking Skelo's path. Skelo sucked his teeth and slapped the cup in Machete's hand.

I was already moving and well away from my desk by the time the cup struck the wall behind my chair.

Malan came running. 'What happen!'

In the office space, the conversation died, every head turned in our direction. A telephonist sucked her teeth, turned hateful eyes on Skelo and sucked her teeth again.

I pushed past Malan, went to the toilet, pulled off my shirt and tore away the pocket. At the cooler, I grabbed a plastic cup, hurried over to my desk and dropped the fabric in the pool of liquid on the tiled floor. I took off a shoe and used the toe to nudge it into the cup. If Skelo threw something at me, it couldn't be for my good.

When I raised my head, Switch and his two men were no longer there.

The telephonist hurried over, dropped her eyes on the cup in my hand and asked what happened – her face tight with concern.

'I awright,' I said.

Superintendent Gill came out with another receptionist behind him. 'What they done now?' he growled.

'I awright,' I said.

He looked at the cup in my hand, then at my face. 'What you got there?'

'Dunno yet,' I said.

'I told you to stay away from this place. You didn—'

'I not the problem, Sir. So why you blaming me?'

He looked ashamed of himself, at a loss. I turned my back on him.

There was a patchwork of bleached varnish where the droplets had settled on my desk.

I grabbed my bag and walked out the door.

The three men were at the far end of the car park, their arms stretched out on the roof of their vehicle. Machete showed me all his teeth. The other two were pretending they didn't see me.

I unlocked my car, laid the cup on the back seat and got in. Malan shouted my name. 'Digger, what happen?'

'I'll deal with it.'

'What you got in that cup on your seat?'

'Is what I about to find out.'

'Where you off to now?'

'Why all them questions, Malan Greaves? I don't trust you any more. You the one put me in this situation. I not counting on you to get me out of it.'

'Digger, is not so it was supposed to go.'

'Fuck you, Malan.'

I drove off.

At home, I dropped the cup in my kitchen sink, dribbled some water into it from my tap and left it standing for a while.

I dug under the sink, found the sponge I was looking for, and poured the contents of the cup onto it. The sponge began

162

dissolving into a black mess. Acid – car battery, I guessed. Probably sulphuric acid.

Five missed calls from Malan.

I didn't understand him – hot one minute, cold the next. Miss Stanislaus had also called. I poured myself a glass of water and picked up my messages. Dessie wanted to see me later. Miss Stanislaus asked if I had more thoughts on the Lazar Wilkinson case. Chilman left a wet cough then hung up.

I dialled Malan. He picked up promptly. 'Digger, office-woman show me your desk. What they throw at you?'

'Sulphuric acid – from car battery. I sure.'

'Monkey juice?'

'That's what you call it?'

He'd gone so quiet, I thought he'd cut off. 'Which one of dem done dat?'

I didn't answer.

'I betting is de sickhead – the one they call Machete. I been watchin him! Okay, take dis down.' His voice had gone flat and businesslike. 'Dem three fellas chill out at a gamblin place in Willis name Rock Box, around ten, eleven evenin time. Switch stupid like you, he don't wear no gun. People say he shoot his lil daughter by mistake once. So he not wearing none – he carry a coupla fishknife. You know how to find de place?'

'I'll find it.'

'You bringin de Mad Woman with you?'

'Nuh.'

He went silent, then coughed in my ear. 'Digger, I tell them fellas to leave you alone, becuz they dunno *what* dey bringin down on themself. They never lissen! So! Who can't hear goin feel. Not so?' He hung up.

I threw myself on the sofa.

My mind took me back to my one-year course in England, and a pale-skinned woman with beautiful reddish hair that tumbled off her head in curls reminding me of wood shavings. I carried an image of Nuala Quinn sitting at her desk in front of our class of nine men. We'd come from every part of the world: North America, the Middle East, a couple of West Africans and two English fellas – one black, one white – all wanting to get into forensics.

It was the end of the course. We were seeing our lecturers for the last time. Each came, answered last-minute questions, shook our hands and wished us good luck.

Nuala Quinn was the last – a criminologist whose idea of teaching was to run an extended, barely audible conversation with herself, as if none of us was there. Most of the fellas in class didn't pay attention, they settled down to other work. Me – I was in love with the woman's thinking and I believed she knew it.

On the last day she was silent; sat with her head bowed over a small book in her hand, *A Good Man is Hard to Find*.

I felt let down. I wanted some final word from her, some thunderclap of an idea that I would take back with me to Camaho. But nuh! The blaastid woman jus siddown there reading her book!

At the end of the non-session, people gathered their things and began heading for the exit. I remained seated and didn't hide my dissatisfaction.

It was then she spoke, her lips pulled back in a big smile – a taunting, sing-song Irish voice directed at the back of the room. 'Have you worked out which one you are yet?'

People halted and turned around. The room went silent.

She raised a hand and showed us three fingers. 'There are – roughly – three kinds of policemen: the foot-soldier, the priest and the savage.' She laid the book on the desk and stood up. 'The foot-soldier follows orders because he needs to have his thinking done for him. The priest does not always do good, but he means good. The savage is,' she tossed back her hair with a swift jerk of her head, exposing her face and throat, 'the worm in the belly. He becomes himself inside the agencies of the law. So many opportunities to hurt: break heads, break lives. He's the one that throws you in a van alive and hands you over dead. The law is a cover for his lawlessness. Which one are you? And,' she picked up the book, 'what have they got in common – those three?'

She shouldered her bag and began walking towards us, her brows puckered as if she herself was working out the answer to her own question.

'Control,' I said. 'Or – erm – the desire to control.'

She looked me in the face and smiled, then handed me the book. 'Mr Digson – you think too much. Not good for you, you know.'

Nuala Quinn was wrong; we were all three. Or could be.

27

I turned up at Rock Box at 11.32. A sprawling shed-like structure with a big patio, ringed with coloured bulbs, facing a beach packed with boulders. The outside walls were plastered with posters advertising beverages. Rows of wooden trestle tables surrounded by stools. Switch, Machete and Skelo were together in the far right corner of the space, a dozen or so beer bottles between them. Malan sat with Sarona near the entrance – Sarona in a multicoloured sarong, her back to me.

Malan lifted his drink to his mouth. His lips moved above the rim of the bottle and Sarona rose promptly. She walked towards me with a swinging flowing movement, her eyes locked onto mine. She smiled and stepped past me. I caught a whiff of her perfume. Malan had disappeared.

I was halfway across the concrete floor when Switch spotted me. He lowered his gaze to the leather belt in my hand, placed his drink on the table and grumbled something. Suddenly Skelo was on his feet – lean, spidery under the lights, that long narrow head of his bobbing on his neck. He'd grabbed a lager bottle and struck it against the table. It didn't break. I broke it for him. He was reaching behind his waist when my buckle connected with his shoulder. I heard the crack of bone. He stumbled forward, reaching for his waistline with the other hand. I destroyed his wrist as he hit the floor, then his shoulder blade. Machete jumped the

166

table. I took his right foot from under him and as he hit the concrete, I smashed his upper arm, then the heel of his right foot. The two men lay on their stomachs, wet, chesty sobs gushing from their throats.

Switch had backed himself into the corner. He'd picked up a length of steel from somewhere – the type they used for reinforcing concrete. Or maybe he'd brought it with him.

There was commotion around me: stools scraping, a door slammed heavily inside the building. Switch's eyes – bright and feral – locked onto mine. I sized him up, a new heat rising in my head. I adjusted my grip on the tail of the heavy leather belt. It was then that Malan stepped between us.

'Finish,' he said, a tight smile creasing his face. I kept my eyes on Switch, my nostrils flared, and it was all I could do to prevent myself from shoving Malan aside and throwing myself at the man.

Malan placed a hand on my shoulder, the other on Switch's chest. Switch dropped the bar. 'He save y'arse,' Switch snarled.

'Nuh,' Malan said. 'I save yours. H'was goin to kill you or cripple you. You wasn watchin Digger' face. You dunno Digger' face. I know Digger' face. I told y'all to leave him alone, was a big mistake y'all makin. Now come siddown and have a drink. I done call de ambulance.' He gestured at Machete and Skelo. Machete looked out cold. Skelo had thrown up.

'Next time you dead,' Switch said.

'Den all ov y'all going dead too,' Malan said. 'Becuz is not only me y'all going have to deal with.' Malan was smiling with his mouth. 'In fact, if De Mad Woman did come with Digger – all of y'all arse would've been dead by now. Believe! What you drinkin, Switch? Is me payin. Digger, you hangin round?'

I turned and headed for my car.

167

Sarona stood close to the entrance – out of sight because of the high row of sorrel plants that hugged the side of the building.

She looked like a mannequin under the string of multi-coloured lights that lined the eaves above her. 'Digger,' she said.

I pretended I didn't hear her.

28

Dog Island sat between Kalivini Island and Coburn. If there was a drugs capital in Camaho, Coburn was it – a sort of inter-island commercial exchange for every variety of marijuana grown throughout the Antilles. There were fellas here who could tell the origin of any given weed, the region in which-ever island it was grown and its potency – just by smelling it.

Well-built concrete houses clustered around a wide lagoon – a resting place for small yachts that were more like floating caravans. Hand-built constructions put together with parts of other boats and fitted with lazy diesel engines that helped them drift down to Camaho on the currents from Florida. They were the underclass of America's boating world.

Dessie, Jana Ray and I hung out by the jetty. She'd taken an instant liking to the youngfella. She even whispered to me that he was 'beautiful'.

Malan had phoned and said that he and Sarona were already on Dog Island. He was setting up. Spiderface, our Department's boatman, would pick us up from the jetty.

I surveyed the hilltop houses and asked Jana Ray and Dessie if they'd ever heard of The Actors – Camaho's very own, home-grown drug lords.

'We proud of them,' I said.

Jana Ray threw me a look and grinned. The fella was get-ting to know me.

For the past coupla years there was a new trend in drug trafficking: young boys without parents or big brothers to control them getting picked up off the streets and sent out mid-ocean in boats to collect a brick or two of refined cocaine and return with it – part of the supply chain that kept the tourists happy. Did they know that Camaho had the highest tourist-revisit rate in the region? Well, I was wagering that those bricks had something to do with it.

Sometimes things went wrong. I told them of YouTube videos of kidnapped Camahoan boys being gun-whipped by raging Venezuelan men, demanding their money from the fellas who sent out those kids. Some of those children we never heard about again.

As for the fellas who sent out those boys, we never arrested them. We left them to self-destruct.

I turned to Jana Ray. 'Yunno why?' He said nothing – a new alertness in his eyes. 'Because what happen to them is worse than jail. So much money, so little to do with it. They could hardly count so they pay school kids to tot up their takings. They throw money at the wind. They dunno what to do with themselves. So they run through some videos, choose a movie star they like and start to walk-n-talk and dress like the movie star, until they begin to believe it.'

'Why you don't arrest them?' Dessie wanted to know. She'd draped an arm over my shoulder from behind and was fingering the hairs at the nape of my neck with the other hand.

'They end up killing themselves,' I said. 'Now, Bradley Grange was different.'

I pointed at a big white house that sat like a stranded ship on a promontory over the sea. 'He was a classmate of mine. His father talked some sense into his head, so he built two houses on the old man's land.

'You never knew if he was at home because you never saw

a light in that house. Cleverly built, yunno, with a special air-conditioned basement that was impossible to get into if you didn't know which doors to open, in what order.

'There was a swimming pool on the grounds but he put a permanent canvas awning over it.'

'What made him different?' Dessie pressed a chin into my shoulder.

'He had a bit of education to start with. And while the other Camahoan fellas took their role models from the movies, Bradley took his from his idea of an English gentle-man: wide-brim hat, yunno, a pipe between his teeth and the most democratic grin a pusson could imagine. In fact, he stopped calling me Digger.'

'What he call you?' Jana Ray did nothing to hide the anticipation.

'Doo-goo-er!'

The youngfella cracked up. Dessie shook with chuckles.

'Okay, y'all laughing. Story done.'

Spiderface arrived and with one fast swerve was beside the jetty. I took Dessie's hand and guided her in. Jana Ray hopped in.

'Finish it, Missa Digger – de story.'

'Is not no story, is fact.'

Jana Ray opened his palms at me.

'Well, one early Monday morning we found Bradley drowned in the swimming pool that nobody knew was there.'

I held him in my gaze. He looked away.

We chose a cool and grassy grotto in a glade along the hillside. Dessie, her chin lowered, passed underhand glances at Sarona, her eyes shifting to Malan then back at the woman. I wondered what she was thinking. Sarona wore a sky-blue sarong around a yellow swimsuit. Malan was cool with Jana

171

Ray – the usual policeman stiffness with teenage males – but he was not unfriendly.

Malan and I stood looking out at a promontory about a mile ahead. He wore a tight smile on his face. 'Pretty wimmen – both of em,' he said. 'I like dat. I not comparin, yunno, but—'

'That's why you ask me to bring Dessie?'

'Nuh, I pleased with what I got. I here for de goat.' He pointed at the rise above the cliff.

For a moment I didn't understand his words, then they registered.

I shook my head. 'Nuh.'

'I bring de SWS.' He raised his chin at the long canvas bag propped up against the trunk of a manchineel tree a little way behind the women.

'What you want to prove, Malan? Leave the fuckin goat.'

And suddenly the heat rose in him. 'Digger, fuck you. Man do what man want to do. Man want goat meat an' man goin to get goat meat.'

For months there had been talk among the fellas in the army and San Andrews Central about a goat they wanted to shoot. A Dog Island ram, with a curving crown of horns, that you could see against the skyline from a mile off. Problem was, before they could make the curried goat they fancied, they had to get on a boat. And so it never happened.

Years before, someone had let loose half a dozen of the animals on the island. They grew wild and thrived unmolested on the sparse grass. Fellas from Coburn claimed they could smell the males, especially in dry season, and though they barely saw them, the animals reminded them of their presence by the tracks they left on the hillsides.

An alpha male had sprung up amongst them. Evenings, it stood on the lip of a precipice above the ocean, facing the sunset – a magnificent bearded thing that stayed on the clifftop for the half-hour the sun took to set, its body darkening with the fading day. Evenings, children came out on the jetty in Coburn to stare at it, some of them remaining long after it was lost to the night, until their parents' voices pulled them away from whatever they were dreaming.

I knew this because I too had seen the animal, and felt, I think, what those children must have been feeling when they looked at the creature standing straight-legged, head up, staring out to sea. A living thing, at ease in its world and sufficient unto itself.

I returned to Jana Ray, Dessie and Sarona. The women were listening to the youngfella talk about sea urchins and seahorses. They looked fascinated. He had a lovely laid-back way of speaking, voice low but resonant, neither show-off nor arrogant. Just excited by his own words.

He broke off when Malan hailed Sarona. She rose from the grass and hurried over to him.

Jana Ray was staring closely at me.

'What?' I said.

He shrugged, smiled. 'Thought y'was upset bout somefing. The Sarona woman ask me if you'z my brother.'

'And what you told her?'

'I say we, erm, friends. Kind ov, I—'

'You should've told her yes.'

His face softened. He didn't know where to look. 'Cool,' he muttered, smiling at the sky.

Dessie dozed off, her head in my lap. Jana Ray muttered that he wanted to walk to the side of the island.

I stared at the long canvas bag, something stirring in my gut. The animal would be a long way off but I'd seen Malan take down men before with that rifle.

He was out there with Sarona, at the edges of the water, the woman cleaving to him, looking up into his face, the water washing around their feet.

I must have dozed off too because the sound of Spiderface's engine brought me back. Dessie sat up with me.

Sarona joined us, her cropped hair making a halo with the sun behind her. I could see the fine hairs on her skin. That underhand gaze again from Dessie. I looked at my watch, then up at the promontory. Malan retrieved the canvas bag and headed for what looked like a primitive stone jetty further down.

The sun was yellowing the waters when the animal appeared. Dessie followed my gaze and gasped.

'My God,' she breathed. 'It's—'

'Beautiful,' I said. 'Malan about to kill it.'

She swung her head at me. And I could not tell whether her expression was one of excitement or disbelief.

'What go on?' Jana Ray said. He dropped himself beside me.

'Malan about to kill a goat.' I pointed.

He looked up at the creature then at each of us in turn. 'Why?' And I could have hugged him, because suddenly he was angry. 'Is a waste.'

He sank into silence. But then he raised his head again. 'Where's he?'

I pointed down at the stone jetty. Jana Ray angled his face up at the silhouette, then swung his gaze across and downwards towards the stone jetty.

'Too far,' he said and smiled.

As his face relaxed, we heard the crack of the Sniper Weapon System rifle. Saw the animal buck, its forelegs raised high and clawing the air. Then it slipped over the cliff, a black shadow falling to Jana Ray's screams of indignation.

Sarona's eyes were like two dark pools on my face, her lips

working, softly, slowly. We locked gazes, me aware of the flare of her nostrils, the fine hairs along her jawline, the pink pearl of her earrings.

Dessie stirred behind me. 'Digger, let's walk.'

I followed her inland through a grove of trees. She stopped with her back against a trunk, her head lowered, her eyes turned up at my face. She gestured and I stepped into her arms.

'Y'awright?' I said.

She nodded, took my hand and rested it against her thigh. 'If you want to—'

'What's the matter, Dessie?'

'I can't like her. I never liked—' The rest of the words got lost in a mumble. 'I don't like the way she was looking at you. I don't like how you—' Dessie sucked in air, grabbed my hand and straightened up. 'Let's go back.'

Malan and Sarona weren't there. I thought I heard Sarona's love cries in the near distance. Then again, might be the gulls.

Jana Ray lay on his back, his blue bum-bag under his head, legs crossed, staring at the sky.

I lowered myself beside him. He looked me in the face – a steady resentful glare. 'Fucker,' he said.

And I wasn't sure whether the word was meant for Malan or me.

29

I went to San Andrews Central to see Staff Superintendent Gill. He must have been waiting for me to come in because he was at the door when I arrived. The place felt more relaxed, and it certainly was louder. The secretaries at their desks were running an animated conversation about play-play men and real men.

Superintendent Gill was wearing a grave expression. 'Digson, you mind following me to my office?' His voice was gruff and loud enough to reach the furthest room. I prepared myself for a dressing-down and followed him into his office.

There was a tray in the middle of his desk. A pitcher of what looked like sorrel sat on it with two down-turned glasses.

He manoeuvred himself around his desk, sat and raised his head at me. Now I was looking at a different man. A big smile spread across his face. 'Young Digson, you want a drink?'

Before I could answer he upturned the glasses and began pouring. He handed me one. 'Sorry about my demeanour out there but I have to keep up appearances, yunno.'

He raised his glass. 'DC Digson, I didn't celebrate your arrival, but I have to celebrate your departure.'

'You kicking me out?' I smiled.

'Yes! And,' he lowered his voice, 'I thanking you same time! Now, youngfella!' He dropped his voice even lower. 'I heard what you did, but not how you did what you did to certain hapless dogs who shall remain nameless in my office. You could regale me, just a lil bit, with some of the finer details of the encounter – some of which I'll pass on to the ladies out there? With your permission, of course. They are very, very interested.'

'No consequence for my actions?'

'Of course,' he chuckled, pointing at the drink. 'Right there!'

Then he got serious. 'The problem that every superintendent still got on this island is the bad seeds. They spring up like weed! I got a whole theory about why that's so. If you lived through the sixties and seventies like me, you'd know exactly what I talking about. The Machetes and the Switches and the Skelos of the Force used to be the eyes and ears and guns of the fella who believed this island belonged to him. They were,' he widened his eyes, 'in the majority.'

'I not putting it on record, and if you quote me I'll deny it, but I glad you passed through here and I sorry to send you off, but Chilly say he want you out of my station because I neglected my duty of care.' He laughed out loud.

'I told him DC Digson don't need no protection from nobody. Is my officers that need protection from him! The youngfella don't look like it, but he is a proper enforcer. Look at what he done to Buso! And Machete and Skelo string up like two man-crabs in the hospital, and Switch 'fraid to come in to work. So, I agree, you have to go, else you'll indispose the whole of Central.'

'Malan Greaves goin do a better job filling you in, Sir – that alright?'

He smiled broadly and stood up. 'I got the details – proprietor called and complained. Said it was like a movie. I just wanted to compare your version with his.'

He walked me to the door, dropped a hand on my shoulder.

'Chilman told me if I don't kick you out, he's coming to do it himself. I don't want to cross thread with him. So is go y'all going.'

'Malan too?'

'Chilman offer him to me. I tell him thanks, but no thanks. I didn't ask about the young lady. How's that going?'

'Which young – oh, Miss Stanislaus!'

'She bad as you?'

'More bad,' I said.

He shook his head. 'So, what Chilman feeding y'all up there?'

'We got no more place "up there". Justice Minister lock us out.'

'Place alarmed and guarded?'

'Don fink so.'

'So what preventing y'all from breaking in?'

'Sir, you suggestin . . . '

'I not suggesting anything, Officer Digson, I just thinking aloud. That Beau Séjour case y'all working on – y'all need resources, not so? Resources that we at Central don't have?'

'We kin manage—'

'Nuh, y'all can't manage! That's the point! You need your resources! So, to access one's resources one does as follows: one breaks in, one changes the lock and one ensconces one-self therein.'

'Never thought of it, Sir. Is good advice.'

'I not giving no advice, Digson. I just thinking aloud.'

'So, I not s'posed to be hearing you?'

'You definitely not!'

30

I was sipping on a cup of hot cocoa when the duty officer in San Andrews Central called me.

'We just fish out a youngfella from de sea, Missa Digger. The name I got is Jonathon Rayburn.' A fisherman, he said, had found the youth floating face-down in the shallows a mile down from his house.

Something in me convulsed. 'Can't be,' I said. 'What he look like?'

'Youngfella, tallish, slim.'

'Can't be,' I shouted. 'You better don fuck with my head this morning, because—'

'Is the details I got here, Missa Digger! People identify de fella—'

'Where?'

'Cayman Beach. I done pass on de message to Rumcake.'

I cut him off, tossed the cup in the sink and ran out the house.

A bright Tuesday morning, busy with minibuses on the main road.

I was breathing hard when I got to Cayman Beach, could barely hold up myself.

They'd laid him out on his stomach, naked but for a pair of shiny yellow shorts, the long arms straight down his side, as if he were asleep. A jagged eel of a scar ran obliquely from just below his shoulder blade to the right side of his lower back. Two officers from East Division had their backs half-turned, heads bobbing in conversation.

Rumcake, the pathologist, passed me his notes. I took them with shaking hands. The old man licked his lips and scratched the stubble on his face that looked white and prickly like a sea urchin's. 'On-for-chu-nate, Digson. Vory on-for-chu-nate. Messy business, won't you say – life and death?'

I barely heard his words. The watery grey eyes were fixed somewhere beyond my shoulders. 'I've arranged the pick-up of the body – blowflies and all that. Thought you wouldn't mind?'

A wind came off the sea and tossed fine sprays of water in my face.

He'd measured the boy's core temperature by inserting a thermometer into his rectum. Estimated time of death was no more than two hours before he arrived. That made it six in the morning or thereabouts. I never doubted Rumcake. With a head full of whisky he could work out the freshness of a fatal wound or time of death with an accuracy I envied. What happened in his head was quicker than math, and better. During his fifty years on Camaho, Rumcake had recalibrated his knowledge of thanatology. The old whitefella could factor in the nuances of temperature, humidity, exposure to air, and tell the time of death almost at a glance.

His conclusion about this dead boy's passing:

Accident. Cause – asphyxiation by drowning.

All the indications were there: white froth around the mouth and nose, inflated stomach, the beginnings of lividity in the neck and chest.

I handed Rumcake his notebook. He swung his canvas satchel onto his shoulders and buckled it shut. The damn thing looked so tattered I was surprised it still had buckles.

'Beautiful specimen, isn't he? Terrible waste. It gets to you, you know – the young ones especially. Anything else I can help you with, young man?'

'That's all, thanks. Can you tell the mortuary to hold him until – erm – the Department authorises his release?'

The white eyebrows climbed his forehead like two hairy caterpillars. He showed me a row of cigar-stained teeth. 'Double-checking – yes?'

'I not doubting you, Sir. I just ... yunno ... '

Rumcake and I were a running joke in the Force. Until I started the job, the Englishman's words were better than gospel in a court of law. I'd heard it said that in his drunken moments – which were almost always – he pronounced me a whippet of an island-lad who'd reduced the noble business of death to chemistry. In my presence, though, the old fella was polite and helpful. I didn't give a damn about the rest.

'You'll contact next of kin?' he said.

'Yes, and thanks again. You'll handle this bit of it for me – I mean the pick-up?' I gestured at the body.

The old fella nodded. His watery eyes were steady on my face. 'Relative?'

'Like you know, on Camaho, everybody is family.' I turned and headed for the road.

Up ahead I saw the ambulance men approaching: two grim-faced fellas, one with the stretcher on his shoulder, the other tripping quickly behind him. A small crowd trailed after them.

I stepped aside to let them pass, acknowledging their nods, my eyes on the smaller group behind: a dozen adults, an animated babble of children, a knot of teenage girls. I picked out the clean-limbed one, about seventeen, a well-groomed head of hair. I curled a finger at her.

'Uh-huh?' The big eyes flashed me with impatience.

'You know Jana Ray, not so?'

Her hands flew to her mouth. 'Is – Is Jah-Ray down there for true?' I watched her face crumple. I took a breath and nodded.

'He come down here regular, Miss, erm?'

'Nadine.'

'He go down there regular?'

She was in a fever to get away, kept switching her head in the direction of the bay. 'Most mornings except Sunday. He go for a swim. I – we – watch im from up dere.' She pointed at a nest of wooden houses on the hillside. 'I hear talk say something happen to Jah-Ray. I say it can't be Jah-Ray cuz Jah-Ray swim like fish. Is him for true?'

'For true,' I said. 'I sorry.'

She shot off with flailing arms and hammering heels, her cries sharp in the air.

At home I sat on my steps, swallowing on the tightness in my throat, watching black cowbirds tussling in a hoq plum tree across the valley.

I fought with the heaviness in my guts, the throb at the base of my throat. And just when I thought I'd gotten a grip on it, the image of an outraged Jana Ray on Dog Island, watching a wild ram die, flooded my head. I covered my face with my hands and cried.

31

Maybe I didn't want to believe Rumcake's conclusions about the way Jana Ray died. But from the moment I saw him lying on the beach, I felt that nudging in my brain like when I'm about to set off to work and I forgot to lock my door.

I picked up my phone.

'Hullooo! Missa Digger?'

'Miss Stanislaus, you got thick clothes?'

'I got clothes.'

'Thick, Miss Stanislaus – like for overseas weather; you got that?'

'Missa Digger, what happen?'

'I taking you out tonight round midnight. Dress for the cold, y'unnerstan?'

'Uh-huh.'

'Catch some sleep before.'

'Uh-huh.'

'See you tonight.'

'Uh-huh.'

I pulled out the lower compartment of my little fridge, withdrew containers, spray bottles, measuring beakers – part of the paraphernalia I'd ordered over the Internet from the time I finished my forensics course in England. I spread two newspapers on the floor and sat down to prepare.

I could live with Rumcake's diagnosis, but I could not go

along with his conclusion. The old whitefella was not wrong about me. When the grieving and the rituals and the shock of death are over, what remains of the physical self is nothing more than chemistry. Like I kept telling Miss Stanislaus, a murdered body rails against it own death. It will record every second of its passing. The trick was to know which chemistry to use to make that body talk to you.

I called Daryl who worked at the mortuary. 'You on night shift, Daryl?'

'No, Francis on tonight.'

'You kin swap with him for tonight?'

'Missa Digger, you think dis man like lookin' at dead people all de time?'

'You don't? You know Jonathon Rayburn?'

'Jonathon who?'

'Jah-Ray. Nice youngfella from Beau Séjour.'

'Jah-Ray! I know Jah-Ray. Why you didn' say Jah-Ray. Me an Jah-Ray go down good.'

'He dead.'

'He . . . ? Missa Digger, you jokin.' His voice dropped to a whimper. 'That don't make no sense. How come?'

'Is what I want to find out tonight. You comin in?'

'Lemme call Francis.'

Miss Stanislaus put on so many layers she looked like an overstuffed teddy bear – a tropical one – with all those layers of colour on her person. She flashed a look at me as if to say, If is the arse you playin, you better watch out.

On the way, I briefed her. She said she already knew about the boy from Pet. Did I know they'd announced it on the radio?

At the high steel gate, I rang the bell. Daryl came out in a heavy coat and boots. I checked my watch – just past 1am.

'Missa Digger,' he yawned, 'you reach?'

'You sleepin on the job?' I said.

'Man tired. I really sorry for the fella. People does dead so stupid.'

'Daryl, say good night to Miss Stanislaus.'

Daryl muttered something polite and turned to lead us in. He swung back his head to look at Miss Stanislaus. She had that effect on fellas. Always.

'Unit 3, third shelf from the bottom.' Daryl swung open the heavy door.

The cold hit me in the face and on the skin of my throat. Miss Stanislaus lifted her shoulders and dropped them, settling the layers on her body.

'Stay close,' I said.

She nodded.

Daryl slid out the shelf. He looked upset. I understood that. Grief is adjustment before acceptance settles in. I asked him to switch off the florescent, then handed my regulation torch to Miss Stanislaus. 'Point it at the ceiling.'

In the diffuse glow from the torch, I could see the whites of Daryl's eyes.

'Remember what I tell you about your profession, Daryl?'

'Nuh.'

'Confidentiality.'

'No worries, Missa Digger. I born confidential. I don't ask nobody nothing about their bizness. What y'all doin to the fella?'

'Stay quiet or I'll ask you to leave.'

'Wake me when you ready.' Daryl slipped out the door and closed it.

'Missa Digger, you cryin,' Miss Stanislaus mumbled. She rested a hand on my shoulder.

'I'm not,' I said and shrugged her off.

I took out the six spray bottles I'd prepared before leaving my house, lined them up on the floor and pulled on a pair of Neoprene gloves.

I turned to Miss Stanislaus. 'To explain what I about to do, I have to confuse you first. I going to talk to Jana Ray and if he answer me, is going to be with light.'

She shifted her feet and nodded.

'You ever wonder what make firefly backside light up?'

'Tell me,' she said.

'Well, firefly mix something called ATP with a coupla other substances that got the devil name – luciferin and luciferase. Firefly combine them in doses and that make their backside blink like the indicator of my car. People call that bioluminescence.'

I took up one of the spray bottles. 'What I have in here is luminol. When I combine it with blood, it will give off a glow. I got another one here call fluorescein, but tonight, I using luminol. If there's blood anywhere on this youngfella, the dimmest trace of it, any kind of bruising, what I got in here will show me. Forty-five seconds is all I have before the glow disappear. Should be enough time to get a coupla pictures. You follow me?'

She nodded.

'I doing his front first, toes to head. When I finish, Daryl will help me turn him over. Then I starting from the feet again. Is going take us until sun-up.'

I felt her shiver; couldn't tell whether it was from the temperature of the room or what I'd just told her.

I began the slow, energy-sapping work: a fine spray along the limbs and trunk, the wait, then moving on – always worried that I might have missed an area, and so going back on myself from time to time. Now and then, the torch in Miss Stanislaus's hand wavered, but she held it steady for the most

part. By the time I got to Jana Ray's face the cold had begun
to seep into my bones.

I glanced at my watch – 3am. I straightened up and
stretched my limbs. 'Miss Stanislaus, you want a break?'

'Nuh.'

'Let's get Daryl.'

I opened the door. 'Daryl, I want to turn the fella over.'

Daryl strode in and with a movement of his hands and
shoulders, flipped the body over.

'Jesus!' I said.

'Is not Jeezus, Missa Digger, is me.' He chuckled and
left the room.

Another three hours crouched in a room cooled to four
degrees centigrade began to slow me down. Miss Stanislaus
lowered the torch and folded her arms around herself.
'Mebbe is not what you think, Missa Digger? Mebbe is
just . . . '

'Only the head now,' I said.

Like most youngfellas his age, Jana Ray cropped his hair
close to his scalp, with a designer tuft on the top. I was on
my last bottle and it was already half empty. I ran my torch
across the scalp. No sign of bruising or contusion, but that
proved nothing.

I inched my way up from the nape of the neck and was just
over to the right ear when I straightened up and beckoned
Miss Stanislaus.

She leaned forward and pressed a shoulder against me.

'See anything?' I said.

Miss Stanislaus shook her head. I sprayed more heavily this
time, felt her body heave and subside.

'Tell me,' I said.

'Blue light, not so? Deep blue.'

I hadn't told her what colour to expect.

187

'Now I betting you we find the same result on the other side.'

I eased the head the other way and sprayed. And there it was, the deep blue glow between the short hairs on the scalp like the hint of a rippling sea. I asked her to shine the light obliquely. I sprayed more generously, took a picture with my phone. It wasn't a steady shot but it would have to do.

'You wondering what I make of all of this?' I said.

She'd pulled her lower lip between her teeth, making chewing motions with her jaw.

'Somebody drowned Jana Ray. Somebody with good-sized hands.' I placed one of mine behind her head and pressed forward slightly. 'Must've kept his head down in the water that way. He struggle – of course, the youngfella struggle. Is where the thumb and index tighten round his head to keep him down that you have the abrasions on the scalp. You can't see them with your naked eye, but they there.'

She placed a hand on my arm. 'Missa Digger, you cryin again and that upsettin me. You leavin this place with me right now!'

Once outside, Miss Stanislaus was all business. 'That remind me, is time to see that woman again – Laza Wilkins' mother. We going to be needing a warrant, I fink?'

I cleared my throat. 'Why?'

'Becuz, I going be needin it.'

32

Jana Ray's death shifted something in me – a gnawing deep-down rage and helplessness. Staff Superintendent Gill was right. I could not work in Central. The place wasn't safe, the hours were too regimented and they treated me more like a curiosity than as a member of Camaho Police Force. To deal with Lazar Wilkinson's and Jana Ray's murders I needed the territory I was accustomed to: my desk.

I broke into the office at 10pm the following day. I called my friend, Caran, from the Bush Rangers. He arrived with his crew.

In half an hour we were inside. The place looked desecrated. The photocopier had been unplugged and moved to the middle of the room. Our desks were rearranged, the water cooler gone, and the old, precious fax machine that we used for inter-island exchanges was on the floor near the bin. Miss Stanislaus's vase had disappeared. The storeroom where we kept our munitions and other important stuff was still locked. We'd reinforced the door with Titan locks in two places. Somebody had taken an instrument to them but they'd resisted the break-in.

A rolled-up poster lay on the floor with the MJ's name headlined on it. Stacks of campaign leaflets.

Caran hesitated when he saw them. 'Digger, you sure?'

'I sure,' I said. 'Looks to me like the MJ didn't just kick us out, he's setting up his party office here.'

I thought of the Commissioner and felt let down, almost ashamed of him. All my old childhood resentments returned. I began wishing again that he wasn't my father.

We rearranged the office as it used to be.

I checked that the phones were still working and the number hadn't changed. I texted Malan and Miss Stanislaus and told them that the office would be up and running from tomorrow night. I told Pet I wanted blackout curtains for the windows because I'd be working at night in the meantime. Pet was feverish with delight. Then I called Chilman.

'Is like you prepare to lose your job?' the old man said. I could hear the big smile in his voice.

'What he getting away with is illegal,' I said. 'If Commissioner Lohar don't have the balls to take back his job from that man, he should resign. And I going to tell him that.'

'You prepare to lose your father too?'

'I ain got no—' I stopped short. Felt so choked, I had to swallow hard.

'Okay, Digson, you upset. Is obvious.' The old man's voice was gentle. 'Them killin that lil friend ov yours got to you, not so?' He went quiet for a while. 'Is another argument for me to keep my department runnin. Go easy, youngfella.' Chilman clicked off.

I sat back and reviewed what Jana Ray told me about his connection with Lazar Wilkinson. That something big was going down, I had no doubt. I sensed it in what Jana Ray refused to talk about and the shivering fear that seized his body when I broached the subject of Lazar's murder, and that name – Shadowman.

I tried to recall every minute of my encounter with the youth – from the time I cornered him in the roadside bush in Beau Séjour to my standing over his body in Cayman Bay.

I made notes and at the end of it, stretched out on the floor to catch a nap.

When I raised my head, the sun was streaming through the window of the office and the MJ's secretary was getting out of her car with a roll of posters in her arms. She was a small woman, long in the face with the glazed eyes of a sheep. She was wearing thick clothes for the Arctic conditions of the MJ's office. I wondered if she ever smiled.

I grabbed my bag, stepped out the door and locked it behind me.

'Sorry, Miss, Office reclaimed,' I said. 'Tell the Minister of Justice,' I bit down on the last word, 'that we got two murders dealing with right now. Y'hear about the youngfella who throat got cut last week?'

She remained as impassive as stone.

'Well, the other one got killed yesterday, and people from the press going be asking what San Andrews CID doing about it. We don't want to tell them we can't do nothing about it cuz Justice Minister lock us outta the office where we work. We don want him to have to answer that in public.'

She slid expressionless eyes over my face. 'What's your name?'

'Digger.'

I was on my way to the market square when the Commissioner phoned. 'Michael, the MJ just called.'

'Yessir, what about him?'

'Well, he said—'

'Commissioner Lohar, I don't want to hear what the MJ said. You the one should be standing between him and us. You the one should be fighting back on our behalf.' I was so choked up, I could barely speak.

'Michael—'

'Don't Michael me, Sir! You letting me down again. You didn stand up for me as a father, and you not doing so as my boss. What I s'posed to do? All my fuckin life, when I need your support, you been leaving me out in the cold. So don—' I cut off, pressed my back against a storefront, closed my eyes and filled my lungs a couple of times until I calmed myself.

When I opened my eyes, a white car had slowed down in the road in front of me. Switch sat in the driver's seat, his elbow hanging out the door. Staring at me with that mouth of his screwed down.

'This time,' I breathed to myself, 'I goin to have to deal with him.'

Switch raised his brows, nodded and drove off.

33

Miss Stanislaus called twice to remind me about seeing Lazar Wilkinson's mother, and could I also get her a warrant? She didn't want plastic cuffs, she needed the ones made of steel.

She sounded brisk and businesslike on the phone.

'Steel cuffs went out with the donkeysaurus,' I explained. 'Like you know, what people nowadays use is plastic. Nobody ever break loose from one.'

'I want steel,' she insisted.

'Why, Miss Stanislaus?'

'Missa Digger, you shoutin. You'll see – that's all.'

I left the office mid-morning, picked up the warrant from Central then drove to her place to meet her.

'Where's the hankuff, Missa Digger?'

'You'll get it,' I said.

An idea had struck me at the last minute: given his length of service in the Force, Chilman would probably have a pair of metal handcuffs. When I asked him, the old fella even offered to bring them to us.

When we arrived in Beau Séjour, DS Chilman's half-dead Datsun was parked by the seafront. I noticed that the grass had begun to cover the scar that Lazar Wilkinson's burnt-out vehicle had made by the side of the road. Boats rose and fell on the water in the bay. A dazzling mid-afternoon sun had turned the water into molten silver. The deserted beach, with its pile of black rocks at the southern end, looked desolate.

He held the cuffs out through the window. Miss Stanislaus sent me to get them.

The rum-fired eyes sought mine. 'What y'all up to, Digson?'

'Doing the government work, Sir. That alright?'

He looked me up and down, pulled his lips to one side. 'Digson, you'z a . . . '

'Dog, Sir. I know.'

'Correct!'

I jangled the handcuffs. 'Thanks for the relic.'

He winked at me before chugging off.

Miss Stanislaus dropped them in her bag. 'Missa Digger, what's de worse thing a woman kin do to another woman in Camaho?'

I thought about it. 'Embarrass her, Miss Stanislaus, bring down shame on her head.'

She shot me a look. 'You know too much! Shall we persevere?'

Lazar Wilkinson's mother was pulling her washing off the line. The woman next door turned from entering her house and planted both elbows on the wall of her veranda, hands propping up her chin.

Miss Stanislaus followed Dora Wilkinson inside her house, fluttering the warrant. I stayed in the yard. From there, I had a clear view of the inside: a six-ringed gas stove, a tall white fridge with the Styrofoam still fitted on the top. Bags of dry goods – wholesale size – heaped against the kitchen counter. In the living room beyond, a flat-screen colour TV on an aluminium and glass stand, with stereo components stacked below it. Four plump sofas arranged around a low glass table.

'Miss Wilkins, I got a warrant to search your house.

Dependin on what you say – in fact, no matter what you say – I going have to arrest you.'

I lowered my head and smiled. Wait till the fellas in the Force hear this version of the Miranda warning!

Miss Stanislaus dropped the handcuffs on the kitchen counter with a terrible clatter. Dora Wilkinson jumped as if she had been struck.

'Who give you de money to buy all dem things in here?' The woman's eyes were on the handcuffs and I could see that she was terrified.

'Well, I . . . I . . . nobody didn . . . '

'Don bother lie for me. If you lie for me, I take you outta here in this.' Miss Stanislaus raised the cuffs, shook them in the woman's face. 'When I put this on you, Miss Lady, you'll never forget the shame from people seein you walkin behind me in it. Where you get the money from?'

'I dunno, the man.'

'Which man, what's his name?'

'Dunno, he ring me, say money wire to my account and is to make up for what happen to Lazar. He say everybody sorry. He say they look after their own people, and he know how hard I take it but nothing they kin do now. Then, same night, Shadowman come outside my door an say dat now I get de money I not s'pose to talk.'

'You could tell me and Missa Digger what the Shadowman look like?'

The woman looked about her as if she might be overheard. 'Is night he come. I-I didn . . . '

Her throat was glistening with sweat.

Miss Stanislaus dropped the cuffs on the counter.

The woman's body stiffened. 'I hear say he's a big fella. Mebbe bigger than that man there.' She directed a shaking hand through the window at me.

195

'Where we find him?'

'I dunno. I swear to God, I dunno.'

'How much they pay you for your boy' life?'

'Dunno, I . . .'

'How much?'

Dora licked her lips, threw a helpless look at me. I almost felt sorry for the woman.

'How much?' Miss Stanislaus raised the warrant from the counter.

Lazar Wilkinson's mother muttered something.

'How much you say?'

Dora Wilkinson mumbled again.

'Ten thousand dollars! That's what your boychild worth to you?'

The woman kept her head down. She looked haggard and deflated. Her hands were still trembling.

Miss Stanislaus passed me a quick sideways glance. I hopped up the steps and entered the house.

I cleared my throat. 'Your bank book, Miss Dora. I want to see it.'

She began making soft stomping motions on the floor with her feet. I leaned against the doorway and held out my hand. 'The book?'

Lazar Wilkinson's mother did not move.

'Okay, Missa Digger, we done here. I take her with us.' Miss Stanislaus reached for the cuffs, slotted in the key and snapped them open.

'I gettin it, I gettin it.'

I listened to the woman shuffling in her bedroom. Something grated on the floor, then came the whisper and flutter of fabric. She returned and dropped a small green book in front of me.

I flicked through the pages. 'Twenty-two thousand

deposited middle of last week. Twelve thousand, forty-two cents in there now. The ten thousand, I s'pose, was for all this?' I made a circular gesture.

I didn't expect Dora to answer me. She didn't.

Miss Stanislaus held open the bank book while I photographed the pages. Finished, I handed it back.

Miss Stanislaus touched my elbow and we left.

With a hand on the car door, she raised her head at me. 'Missa Digger, how I do?'

'You born for this,' I said.

'Fank you. I decide you not so bad yourself.'

'Fank you too, Miss Stanislaus!'

She drew the plasticuffs from her bag, shook them in my face. 'You fink I could've make that woman talk with this?'

'What made you think they would try to buy her off?' I asked.

'Common sense, Missa Digger. Lazar is the woman' son. They know she goin be hurtin-an-complainin, and whatever little she know, she goin tell it to de world. They make sure they buy her mouth.'

She went silent for a while, her eyes lifted at the peaks of the Belvedere mountains.

'Missa Digger, tell me the truth. You fink this will pass over?'

'What you talking about now?'

'What waiting for me in two weeks an' four days' time.'

'You mean the hearing? You been counting?'

She nodded.

'Miss Stanislaus, it got to pass over. I got to make it pass over.'

'What you have in mind?' she said.

'Maybe I get a breakthrough. Maybe I beg. Maybe I blackmail. Dunno.'

197

'You do that for me?'

'What you think?'

She shrugged. 'Mebbe I do the same.'

'For?'

'Missa Digger, you like fry-breadfruit? I got some in my bag for you.'

'I ready to have it now,' I said.

'Nuh. You eat it in the car.'

34

The hillside on which my house was built climbed another half-mile up to a giant rock formation on the summit. A few families had built their homes in the valley directly under those rocks, and I always wondered how the inhabitants down there could go to bed knowing that several megatons of granite were perched above their roofs. Rock Top was a barren place with a line of glory cedar trees, stripped of their leaves and tormented by a steady chilling wind that rose off the ocean a couple of miles away. But I liked the isolation that I found when sitting up there. It cleared my mind and drowned the static in my brain.

I ran through the list I carried in my head. These days I felt weighed down by them.

I had no results from the old women on Kara Island about finding the body of Miss Stanislaus's great-uncle, Koku. The last time I spoke to Benna she told me, 'Koku not buried in dis soil, Missa Digger. Else he would've reveal himself to me.'

'I don't unnerstand,' I said. 'You been searching? I mean actual searching—'

'Why you doubting me?' she said.

'I not. I sorry. Call me if—'

'Somefing cross my mind last night, Missa Digger. Just one idea.'

'Tell me.'

'Nuh!'

'Benna, you not helping me or Miss Stanislaus at all! I need to know.'

She must have picked up my distress because when she answered, her voice had softened. 'We got other islands round here. Kara Island not the only one, yunno.'

'Do your best, Benna. Please!'

'Uh-huh,' she said and hung up.

I could hardly bring myself to think about the hearing, couldn't bear the thought of Malan striding out of whatever room in which the meeting was held with that sneering mouth and his eyes locked on Miss Stanislaus's face.

When my father, the Commissioner, had asked me how far I was prepared to go with this, I'd told him the truth. I would go as far as I felt I needed to, and that included losing the job.

Was it all because of Miss Stanislaus? Nuh . . .

Like Chilman said, the MJ's actions stank of the kind of control that Camahoans had died from before and I didn't have to look far to find an example. It was the words that came from a Justice Minister's mouth that unleashed a posse of officers on women protesting on the streets in '99 against the rape of a schoolgirl all those years ago. It resulted in the murder of my mother and the disappearance of her body.

But how could I even begin to take on a man with the MJ's clout? I had no illusions about what he was capable of. I'd learned of a personal assistant of his who'd rejected his advances and walked off the job. A few months later she fell seriously ill, had to leave Camaho for treatment in Canada. The MJ had her passport seized. Her sister sneaked her off the island on another woman's passport. Pet said she knew the woman.

And there was Jana Ray . . . However much I tried to blank the youngfella from my mind, my thoughts always ended up on him. There was so much I didn't have a chance to drag out of him. He'd admitted to working for Lazar Wilkinson. Seemed disturbed by the change he noticed in the stuff that they were handling and wanted to get out of it. The way I saw it now, those changes might have contributed to his and Lazar Wilkinson's murder. Might indeed be the cause of it. Dunno! That their deaths were connected in some way, I had little doubt.

I'd learned in that Forensics course in England that there were many points of entry to investigating a crime. The most obvious was not always the best. And depending on the one you chose, you can either arrive at a dead end or a break-through. For the moment, I decided to focus on Jana Ray.

I stood up, dusted the seat of my trousers and headed back down the hill.

The hillside houses were quiet when I got to Jana Ray's place – the sea flat grey in the distance. The chill of the mountain air that settled over the village at night had not yet been lifted by the early sun. Somewhere in the near distance came the *thack-thack* of a machete attacking wood.

I pushed open the door, stood in the middle of the front room. Jana Ray's books were packed as usual on the floor, his utensils upturned. A hand of rotting bananas against the foot of the dresser, writhing with ants and aphids. A small canvas purse on the floor, the tip of a five-dollar bill sticking out. A kingsized Anchor matchbox sat on the edge of the stove. I reached over and slid open the drawer of the box. Empty.

My eyes fell on what looked like a digital clock beside a small card stamped Amazon.com. I picked it up, brought it to my face. The print on it said: thermometer/hygrometer. Made in China.

I stuffed it in my bag.

I switched on my torch and walked into the gloom of the bedroom. The mattress on the floor had been gutted – the coconut fibres strewn in clumps across the space, the floorboards in each corner raised. A small cloth suitcase lay with its flap unzipped. I opened it and pulled out the jumble of shirts and underwear I'd bought him, crumpled but unworn. I fingered the lining of the suitcase.

As I was straightening up, I spotted a book against the wall, half-opened, obviously tossed aside. *Hydroponics: Principles and Practice* – heavy, thick cover, cloth-bound. Expensive. A card promoting Amazon Prime peeked out from the pages. On the inside cover a few handwritten words, *Fr. your star-apple*. Underneath it, barely visible in the gloom, the book I'd lent him. I stood there for a while, my head pulsing with the headache I'd been ignoring since I woke.

Footsteps outside. I closed my eyes and listened. Woman . . . heavy. Breathing loudly from the climb. I shoved the books into my bag, strode across the floor and pulled open the door.

Brown feverish eyes settled on my face. She stood barefoot on the bank above the entrance, a rusty machete in one hand, her body pushed forward as if she were about to throw herself at me. 'The boy gone, why y'all don't leave im alone. Why y'all diggin up his place? Y'all don't do enough already?'

I pulled out my ID and turned it towards her. 'I'm DC Digson, San Andrews CID. Who's "y'all"?'

She shifted sideways, glanced quickly behind her. 'People! Fuckahs! Doin all kinda wickedness round here and people can't stop dem. Is a gun I want for them. Take people chil'ren . . . donkey . . .' The rest of the words got lost in her throat.

I felt my body stiffen with annoyance. 'Is names I want. Gimme some blastid names!'

I stepped down from the doorway. The woman pulled back

abruptly, her heels beating a heavy rhythm down the path. I followed her as she swung into a track between a row of houses. A brace of pothounds, all ribs and bared teeth, rushed out and blocked my path, their racket raking against my ears.

'I coming back,' I snarled. 'Is come, I coming back.'

I returned to the house and closed Jana Ray's door.

I called Dessie.

'Dessie, Digger here. How you?'

'Digger! I so cut-up about your little friend.'

'I cut-up too, Dessie.'

'When we seeing?'

'Dessie, is a favour I call to ask you. I want you to check an account for me. It belongs to one Dora Wilkinson. I told you about the necktie killing?'

'It was all over the radio, Digger.'

'Well, Dora Wilkinson is the fella' mother. She received a payment of twenty-two thousand dollars, middle of last week. I want to know where or even better who the money got transferred from.'

'Hold on Digger, you going too fast. Give me the name again.'

I gave her the name again.

'You sure she has an account with us?'

'I sure.'

'I'm sorry to say, it's not that simple. We have procedures, you know.'

'Dessie, I could get a court order but I prefer to keep it simple, that's all. You still there?'

'You have the account number?'

'Hold on,' I said. I pulled out my phone and brought up the photo of the bank book.

'09434. Name, Dora J. Wilkinson; address Beau Séjour, San Andrews.'

203

'I think I see it.' She lowered her voice. 'You free later?'

'Nuh. Sorry. Lemme know what you find. Fax it to the office if you want.'

'I'll text,' she said.

'Thank you, Dessie.'

A couple of minutes later, Dessie called back. 'Money was deposited by the customer, Digger. Not transferred.'

'You sure?'

'Of course I am.'

I sat on the seawall facing the ocean. The bay was empty but for a small group of boys tossing water in each other's faces at the northern end. Someone had planted a black flag on the spot where we'd found Lazar Wilkinson's body. Probably his mother. The houses on the hill behind me had begun to brighten in the early-morning sun. To the side of them, further up the hill, Jana Ray's place. All I could see from here was his rusting roof, like a scab against the green.

I jumped off the wall and walked to the beach. The boys' shouting died, their heads now swung in my direction. They began leaving the water and were out on the sand by the time I reached them. Lean, bony kids with scooped-out collar bones, scarred hands and welts along their legs and shoulders. A picture of the scar that ran all the way down Jana Ray's back popped into my head. They watched me watching them, mouths partly open. The night I returned to Beau Séjour with Miss Stanislaus and chased down Jana Ray, I'd shared my food with two of them. The one who'd said his name was Eric wasn't among this bunch.

'Tell me about them marks on y'all skin,' I said.

They bolted, almost as if they'd rehearsed it – became fast, zig-zagging shapes through the trees.

I shouted at their disappearing backs, the same thing I'd said to the dogs.

35

I arranged to meet Miss Stanislaus at the office. She was hesitant at first.

'We ain got much to lose,' I said.

I ran a damp cloth on the surfaces of the desks, fussing over Miss Stanislaus's especially. I'd already re-positioned the bits of furniture to their original positions and swept up the grit that had been left on the floor. I'd stacked the MJ's leaflets and posters in the corner by the door. But wherever I turned, my eyes were drawn to them. I finally placed them in the storeroom.

Chilman walked in before Miss Stanislaus. 'Digson, you look sick. When last you sleep? Place change,' he grumbled.

Miss Stanislaus arrived an hour later. 'Office don't feel de same,' she muttered. She ignored her desk, pulled a chair and positioned herself to face the window.

'Pet and Lisa not here,' I said. I didn't tell them Pet had said she doubted Lisa would return.

Malan turned up late afternoon. He poked his head through the door and gestured me outside. He had a hand under his chin. His brows were clenched.

'Digger, I decide they wasting me down in Central.'

'What you want, Malan?'

'Staff boss, Gill, say he still doin de paperwork for my job.

And,' Malan looked away, 'like Sarona say, I got de time so ain't no reason why I can't help out. I think Sarona right.'

'You sure is Sarona who make you decide? Mebbe the MJ called you and told you he got no use for you no more?'

Malan could barely look at me. 'Nuh, I call him. I tell him we need de Department; was a mistake I make. I tell him about the case you chasin—'

'We! Me and Miss Stanislaus.'

'I tell him nobody else kin handle it – San Andrews CID specialise in that—'

'And Miss Stanislaus?'

'Is the only fing he not letting go. He say he want the hearing. He say the rest is awright in the meantime.' Malan looked at me. 'Digger, what he got against you? Becuz is a lot of questions the MJ ask me about you. He want to know where you live, where your family from and even the name of the woman you going with. I only tell im about your bourgeois woman – the Manille girl. That slow im down, becuz he know he can't fuck wid that family. They prob'ly the one dat make him minister. And they kin suttinly take him down.'

'Why he not dropping Miss Stanislaus?'

'Becuz of you, I fink. He know you partnering with she, and y'was on the scene. Mebbe he decide he can, erm, im-pli-cate you too. I show you somefing.'

Malan pulled out a sheet of paper from his pocket, unfolded it and turned it to face me. It was a drawing of a prostrate man that took up the whole page. There were circles on the shoulders, the thighs, the knees, the groin and sternum.

Malan cocked his chin at me, the black eyes flat and light-less. 'Mibo from Kara Island send him this. I suspect the MJ ask for it. You seein what I see?'

'Tell me,' I said.

206

'That's a map of the bullets on Juba' body. Check the placement of them shots. Keep in mind y'all say the fella was a movin target and it was night-time. You see what it sayin?'

I lifted my shoulders and dropped them.

'Digger, you gone blind?'

'For the time being, yes.'

He licked his lips and blinked at me. 'You don't see? That woman place every fuckin bullet as if she reach out 'er hand and stick them on the fella. Digger, she almost as good as me.'

'Almost?'

I didn't think Malan heard me. He was staring at the silhouette of Miss Stanislaus in the office. 'If you teach De Woman to shoot like that, you stupid. I not teachin no woman to do nothing better than me.'

I turned towards the door. 'You finish with me?'

'MJ say is impossible for woman to shoot like dat, night-time. I almost believe him. He make it clear to me that she must've wounded Juba first – gone close to im after she disable im and done the rest in cold blood. He conclude was an execution – she use the cover of the law to get revenge. A clear case of pre-med-i-ta-tion. I tell im you was there. He say that you'z a liar, Digger. You sure it happen the way you say?'

'When you talk to your boss again, tell him I sticking to my story.'

'I know he don't like de best bone in you, Digger. But what de MJ tell me make sense. I soften him lil bit, yunno, but he say he got to take action against de Department becuz he got no argument in his cabinet meeting to explain why you and De Woman shoot down dat fella. He ask me what evidence y'all got dat Juba is a murderer. I tell him I dunno.'

'So what you saying?' I said.

'Is not me saying, Digger. Is him. S'far as I see, de MJ got to get an argument for cabinet. So give him de argument. Prove that Juba is de murderer that y'all say he is.'

'I confused,' I said.

'Your problem,' Malan said. 'And I decide that I not helpin y'all.'

I wasn't angry with him any more. What I felt about Malan was worse. He'd lost my trust and whatever respect I had for him. He was a danger to himself.

'I been thinking, Malan – even if it did happen like the MJ believe – mebbe every girlchile in Camaho should be like that, yunno. After a fella two-three-four times her age rape her, she don't bother to report it. She hold it in until it turn poison in her heart. She bide her time, and when time reach she take him down herself.'

'You should hear yourself, Digger, you talk like a fuckin criminal.'

'I learning from you,' I said. 'You coming or you going?'

'I going,' he said. 'Fings change in there, not so?' He raised a hand at the office.

'You not running the place no more.'

'Nuffing change, then. You givin me a key?'

'You not working here no more.'

I remembered DS Chilman's advice. I fished out my key and handed it to Malan. He plucked it from my fingers. 'Call me when you want me.'

He ambled to his car, dragged open the door and slid in behind the wheel. Malan drove off without looking back.

Miss Stanislaus was stepping out the door when I turned around. 'Missa Digger, I see you give that man a key. I not goin to be sittin down in there lissenin to him no more.'

'Me neither, Miss Stanislaus.'

'Then you shouldn've give him no key.'

'Your father said to treat him same way.'

208

'For what, Missa Digger? For what? He don't mean nobody no good. Why you still holdin onto him when he nearly got you kill?'

'Miss Stanislaus—'

'He nearly got you kill, an you never tell me about it. Why you didn' tell me?'

I shrugged. 'I handled it, Miss Stanislaus.'

'Malan is trouble, he's trouble to his own self.' Her words came fierce and urgent. 'I tell you this, Missa Digger, if any-fing did happen to you down there in that Rock place – I'd've been in a lot more trouble becuz is not them police fellas I'd ha been going after. Is him!'

She swung around and quick-stepped past me to the road.

I got into my car, drove until I drew up alongside her. I stopped, leaned across and opened the door.

She kept on walking, her head straight. I did it again a couple of times. 'We need to talk,' I said.

She sucked her teeth, threw me a fire-and-brimstone look and kept on walking.

I watched her disappear down the road to the marketplace. I felt so abandoned I decided to go home.

On my way back to my place, I was forced to a crawl on Old Hope Road. Both sides of the road were lined with young children and teenagers. They assaulted my ears with distorted versions of my name: *Dig-dug! Dig-who? Digger who Dug her!* I put it down to the spillover violence from a cricket match they were playing on the only straight bit of road in the village. Old Hope versus Mont Airy.

I was shaking with exhaustion when I finally pushed open my door. I mixed myself a mauby drink with a sprinkling of rhum agricole and fed my player Third World's *Journey to Addis*. I selected 'Fret not Thyself'. The words were biblical and assuring and loaded with so much history it turned my mind to the old women of Kara Island.

That heaviness in my chest returned – that lump in my throat I could not get rid of and the embarrassment of being close to tears every time I paused, which was why I could not allow myself to stop.

He remind you of yourself. Miss Stanislaus had said that about Jana Ray after she'd gotten over the fact that I did not arrest the youngfella the first time I cornered him in Beau Séjour. It didn't occur to me until she said it, and even then I decided she was wrong. Jana Ray brought home to me what I didn't have enough of – family.

I'd taken a picture of him when we were on Dog Island.

The youngfella was standing with his back against the sea, his blue bum-bag dangling from his hand – a tall, sleek-looking man-boy, proud and poor-arse like I used to be. Jana Ray hid his intelligence behind that shy reserve of his. An athlete too, if ever there was one, and in whom the gift was not so much wasted as ignored. I recalled him glaring at me and pointing at his head that last time he visited my place. *I have plans, Missa Digger. Gimme a couple more years and I off to university.* University meant money. A lot. Jana Ray had set himself a deadline and was so sure of achieving it, he was prepared to bet me. That suddenly gave me an idea.

Next morning, I drove to San Andrews under a cloudless mid-August sky. Already, the day had begun to heat up. At the office, I ran through the ansaphone messages from stations around the island. It seemed that they'd dropped the search for the two whitefellas and Tamara, the woman that Miss Stanislaus and I wanted to question in relation to Lazar Wilkinson's murder.

Nobody here see no woman who carry dat description. She probably with a fella.

She a young-girl y'all say? Then she must have a man. Find out where the man is and she mos' likely with de fella.'

Y'all call y'all self detective? So how come y'all can't find she?

A couple of them sounded drunk.

I made a list of the banks in San Andrews, worked out a trajectory in my head and hit the road on foot. I figured if Jana Ray had the kind of money to pay for a university education, he would not keep the money in his house. I did the rounds of all eight banks and the response was the same from each – no account holder by the name of Jonathon Rayburn. On a whim I made my way to the Credit Union – an ancient, recently spruced-up brick building overlooking the Carenage. I went through the routine of raising my ID at a teller and asking for the boss.

A woman approached from the back of the space – stiff-backed, pressed hair hugging her scalp. Skin tight and glossed like a star-apple fruit.

'Sorry to bother you, Miss erm . . . ?'

'Blackwood.'

Mid-thirties – give or take a coupla years. Coal-black eyes.

'I'm DC Digson. Quick enquiry, yunno. Youngfella name Jonathon Rayburn. Goes by the name of Jana Ray. I just checking whether he got an account here.'

Her eyes made quick darting movements from my face to my feet. 'Yes, he has one.'

'You know Jana Ray?'

'We all know him. It was in the papers.' She raised her head at the row of tellers. 'Bright young man. Pleasant.'

'I'd like a printout of his transactions, please, from when he opened the account to the last time he accessed it.'

A small tensing of her brows. 'Mr Digson, I don't think—'

211

'I could get a warrant, Miss Blackwood. I could make a fuss and draw everybody's attention to what I'm here for. That's what you want?'

I watched her retreating back till her head disappeared behind the high partition at the far end of the room. The tellers at the service counters had their eyes on me. Thirty-two minutes later, Miss Blackwood returned with a wad of papers, pointed at a desk and dropped them on it.

I dragged a chair, my shoulders tense with the atmosphere that my presence had created.

I traced a finger down the right column on the paper. Twenty-eight thousand and ninety-two dollars and a penny over a two-year period.

I dropped an index on the figure and looked at the woman. 'I happen to know that's about twice the annual salary of an office worker. Jana Ray not working but he's putting down regular deposits every Saturday. Ninety dollars every time. That make a certain kinda sense, Miss Blackwood. A spliff costs thirty dollars. So Jana Ray decided to bank three spliffs' worth of money every week. The pattern changed last December – weekly deposits rising to five hundred dollars with a coupla hundred here and there. Then,' I pointed at the last two deposits, 'one thousand dollars, and another thousand dollars ten days later. Your job is to review accounts? Not so?'

'It is.' She looked completely unflustered.

'And what this tell you – a poor-arse youngfella, still in school, with this amount of money in his account?'

'You're the one telling me, Mr Digson.'

'You had an idea where the money was coming from, not so?'

For a moment, I thought she was going to deny it. When she spoke her lips barely moved. 'I encouraged him to save his money. I opened the account for him. I'll take

212

full responsibility for that.' For all her self-control, she couldn't prevent herself from glancing at the big glass door marked, MANAGER.

'My job is to bank money, not—'

'Drugs money too?'

'You not letting me finish,' she breathed. 'It is to further his education. You know what it is like to be poor-arse like you say and fight life on your own?' She'd dropped her eyes on my blue silk shirt.

'Enlighten me, Miss Blackwood.'

Now her voice was low and throaty. 'Last June he came in with a little exercise book. He showed it to, erm, me. He worked out the cost of his university in Trinidad for the four years he was going to be there: tuition fees, rent, books, how much more he needed.' She paused, blinked at me and swallowed. 'Guess what he left out.'

'Save time, Miss Blackwood. Tell me.'

'Clothes and food.'

'You his family?'

'I live a few houses down from him.'

I scrolled through my memory of the residences that stood on the hillside below Jana Ray's place. 'Blue concrete house. Beige veranda, garage on the right side, soursop tree hanging over it – that one?'

'That one.'

I stood up, slotted the printouts in my bag. 'Everything you tell me makes sense, Miss Blackwood. Is not you I after but I not done with you yet.'

I scribbled my name and number. 'Gimme a call if anything comes to mind and you think I should know.'

She saw me to the door. Fixed me with those black-agate eyes. 'People find themselves in a hole, they'll do anything to dig themselves out of it.'

213

'You think I dunno that?'

'Thanks,' she said.

'For what?'

She probably didn't hear me. She was hurrying across the polished floor towards her office.

I walked out into a sizzling Camaho afternoon. A tourist liner sat beside the mile-long jetty, dwarfing the buildings and the streets. Pale, straw-hatted bodies packed the sidewalks, their multicoloured shirts and wraps patterned with parrots. I watched the throng of foreigners smiling foolishly like the natives they were meant to be observing and not mingling with. A young, heavily muscled Camahoan fella we knew as Bad Talk, with short bristling dreadlocks and misaligned teeth, was feeding the tourists what he thought they wanted to hear – his own invented history of the island and its people. His claims were so outrageous, I was tempted to arrest him.

Street vendors sat under parasols, selling beads and shells, in fact anything that could take a shine – as foreign to me as they were to the tourists. Sensible Camahoans sought refuge from the heat in air-conditioned doorways or beneath anything that cast a shade.

I called Miss Stanislaus and told her I thought I had a breakthrough with the Jana Ray case and probably Lazar Wilkinson. I gave her a quick update.

'You still fink Jamma Ray was a good fella?' she said.

36

I sat at my kitchen worktop, pulled out the books I picked up in Jana Ray's bedroom. He'd desecrated mine. Not only had he wrecked the covers, he'd had a field day scribbling and drawing all over the pages. A line of stickmen climbing up a gradient with boxes ten times their size ran across the bottom margin of the inside cover. On the adjacent page were what looked like six badly drawn electric fans turned upside down, with the same number above each one. I couldn't bear to look any more. Jana Ray's own book was in perfect condition. 'Sonuvabitch,' I breathed and tossed the thing aside.

What the hell did he want with a book on growing plants without soil, anyway?

I fed a Chronixx CD into my player, mixed myself a mild rum cocktail and settled down to Jana Ray's *Hydroponics: Principles and Practice*.

There was a whole section in there, heavily annotated, on plant genetics and a type of marijuana named kush. On the last few pages were two columns of tightly written script about medical marijuana and techniques for extracting mar-ijuana oil. When I closed the book, I had a reasonable idea of what Jana Ray had been up to and if my conclusions were correct, that youngfella was a liar and a genius.

Miss Stanislaus was right, I didn't know Jana Ray at all.

At five o'clock, I changed into a pair of cargo trousers with oversized pockets, a thick cotton shirt, a heavy pair of boots. I retrieved my Remington, hefted the weapon in my hand and hesitated over it. I'd never had a relationship with this thing – not like Malan, for whom a gun was an appendage. He'd told me once that he felt naked without the big Sig Sauer sitting against his body. Miss Stanislaus's Ruger – I wondered if she was getting on any better with the Glock – was like a deadly piece of jewellery that she would never leave her house without.

A gun in my hand felt heavier than its weight. It threw me out of myself. In my mind, it was the thing that killed my mother. It was never what I reached for first to save myself. I unhooked my heavy leather belt from the bedroom door and threaded it through my trousers.

Night had begun to dust Old Hope valley. I'd packed my knapsack with my tools, a few tins of sardines, biscuits, a pack of candles, a multi-tool knife, a litre of tap water, an exercise mat that would serve as a mattress and Jana Ray's thermo-hygrometer. My Remington R1 was in the hood of my bag.

I parked two miles down from the village and walked to Jana Ray's place. I lit a couple of candles, sat on the floor, paging through his school texts, my ears trained on the darkness out there – so thick, the night felt like a living, breathing presence. A couple of times, I raised my head at the thud of footsteps on the path below. I placed the Remington on my lap when footsteps continued up the hill and seemed to stop a few feet from the house. They neither retreated nor came nearer and the oddity of the sensation raised the hairs on my neck.

Close to morning, I stretched out on the mat and took a nap, then got up and fed myself. Mid-morning I opened the door and took to the hills.

Ahead of me, the rising peaks of the Belvedere mountains, jagged and forbidding against an almost violet morning sky.

I navigated giant ferns and reeds, dripping soil, cascading vines, deep patches of darkness where forest trees laced their branches together. Old Hope was a place of water, wind and forest too. There was no one I knew from my village who could not navigate the bush.

I kept my eyes on the thermo-hygrometer.

I was looking for a wind-sheltered area, but with good air circulation, on the side of one of these mountains where the temperature was close to 74 degrees, humidity between 51 and 61. An hour later, the instrument told me I was in the zone. I began a circular hike around the mountain. A couple of hours later, I skirted a sheer drop down to a ravine full of stones, and there it was in front of me – a clearing in the middle of which a large tent-like structure stood: perforated plastic covering, propped up by bamboo.

Inside the tent, a garden of deep green plants, thick-headed and squat with clusters of knotted, purple-tinted buds. Beautiful and strange – their pistils glowed bronze in the diffuse light. The plants sat amongst a scattering of powdered limestone. Outside, at the back of the structure, was what looked like a trench, the evidence of burnt charcoal still in it. An array of bamboo pipes hung over the trench, all leading into the makeshift greenhouse – Jana Ray's very own invention for delivering carbon dioxide to the leaves of the plants. The garden gave off the smell of pine.

Having read his notes, I could have guessed the acidity of the soil was somewhere between 5.7 and 6, the temperature of the root zone of these plants 20 degrees Centigrade or thereabouts. Jana Ray had created his own strain of high-yield kush, and found a way to grow it here in Camaho. And this, as far as I could tell, would have been his first crop.

I took out my phone and Googled 'kush price per ounce'. Result: 375–500 US Dollars.

More expensive than cocaine. No wonder he was not interested in Dessie's job offer.

My watch said 4.07pm. With my gun in my lap, I sat on a patch of dead leaves outside the greenhouse and ate the sardine sandwich I had made.

Heads and eyes – they tell you everything if a pusson knew what to look for. I learned that from Miss Stanislaus. I thought of the sideways shift of Jana Ray's eyes when I pushed him hard with questions, his carefulness with words when pressed for details of Lazar Wilkinson's dealings, that look on his face, and the odd folding of his shoulders as if to shield himself from a chilling wind. My mind returned to the ridge of flesh that branded his back. On the beach, when I asked the boys about the source of their scars, they raised their chins up past my head. Their eyes gone dark with fear before they ran off.

I threw on my backpack, edged my way down to the bottom of the ravine, following it till I came to a patch of silk cotton trees. A break in the bank led me onto mud-smeared stones, the track curving down and around a sea of dripping ferns. The climb took me to a ledge, then a field of giant volcanic boulders with a narrow path winding through them.

I followed it, found myself in a wide leaf-covered space, fenced in by mapou trees.

I entered the gloom and surveyed it: about twenty yards long, ten yards wide. Five giant cocoa baskets, their insides blackened by charcoal dust. Small metal drums, pots and pans strewn along the floor. Six bottle torches – a couple still filled with kerosene. In the centre, a row of twelve fireplaces, about four feet apart. On my left, seven six-foot sheets of corrugated galvanise, the type used to cover roofs. Five green plastic buckets, eight short lengths of wood shaved down at one end to look like pallets, four balls of string, brown wrapping, a couple of old rucksacks, an unopened packet of condoms.

I unrolled a heavy sheet of canvas to reveal an ornamental stick and a tamarind whip – the kind that cruel parents took to the skins of their children. This one was thick, its branches plaited – designed to draw blood.

I retrieved sachets from my bag, scraped the bottom of the drums and containers and dropped the sediments in separate bags.

I felt the hairs on my neck stir, straightened up and reached for my Remington. Stood still, listening. Nothing but the slur of disturbed leaves.

I stood in the gloom, the gun in my hand, until only the sounds of the mountains returned.

The hills were sinking into darkness and with it came the rising mountain chill. I wrapped the whip with wild sigin leaves, laid it across my shoulders and began my downward trek, halting at every rustle until my feet hit the climb to Jana Ray's place.

From there, I looked up at those high indifferent hills, full of odd sounds and a raging sadness that perhaps only I could hear.

I phoned Caran and described the place to him. 'Sound like a helluva cocaine factory, Digger.' He sounded incredulous. 'You sure that's the size of it?'

'You tellin me that's not normal?'

'Not for Camaho. Is not. Tomorrow we'll check it out. That got anything to do with the Wilkinson fella and that lil friend of yours they kill?'

'I not sure yet. Look to me like they finish whatever they been doing here.'

219

'Careful, Digger, the kinda people who operate that bizness won't have no problem killing you.'

'I know.'

I hurried to my car and as soon as I got home, I extracted a bottle of pale brown liquid from the bottom of my little fridge, pulled down one of my notebooks from my shelf and ran a finger along one of the pages I'd bookmarked.

Scott's presumptive test:

Cobalt thiocyanate, distilled water, glycerin, hydrochloric acid, chloroform.

Cocaine will turn the liquid blue.

Note: Presumptive tests cannot definitively confirm the presence of a drug, as other substances may cause false positives.

I emptied one sachet of the scrapings I'd taken from the metal drums in the mountain into a beaker.

I held it up against the light.

Is not no false positive here, Missa Scott. Is blue. Is true. Is true-blue. Is cocaine!

37

Two weeks after I broke into the office, we were fully up and running. Chilman had taken over Malan's office – it used to be his before he retired.

This morning, he planted himself in our office space, his head jerking like a turkey's as he followed our movements and conversation. Miss Stanislaus, as usual, pretended he wasn't there. Caran had dropped in with his team after visiting the hill where I'd uncovered the cocaine processing operation. He sat with his back pressed against a chair, legs outstretched, his cinnamon-brown face clenched with concern. I'd never seen him look so worried. His three Bush Rangers remained standing like the soldiers they really were, with their rifles cradled in their arms. Inscrutable as stone.

Pet couldn't keep her eyes off Toya. Caran's lieutenant was a taut young woman – dark-eyed and unsmiling, with a Remington Bushmaster ACR slung from her shoulder. Her right index was always on the trigger guard of the rifle. The only people who could get a sentence out of her were Caran, her companions and, with no small amount of envy on my part, Miss Stanislaus. The rest of us were treated to grunts and monosyllables. Apart from those four, I wondered if Toya Furore liked humans.

Pet had walked off her job in Customs. When the Chief of Customs called her cellphone, she told him she was back at work. He must have told her something that annoyed her. 'You don't want me back there, Missa Torville, I telling you, because I sure to report one of your man-staff for sex harassment.'

She put down the phone and raised her head at us smiling.

'What's the name of the fella who harass you?' Chilman growled.

'Is not a fella,' Pet replied.

'Is who then?'

'Nobody yet, Missa Chilman. I just jumping in front becuz one of them sure to try it.'

Chilman sucked his teeth and mumbled something.

The DS dragged a chair to the middle of the office space and we made the usual semicircle around him. He fished out a biro from his pocket and the tiny notebook he always carried.

When the old man raised his head at us, he was like a different person. The yellow eyes were unblinking and aggressive, his expression thuggish – that I-not-taking-no-bullshit-from-nobody-right-now attitude that sent a thrill down my spine, even while I hated the Old Dog for it. I prepared myself for a grilling.

'Okay, Digson, let's see what we dealing with. Two young-fellas murdered in the village that I pass through every day. Name them.'

'Lazar Wilkinson and Jonathon Rayburn, Sir. I think—'

'I don give a damn what you think right now. You find out why they got killed?'

'I believe is drugs, Sir.'

'You believe! You gone religious now? Gimme the blaastid evidence!'

Miss Stanislaus stirred in her seat. Chilman glared at her. She began inspecting her nails.

'Like you know, Sir, we just located the camp where all the drugs were processed. I can prove it was cocaine.'

'And I kin prove that I got two hands! Is useless information, Digson, unless you find a link between the factory and the two deadfellas.'

'Jana Ray admitted they were handling drugs before they killed him. He confirmed that Lazar Wilkinson employed him. And it is the same village, Sir. I can't see them not being connected.'

'Connected how, Digson?'

'We working on it.'

'You call that a proper answer?'

I shrugged.

'So it boil down to this: two youngfellas dead, y'all *fink* you work out how they dead but you got no evidence to show why. And you dunno who kill them. Not so?'

I said nothing.

Chilman threw us a sour look, pushed himself off his seat and walked into the toilet.

Pet was passing me glances. The woman looked worried for me. Caran cleared his throat and readjusted his chair.

The Old Bull returned and sat back down. 'The young woman and the two whitefellas y'all been chasing after – what they done to deserve y'all attention?'

'We figured Lazar Wilkinson was murdered by at least two men and that a woman was involved. I already told you that.'

'Tell me again!'

I gave him a quick recap. 'Besides, a youngfella named Eric gave a description of the woman who was with Lazar Wilkinson a few days before he got killed. She happened to fit the description of a young woman I met at The Flare with the two whitefellas in question.'

'So is only speculation?'

'Reasonable speculation, Sir.'

'What's the difference, Digson? Why y'all picking on the

two whitefellas – and I ask out of special concern for the tourist trade.' He soured his face. Pet laughed.

'At least one of the men attempted to kill me, or to maim me, Sir. He pulled a knife on me when my back was turned. In other words they got no problems killing people. In fact, Miss Stanislaus is concerned that the young woman with them, Miss Tamara, might even be in danger.'

That paused him for a second. 'They try to kill you, you say? How come I didn know that?'

'Because you wasn there, Sir.'

Pet brought her hand to her mouth, converted her chuckle to a cough. Chilman threw her a scalding look.

'At least we have to eliminate them from the investigation,' I said.

'But you dunno how to find them,' he threw back. He turned to Caran. 'That factory Digson find in the bush – is really as he describe it?'

I raised a finger to object. Miss Stanislaus threw me an urgent frown. I sat back.

'We talking bout millians-a-dollars' worth of stuff they been cooking up there,' Caran said.

'Is true,' I told Chilman. 'Is like a laboratory in them hill up there: hydrochloric and sulphuric acid, potassium permanganate, ammonia – you name it.'

The DS blinked. He looked confused. 'So what we do about it?'

'Lock down the village,' I said.

'Impossible,' Chilman said.

'Why not?'

'Is where the man who run this country grew up. Is his people. And if you dunno it yet, he's a vindictive little so-and-so. He'll shut down San Andrews CID in no time.'

'Technically, we already shutdown,' I said.

'Then what you doing here?'

'Dis is not two fellas playing cook in a kitchen.' Caran was almost pleading.

When he returned from the hills, he'd handed me a memory card of the photos he'd taken.

Chilman smacked his lips. 'I still say, no! Is suicide.'

'For who?' I threw back. 'You prefer to fill up Camaho with poison?'

'The poison is not for Camaho, Digson. It can't be for Camaho! Use your blaastid brains. Whatever drugs them fellas was making up there, is too much for one lil island. It got to be passing through. Them young-people who get beat-up-an-kill' is not what's important now. Them's what Obama-in-America used to call co-oo-lateral damage after he drop bomb on poor-people arse in their own country and say it was a mistake, and that was only them theorist he was after.'

'Terrorist,' I said. 'Not theorist.'

'Digson, haul y'arse. You not askin the right questions! These is de right questions.' Chilman made a machete of his arm and swung it. 'Where aaaall dat cargo come from. Who bring it here and how, where they have it now, where they takin it to, and—!' He froze the hand. 'The best way we kin stop dem. For good! Forget about dem two dead-fellas, and locking up poor-people in deir own house! Concentrate on that.'

He zig-zagged towards the door and pulled it hard behind him. Outside, the Old Dog threw us a nasty look before driving off.

In the silence Chilman left behind, I could hear the click of insects on the glass of the window, the hum of the fridge and photocopier. The whisper of Miss Stanislaus's finger on the page of my destroyed book which, after complaining bitterly

225

to her over the phone, she'd asked me to bring in. She closed the book and turned her chair to face us.

'Why y'all feel so strong bout lockin up a whole village?' Miss Stanislaus said.

'Everybody there got something hanging over them,' I said. 'I never see that kinda frighten before. I ask meself what it take for a woman to lose her son and accept a few thousand dollars as repayment. Is not greed. Is not that she don't care.'

'Is what, then?' Caran said.

'Is what she knew was going to happen to her if she talked. She's afraid.' I picked up the tamarind whip I'd brought down from the mountains, unwrapped it and dropped it on the table.

A whinnying sound came from Pet.

Caran dropped deep expressionless eyes on the whip then turned his gaze on me.

'Was a lil slave operation they had up there,' I said. 'I could walk into that village right now and pick out boys between ten and fifteen by the marks on their skins, including Jana Ray. They couldn't get tired or fall asleep because this whip was there to wake them up. I still say lock down the village.'

'What good that going to do?' Miss Stanislaus wanted to know.

'Like Digger say. All of them benefiting from the operation,' Caran told her.

'Dat's not what I hear him say, Missa Crayon. I hear him say they frighten. You don fink dat lockin dem up or down or upside-down goin frighten dem even more?'

'Okay, Miss Stanislaus – whatever you say, I go with it. Digger, you identify the fella who been using that thing?' He was staring at the whip. He looked up suddenly, as if we'd caught him out.

'He's like a superstition among them. They 'fraid to say his name because they believe he will hear them. Even Jana Ray. But the fella real. The proof is this.' I knocked the whip onto the floor. 'What I want to know is what Camaho people got with whip! Is always—'

'You didn say the fella name,' Caran said. Again that stillness in his face.

I thought back to my last evening in the mountains when I'd sensed eyes on me, the brief disturbance of the bushes followed by the shuffle of quickly fading footsteps. 'Shadowman,' I said.

'He live in de village?'

'Nuh.'

'How you know?'

I recalled the woman with the machete who confronted me at Jana Ray's door. 'One of those village wimmen would've already poisoned him or killed him in his sleep by now. I sure of that.'

He addressed Miss Stanislaus with that polite voice and shy-boy smile he reserved only for her. 'Lock down or not, somebody got to get him.' He stood up. 'Call me when y'all find out where he is.'

Caran man-hugged me, and took Miss Stanislaus's hand in his as if it were a flower. He waved at Pet and was off with his crew in their brown Land Rover.

38

Where aaaall dat cargo come from. Who bring it here and how, where
they have it now, where they takin it to . . . ?

Chilman's words kept looping in my head, my mind
stopping always on the whip and the two deadfellas he was
advising us to forget.

Miss Stanislaus's voice broke into my thoughts. 'Missa
Digger, I decide you need to see me urgent. We take
some breeze?'

I followed her to Kiran's Food Palace – a no-frills restaurant laid out like a giant kitchen. We chose an eating area
that looked onto the mile-long jetty built by the Chinese
who'd brought their own workforce, reducing the Camahoan
unemployeds to observers.

The air around us pulsed with the throb of minibus
engines, conductor's calls and the beehive hum of outer-
parish shoppers preparing to vacate San Andrews.

Miss Stanislaus sat facing me. She dropped her bag on
the table and passed a hand across my cheek. 'You should
see yourself. That pretty face of yours gone rough and sour
for true!'

She pulled out my book and laid it on the table. 'Missa
Jamma Ray was smart. I never see nothing like it before. You
see, Missa Digger, I figure the youngfella would never touch
your book if he didn have good reason. He borrow your best

book because he figure you going be so damn vex, you will examine the damage while you cussin him. Is what normal people do, but not you – all you do is fling it away. You never ask yourself why Missa Jamma Ray going do a fing like dat.'

She stood up the book on the table squinting at the thing as if in some kind of wordless communication with it, the light settled on her face and hands as she slid her palms around the inner surfaces of the covers. She paused over the handwritten words, *Fr. your star-apple*, cocked her head and threw me a quick smile. I waited out the performance.

Miss Stanislaus laid the book flat on the table and opened the back cover. She slid her hand into her bag and brought out a razor blade. She began to cut away at the inside fabric of the back cover.

'Nuh-nuh-nuh!' I reached out to grab it from her.

She stopped me with a look, peeled away the rest of the fabric to reveal a small blue book. A Camaho passport. Miss Stanislaus handed it to me – a flimsy thing, half the size of previous passports and valid for half the number of years – the government's latest scam for making money off the travelling poor. I took the treasury receipt, glanced at it, then at the photo page from which Jana Ray looked out at me with a soft face and radiant eyes. I flipped through the pages of the passport.

'Never used,' I said. 'He got this last month on the third. Paid the extra hundred and twenty-five dollars for express service.'

'One week before they kill Missa Laza Wilkins. Two weeks before they kill your boyfriend.'

'He was not my boyfriend.'

'H'was a boy, not so?'

'Uh-huh.'

'And h'was your friend, not so?'

229

'Uh-huh—'

'So! How you call that? Now look at this, Missa Digger.'

Miss Stanislaus opened the book and pointed at the drawings.

'I saw them, Miss Stanislaus. Is the kinda thing I used to do in school when I thinking through stuff.'

'You draw sea tings?'

'Anything.'

'Nuh,' she said.

'Nuh what?'

She opened the inside back cover, dropped a thumb on the drawing of a boat. 'Dis boat same as de one in front except it different.'

'Jana Ray was bright but he couldn draw, Miss Stanislaus, that's all.'

'Missa Digger! I tryin to show you someting! And you not lissenin!'

She placed an index finger on the drawing of the boat at the back. 'Yuh see?' She flipped the book over to the other cover. 'Yuh see?'

'Nuh.'

'Same boat, you agree?'

'Not sure, Miss Stanislaus. Mebbe is the only way he know to draw a boat.'

'Same boat,' she snapped. 'This tell me so.'

She pointed at a couple of hash marks on each drawing on the hull, so small I had to squint. 'Front-picture boat low in de water. Back-picture, boat high in de water – what dat tell you?'

'Boat loaded, then boat unloaded.' I took the book from her, began paging through it. I went back to the row of stick drawings of people heading up an incline, then the six fans, each with the number 7–557 above it.

'Okay, let's say you not wrong. Let's says the stickmen is them lil fellas carrying all that stuff up in the mountain ... What else he trying to say?'

Miss Stanislaus pulled a tissue and patted her cheeks. 'That he know they was goin to kill im.' She took up the passport. 'H'was tryin to run away.'

For a moment she looked as if she wanted to cry. Miss Stanislaus closed her eyes and took a breath and pulled herself together. 'Missa Digger, we got a lotta work to do. An I needin time to do it.'

My heart flipped over. She was reminding me that the hearing was due in ten days' time.

'I working on it, Miss Stanislaus. Right now I got to go back to Beau Séjour.'

'Becuz of the book?'

'Yes, the other one – the one he didn't touch. And the lil dedication there.' I dropped my finger on the handwritten line, *Fr. your star-apple*. I damn sure I know who write that.'

'I come with you?'

'Nuh, is only going to complicate matters.'

39

It was late evening when I got to Beau Séjour.

I waited by the side of the road until Miss Blackwood parked her car and entered her house. I gave her another thirty minutes to settle down.

She did not unlock the door until I said my name, and even then I caught a movement of the blinds at the window on the far right of the house. A minute or so later she let me in.

She waved me into a small living room: clean, uncluttered; a mahogany table with square mats weaved from wild pine. A single light with a big lampshade suspended over the table.

Stacks of Mills & Boon and Denise Robins romances in a wide glass-fronted cabinet. A few saucers filled with decorated seashells. She brought me a glass of sorrel, sat at one end of the table with those enigmatic eyes on me.

'You know why I here, not so?' I dragged my bag and opened it. I dropped Jana Ray's book on the table. 'You bought this for him, right?'

She nodded.

'And this?' Her eyes moved from my face to the thermohygrometer. She made a series of little movements with her lips, then blinked – a slow shuttering of her eyelids. I took that for a yes.

A new hardness had risen in my chest. 'I telling you this right now, Miss Lady, don't try to hide nothing from me, and with all due respects don't gimme no bullshit either. Why you so slow to admit you buy this thing for him? What you think you hiding?' I flicked the Amazon shipment card across the table towards her. 'Is easy to figure out. I just didn't have time to think about it. Jana Ray ain't got no credit card to open no Amazon account. It got to be somebody who done it for him. I could bet my last dollar it was you.'

'He wanted things and I could help him.' She'd put on her bank-teller's voice. 'He would never ask for something unless he really wanted it, and even then—'

'He'll find a way to pay you back,' I cut in. 'Miss Blackwood, he's all over you.' I pointed at the polished seashells, then at the gru-gru ring on her index. I opened the book and turned it toward her. 'From your star-apple. No signature, of course, but that's your handwriting, not so?'

She didn't answer me. Her hand was turning the gru-gru ring.

'So! Jana Ray was not just a youngfella you been helping out. I believe you been intimate with him. I not saying you start it, I dunno and I don't care. You in your mid-thirties with a respectable job and a reputation to protect, and Jana Ray is eighteen. So I unnerstan if you prefer that nobody know about it. S'far as I see, Jana Ray had more sense in him than a whole heap of big men put together. So I not here to judge you. What I want to know—'

She got up abruptly and strode over to the kitchen.

I heard the sigh of the fridge door, liquid being poured. She returned with a glass brimming with water and rested it in front of her.

It was then I realised that I'd raised my voice. 'Sorry,' I said and sat back. 'I s'pose what I saying is that he must've said some things – called names, yunno.'

'You right,' she said. Her voice had dropped to a whisper.

233

'He talked about Lazar all the time. He liked him. Shadowman was the one he hated. Always said that Shadowman is the devil, erm – the devil's spawn.'

She'd pushed her head so close to mine, I could smell the pomade in her hair. 'People don't call his name round here. They convinced he always hears them. Somewhere on the coast,' she breathed, 'is where they say he's living.' She sat back rigid, her head cocked as if listening to the darkness out there. The fear was so strong in her, I could almost taste it.

I found myself leaning towards her, my voice dropping to a whisper too. 'When was the last time you saw him?'

She shook her head. 'Shadowman—'

'Is Jana Ray I talkin bout.'

'Oh! The night before y'all found him.'

'So you got his blue bag?'

She nodded, looked stricken, then got up with a sigh. She retreated to her bedroom and returned with Jana Ray's bum-bag.

I dug into it, pulled out a small notebook and dropped it on the table. My fingers returned to one end. 'You got scissors?'

She left and promptly returned with a pair.

I made a careful incision in the fabric, extracted a sachet of seeds labelled 'MM' and a four-gigabyte SD data card wrapped in plastic.

'I'll keep these,' I said. 'Anything about his behaviour changed? I mean before he—'

She shook her head.

'You sure?'

'Except, he started, erm,' she began picking at her sleeve, 'visiting almost every night – three, four weeks ago.'

'And before that?'

'Once a week – sometimes twice. Depending.'

'On what?'

She slid an eye at me, then looked away. 'The work . . . '

I raised my brows, gave an interrogatory shrug.

'He wouldn't say what work. Told me is better if I didn't know. The last time,' she shook her head, 'he look like he been through hell.'

'You say he started seeing you almost every night?'

'To talk or sleep.' She slid a hand along her arm. Her eyes went wide and dreamy. I listened to the new husk in her voice. 'As if . . . '

'As if?'

'He wanted to, erm—' She stopped. I watched the movement of her lips, the shift of her hands on her lap. 'Hide himself, yunno.'

'No, I dunno.'

'In, in me.' And then she folded over, her hands covering her face, and she was shaking with sobs.

I got up. 'I sorry to distress you.'

I walked out the door and pulled it behind me, stood on the veranda and took in the night, thick with the clink and scrape of insects, the cough and sigh of the waves in the bay beyond. Then, close by, the abrupt shuffle of bush. Beyond the road – barely visible against the skyline – stood the high dark fence of mangroves.

I tapped the door and opened it. 'You got a friend or family you kin stay with for a while? The further from here the better.'

She rolled startled eyes at the window. 'Something happen?'

'Pack a bag, take everything you need. Then lock up. I'll wait.'

The woman reached for her cellphone. I stepped out the door into the cool of the night, listening to the fast pulse of her voice, the sudden urgency in it. I counted to forty before she was out on the veranda.

'Golf Course,' she muttered.

I took the small suitcase and waited while she locked up, then I walked her to her car. When she buckled herself in, I slipped into the passenger seat. 'I parked a coupla miles down. Drop me by my car. Then I'll follow you.'

She threw me an alarmed glance. 'Something happen?'

'Just a feeling – that's all.'

I trailed her car the nine miles to Grand Beach Road, then uphill to the Golf Course, past rows of opulent bungalows that sat in front of wide front gardens studded with fan-leaf palms. Their wraparound verandas glowed warmly under low-hanging lamps. She stopped at the last one.

A tall, toffee-coloured man, bald as a polished coconut, stood at the door with a dog at his side. I'd expected a woman. Miss Blackwood lifted a hand in my direction. The man raised his head and nodded.

For a while I kept my eyes on the donkey-sized Alsatian making happy circles around Miss Blackwood's legs, then I tapped my horn and reversed.

40

The sun hadn't yet risen when I began tapping on doors in Beau Séjour. Heads popped out. Faces stupefied by sleep squinted at me. A few mumbled words. I followed the pointing fingers till I came to a narrow yard with a small burnt-out house in the middle. Eight yards or so beside it, a smaller structure, awkwardly put together with sheets of MDF. I tapped the door. The woman who opened it was in the same dress that I'd seen her in at Jana Ray's place. I still had that picture of her in my mind: standing barefoot on the bank above the entrance to Jana Ray's house, a rusty machete in one hand, glaring hatefully at me and wanting to know what the hell I was doing in the dead boy's place.

At the sight of me, she looked dumbfounded. 'My boy didn do nothing!'

Inside, approaching footsteps. 'Stay there,' she snapped. She was fully awake now, eyes hot and hateful on my face.

'I not after your boy,' I said. 'I want to know where I kin find Shadowman.'

'S'far as I see, de fuckah everywhere. I dunno where he is.'

'He got to be somewhere.'

'He's a devil. See what he done to my boy.' She reached an arm behind her. A head appeared under it. Eric, the little boy I'd offered food the night after the murder of Lazar Wilkinson, which he could barely lift to his mouth. He was looking up at me with big wet eyes. I reached out and passed my hand along his arm. Dislocated shoulder.

'How long he had this?'

'More dan two weeks,' the woman said.

'And you didn't take him to hospital?'

'First time I try, Shadowman put fire to my house. Middle of de night when we sleepin.'

'If this shoulder heals like that, he'll never be able to use it proper again. Hold on.'

I phoned the ambulance.

'Digger, is early mornin,' Pedro grunted.

'Pedro, I have a lil fella here in Beau Séjour. Come take him to the hospital.' I explained the problem and gave him directions. 'Make it quiet, okay? No showin off with y'all siren.'

'I don't want no trouble,' the woman said.

'S'far as I see, y'all got trouble already.' I turned to the boy. 'Tell me where I find Shadowman.'

Shadowman lived somewhere up the coast. He believed it was Victoria. He described a 'harden-back' man, strong, very strong. 'He got short knotty hair and a cloth tie round iz forehead. He say is for the sweat. He always sweatin. He—' Eric had become almost speechless with fright.

'What's his real name?'

'Sha-Shadowman.'

'His real name.'

He shrugged. 'Shadowman.'

'Why they call him that?'

Eric thought for a while. Then gave me one of the most honest, open looks I'd seen from anyone. 'Becuz he is a shadowman.'

'Put on some clothes,' I said. 'I'll take y'all myself.'

I called Pedro and cancelled the ambulance.

238

'I not coming,' the woman said. 'I not dress' to go nowhere.'

'They might keep him in,' I said. 'Mebbe a coupla weeks.'

'Fanks, Missa . . .'

'Digger.'

'That your real name?'

'For now.'

I waited for the boy to change: same trousers and what looked like his school shirt. A pair of rubber sandals. He came out with a comb in his hand, threw a doubtful look at it, then handed it back to his mother.

'He didn have no time for brekfas',' the woman said.

'No worries,' I said. 'C'mon, youngfella. I feed you first and then we talk. Then I take you to hospital. That awright by you?'

He nodded without looking at me.

'You sure Shadowman live in Victoria?'

'I dunno for sure. S'only what I hear.'

I took Eric to God Fries Eat Inn, a little food place that overlooked the market square. The boy's eyes were everywhere. He twitched at the sound of raised voices out there. A vehicle backfired in the near distance and he jumped. I observed him closely, the film of sweat on his upper lip, the damaged hand. I felt sorry for him.

Eric stared at the food counter, then at my face. 'I could eat what I want?'

'Of course – what you want?'

'A lil bit ov everyting.'

'Makes sense.' I raised a finger and winked. 'That mean some serious negotiations.'

'You could afford it?'

'Hope so.' I got up and went to the counter. I did some explaining to the aproned woman behind it. She pushed out a hand. I paid. 'Coming up,' she said and disappeared through the adjoining door.

'Coming up,' I said to Eric. I pulled a seat to face him. 'You never come to town before?'

'I don like it. Too much noise an' ruction,' he said.

'That bother you – noise and ruction?'

'I like quiet more.' He sniffed and wiped his nose.

'Is quiet up in the hills, not so?'

Eric looked as if he expected me to strike him any minute. And I guessed that kids as brutalised as he was would think that it was normal.

'Eric, I want you to tell me everything you know about Shadowman, what he look like and where I kin find him. I want to know who been visiting him, who been visiting Lazar Wilkinson and how close Jana Ray was to them. I want to know everything you saw and heard from the time they got you climbing them Belvedere mountains with heavy load on your head. What I saying is—'

His eyes switched to the door. 'I-I 'fraid, Missa Digger. I—'

'I promise you this, Eric: nobody going touch you from now on. Whatever need to get fixed in Beau Séjour going to get fixed.' That awful tightness in my throat returned. I filled my lungs, trying to blink away the image of Jana Ray. Eric's eyes were on my face, his lips twitching, his head cocked sideways as if he were tuning in to the current of emotion running through my body.

The woman arrived with a wide plastic tray with the 'lil bit of everything' I'd ordered: fish – fried and stewed, a small bowl of breadfruit and potato chips along with a plate heaped with rice, sweet potatoes and fried plantains; and to top it off, a barbecued chicken leg.

Eric sat blinking at the food a while, and after seeming to have worked out a strategy, he attacked the chicken first.

I felt like crying just watching this lil boy with his displaced shoulder struggling to feed himself.

'How that happen – the shoulder?'

'Shadowman lift me up an throw me.'

I winced.

'He bigger than you,' Eric said. 'He got more muscles. You can't hear him when he walk.'

'You worrying about me?' I smiled.

'Uh-huh.'

When he paused from eating, I passed him a tissue and dropped my elbows on the table. I looked into his face. 'Talk to me, Eric. How they got you involved in this?'

'Lazar,' he said. 'He give us money to take some fings from de boat in de bay up to de mountain. Shadowman was up dere waitin for us. He tell us what to do.'

So after all, Miss Stanislaus was not wrong about her reading of Jana Ray's drawing. I felt a flush of admiration for the woman – *boat loaded, then boat unloaded . . .*

'Who run things – Shadowman or Lazar?'

He lifted his shoulders and dropped them. 'Not Shadowman, not Lazar.'

'How you know?'

He shrugged. 'Shadowman didn like Lazar. Shadowman don't like nobody. Lazar didn like im either and Lazar use to tell him dat. Specially when he beat us.' The boy threw me an appealing look. 'You say you goin proteck me, not so?'

'I promise.'

'Becuz Shadowman say he kill us if we tell anybody what we do up in de Hole.'

'That what you call the place in the mountain – the Hole?'

He nodded.

'What part Jana Ray play in all ov this?'

'Jah-Ray do the pourin and de mixin. De rest ov us cook

241

an stir. Shadowman hit Jah-Ray once cross his back wiv his whip.'

I visualised Jana Ray lying face-down on the beach. The laceration, gone pale in death, running across his back.' I took a breath and looked Eric in the eyes. 'You witnessed that?'

'Everybody was there. Jah-Ray didn come back for two night. Jah-Ray wasn 'fraid ov Shadowman. Shadowman couldn make im 'fraid.'

'Why – what Jana Ray done to get hit?'

'Shadowman always askin Jah-Ray for his marijuana seed and Jah-Ray give im de wrong one. Mebbe dat's why he hit im.'

'And what happen after Jah-Ray left?'

'He come back.'

'Why?'

'Cuz, Lazar say de Townman ask Jana Ray. I hear Townman threaten Shadowman an say Jana Ray the only one know how to do the mixin. And they ain got no time to teach nobody else.'

I sat back. 'Who's the Townman?'

'I never see him proper. Was night when he come. I – I see.' He looked uncertain now.

'What you see, Eric?'

He hesitated, licked his lips. 'I see his hand.'

I frowned at him.

'H'was in a car. Lazar was by the road talkin to im. He was pushin iz hand outta de car an pointin it in Lazar face.'

'Was night, not so?'

'Uh-huh.'

'So, how come you see the hand?'

'Was moonlight, Missa Digger.'

'How long that was before y'all find Lazar dead?'

He shook his head. 'Dunno, mebbe a week, mebbe—'

'You don't remember days?' He shook his head.

'Or dates?'

That look again as if he expected me to hit him.

'What the hand look like, Eric?'

'Was night, Missa Digger. I couldn see proper.'

'But you jus tell me was moonlight.'

He blinked a couple of times.

'Okay – what you *think* the hand looked like?'

'I fink was a fair-skin hand.'

'You sure?'

'I tell you it was night.'

'Moonlight night,' I said. 'Okay.' I eased back on the chair. 'You want to finish your food?'

'I full. Didn know I would've been so full so quick.' He looked distressed.

'One last thing, Eric, then I promise we get outta here – you want to rest a lil bit?'

'Nuh, let's finish.'

'Tell me about the boat.'

I figured that given what we called the *makoness* of Eric – the way he took in information and remembered things – I needed to get as much as I could out of him.

After we tracked down Tamara's home from what we learned from the children we met on the road, Miss Stanislaus told me that children were the real truth-givers of Camaho, because they hadn't yet learned to lie. Which was why, she said, so many 'big-people' – the ones with things to hide – were uneasy in their presence and often feared them. Children, she sniffed, were a completely different tribe. Surely, I thought, chief of that tribe had to be this young boy sitting in front of me with a dislocated right shoulder.

He said it was late at night when the boat arrived. Lazar Wilkinson had knocked on his mother's door and called

243

him out. He'd never seen a vessel like that before. It looked like two boats in one. It was so unusual, he could hardly find the words to describe the thing. He was certain it was black and didn't have a proper cabin, just what he called a windshield.

Apart from the carriers like themselves, who else were there? I asked.

He blinked and rolled his eyes as if he were looking into his head.

Jana Ray, Shadowman, Lazar Wilkinson and the two drivers of the boat.

'What the drivers look like?'

One tall, one short – the taller of the two in a tight-fitting wetsuit.

'Thanks,' I said. 'You saw when the boat left the bay?'

'Nuh. But I hear it from up in dem hills. I ask Jana Ray why it so loud. He say it got six engine.' He stood up. 'You finish, Missa Digger?'

I dropped an arm across his shoulder. 'Come with me, Eric. We go buy some stuff.'

I took him to one of those stores on Cranby Street, whose goods spilled out onto the sidewalk. I pulled some shirts – one white, two blue – from a rack, a couple of T-shirts and two pairs of trousers. Cheap synthetic material, but they were better than nothing. I sent him into the small cubicle that served as a fitting room and waited while he tried them on. Eric came out in a new shirt and trousers both buttoned up the wrong way. He looked helpless and frustrated. 'Don't worry, is your hand,' I said. I knelt in front of him and fixed him up. 'Where's the ole-clothes?'

He jutted his chin at the cubicle.

'You don't want them no more?'

'Nuh.'

I paid and stepped out with Eric into a dazzling day. Somebody turned up the music in one of the cars across the street and he cringed.

I drove up the hospital road with Eric sitting quietly beside me. He looked relaxed, even contented.

'You in school?' I said.

'Sometimes – when Mammy could afford.'

'You got to go to school. Use that memory ov yours to learn. It kin get you far. Y'unnerstan?'

He nodded.

A thought struck me. 'The car, Eric – the one the Townman was driving. You remember the number?'

'It didn have none,' he answered promptly.

I took him through the hospital gates and had a long talk with the doctor who'd come down to reception. The woman examined the boy's arm and looked appalled. They'd have to keep him in, she said – at least two weeks. They'd have to break the shoulder and reset the bones – she glanced at Eric and shut her mouth abruptly. Then she turned on me. 'Why you didn't bring him sooner?'

'His mother couldn afford it,' I said.

'This is the general hospital. It's free.' Her voice was tight with accusation.

'*He* wasn't,' I said. 'And I have to let you know, Doctor. I just a very concerned citizen – so don't look at me like that.'

I returned to the office, dizzy with the information I'd extracted from Eric. I grunted a general hello and hurried to my desk. I spent the rest of the morning scribbling what I'd learned from Eric. When I lifted my head it was past noon.

I spent another thirty minutes researching Eric, or rather his particular brand of recall. I eventually found it: *eidetic memory – ability to recall images from memory vividly with high precision ... not limited to visual aspects of memory ... includes hearing. Found in 2 to 10 per cent of children aged 6 to 12.*

I sat back and could barely believe my luck.

I pulled my chair across the floor to face Miss Stanislaus.

'Miss Stanislaus,' I said, 'I discover Eric was a special lil fella. He's like a video recorder. He give me reasons to believe that we looking for a boat that been here at least two weeks. Eric was one ov them stickfellas that Jana Ray draw carrying up the cocaine base up the mountain. He describe the boat as two in one. I thinking catamaran.'

'He member de people with de boat?'

'Yes: Jana Ray, Shadowman, Lazar Wilkinson, the two men that fit the description of the fellas we identify with Miss Tamara – they the ones who drive the boat.'

Miss Stanislaus stirred her shoulders. 'Lil Eric was among dem?'

'Yes. And he mentioned a Townman. He didn see much of him because the fella was in a car cussin out Lazar Wilkinson. All he saw was a hand.'

'A hand?'

'A hand!'

'What about the hand?' She was smiling at me with lifted brows.

'Fair-skin hand, he say.'

A burst of chuckles came from her.

'I serious,' I said.

'Really?' And she started laughing again. 'Is a lil makoman you got there.'

'The boy talented.' I pushed back my chair and stood up. 'First things first, Miss Stanislaus. We got to find Shadowman. Eric say he live Victoria, Miss Blackwood say somewhere on the coast and Jana Ray say he dunno. I think we should do the whole west coast – top to bottom. And then ...'

246

'And then?'

'If what Eric tell me is true, Miss Stanislaus, Shadowman not the one behind this drugs bizness. But I want him – I want that fella bad.'

'You know what he look like?'

'Big fella, knotty hair, a cloth or bandana tie around iz head.'

41

Miss Stanislaus and I took the Eastern Main, headed for the northern tip of Camaho, then west through the blue foothills of Saint Catherine Mountain. A lazy day, cool because of a covering of clouds that sat like a white lid over the island – the kind of day that reminded me of my childhood and the miraculous light of Easter.

We did not find Shadowman in Victoria. No one admitted to knowing him, although, with some of them, I recognised the fright in their eyes.

Halfway down the coast, in Kanvi, I approached a young man sitting on a culvert over the river that ran through the town from the Belvedere mountains. He looked us up and down, shook his head and strolled off. Miss Stanislaus kept her eyes on his back as he swung towards the rows of houses that faced the beach and disappeared amongst them.

'He know,' she said, her voice low and urgent. I followed her into an alleyway. An old man, bone-thin and shirtless, lowered the corn cob he was sucking on and angled his head at the beach. The ole fella even winked.

Miss Stanislaus was hurrying ahead of me. I spotted a man about fifty yards up the beach, on his knees, slapping the side of a boat as if testing it for soundness. All I could see of him was his back, the muscles rippling like live snakes under his skin. A blue bandana circled his head. Miss Stanislaus was almost upon him.

I called out to her and broke into a sprint.

It was then the kneeling man rose with an explosive movement, his hand rising and coming down on the side of her face. He threw her off her feet. Then he was gone, up the beach towards the houses, gliding through the alleyway like a spectre. I plunged after him, remembered Miss Stanislaus and swung back.

She was lying on the sand, her face among a scattering of wood shavings, her shoulders heaving, a thread of blood trickling down the side of her mouth.

I raised her upper body and eased her weight against my chest. She muttered something.

'Don't talk,' I said. I pressed my nose against her hair and held her close. That cry that came from her — I knew the blow had damaged something. She was trying to move her lips. What came out was a gurgle.

Pet picked up promptly.

'Miss Stanislaus down. Send an ambulance.'

'Miss Stanislaus? O'Gord! Digger, you serious?'

'Get a fuckin ambulance, Pet. Right now. Kanvi Beach.'

I heard the sob in her voice before she cut off.

I cupped Miss Stanislaus's face with my hands and said the same thing over and over again. 'You goin be alright, Miss Stanislaus. You goin be alright.' Said it until it sounded like a lullaby, while I kept my eyes on my watch.

The villagers came running — a thick gathering of children and adults, edging closer by the second. A woman and two young men broke away from the bunch and began approaching.

'Stay back,' I snapped.

They backed away, muttering.

My phone buzzed. I picked up. 'Spiderface there yet?'

I realised what Pet had done. An ambulance meant a

249

forty-minute drive from San Andrews. A speedboat, fifteen minutes or less. I spotted the craft cutting a fast white path towards us from the south.

Spiderface swung almost onto the sand, the big Honda engine growling. He tossed out an inflated bed – the type tourists sunned themselves on. We eased Miss Stanislaus onto it, then into the boat. Spiderface looked mortified. He could barely keep his eyes off Miss Stanislaus while the boat cut water for San Andrews.

The ambulance was waiting on the Esplanade. Pet stood on the concrete walkway edging the sea, a tiny decorated handkerchief pressed against her mouth.

'I handle it from here,' Pet said.

'Sorry to cuss you, Pet. I was—'

'I don't care bout that,' she snapped. 'Let's get Miss Stanislaus outta here.'

42

I left Miss Stanislaus at the hospital with Pet fussing over her and stopped off at the market square. I returned home with a bag stuffed with vegetables and a couple of pounds of fresh butterfish. I washed my hands, then showered. I washed my hands again before going to the cabinet and mixing myself a drink. I wanted something strong to take me slightly out of my head – rhum agricole with a few drops of nutmeg syrup.

I unlocked my cabinet and took out my Remington, spent half an hour inspecting it; then cleaning and oiling the weapon. I shoved it in my bag and cooked the food I had bought.

I left home late evening in a thick grey cotton shirt, a pair of trousers and gym boots laced up to the ankle.

Miss Stanislaus was up – a bevy of young nurses around her bed. They'd laid out for her what the hospital could afford: a bowl of tomato soup, a plate of rice with a tiny toss of salad on the side, and something that looked like luncheon meat. I took the bowl from Miss Stanislaus's hand and placed it on the tray.

'Sorry, ladies, I bring real food.'

I took out my food carrier, pulled a chair and spooned the fish broth into the bowl I'd brought along with me. We were quiet as acolytes while we watched Miss Stanislaus eat.

'She your lady?'

I looked up at the nurse who spoke. She was the tallest of the four. Small, deepset eyes. 'More than that,' I said.

As soon as Miss Stanislaus finished eating, there was a tissue in front of her, pushed firmly forward by a nurse with an impossibly neat hairdo and direct, territorial eyes.

'He kin cook,' Miss Stanislaus told her as if that would stop the stand-off between the boldface woman and me. The left side of Miss Stanislaus's face was swollen, otherwise she looked fine.

'Where's Daphne?' I said.

'Fwens,' she mumbled. 'Mither Digger, I caan't thalk.'

I poured a glass of juice and held it out. She shook her head. 'All kindsa things in this, Miss Stanislaus. Forest fruits from all over the island, y'unnerstan? You grow back muscles straight away, in places you didn even know you had muscles. Just a coupla sips and I leave you alone.'

The side of her face shifted. She winced. Suddenly the glass froze at her lips and she began to do that reading thing with her eyes, taking me in from foot to head.

'Nuh,' she said.

I got off the chair.

'Nuh,' she said again, pushing herself to her feet.

Four pairs of hands shooed me out of the room. One of them muttered, 'Dog!'

'Mitha Digger, stay. Come thalk to me.'

I shouldered my bag and hurried along the wards.

I was at the gate when DS Chilman rolled up in his tin-can. He prised himself out the thing, a plastic bag in one hand.

'What you got in there?' I said.

'Is my business, Digson.'

'I hope is not food because she done eat mine already.'

'Digson, haul y'arse.'

252

'I just want to make sure you not giving her nothing that will make her more sick, y'unnerstand?'

'You the blaastid doctor? Is fruits I got here.'

'That's alright then.'

'Thank you, Sir!'

'Don't stay too long either. She kinda tired, yunno.'

Chilman showed me his teeth. 'Whatever you two got, y'all got it bad, is all I can say.'

He ambled off, raised the bag above his head and shook it. 'Come pick up some tomorrow.'

'I might,' I said.

'Suit yourself.'

I was about to get into the car when Malan pulled up in a spray of gravel. He too came out of his vehicle with a bag. 'Digger, I glad I see you. I just figuring out how I goin get dese fruits to De Woman.'

'Malan, you confusing me! She not going to take nothing from you. That's for sure.'

'Wait for me,' he said and strode off towards the gate. I leaned against my car, observing him. Malan said something to the guard and passed over the bag to him.

When he returned, he dropped his back against the car beside me. Night had already fallen, the town below lit yellow with street lamps.

'Update me, Digger. What go on in de office?'

I filled him in as briefly as I could.

'I intend to come in to work, Digger.' He sounded defiant. 'Y'all can't keep me out. Gill at Central tell me he don't want me down there, I should follow you.'

'You got a key,' I said. 'Just don't expect it to be the same at the office. How's Sarona?'

'Saro quiet,' he said. 'She love de sea. I got Spiderface taking her about. She prefer it to de road. Saro teach me one thing, Digger. We should use de sea for traffic, not no road. Is faster and is nicer. We don need no cars.'

He'd folded his arms, looking out at the horizon, his voice gone low. 'I should've meet Sarona long time ago. I would've been a better fella. She the first woman I ever tell I love – yunno that?' He chuckled and shook his head. 'First woman ever give me back-chat and I don't want to shut 'er up. First woman I want round me every minute of de day. Woman bewitch me, and I like it.'

He sucked his teeth and turned to face me. 'Digger, I decide to keep a foot in Central too. Gill can't drive me out. Yunno, I overhear Switch bad-talkin you, tryin to get iz new friends to catch you out on your own somewhere. I walk up to im in front of dem. I ask im about de promise he make to me after you straighten he and his pardners out. I tell im to leave tings alone, don push it, else ...'

'Else what?'

Malan went quiet again. 'I tell im I goin stop im for good. Not for you, Digger.'

'For who, then?'

'For de promise he make an' break.' Malan jangled his keys and shoved off. 'I gone.'

43

Every location on the island has its own voice. I told Dessie that once and she laughed at me.

The slope of a hill, the type and thickness of the vegetation made a sound when the wind ran over it, that a pusson heard nowhere else in the world. Up here, among the ferns and bamboo and ancient thick-headed trees, the Belvedere mountains sobbed and mourned.

I was a child when my grandmother told me about this world known only to hunters of bush-meat, and those who made the illicit rum she called mountain-dew. The Belvedere mountains – a place of restless spirits, populated once by the 'People Above the Wind' – women and men who, before her time, fled the plantations in the lowlands and built themselves whole villages and roadways among the trees. Maroons.

With Jana Ray's weed-garden a few yards below, its plastic covering ghostly in the moonlight that filtered down on it, my grandmother's stories were easy to believe.

I sat with my bag in my lap, my back against a tree, the thick shirt buttoned up against the chill.

I must have dropped off because I opened my eyes to watery morning light and the vegetation further down covered in a fine mist. The crackle of the plastic covering had pulled me out of my doze. A blurred shape moved amongst the plants in Jana Ray's greenhouse, crouching over one row, straightening up and moving to another.

He stepped out into the open, rippling with muscles, dark as the trunk of the gumbo-limbo tree a couple of feet on his left. He hung there a while, lifted his head at the groans of a bamboo grove somewhere in the distance.

He walked around the construction, inspecting the pipework that led into the greenhouse; began gathering leaves and kindling. He made a nest in one of the firepits under the bamboo pipes, doused the mound with kerosene from the yellow demijohn in his hand, then dropped a match on it. The whole thing flared up and sent him leaping back.

'You'll never work it out. You ain got the fuckin brains,' I said. 'You kill Jana Ray for nothing. You fuckin stupid snake.'

My voice spun Shadowman around, his head switching from side to side. I stepped forward, my gun raised, and in that instant he'd disappeared. Just a rustle in the bushes further down.

I pressed my back against a tree, my head lowered, my heart hammering, my finger tensed on the trigger of the Remington. A grunt behind me. I threw myself flat just as something crashed against the trunk and splintered. He was on me before I recovered my balance. A hammer blow to my head dimmed my vision, the gun slipped out of my hand. Then an arm locked around my throat, dragging me upwards, then backwards, then downhill. My heels digging into the forest floor.

I realised immediately that Shadowman was dragging me to the fall above the ravine. I made myself a deadweight for a second, pulled my feet up under me and drove my weight into him. He stumbled forward, and by the time he braked, I'd broken loose. Perhaps he expected me to run. Perhaps he

256

was accustomed to a fast and frightened retreat. Me – I hurled myself at him. His arms closed around my waist, and it was all I could do to hold back the scream as the pain rode up my body in waves. I felt my feet leaving the earth, glimpsed for a second his upper lip peeled back, his narrowed eyes, the tendons pushing against the skin of his neck, as he tensed himself to fling me. I brought my forehead crashing down on his. Felt his body shudder, butted him again, the recoil travelling down my spine. A gurgling groan came out of him.

I pulled myself loose and rammed my shoulder into his gut. I watched him totter backward, a forearm swiping at the blood on his forehead. Then, suddenly, he was no longer there.

I stumbled back to Jana Ray's greenhouse. It took me a while to empty the demijohn. I struck a match and tossed it inside the enclosure, retrieved my gun and began limping my way down the Belvedere.

I opened my eyes to the familiar pattern of my rafters and Malan's face above me. I was on my sofa.

'What happen?' I said.

Malan pulled a chair and sat beside me. 'You in your house, Digger. You pass out. Driver find you by the road. He figure you been lying there a long time. He call San Andrews Central.'

'You know the driver' name?'

'Mokoman, I fink. Hear dis: San Andrews Central forward the call to Pet. Digger, I never hear nothing so. Pet cuss them police arse in Central for negligence. Receptionist say she hear Pet on another phone, same time, instructin ambulance how they must pick you up and put you down. Receptionist call me. I decide to pick you up meself.' He chuckle-hissed and straightened up.

257

'Miss Stanislaus awright?' I said.

'Lisa say they lettin De Woman out today.'

'Lisa back?'

'Nuh, Pet tell 'er and she tell me.'

'Miss Stanislaus know what happen with me?'

'Not yet. Pet say she not coming to see you till she cool off. She say you behave like an arse becuz you could've dead up there and nobody would know. She say you should've gone with reinforcement. Digger, she right! An' doctor say—'

'Doctor!'

'Doctor was here. Pet send doctor with instructions.' Malan scratched his head. 'Anyway, de dognoses is you more tired than beat-up – somefing about exhorshun an con-cushion.' Malan chuckled again. 'You an' De Woman plan this?'

'Enjoy yourself,' I said.

I rolled off the sofa. The room rolled with me and I hit the floor. I felt a ripple of pain across my back.

Soft hands helped me up. A breath of perfume.

'Take it easy.'

I wasn't aware that Sarona had come with Malan. I smiled at her and thanked her.

'Malan said somebody attacked you?' she said. 'You better now?'

'Fink so – is part of the job.'

'Seriously?' She'd directed the question at Malan. Her manner with him was soft, delicate. Almost like Dessie was with me. Sometimes.

'Digger never take precautions,' Malan said. 'That couldn've happen to me.' His tone was low, reassuring. She seemed satisfied.

I gestured at the door. 'Where you find my keys?'

'Your pocket,' Malan said. 'Tell me, what happen to you in de bush?'

I told him, struggled to my feet and poured myself a glass of water. I could barely lift my arm. There wasn't a part of me that wasn't hurting.

Malan jangled his car keys, dropped an arm around his woman's shoulders and strolled out the door. They looked good together – he nutmeg, she cinnamon.

I dropped myself back on the sofa, suppressing the urge to call Miss Stanislaus.

I lay in the darkness of my living room, letting the sounds of the Old Hope evening wash over me: children squeezing in the last bit of play before adults bawled them inside. There came the wash of birdsong in the valley, the bang and rattle of closing doors and windows.

Pet called. 'Digger, y'awright?' Her voice was worried, intimate.

'I better, thanks, Pet. Thanks for everything.'

'I-I kin come see you? If you ... never mind, Digger.' She hung up.

When Pet spoke to me like that, she became a different woman. Her voice lost its edge, dropped an octave lower and the uncertainty in it was unbearable. The only time I'd heard Miss Stanislaus chiding her was the lunchtime I walked into the office and overheard them in the toilet.

'Make yourself forget him, Miss Pet. Where woman concern, Missa Digger dunno what he looking for.' I'd dropped my keys on the desk, cleared my throat and bit into my fish burger.

My thoughts looped back to Jana Ray, the beauty and the promise of the youth, and the way Shadowman had killed him. Not just to steal his work. Those imprints on the base of the young man's skull were where Shadowman's nails had bruised the scalp. Each small cut marked the number of times he'd adjusted his grip on the boy's head. My blood curdled

259

at the image of Shadowman bringing Jana Ray's head up for just that little bit of air each time, to prolong his asphyxiation. The third time he had kept Jana Ray down.

Crime was not just wickedness, it was wasteful.

In my head, I tried to bring together all the events of the past few days: that first call by the bus driver named Mokoman about a body by the road, the fear that squatted over the little seaside village, the helplessness and outrage of the woman who had confronted me in Jana Ray's ramshackle house, the cave in the mountains that Eric called The Hole. The messages Jana Ray had left me in my book.

Those drawings were as clear to me as daylight now. Like Lazar Wilkinson, Jana Ray had gone down fighting.

Slow footsteps coming up the driveway, halting at my door.

DS Chilman let himself in and cleared his throat. His hand fumbled at the wall. The lights came on.

'I didn hear your car,' I said.

'I coast, Digson. The coupla pints of gas I got, just enough to take me home. Offer me a drink, youngfella.'

'I have juice.'

He curled his lips at me, walked into my spare room, rattled round a while and returned with a bottle of my finest vintage rum.

'Easterhall X10,' he breathed. 'Digson, you'z a petty bourgeois.' With a twist of his wrist the bottle was open. I slid a glass across the worktop.

He smacked his lips, gave me a slow wink.

'Difference between me'n'you, Digson, is that I not a hypocrite. I prefer honesty. Rum is rum. I take it straight. Not like you who prefer to dress up the holy spirit with cosmetics. You, Michael Digson, does make a whore of the blaastid thing and call it cocktail.'

260

He raised the glass face level and addressed it. 'Gimme the real reason that drive you up in the hills all night last night till morning with a gun in your hand – a gun, mind you, that nobody could persuade you to carry before.' He turned around to face me. 'Why?'

'Dunno what you getting at, Sir. I was doing my job.'

'Nuh! Is becuz the fella lay his hands on Kathleen. Biggest mistake that Missa Shadowman could make was to hit a woman that you care about. You think Kathleen dunno that? Is why she was so agitated soonz you left the hospital.'

I strode across to the fridge and got myself a glass of water. He followed my movements like a cat watching a lizard.

'First time my daughter ever ask me for anything. And that was to beg me to stop you from sinning yourself or getting killed. First time I hear my daughter nearly cry.'

He poured himself a drink, knocked it back and gave me one of his awful yellow-eyed grins.

'Well, I tell her the truth. I tell her is nothing me or Camaho Police Force kin do when Digger Digson catch afire. He can't help it. She just got to wait and pray to all them orisha-women she believe in, and hope he come back alive.'

'You giving me grief for doing my work!'

'Nuh, I givin you grief for forgetting your work! If you wuz doing your work, you'd ha gone up there with officers, corner the fella and bring him in for questioning becuz he got all the answers. You'd've break his leg if you had to. You'd've lay down a red carpet for Shadowman if it was the only way to bring him in. And the case would've been wrapped up in a coupla days.

'What I saying, Digson, is you went to kill the fella, and if you did manage to kill him, you'd've killed the case.'

He downed the drink and slammed the glass on the work-top surface. 'What I want to know is when you going to

261

let go of her.' He was pointing at the picture of my mother on the wall.

'Leave my fuckin mother out of this.' I got up, opened the door, walked out into the night and pulled it hard behind me.

Half an hour later Chilman came out. He lowered himself beside me on the step, his old satchel on his lap.

'Good rum,' he said. 'A lil too polite, though. But nice.' He pressed his shoulder against my side and nudged me with an elbow. 'Digson, you think I come here to downpress you? You think I don't unnerstand? I had a pardner name Cello. We work fifteen years together. We face everything together: madman, thief, gunman, bad weather – whatever! Cello was the one pusson in the world I know would die for me, no question. Was the same for me. I kin call him any time of day or night if I in trouble and he'll get off his woman, ask her for excuse and come and find me. I do the same for him. My wife couldn understand it. She got my money, she got my children and my body, but she feel that whatever Cello getting from me, she want that too. I tell her I can't give her that. Is the job, is what happen when you spend your life facing trouble together, and you know you only come out of it alive because the other person throw their life in the ring with yours. If you lose that pusson, is like you lose part of your brain. Ain got no name for it, Digson. All I saying is, you got to watch that. Keep a very close eye on it becuz the woman you sharing life with never going to understand it.'

'You think I dunno that?' I said.

'Digson, what's going to happen to my daughter?' he said. And he'd suddenly become a tired and scared old fella looking into my face.

'I doing my best, Sir.'

'I know,' he said, dropping a hand on my shoulder and pushing himself to his feet.

He picked his way down the driveway. The Datsun shuddered into life. We called it The Donkey, because Chilman swore on his children's life that the vehicle knew how to get him home. I never doubted that.

My thoughts flicked back to the first time Dessie spotted me with Miss Stanislaus at the entrance of the Fire Station.

She came over to my place that night.

'Tell me about that woman, Digger – the one who was with you.'

I told her about Miss Stanislaus. Dessie listened as if she were absorbing my words with her eyes, a finger pressed against her lower lip. She curved her body forward on the sofa, her arms around her knees. 'Digger, I want the truth. You in a relationship with that woman?'

I never thought of Miss Stanislaus as 'that woman', I said. I never stopped to examine the way we worked together. It was like asking me how I felt about my head. You don't think about it unless it's hurting you. And when it hurts, you do something about it. Like when a market seller named Cocoman had the blade of a machete against Miss Stanislaus's throat. It didn't feel as if another officer was in trouble, it felt as if I was the one that Cocoman was fuckin with.

'Dessie, I don't have the words for it,' I said. 'But what I know is that I would do what I need to do to make sure Miss Stanislaus awright. And I sure she'll do the same for me.'

Dessie sniffed and covered her face with her hands. Then she rose to her feet. 'So, y'all have a relationship?'

'You my woman, Dessie. She's not.'

'I would've preferred you didn't tell me.'

'I would've preferred you didn't ask me. Is like you pushing me to choose between air and water.'

'Which of us is air, Digger? And which is water?'

'No choice, Dessie. They both important.'

'Digger, any number of man wants me.'

'Then go with any number of man. I got strong feelings for you, but that don't mean I going to lie.'

A couple of hours later, I walked her to her car. Dessie looked stricken.

44

A tap on my door pulled me out of my thoughts. I turned off
the stove, straightened myself and pulled the door open. Miss
Stanislaus was out there. The late-evening gloom behind her
was speckled with fireflies.

I pulled the door wider and stepped aside, zoning in on
her face. She looked calm but I sensed the agitation in her.

'What's happening?'

'I decide you going to cook for me.'

'Just in time,' I said. I gestured at the pots sitting on the
stove, then pointed at a chair. Before she sat, I caught a look
from her, self-conscious, almost shy.

'How's the face?' I said.

'Face fine, Missa Digger. And you?'

'I good.' I laid the food on the table. She extracted a tissue
from her bag and slipped it up her sleeve.

'I hear *he* come to talk to you?' '*He*' was Chilman.

'Uh-huh.'

'What *he* say?'

'You like my salad dressing?'

She plucked a string of grated carrot, dipped it in the dressing and tasted. 'It good,' she said.

I loaded a Country and Western CD into my player. Her
kind of music.

I switched it on and turned the music low. She raised her

265

head at me. 'Missa Digger, you never tell me you know dat Malan lef iz wife.'

'Malan never tell me that he left his wife, Miss Stanislaus.'

'Pet tell me that she keep callin de office to talk to him. Is not right to cause dis kinda sufferin. Is why I never consider meself to be no proper police. Becuz,' she was hissing with indignation, 'police do what's right becuz they get a salary. I do what's right becuz is right!'

'That's why you upset?'

'Uh-huh.'

'You sure?'

Miss Stanislaus didn't answer me.

I spooned out the stewed fish into a bowl. Then the steamed vegetables. Miss Stanislaus looked at me with something like reproach in her eyes. I got up and fetched a couple of napkins. That appeased her.

'Miss Stanislaus, your father came here last night, drink a bottle of my best rum and cuss me stinking. He say I wasn't acting as an officer when I went chasing after Shadowman. He say what I did was selfish. It hurt but he was right. Only thing I don't accept is that I would've mash-up the investigation.'

'He's right!' she said. 'How you know where to find the Shadowman?'

'I figure he's the one killed Jana Ray for his marijuana garden, and if that was so, I would find him up there. Jana Ray was an asset. Why they going want to murder him? I figure it had to be for something else. Jana Ray been setting himself up selling marijuana oil and kush. There's a lotta money in it. Shadowman was after his plants.'

'I really upset wiv you, Missa Digger, for goin after that man on your own.'

'You ask me a question, Miss Stanislaus. I tryin to answer it.'

'Go ahead,' she muttered.

266

'Well, when I searched Jana Ray' house, the whole bedroom ransacked, none of the obvious things taken, but
somebody been in there looking for something. I believe it
was Shadowman looking for Jana Ray' stash of seeds.'

'What make you so sure, Missa Digger?'

'The lil fella name Eric told me that Shadowman was
always oppressing Jana Ray for his seeds and plants, accusing the youngfella of giving him dead seeds because they
wouldn't grow. What Jana Ray never told Shadowman was
that the plants survive only in certain conditions. I believe
Shadowman started concealing himself to watch what Jana
Ray was doing. Then it must've crossed his mind that all
he needed to do was to take the whole damn garden from
the youngfella. Thing is, Jana Ray might've left it because
h'was planning to run away. Something must've told him
that Shadowman was going to kill him. H'was a sensi-
tive fella.'

'You finking is different people who got rid of Missa
Laza Wilkins?'

'Lazar Wilkinson was a different kind of killing. I still
believe Miss Tamara and the two foreigners got something
to do with it.'

'Missa Jamma Ray – you say he didn have no interest in
the marijuana weed bush – what he got interest in?'

'Marijuana oil, Miss Stanislaus – a cure for the epilepsy that
killed his mother. His notes told me that.'

'But his mother pass way!'

'It don't work like that in people's head, Miss Stanislaus.
You don't want it to happen again to whoever matter to you.
You rather kill or die to make sure it don't happen again.'

I gathered the plates and laid them in the sink.

Miss Stanislaus eased her hands under the running tap.
'Missa Digger, I finkin you 'fraid that this job going make

you a worser man, yunno. Mebbe is not that. Mebbe the job wake up the fings you already got inside you.'

I followed her out to the veranda. On the road below a car rushed by, leaving behind the quiet and the darkness.

'Why those drug people want to interfere with Camaho, Missa Digger?'

'Camaho is small, we already got a smuggling culture, we have a whole heap of youngfellas on the island who can't get a job. We got a million lil bays and coves where you could hide a boat. And we got the personality – secretiveness is first nature. Besides, the market for the drugs not too far from here: we got Trinidad next door, and once you go past Kara Island, is a straight run up to Florida and Miami. What I saying, Miss Stanislaus, and what your father always knew, is that Camaho is ripe for a takeover.'

I went to my shelf and pulled down the book that Jana Ray had marked. Miss Stanislaus came in. I opened it and held it out to her, my finger on the first two of the six drawings of fans with the numbers above them. 'I was wrong, them is not fans. Them is propellers. The first two look different. I dunno why, I dunno what them numbers above them saying either but I feel sure is connected with the boat.'

She took the book and bent her head over it, her brows pulled tight. 'Same engine, Missa Digger, only difference is pro-puller not fit proper on the first two.'

She raised her head and looked past me as if she were listening to something beyond the room. 'Mebbe they need fixin?'

'I not so sure that's what it mean, Miss Stanislaus. I not—'

'Everyfing Missa Jamma Ray say so far is true,' she snapped. 'So why you doubtin him now?'

I left her there, walked out onto my veranda, staring into the darkness beyond the grapefruit and banana trees that fenced my house. And it came to me that everything about

Miss Stanislaus's visit and her attitude tonight was about the weeks of waiting for a verdict on her future with San Andrews CID. She was expecting me to understand her fears without having to spell them out.

Still, I was waiting for her to tell me. Miss Stanislaus was the only human I knew who, however much she tried, could not sidestep the truth.

She came out and placed herself beside me.

'Missa Digger, I love my job. Bes' fing dat ever happen to me. An' I good doing it, not so?'

'The best,' I said.

'If I lose it, I wouldn fall down an' dead, Missa Digger. But I don' want to lose my living becuz of a man that take so much from me arready. Else, nothing else make sense.'

'Miss Stanislaus, if you go, I go too.'

'Mebbe that's what they want?'

'Mebbe, Miss Stanislaus. Dunno.'

45

Early morning, Benna called me from Kara Island. She greeted me cheerily, apologised on behalf of herself and the others for taking so long. Yesterday, they'd found Koku Stanislaus – or at least the place they were almost certain he might be.

This woman's way of saying things always left me full of doubt.

'Might be?' I said. 'Y'all not sure?'

'We sure,' she said. 'We jus didn take im out.'

'He's, erm, still buried?'

'Yes.'

'So how you know?'

'We know,' she said. 'We done we work, you come do yours now.'

I glanced at my watch. She'd phoned me just after 6am. The first ferry left at 7. Weather permitting, I'd be there around 8.

They were waiting for me on the jetty. Beach Street was humming with clusters of people sorting themselves – probably unconsciously – by age groups. The women had clearly broadcast the news.

Two men, their faces expressionless as planks, stood to one side of Benna and her crew. They were leaning on forks and shovels. I greeted the women, took their proffered

270

hands and bowed. The childhood habit returned so easily, it surprised me.

'Come,' Benna said. The crowd moved aside for her as if parted by a hand. She took me to an eatery across the road, named Delna's Diner. Benna sat me at a table.

'I tell Delna you goin be hungry. She open up early and prepare somefing for you.'

'Where on the island you find the body?'

She shook her head. 'Is not on Kara Island. Eat first, then we show you.'

She watched in silence while I ate, attentive to every movement of my hand and mouth.

'You live on your own, not so?'

'I do,' I said.

'You been doin it a long time.'

'How you know?'

'Is the way you eat.'

I raised my head and looked at her.

'Never mind.' She smiled. 'You tell Kathleen you here?'

'Nuh. I want to make sure first.'

She nodded. 'Kathleen was walkin a clean road before Juba spit on it. Pretty, pretty girlchild she was! An' bright! She used to make us laugh with the things she say and the questions she throw at people. You had to be quick to keep up with her.' She leaned into me. 'Missa uhm . . .'

'Digger,' I said.

'Yes.' She laid her stick across her lap. 'We could've put away Juba long time ago. H'was a burden for all of us to carry all these years. But was not our job to do it. Ain got a pusson here who didn know Kathleen comin back for him. However long it take. Mebbe Juba know dat too.'

'Is the exact opposite I here to prove, Benna. Don't let nobody hear you say that. Specially in Camaho.'

'I not surprised! Camaho people got no culture, and even less common sense. Exceptin you, mebbe.' She showed me a row of healthy teeth. 'Come, we find Koku on White Islan.'

I'd finished eating the soused crab meat and bread, thanked Delna and followed Benna to the jetty. They'd hitched up a big wooden boat against it. The women climbed on board, then the men with their tools. I passed over my murder bag to one of the men and climbed in.

The pilot took us south, following the contours of the island. Once around the southern tip, he veered north. Ahead of us two small islands appeared – one humped like a tortoise; the other, a white sand bank partly covered in vegetation. At one end of it, a round thirty-foot-high rock formation thrust out of the water. I thought of an octopus with its body streamlined for flight.

The women had their heads together, conversing in low tones. I found myself in awe of them.

White Island was more beach than land, the purest, whitest sand I'd ever walked on. They took me towards the 'head' of the octopus, up a slight incline – the boatman in front, flashing his machete at branches and lianas.

We walked into the cool gloom of a Lignum Vitae glade, the leafy floor dappled with sunlight, the roar of the sea in my head. I followed Benna's pointing stick. All the signs were there.

'It might not be him,' I said.

'Is him,' she said. I marked out the rectangle I wanted the men to excavate and they set to work: fast, proficient, their movements economical.

Koku Stanislaus's killer had placed him in a long bag before they threw him in. The fabric was some sort of coarsely weaved material.

'Fish bag,' one of the men said.

'What?'

'Fish bag, yunno. Fellas who hunt big-fish does carry dem in it.'

'You know the people who use them?'

He shrugged. 'Most fishin-fellas got one. Tomas does order it for us.'

'Who's Tomas?'

'Ole fella who got a little hardware shop back of Delna' place.'

'Where Tomas order the bags from?'

The man lifted his shoulders and dropped them. 'Ask him.'

'I intend to,' I said. 'You got a fish bag too?'

'Course!' he said.

'We got work to do,' Benna cut in.

I nodded and turned back to the hollow in the ground.

'Is not going to be pretty,' I said. 'Y'all might want to leave now?'

'Why?' Dada said.

'Okay.' I shrugged. I took out my LED torch. 'Lemme explain what I will be doing. At some point I might be needing the help of y'all fellas. Y'all might want to cover y'all nose.'

They didn't seem to hear me.

Flies and moths and, later, Carrion and Rove beetles had already done what no priest nor prayers could do: stripped Koku Stanislaus of his mortal coil and returned him to the earth.

I took photos, of course, then ran my torch along the length of the bag, pausing on what looked like printed letters at the side, which were so faded I could have mistaken them for stains had I not brought my torch closer.

I turned to Benna. 'I'll have to have our people take him to Camaho. So I could do a proper job.'

'Nuh!' The old woman looked affronted.

'I have to,' I said.

Benna shook her head and tapped her leg with her stick. 'Koku not crossing no long-water no more. He already where he s'pose to be.' She waved her stick in a way that took in the bushes, the sky, the sea, and Kara Island in the near distance.

I thought of Miss Stanislaus and imagined her being similarly outraged.

I could barely hold in my irritation. 'Then you want me to desecrate the body?' I meant it in a forensic sense, of course, but she wouldn't understand that.

Benna tensed, she narrowed her eyes and showed me her teeth. Whatever emotion that ran through the old woman now transformed her. I could see why the whole island deferred to Benna. 'Lissen, youngfella, don't play de arse with me, y'hear?'

'Sorry,' I said. 'By desecrate I mean, I got to take away a coupla things with me.'

She hadn't relaxed. Those pale eyes were still drilling into mine.

'I want the handles of the bag. The zip might be useful, and the side of the bag where I saw what I think is the brand name of the bag. I have to take that.'

Benna relaxed her shoulders then gestured at the men who promptly set to work.

The way I saw it, somebody would have had to lift that bag and carry it. Traces of that person would have been on the handle. I'd read somewhere that in ideal conditions, DNA could last longer than a million years. But this was no textbook situation. Here, with warm weather, very porous soil, a shallow grave and the fact that the old man had been lying there a coupla years, I doubted whether I'd be able to isolate any trace of whoever it was that had brought him here. At least not forensically.

Besides, taking samples and having the lab in Trinidad run a thorough test made no sense. It would take time, and time was what Miss Stanislaus and I did not have.

One of the fellas I knew now as Vaz – short, muscled, with heavy eyebrows and small eyes – handed me the cuttings from the bag that I'd asked for. He'd wrapped them in a bunch of seagrape leaves and seemed anxious to get them out of his hands.

A couple of hours later, a flannel still around my lower face, I straightened up. Under the light of my LED torch, they identified Koku Stanislaus's canvas belt which, they said, the old man always wore. There was no other like it on the island. Or prob'ly anywhere else. Koku had brought it back from his work-years in Aruba long before I was born. The sight of that belt brought down a heavy silence on them.

'I finish here,' I said finally. 'Y'all got to preserve this place. Is evidence.'

I had more than two hundred photos stored in my camera. 'I leaving that to y'all until I send the people from Camaho to do their part.' I glanced at Benna. 'Then we going to hand him over to y'all, his people. Come, lemme explain what I find.'

They followed me through the vegetation to the shade of a seagrape tree on the beach. I extracted the data card from my little Casio camera and slotted it into the seven-inch Android tablet I'd brought along with me.

I sat on the sand while they crowded around.

I pulled up the pictures on the screen. 'His bones and teeth and joints give an idea of his age and the condition of his body before he died. He had strong bones, though his knuckle joints tell me that the ole fella had arthritis, specially his right hand.'

Dada grunted assent.

'No problems with his knees, though. H'was around eighty, mebbe older.'

'You say dat you kin tell what happen to him?' Benna said.

'Yes.' I traced a finger along the picture of the spinal column. 'We call these bones vertebra. Like y'all see, every one of dem got two lil wings on each side, except this one.' I dropped my finger on the left side of the fourth vertebra. 'This one broken. That suggest that something strike the ole fella with great force from behind and break it off.'

I showed them a frontal photo of the ribcage. 'Whatever went through his back and break the bone didn't come through at the front. It hit one of his ribs also at the back but higher up. You would expect it to hit the front part of the ribcage, if the weapon was straight like a steel rod, or something like that. But no, it hit the back. I asking y'all, what could enter a pusson from the back with such force and not go through his front?'

I raised my head at them. 'It's got to be something that curve back on itself.'

One of the men cleared his nostrils, a harsh scraping sound. 'Hook.'

'Gaff,' the other said.

'It also mean the person was behind him when they strike.'

I rose to my feet, stood behind one of the men and showed them the blow that would achieve this.

One of the women covered her face.

'Something else: a blow like that is only possible with the left hand.'

There was a long silence, filled in by the sound of the water licking the sand.

276

'Juba carry dat gaff in iz right hand. Always,' Vaz said, and looked to the other for confirmation.

'Y'ever see him use it?' Benna said.

The fella shook his head. He appeared stunned by the idea.

'I witnessed it myself,' I said. 'The night Juba tried to kill Miss Stanislaus and me. When I saw him on the road that night, he was carrying the hook in his right hand. When he was about to strike me down, he switched it to his left.'

'What come after this?' Benna wanted to know.

'I might need y'all as witnesses.'

Benna nodded. The others looked unsure.

Dada soured her face. 'I don like Camaho, y'all kin bring the courthouse here?'

Benna sucked her teeth. 'Woman, you too fool!'

One of the men laughed out loud.

'We can't keep dis from people,' she muttered. 'We got to let everybody know.'

'Go right ahead, Benna. Let everybody know.'

'Anyfing else, youngfella?'

'Yes, I want to visit Missa Tomas. After that I going to find Officer Mibo – y'all kin tell me where he live?'

'Is time.' Benna nodded. She turned to the men. 'Put some branches over Koku. Let im know we comin back for him.'

The men hurried off. Benna waved me into the boat.

46

Tomas's place looked at first glance like a rectangular hole cut into a peeling brown wall. An old man with a face wrinkled like a raisin was resting his head against it. I looked past his shoulders into a gloomy room, as narrow as a corridor, with a confusion of fishing tackle on either side. The old fella seemed indifferent to the sizzling heat of the midday sun. Not a bead of sweat on him.

'G'd afteroon, I looking for Missa Tomas?'

'He here,' he said, nudging a finger at his chest. He looked me up and down, then up again. 'What you want?'

'I got a coupla questions,' I said.

'Questions is not money; you want to buy somefing?'

'I want some answers,' I said.

'You won't find none here.' His face shut down. He might as well have turned his back on me.

I opened my bag and pulled out the pieces of the bag we'd found Koku Stanislaus in. I held out the handle that we'd cut off in front of him. 'Yunno what kinda fish bag these might belong to?'

He didn't answer me.

'You sell fish bag, not so?'

'You want to buy one?'

'Nuh, I want to know who buy this one from you.'

He threw a quick look at my hand and chuckled. 'Damn small bag,' he said. 'You carryin ants in dat?'

His grumpiness reminded me of DS Chilman and Dada.

'We just find Koku Stanislaus body in a bag on White Island. Them is the handles of the bag. Somebody kill' him and bury him in it.'

The yellow eyes shot wide and froze on my face. 'For true?'

'Ask Benna,' I said. 'Is two years now Koku disappear and you telling me y'all didn notice it? Is a lil island y'all living on. Not a continent.'

He shook his head. 'For true?'

'Yes, Koku dead for true. I got good reasons to believe Juba Hurst kill him.'

The old man licked his lips and blinked at me. 'Koku kept to himself. Me and he – we never use to get on. People say he went to live in Camaho wiv the girlchile he adopt – the one dat come back here an' kill' Juba. Me, I never trust dat girl—'

'I do! I was with her when she took down Juba. You going answer my questions?'

He nodded.

'These come from your shop?' I handed him the handles of the bag. They were made of some thick nylon fabric and were padded – blackened now by the soil they'd been covered with.

The old fella bent his head, his thumb exploring the fabric, his lips moving as his fingers rolled away the grit. When he looked up, his eyes were distant, his voice gone low. 'Is not mine,' he said. 'It feel expensive. That the only part ov the bag you got?'

I reached into my case and pulled out the piece that had been cut from the side.

Tomas took it from me and began doing that rubbing thing with his hand. 'Like I done tell you, is expensive. De material make of hemp. Is what you find Koku inside, for true?'

279

'You would notice one of these if somebody carrying it around, not so?'

He shook his head. 'It different from de rest,' he said. 'But I hardly leave my place. I wouldn know. How big you say de bag was?'

'Six or seven feet,' I told him.

'You wouldn buy a bag like this unless you dolphin huntin.'

'You got dolphin hunters round here?'

'Eastward Island people.' I visualised the place – a couple of miles off Kara Island with big concrete houses rising from it like fortresses.

'We don't eat dolphin.' Tomas coughed into his hand. 'Vincen Island people pay good money for the meat, though.'

'I happen to know dolphin meat is poison,' I said. 'They pick up mercury from the ocean. Pollution, yunno, from all that gold they processing in Guyana.'

'Who you after?' he said. The old man looked worried.

'You mention dolphin hunters from Eastward Island. Ain got no Kara Island fellas here who hunt dolphins?'

He shook his head, shook it again then dropped his eyes on his rubber slippers.

'Tell me,' I said.

'Dunno,' he said.

'I know you know, Missa Tomas. I listening.'

He kept shaking his head.

'Okay.' I took the fabric from his hand. 'I going to ask Benna to get the information from you. You prefer I do that?'

'De only pusson I know round here who dolphin hunt is my family and my family will never . . .'

'Go on.'

He flicked a hand at the fabric. 'That kin never involve my family.'

'I listening, Sir.'

'Is not de kinda fing Mibo going—' Tomas stopped abruptly.

'Missa Tomas, from the time you put your hand on this,' I waved the cuttings at him, 'you know it was Mibo' bag, not so?'

The old man smacked his lips, blinking rapidly.

'What's Officer Mibo to you?'

'My youngest brother' child. Mibo is the last one.' He spoke as if that explained everything. The old man threw me a fast furtive glance. 'Queenie know bout this?'

'Who's Queenie?'

'You call her Benna.'

'Where you think Mibo got the bag from?'

'Is a surfin bag, Missa erm . . . '

'Digger! You order it for him, not so?'

'Is what 'Merican surfin fellas carry their surfin board in. We use it for dolphin.'

'You didn answer my question, Sir. You order the bag?'

Tomas kept swallowing and shaking his head. 'Uh-huh,' he said finally.

'From?'

'Not far.'

'From?'

'Miami. Queenie know bout this?'

'Not about Mibo. Not yet.' I lowered myself in front of him. 'What I got right now is a link between you and a bag that had Koku Stanislaus' body in it. You say y'all didn get on, so you might have your own reason for killing him. That make you a suspect, Missa Tomas, at least. Unless you kin prove otherwise, y'unner—'

The old man shot to his feet and marched through the door. He slammed it shut behind him. I heard a series of bangs and rattling as if he were pulling apart the place. I felt relaxed. The good thing about Kara Island was that there was nowhere to run.

Tomas returned with a black hard-cover A4 notebook. He opened it and turned it towards me. I could hear his breathing. I never knew a person could communicate so much indignation by their breathing.

Neatly lined pages.

Seven columns: name of buyer, item ordered, date of order, amount deposited, amount owing, date of arrival of the item, date of delivery to the buyer. Mibo had paid the full amount in advance. He'd received the item three weeks and four days later. That was three years ago.

'You got the order–invoice?'

He left the book in my hand, turned and marched back inside. I retrieved my camera and photographed the pages of the notebook.

Tomas returned and held out the invoice. The address:

Surf Edge Supply
Miami Beach, FL

The price: US$ 269.95.

'Expensive bag,' I said. I took a picture of the page.

'A coffin cost more,' the old man said.

'You know where Mibo live?' His face had gone grim; his expression vengeful.

'Benna told me,' I said.

The old fella raised a hand and shooed me off. He looked as if he'd just received a beating.

47

Officer Mibo had built his house a couple of miles outside the town.

It stood among smaller residences about one tenth its size. The place still smelled of raw concrete, built in what someone thought was Roman-style architecture: a lion's head on each gate post, wide curved steps and columns leading up to a doorway that was arched at the top. A paved yard with four cars including an SUV. I wondered what he did with such a vehicle on a 12-square-mile island.

I climbed the steps and knocked on the big glass door. Mibo appeared from a sideroom – thin as drought, skin so tight on his face I could see the bone structure of his head. He was in a pair of floral shorts and rubber slippers. There was a remote control in his hand. A cinema-sized wide-screen TV shimmered blue in the living room behind him.

'Digger here.' I showed him my ID. He knew who I was, of course, but I wanted to unsettle him with my attitude. Mibo blinked, tried one of those brotherly police smiles. I did not return it. His face froze.

'You heard what happened to Officer Buso, the policefella I arrested for running over—'

'I hear about it,' he said.

'So you know what I was forced to do to him!' I looked at my watch, then at his clothes. 'Is one o'clock. You on lunch break?'

He muttered something about 'not feelin so good today'.

I looked him in the eyes. 'Coupla days ago, I had a conversation with the Commissioner of Police. Officer Mibo, I want you at the station right now.'

His eyes popped wide. He licked his lips. 'Something go on?'

'A lot! If you got doubts about my authority for being here, give the Commissioner a call.' I pulled out my phone and held it out to him. As I expected, he declined. 'Go fix yourself, Mibo. I waiting.'

I descended the steps and surveyed the yard: fishing tackle – lots of it, a couple of dinghies out back, a sleek grey speedboat with a big Yamaha outboard engine.

Mibo came out buttoning up his shirt, his belt undone. The woman I'd met at the station when I went looking for him before followed him out on the veranda. She stared at me with intense unreadable eyes.

Mibo headed for the SUV. I pointed at the blue and white Toyota at the far end of the yard marked POLICE.

We drove in silence. I'd taken out my Remington and rested it, Malan-style, on the dashboard. I could smell the sweat on the man. Mibo drove with his arse pushed hard back against the seat, his chin almost on the steering wheel, both elbows jutting out at right angles.

'Officer Digger—' he said.

'Talk to me in the station.' I'd rehearsed all this in my mind – my own version of Chilman's approach to sharing out justice: *Keep opponent off-balance always*. But right now, sitting beside Mibo with the muzzle of my Remington angled 'accidentally' towards him and my memory of the old man's remains on White Island, this was as real as it could get.

By the time we got to the station, I was in a stinking mood. I was thinking of the terrible toll that a single person's greed and selfishness took on other people's lives. I was thinking of the pressure Miss Stanislaus was under partly because of this fella's report.

I followed him into the station, my eyes on the nape of his neck.

An old desk in one corner of the room, a broken keyboard sitting in the middle of it, the telephone handset the woman had tried to warn him on the last time I came, a stack of biros and an A4 notepad.

'Where the others?' I said.

He muttered something about holiday. 'Nice life,' I said. 'Benna say you one of the best navigators on Kara Island with boats. That true?'

He shrugged.

'Officer Mibo, you not talking much. Why?'

'You not givin me a chance,' he grated.

'I giving you a chance now. Talk!'

He threw me a red-eyed, hateful stare. A coward, I decided – despite his size and demeanour.

'You 'fraid to talk because you dunno what might leak outta your mouth, you got so much to hide – that's why.'

'I ain got nuffing to hide. I dunno why you come here giving me grief!' He'd bared his teeth and widened his eyes at me, and now I saw the nastiness in him.

I dragged the only two chairs in the room and placed them side by side. 'Siddown, Officer Mibo. I got some pictures to show you.'

He made as if to leave.

'If you run out of here, I'll take out your legs from under you. I serious!'

He lowered himself on the chair, his eyes on my face. It took a special kind of policeman to be like him – to surrender so much of himself for money, an ugly house big enough to accommodate a small village, a car you couldn't drive a coupla miles before ending in the sea.

I retrieved my tablet and switched it on. I sat with my shoulder pressed against his. He didn't like it, but he could do nothing about it without falling off his chair. A trick I'd learned from Chilman.

I began swiping through the photos with Mibo's face in my peripheral vision. He remained expressionless. I stopped at the photo of the old man's belt, felt the abrupt convulsion of his body. I pulled up a photo of the old man's remains in the bag. Another convulsion.

'That your bag, not so?'

'Nuh! I never had no bag like dat.'

'You sure?'

'Of course, I—'

The pictures I'd swiped and raised in front of him had cut him off: the old man's record of their transaction and the invoice. 'You still sure?' I said.

Mibo's lower lip was twitching.

I positioned my chair to face him. 'If Juba was alive, I'd have the evidence to lose him in jail for murder. I wouldn't've found out about your part in this killing and your links with Juba Hurst until you exposed y'arse by filing a bad-minded report to the Justice Minister and the press. Why?'

He threw a quick look at the door.

'Run if you want to die, Mibo. Go right ahead.' I raised a finger at his face. 'Next coupla days is the hearing. If Miss Stanislaus go down, you go down further. I'll send you so far fuckin down, you'll wish you never born. I will make it so you never leave jail, because I got strong enough evidence to show that you took the old man' body to White Island in one ov your boats. You probably the only person round here to brave them badwater out there, night-time, with the old man's body in your boat. And the bag – you had to use your expensive bag becuz I sure you find out how a dead body could fight you back – four limbs and a head that won't stay where you want them to stay. A dead body don't help you to lift or move it. You feel as if it resisting you. If you drag it, it heavy like concrete, not so? And it leave a trail ov blood or shit behind it, or both. So you had to hold it together in your dolphin bag. The first thing you learn in forensics, Mibo, is that dead or alive, a body never stops talking.'

I felt so choked up, I had to swallow hard.

Mibo shifted in his seat. I could see the strain on his face. The fear. It crossed my mind that if I spoke to Benna about this, Mibo would probably be dead by tomorrow. Like Chilman said, Kara Island people needed no police. Controlling forces more powerful than us ran this island – some system of justice and retribution that I'd only got a glimpse of through the old woman that even an old fella like Tomas seemed to fear. I picked up one of the biros, pointed at the notepad with the letterhead of Camaho Police Force on it. 'I want a signed statement from you confirming that all the claims and allegations against Miss Stanislaus were hearsay. In other words, you make them up! I want you to state that you had a personal grudge against Miss Stanislaus – make up the reason if you have to – and you have no grounds for doubting Miss Stanislaus and my account of what happened the night we shot Juba.'

I stood up, looked down on his head. 'If I not satisfied, I going to make you do it again. After that, I got a couple of questions for you about who instructed you to ignore procedure and give your opinion on the radio about a police incident almost as soon as it happened. I giving you half an hour.'

I stepped out of the tiny concrete room. I felt drained. The heat of the day was suffocating and unbearable.

After half an hour, I went back in, my belt rolled around my hand.

He'd written the statement, of course, just in case. But he wouldn't let me have it if he could help it. Too much to lose. I knew that before I'd ordered him to do it.

He rushed me with the keyboard – a murderous swing at my head. I ducked and back-pedalled out the door. The sight of the raised gun in my hand sent him scuttling backward.

'Okay, letter done,' I said. 'Now for the conversation.'

I spent an exhausting three hours with Mibo. I found myself battling with a liar. The cunning and deceit came out of him as naturally as the sweat trickling down his face. I learned to read him quickly. Before he told a lie, he licked his lips. A thumb folded tight inside his fist was a sure sign that the question I threw at him would shut him down or scare him. I learned a lot by what he didn't say. Miss Stanislaus would have been proud of me.

48

Killing Juba Hurst upset 'a lot of things', he said. Juba had set up a cocaine-cooking operation on the piece of land he killed Koku Stanislaus for because the old man refused to sell.

Mibo confirmed everything Benna had told me, and told me a lot more: the boys Juba brought over from Vincen Island to help him, the sprint boats that arrived late at night to collect the processed cocaine, before heading off to Trinidad, Miami or Florida – that was until the old women began their guerrilla war on the camp and drove Juba off Kara Island, because, according to Mibo, 'it wasn worth de boderation'. No it wasn't! From what I observed, if Juba had laid his hands on any of those old women, Kara Island would have probably burnt them alive.

Killin Juba upset a lotta things . . . What the hell was *things*? The processing operation? People? Both? Who was *people*?

I made the leap. 'What's Juba's connection with Shadowman?'

He lifted his shoulders and dropped them. 'Cousin,' he mumbled.

'That make him your cousin too, not so? Shadowman come from Kara Island?'

He nodded.

'What's his real name?'

He muttered something.

'Never mind, I'll ask Benna.'

'Ronald Hurst,' he said.

I stood up. Mibo flinched as if he thought I was about to hit him and my mind shifted to Eric. 'So, I take it that Camaho is where Juba set up after Benna chase him out! That operation in the Beau Séjour mountains was Juba's, not so?'

He did not reply.

'Look, you already deep in shit. You a policeman involved in drug-dealings and you'z an accomplice to one of the nastiest murders that happen here on Kara Island. You can't get any deeper. All I need to do is pass the word to Benna and her people that you involved in the old fella's murder.'

I sat back on the chair and leaned into his face. 'Now if you dunno it yet, you part of some runnings that done kill three people: Koku Stanislaus, Lazar Wilkinson and a youngfella I happen to know.'

I brought my face so close to his, he was forced to lean back, now only the back legs of the chair supported him. 'Yunno Lazar Wilkinson, not so?'

He nodded stiffly.

'Who kill im?'

He lifted a hand in what looked like an attempt at denial, thought better of it and steadied himself on the teetering chair.

'All I hear was he turn greedy. He say Beau Séjour is his area. And he don't want no fee for processing the cargo, he want a percentage.' Mibo sounded indignant. 'The fucker been pressuring de bossman, uhm, Juba, I mean . . . he say he goin expose the whole thing to y'all.'

I watched him wipe the spittle from his mouth with the back of his hand. I pushed my chair backward. 'By "y'all" you mean the police. Right? You not a policeman too?'

Mibo's eyes froze on my face.

I stood up and unrolled my belt. 'Now, if you think I got

any problems fuckin you up right now for holding back on me, I'll prove to you that you wrong.' He saw what was coming, raised both hands to his face, his palms turned towards me.

'What's the bossman name?' I said.

'I didn say "bossman".'

'You just said "bossman". You said Lazar Wilkinson was pressuring the bossman. I happen to hear he's a pale-skin fella – what's his name?'

He'd licked his lips. 'Is Juba I call bossman.'

'Mibo, you lying. This is what I want to know: where the cocaine base come from? Who bring it here? Who running Juba, Lazar Wilkinson and Shadowman? Becuz is clear to me that after Juba dead the operation still going on as if nothing happened. And I want to know about that boat that I been hearing a lot about recently. What you know about the boat?' I snapped.

He licked his lips and nodded.

He didn't *know* about no boat for sure but he *heard* about one – a speedboat. It arrived in Camaho from Venezuela a coupla days after Miss Stanislaus shot down Juba. He'd *heard* that it was transporting cocaine base. Juba, *he believed*, been handling arrangements. And becuz Juba couldn't risk no problem from no ole wimmen on Kara Island, he got the order to move to Camaho. And yes, *from what he picked up* from Shadowman, there'd been a big hold-up – some kind ov problem with engine transmission.

'Where's the boat heading after it leave Camaho?'

'Word reach me that is Europe,' he said. Mibo wouldn't look at me. I thought back to the description that Eric gave me of the craft he said he'd helped unload. Small enough to be brought into the little bay in Beau Séjour, no cabin, just a windshield. A trip across the Atlantic in a craft like that made no sense and yet Jana Ray had said the same thing.

'Impossible,' I said.

'Is what I hear,' he said.

'Who ordered Juba to move to Camaho?' I said.

'Dunno. I didn say nobody order nobody.'

'You just said Juba got the order to move to Camaho. Somebody had to give the order, Mibo.'

'I hear talk bout bossman an' bosslady. But I didn listen to that.'

'"And bosslady"?'

'I didn say bosslady.' He shook his head and kept it lowered.

I didn't press him, he'd clamped his hands down on both thumbs.

I left him standing at the back door of the station, his arms folded tight around his chest.

'You dead and you don even know it yet,' he shouted at my back.

And you in jail, I thought. *Becuz I coming back for you.*

'The bossman going to do it?' I threw back.

I saw the panic in his eyes and smiled.

49

By the time the ferry swung into Blackwater, the headache that I'd been dodging for the past few days tightened its grip on me. I stood on the deck, holding onto the protective railing. Every dip and shudder of the boat felt amplified. For a moment everything around me became smeared and fluid. I threw up. Fell onto my hands and knees and began crawling towards the doorway of the cabin.

I didn't know if I made it.

When I opened my eyes, the boat was docked in Camaho. I was lying on a stretcher, the ambulance almost on the sidewalk of the Carenage. A woman in a light-green smock was bending over me. I recognised her as the doctor I'd seen in the hospital when Miss Stanislaus was there.

From somewhere behind, I heard Chilman's cough. Pet had a hand on my neck.

'I'm Dr Venfour,' the woman said. 'How you feeling now?' She had the most musical voice I'd ever heard.

'What happen?' I said.

'Did you have breakfast or lunch?' the doctor said.

I blinked at her and nodded.

'When last you slept?'

I thought about it and showed her four fingers.

'Four what? Days?'

I nodded.

'You haven't slept for four days!' She sounded so outraged, I thought she was going to leave me there and head back to her work.

'Ease him up,' she said.

I felt better when I came to my feet.

Chilman took me home.

'Where's my car?' I said.

'Don't worry,' he said, pointing at my sofa.

I must have dozed off because when I opened my eyes, it was dark out there. The slam of my door had woken me. Chilman must have hung around a long time.

There was a pot of pasta on the stove, still warm; a saucepan of cooked corned beef, done up with garlic, onions, cherry tomatoes and ginger. A small bowl of salad with a slice of lime and a rum glass of olive oil between them.

There was a note on the lid of the pot.

Call me when you up. Important.
  PS – I borrowed a bottle.

I imagined the old fella scribbling the note, with a bottle of my best rum secured under his armpit. I shook my head and chuckled.

Next day, in the office, Miss Stanislaus took the news of her uncle's death quietly, her hands folded in her lap, the tears dripping down her face. Pet was out for lunch.

'I sorry,' I said. 'I believe Mibo was the one who take your uncle out to sea.'

'H'was never good.'

'After the old wimmen drive Juba out, Juba moved the camp to Beau Séjour – that was three months ago. Shadowman is Juba' family – proper name is Ronald Hurst. Mibo said he stopped Juba from attacking the women. I don't believe him. Miss Stanislaus, what's Benna to these people?'

'"These people" is us, Missa Digger.'

'Who's Benna?'

'One old woman, Missa Digger.'

'Tell me. Please.'

Her silence became a wall between us. I felt shut out.

'You don't trust me?' I said. 'I been doing all this becuz of you, Miss Stanislaus. I went all the way to Kara Island to clear your name—'

'Your name too, Missa Digger.'

'I not the one facing a hearing next coupla days.'

'Not yet, Missa Digger. After me, the MJ coming for you.'

'Okay.' I gestured at my notes. 'I'll finish this. Mibo admitted that Juba had a shipment to process. Juba got killed two days before the shipment arrived in Camaho.'

'Missa Digger, you talkin to me like if you vex with me. You vex with me?'

'I giving you the information, not so?'

She muttered something, then shook her head.

'Miss Stanislaus, you not interested no more?'

'I don like your attitude, Missa Digger.'

'I don't like yours either, Miss Stanislaus.'

I pushed back my chair and stood up. 'The important thing I want to tell you is Mibo confirm that everything we been thinking so far is true: we got a boat somewhere on this island and Juba was part of it but he not the one behind it. We killed Juba coupla days before the boat arrived, and bizness going on as usual. Is some "bossman" and "bosslady" behind it. I got my suspicions who the bossman is. Why you looking at me like that? I done you something?'

'You ain got no feelins, Missa Digger.'

'You not the one always telling me I got too much?'

'You jus tell me my uncle got kill' like you telling me the price ov fish, and then you go on talking as if nuffing happen! Den you insult me by gettin off the chair and walking off.'

'I tell you I sorry, not so? And I didn' walk off. I still standing here.'

'Would've been better if you walk off.'

'Jeezas! I dunno how to please you.'

'No, you dunno!'

'Thank you!'

I returned to my seat.

She sat there glaring at me for a few minutes, then she got up and walked out.

I called Chilman.

'Digson, you sound upset! What happen?'

I filled him in and ended with Mibo's connection with Koku's murder.

'That don't relate to y'all shooting down Juba.'

'The cocaine-cooking factory directly related, Sir. Killing Lazar Wilkinson and Jana Ray is part of it. I can argue that at the hearing. The rest is persuasion.'

'Who will do the persuading, Digson?'

'Me,' I said.

'You can't. In Red Pig mind, persuasion is provocation from you.'

'I don unnerstan, Sir.'

'The MJ – he don like you, Digson. Something about you frighten him. All of this is about you, from the first big case y'all do two years ago when y'all expose his dealings with that preacherman name Bello.'

'Then I'll pass the files to you.'

'Fank you,' he said and cut off.

Miss Stanislaus returned, slowed down at my desk and dropped something on it. I smelled fish roti. I raised my head at her, uncertain of her mood. There was a question in her eyes. I thought I understood it.

'Was sudden,' I said. 'Missa Koku hardly feel any kinda pain.'

'Okay,' she said.

I held up a folder. 'I want to rehearse this with you. For the hearing.'

'Nuh.'

'You don't want to go through it?'

'Nuh.'

'It will help if you rehearse it.'

'You don't rehearse the truth, Missa Digger, you tell it.'

'Your father will be defending your case tomorrow. I want him to go there half-drunk.'

'Missa Digger, you know what you sayin?'

'Yep! His mind work quicker when he half-drunk – a lot quicker.' I turned my chair to face her. She was patting her brows with a tissue. 'Miss Stanislaus, answer me honest. How you going to feel if the hearing never happen tomorrow? Cuz is going be hell for everybody.'

The tissue froze. 'Is possible?'

'Dunno, I kin try. But mebbe you prefer to fight back?'

'I been fightin from de start, Missa Digger. In here.' She pointed at her head. 'And it worry me an make me tired.' She turned her head away.

I picked up my file. 'I tired too, Miss Stanislaus.'

I called the Commissioner's office and asked his secretary to inform him that Mr Michael Digson was on the way. She told me he was busy for the next couple of hours. I said I would wait.

50

An old wood-panelled room with big windows. On the wall, portraits of all the Police Commissioners who had gone before. The history of the island was in those pictures, a long row of portraits of white stiff-backed colonials; after them a couple of light-skinned Barbadian mulattoes, after them the 'brownings'; and now the milked cocoa of my father. Another coupla decades or so, they'd probably be obsidian.

A parade of men in too-tight suits and shirt-jacks trailed in and out with suitcases in their hands. My father's voice was a pleasant baritone, always with a hint of humour. It felt as if I didn't know him at all.

Finally my name.

I walked in. He gestured at the chair directly facing him. 'You look harassed,' he said. 'What's happening with you?'

'I'm alright,' I said. 'For the hearing tomorrow, I brought some information. I know you s'posed to get the information same time like everybody else—'

'But?' he cut in, smiling.

'I giving you a head start, Sir.'

I placed the file in front of him. In seconds, he was deep in it. I liked watching him concentrate, brows pulled tight, his eyelids like half-closed shutters, his mouth a clenched line. I would never let him know that.

When he finished, he sorted the papers into two neat piles. 'This,' he said nudging the pile with the notes and photographs of Koku's murder, 'is useful. In fact, important. That,' he lifted the other pile with my notes on the MJ's indiscretions and slid them back at me, 'is suicide.'

He sat back. 'It is a bomb in your hand, Michael. If it goes off it will destroy you too.'

He stood up, looking down on my head. 'I told you before, you can embarrass a man in the MJ's position and get away with it. Humiliation is a different matter.' He reached for the pile he'd just pushed back. 'This might win the opposition an election. They'll thank you for it. But they'll know that you're a danger to them too.'

'The MJ got something on you?' I said.

He sat back. 'No, Michael. My one indiscretion is you. And you're the person who doesn't want me to broadcast it, because I'm very proud of the fact. You wouldn't come to my office unless you want something. What're you asking for now?'

I looked him in the eye. 'For you to take back your job from the MJ, so I could respect you. I, erm, I want to feel good about you as my father. And I don't want this hearing to happen, either, because,' I pointed at the notes that he'd rejected, 'I'll use whatever I got at my disposal to defend myself and Miss Stanislaus.'

He stared out the window. Our silence lasted minutes.

I stood up and gathered my papers.

He roused himself and reached for the phone. 'Sharon,' he said, 'get me the Prime Minister's office.'

He re-cradled the handset, pointed at the documents in my hand. 'I'll have those too. All of them.'

He nodded me out of his office.

Back at my desk in San Andrews CID. My roti had gone

cold. Miss Stanislaus stared at it, then at me, her mouth twisted with displeasure.

The office phone rang. Pet answered. She handed it to me. It was Sharon, the Commissioner's PA.

We were not required at the meeting tomorrow, she said.

'Not required – that means it's happening anyway?'

She hesitated before asking me to hold on.

'Michael? There's going to be a meeting. I've insisted! But there's not going to be a hearing. And,' the Commissioner sounded belligerent, 'just to inform you, I'm having Officer Mibo arrested today!'

I passed on the news to Miss Stanislaus and Pet.

Pet broke out in sniffles. Miss Stanislaus hurried off to the bathroom.

I walked out to the courtyard, struggling to control my breathing.

51

Chilman decided to call in his 'forces' for a 'head-knocking' session. That included the Commissioner. I told him I needed a full day to pull the information I'd gathered together before that happened. The Old Bull agreed.

I passed the time at home with a mix of vintage rum and coffee at my elbow, my laptop and several sheets of grid-lined paper. I needed to piece together and crosscheck everything I'd learned so far from Eric, Jana Ray's drawings and what Mibo had told me.

When I turned up the next day, a table sat in the middle of the space, a dazzling white tablecloth laid out on it with the kind of food that had me grinning foolishly at everyone.

Cornky wrapped in plantain leaves, potato pone, cassava bread, corn bread, tania porridge, stuffed crab-back and cray-fish done in the way that Miss Stanislaus claimed only she knew how: marinaded and baked then blessed with peppery sauce. From time to time, she presented me with a bit of one or the other, but never the whole assembly.

'Everything here for me?' I said, jigging around the table. I took Miss Stanislaus's hand and bowed the way I did with the old women on Kara Island.

Chilman burst out in a series of dry chuckles. 'Digson, you'z a jackass!'

Pet threw me a sidelong glance, smiled and shook her head.

Miss Stanislaus was fluttering like a butterfly. 'Missa Digger, why you so chupid? Is just a lil somefing, yunno. A lil bit of light, becuz we come out ov all that darkness.'

'The woman is a poet too,' I said. I fetched some plates from the tiny kitchen at the back, served them first then packed my plate.

'Digson, yuh brain in your blaastid belly.'

I wagged a crayfish in his face. 'Correct! Along with lobsters, crayfish is the only creature that got a belly where the brain should be.' I tilted my head and dropped the whole thing in my mouth.

Caran turned up late afternoon with his troop. He dropped a bag of mangoes in the middle of the office, gave me a high-five and dragged a chair.

Spiderface, our boatman, sat beside the door, his head down, looking jittery. He'd just returned from taking Sarona, Malan's woman, to Grand Beach by boat. Pet, her hands poised over her keyboard, was a living picture of a don't-play-de-arse-with-me office admin. Caran's crew stood like a group sculpture in the far left corner of the room.

Malan had a shoulder against the door. As chance would have it, he'd dropped in to hand over Miss Stanislaus's Ruger and 'to see what go on' and nobody couldn stop him. Truth was, I'd messaged him about the meeting.

The Commissioner arrived dressed for the beach – in khaki shorts, sandals, a short-sleeved shirt and a small towel on his shoulder. He nodded at the room and took a chair beside Chilman.

'Start shootin', Digson!' Chilman said.

As always, I raised my brows Django-style. 'You sure?'

I received the usual sour-faced grin from him.

'Is all one case,' I said. 'Juba, Lazar Wilkinson, Jana Ray, the drugs factory, the two whitefellas and the boat. They all connected. We chasing after a single case and is all about a drugs boat that we can't find and we *got* to find.'

'What you have so far?' Chilman said.

'Five weeks ago, a black catamaran arrived at Beau Séjour late at night and unloaded a cargo of cocaine base which, from what Mibo told me, came from Venezuela. The aim was to refine the stuff in Camaho and then take it elsewhere. Between the boat arriving and the cocaine base getting processed, Lazar Wilkinson and Jana Ray got murdered – Lazar Wilkinson because, from what Mibo says, he was demanding a share based on the value of the cocaine, not a straight fee. Else, he threatened to report them to us. That threat, it seems to me, might've been the reason for killing him. Somebody Mibo referred to as the bossman had a problem with that. Little Eric talked about a 'Townman' with pale skin that he saw cussing Lazar Wilkinson. I believe that the Townman and the bossman are different names for the same person.

'I not detailing what I think lay behind the Jana Ray murder again, except to say that Miss Stanislaus and I worked out from his drawings that the boat had two broken propellers that need fixing or replacing. Mibo also confirmed that they had what he called a transmission problem. He said Shadowman told him, so he's clearly connected to Shadowman.

'I suspect the boat is still here, and if the boat is still here, the drivers still here too.

'In short, we looking for a boat packed with refined cocaine, somewhere on this island waiting for two propeller replacements.'

'How much engine it got?'

'Six.'

'Six! Digson, you sure?' The DS clearly didn't believe me. He raised a finger at Spiderface. 'That make sense to you?'

Spiderface looked startled. 'If Missa Digger say so, Sah.'

'Digger already say so,' Chilman grated. 'I want to know what you say.'

'I dunno, Sah. It don' make sense to me, Sah.' Spiderface passed me an apologetic look.

'Digson, is facts I want—'

'You want me to hand over the case to you, Sir?'

'Why you frettin now, eh?' Chilman raised a finger at me.

'Cuz *people* don' believe Missa Digger!' Miss Stanislaus addressed the window fretfully. 'And is all this not-believin been causing problem. Missa Digger, persevere, please.'

I persevered. 'What don't make no sense to me is the way lil Eric described the boat and where Mibo and Jana Ray say it will be heading.'

'Where's that?'

'Europe.'

'What puzzle you bout that?'

'Based on what I understand from Mibo and Eric, is a speedboat, with only a windshield to protect them from the weather. It can't make a five-thousand-mile transatlantic run, unless they have a rendezvous along the way with a ship or something capable of doing that distance.'

'So is a ship we lookin for!' Chilman said.

'So why people can't find it if is a ship?' The sneer was in Malan's voice.

'Is simple,' Chilman growled. 'They'll offload on a bigger boat further out.'

'Exact details not important right now,' Caran cut in gently. 'Digger, finish what you saying.'

'From Eric's description, the boat is one of them catamaran types designed for speed and stability – I spent half a night searching around on Google. From his description the boat got no cabin – in other words, no sleeping facilities, and,'

I dropped the report on my desk, 'even drug runners need to sleep. Venezuela to Camaho is five hundred miles – that makes sense. They could cover that distance during daylight in under a day with a go-fast boat. The next stop should be in a day also, or less, and that's definitely not Europe.'

'So Mibo and the lil boy lying!' Chilman said.

The Commissioner cleared his throat. 'If there is a boat and it involves international waters, we have an arrangement with the American Coast Guard. From what I heard they have helicopters. Some time ago – early last year, I think – I met with the Regional Drugs Monitor, one Mister Cunningham—'

'Nuh!'

That was Chilman.

'With all due respect, Edward, er, Mister Commissioner, I recalling right now the Dillon Case last year. Yankee coast guard catch the fella who was a national of Camaho. They disregard the fact that we forewarn them that the fella coming. They seize all the money and the drugs – and I got my suspicions what they done with it – and take all the credit for demselves. They never mention Camaho. All I saw was eight whitefellas on the cover of a Florida magazine posing as if dem is Tarzan' children who just grab some sweeties from the apes. We not no addition to American police. We not suckin on nobody nipple. And we not addressing the problem facing us. Is we, Camaho Police, that got to show drugs people that we kin stop them. Is we to show them that if they tangle with us, we tangle right back with their arse too. And we tangle hard!'

'How we s'pose to do that?' Malan wanted to know.

'You mean how you show them that you not only a man with woman – that's what you asking?'

'That was ah insult! Not no answer to my question,' Malan grated. 'Answer my question.'

'I apologise.' Chilman smiled without a hint of regret. 'The answer is, we use the assets that we born with. Before boats and guns, we had brains! We still have brains.'

The Commissioner shifted in his seat. 'There is an agreement between the islands and the Americans. We can't ignore it. The Minister of Justice will expect to know this time.' He threw me a deliberate look. 'It is also his business.'

'Nuh!' Chilman said again.

The Commissioner stood up. 'DS Chilman, can we have a word?'

They walked out to the middle of the concrete courtyard. No sharp gestures, no agitated lips, just two ole fellas quietly exchanging words.

'The MJ going to know,' Malan said.

'Who will tell him? You?' Pet said.

'Nuh. But he going to know.'

'I sure *people* going to tell im.' Miss Stanislaus did not even look at Malan.

Malan opened his palms. 'Why everybody shootin at me? What de hell y'all take me for!'

'You really don want to know,' Pet said.

Chilman walked back in. The Commissioner addressed us at the door. 'That's it then, folks. I think we've covered it. Like you see, I've only dropped in. I've been open to the advice of officers on the ground. And given the informality of the advice,' he gestured at his clothes, 'it's not going to be recorded.' He turned his gaze on Pet.

'Deleted,' Pet muttered without looking up.

Trickster, I thought. *He not going to no beach.* I couldn't help shaking my head at him, and I was sure the geezer threw me a wink.

'This is what I told DS Chilman,' he said. 'He is risking this unit again by insisting that you handle it yourself without the

306

resources available to the government. If it's a success, you'll have strengthened your hand and more than justified your usefulness. If it's not, well, let's hope it works. Mister Michael, can I have a small tête-à-tête with you?'

I walked out into the yard with him. 'Is Mister Digson, Sir. Nobody calls me Mister Michael. It sounds ugly.'

'You fret exactly like your sister, Lucia, Mister Michael. As far as I see, it's all guesswork.'

'Is all we have to go by, Sir.'

'Not a lot then.'

52

I swung through Dessie's gates, stopped the car and checked myself in the rear-view mirror. I'd chosen a dazzling white shirt – the two topmost buttons unhitched – which Dessie herself had selected. A pair of carefully pressed trousers.

Theirs was one of those old colonial houses, all wood with gables and awnings, a latticework veranda and folding doors. It was built for light and air with a sloping downhill lawn, shaded in places by hybrid mango, dwarf coconuts, damsons and red-plum trees.

Mrs Shona Manille met me on the step, her cotton-white hair swept up in a mound – the kind of middle-aged person you saw in glossy magazines.

'Michael?' she said. 'We met before. You're cuter than Dessie says. Can I offer you a drink?'

I stepped into a wide hall with polished wooden floors. A table laid out with a regiment of twinkling cutlery on either side of plates.

Raymond Manille, the father – a tall, spare man, brown like my father, the Commissioner. Grey-green eyes with not-quite-European hair that had probably been trained to a passable straightness by a lifetime of aggressive cajoling.

'Michael Digson?' He extended a hand as if I'd just entered a meeting. Unsettling eyes on my face, like he was examining every pore. 'Nice of you to come.'

Dessie came down the stairs, said a shy, 'Hi', and placed herself beside her mother. I was clearly on my own.

Raymond Manille gestured at a chair. I sat facing Dessie. She could barely look at me.

Mrs Manille fanned herself, deplored the weather and asked me about my work.

Raymond Manille enquired about my education, didn't wait for an answer but raised his head and said, 'Mildred?'

An aproned woman came out from the back with a food tray on wheels and served us soup.

Raymond Manille gestured at the table. 'Go ahead, Mister Digson.'

It was a test, of course. I was good at tests. I prepared for them, had in fact just rehearsed the basics on my way up in my car.

The order of the cutlery should mirror the order of the courses. Start at the outer edge. Move in towards the plate. Exceptions: you can put a butter knife on the bread plate and dessert cutlery above the plate but parallel to the table edge.

Nice food, though – pumpkin and sweet potatoes, from their own estate somewhere inland and whipped to an impossible smoothness. Ground provisions that tasted familiar but looked foreign as they were cut in decorative slices. Fish, boned and marinated. Salad that sat like a bouquet in a polished wooden bowl.

Mister Raymond asked me about my job again. 'Crime detection,' I said. 'I've been doing for two years.'

'Dessie said you specialised in England? Wasn't it quite involved?' Mrs Shona Manille brought her beautiful hands before her face, steepled her fingers in a prayer shape. Her chin dipped slightly, followed by a slow wink.

I laid my cutlery to rest, patted my lips with the napkin and offered Mister Raymond Manille a minor disquisition on the intricacies of forensic pathology, thanatology and the critical breakthroughs that forensic osteology afforded people in my humble profession.

'But you don't have a degree,' he said.

'That's true, Sir. Not yet. But I'm good at my job and I speak English as well as anybody on this island – if that's any sort of parameter to judge a person by.' I raised my head at him. 'If you don't mind my saying so, Sir. I came here for lunch?'

'Sorry,' he said. 'You're right. Dessima is my daughter. Maybe I'm a little protective.'

Mrs Manille steered us through the rest of the meal with a series of chirpy observations and exclamations about gardening in the tropics and climate change.

Through all of it, I felt Raymond Manille's eyes on me.

He invited me to follow him out into the front garden, pointed out the cattleya orchids and butterfly jasmines that took up so much of Shona's time.

'Digson – haven't heard the name before. Are you related to the Dobsons, the ones on Morne Bijoux? Dessie told you she was married to Luther Caine who used to manage Camaho Co-op? He's got a good business fixing boats now. We all regret it didn't work out.'

'And by that you mean he was the kinda fella who nearly killed her twice, right? Sorry, Sir, I been listening to you trying to make me feel as if I chasing after your daughter and your money. I don't know what impression Dessie gave you, but I got my own place and I know where I'm heading. If Dessie can't find the guts to make her own decisions, then putting me through this is a waste of my time and yours because I'm not going to be with any woman whose parents want to run my life and hers. I thankful for the invitation. But I decide I have to go.'

Shona Manille intercepted me by my car. 'Mister Digson, he's like that with everybody. With Luther too, first time.'

'Then he got to learn to improve his manners, not so? Because I not taking that from him. As for family name, last time I checked, we all arrived here on a boat, and that trip wasn't first class.'

I rounded on Dessie who'd come out after me. 'And what happened to you at the table? Cat eat your tongue? You dunno how to stand up for your man?'

Mrs Manille excused herself and floated into the house. She was in there for a while. Then she sang out Dessie's name.

'Wait a minute, Digger. Please?'

They were in there for a while. Dessie came out, a small indecipherable smile on her lips. 'He's going out in a minute. Golf course. Mom asks you to stay.'

Raymond Manille walked out in shorts, polo shirt and sandals. He aimed his keys at his Hyundai. The vehicle made a startled sound. He threw me a tight smile, dropped himself in his seat and rolled off.

'He told Mom he doesn't think he likes you but you have balls.' She rolled her eyes. 'I could've told him that. All he had to do was ask me.'

'You could've, but you didn't,' I said. 'Dessie, I got to go. I need to meet somebody.'

Lunch with Raymond Manille, the conversation between us, brought my father, the Commissioner, to mind: my history with him, his 'outside' child, or rather the absence of a history.

The rumour had reached him that Dessie and I

were 'meeting'. And again the same old story from the Commissioner: if they knew I was his son, it would help.

'Help with what?' I had asked when he called. 'I carry the name of the woman who catch her arse to bring me up. No late-hour endorsement going to change that. They take me as I am, or to hell with them.'

After leaving Dessie's place, I phoned Miss Blackwood. Would she meet me for a drink? She was hesitant about the venue I suggested.

'Too low class for you?' I said.

'Is not where I normally drink or eat. How about Saint Eloi – near my area? This evening?'

We went north to Saint Eloi, a small restaurant that looked straight out to Salt Point and the international airport. We were surrounded by Camaho's middle-aged, middle-class women – silver-permed with pleasant placeless accents. We talked over a plate of roasted aubergines and courgettes, frittered bananas and breadfruit.

'You cook?' she asked.

'People like my cooking.'

'And who's people?'

'The ones I cook for. How's the golf course?'

'I'm back in my place – I decided I'm not running from nobody. How's the investigation going?'

'Shadowman killed Jana Ray. I went after him once. He got away. He won't get away next time.'

'You don't look like that kind of policeman.'

'How's a policeman s'posed to look?'

She eased back in her chair. 'I would kill him myself if I had the chance.' Miss Blackwood adjusted her napkin on her lap. 'I was married ten years. My husband walked off one Sunday. Last thing he told me was, I was cold. I used to overhear my staff saying the same thing. It was true. And then Jana Ray turned up in my veranda, offering to sell me marijuana oil. It was a cure for everything, he said. I told him I wasn't sick and I wasn't planning to get sick. And then he said "please" and I realised how desperate he was. He kept on coming and then, yunno, love happen. With him—'

'You wasn cold, I know. Something I want you to do for me, Miss Blackwood. You got friends in the other banks?'

'Depends on the bank.'

'Camaho Co-op? Not the manager. I thinking somebody at your level.'

'Uh-huh?' She'd gone wary, almost suspicious.

'Is connected to Jana Ray's death. You know Dora Wilkinson – Lazar Wilkinson's mother. Twenty-two thousand dollars was put into her account a coupla weeks ago. I want to confirm where it came from. I got another coupla accounts I want to get at.' I tore a leaf from my notepad, wrote the names and pushed it towards her. 'You know anybody in there who can do that for you, apart from the manager?'

'You can't go direct?' She looked worried.

'I already went direct.'

'And?'

'I asking you to do it for me. Please! If not for me, then for Jana Ray. You want another drink?'

She nodded and slipped the note in her purse.

Around noon the next day, a neatly dressed young woman tapped on the office door and asked for Mister Michael Digson. I remembered the face – one of the tellers at Miss Blackwood's bank. She handed me a sealed envelope, turned promptly on her heels and walked back to the road.

Three typewritten lines:

```
Payment by LC Enterprise
(Acc. no 105236) $22000.00
To payee, D. Wilkinson.
```

I messaged Blackwood. *Recvd thnx. Who manages Acc?*
An hour later she responded: *Manager.*

53

There were two boat-fixing businesses on the island. Blue Dolphin was owned by a whitefella in Easterhall. A pleasant Camaho voice informed me that Blue Dolphin was closed for the time being because, two months ago, Missa Dudley's heart attacked him and he was still in England receiving treatment. The other was LC Enterprise, owned and run by Luther Caine.

The social calendar of Camaho's middle class had been fixed since before the English declared the island profitless and abandoned it: business on weekdays, cocktail parties on Fridays, tennis or golf on Saturdays, buffet on Sundays with the occasional dip in the sea in-between.

I'd been picking at an idea from the time I returned from questioning Mibo on Kara Island. Besides, it was Friday, I was home alone but had no desire to see Dessie anytime soon. In fact, I was more upset with her than I was with her father.

I phoned Miss Stanislaus. 'You want to be my woman for the weekend?'

'Nuh.'

'Only for tonight, then.'

'Missa Digger! What got into you?'

'I serious. Cocktail party. Residence of Luther Caine. Former manager of Camaho Co-op bank. I want you to wear me on your arm this evening.'

I crossed my legs, laid back and waited through her silence.

'Missa Digger, I not sure I up for that.'

'Okay,' I said, 'I'll take somebody else with me. I was offering you first choice. That's all.'

I rang off, checked my watch. Five minutes later, the handset buzzed. I let it vibrate a couple of times, then picked up. 'Oh, Miss Stanislaus! Long time no speak. How you?'

'Missa Digger, you too stupid! Is cocktail party you say?'

'Yes.'

'So, I got to dress-up like how cocktail-people dress?'

'I don't mind a lil extra touch from you.'

'You not goin be wearin dat ugly belt ov yours? Else I not coming.'

'So that's a "yes"?'

'The belt, Missa Digger.'

'I'll leave the belt. You coming?'

'Uh-huh.'

I left home at 6.30, waited seven minutes at Miss Stanislaus's gate before she appeared.

She'd pulled up her hair in a mound above her head, exposing a forehead and face I had never seen that way before. A gown – dark blue with silver trimmings – flowed from rounded, full-fleshed shoulders. Silver shoes.

'That you?' I said. 'Where's Daphne?'

'She with Miss Iona.' Miss Stanislaus eased into the car.

'What's the perfume?'

'Is my bizness, Missa Digger.'

'Never heard that brand name before. But it's nice all the same – real nice!'

She gave me a quick once-over. 'You awright too. In fact, a lil more dan awright. Missa Digger, shall we persevere?'

'Persevere we shall, Miss Stanislaus. But I, DC Digson, taking my time persevering tonight.'

Luther Caine's house roosted on the summit of Lavender Hill, which overlooked San Andrews. Late Friday evening, the ocean lay still and wide in the near distance like a giant amber lake. Flamboyant trees dotted the lawn around the house, their branches spread like over-sized umbrellas, a carpet of deep red petals bloodying the lawn. A row of stunted palms crested the sweeping downhill flow of Julie and Ceylon mango trees. And I thought to myself if skiing lessons could pay for all this, I was definitely in the wrong job.

We walked into women's laughter, the muted roar of men in chesty conversation, the smell of roasted meat, the prattle and clink of silverware and cutlery.

In the far corner of the big living room, I spotted Passiflores Arielle, Luther Caine's personal assistant when he used to manage the bank. Passiflores – a darker-skinned version of Dessie – was in conversation with a bevy of light-skinned girls, her lovely arms making delicate shapes in front of her. She spotted me and froze, recovered almost instantly, except now, those night-dark eyes kept switching in my direction. Other heads turned with what looked like alarmed curiosity.

I dropped an arm across Miss Stanislaus's shoulders, her skin cool as spring water under my hand. We stood at the doorway for a while, taking in the high ceiling, the thick beige curtains running down the sides of tall glass windows.

Somebody had to make the first move. Luther Caine did. Fair-skinned, grey-green eyes, all teeth – a Caucasoid Negro. Light-blue linen jacket. Matching raw silk trousers holding their own against the movements of his big body. He took Miss Stanislaus's hand and bowed and I noticed the welts at his wrist were fading but still there. Miss Stanislaus curtsied slightly, held Luther's gaze and radiated.

'Mister Digson,' he said. 'Who's the belle?'

317

'My partner.' I smiled at Miss Stanislaus, deepened my voice Schwarzenegger-style. 'Let's hope it stays that way.'

That made him laugh – a short, sharp burst – then his face resettled and he was all cool-eyed again. 'You're welcome, of course, but you don't mind me asking who—'

'Invited us?' I smiled. 'Nobody. I thought you wouldn't mind, seeing as so much of my business tied up with yours these days. Just curious, that's all.' I gestured at the opulence around me. 'Fixing boats looks like good business.'

'We manage.'

'We?'

I saw the shadow of irritation on his face, felt Miss Stanislaus shift beside me. 'You good with outboard engines, not so?'

'I wouldn't advertise it if I couldn't do it. That would be—'

'Criminal, I know,' I cut in. 'Fast engines too?' I narrowed my eyes at him. Something about Luther Caine seemed to change – a reddening of the skin just above the collar, a sudden stiffness. I'd tried to visualise that temper that Dessie had spoken so much about in the days when she stole away from this house to meet me in whatever secret corner of the island we could find. There was never sex between us then. It wasn't about that at all – just a woman seeking some relief from the words of a man – this man, determined to make her believe she was no good.

Miss Stanislaus had gone very still, her face suffused in a dreamy smile, eyes partly veiled by her lashes. She was following the movements of Luther's hands, his face – the rest of him. Reading the fella.

'You didn't answer me, Luther.'

'Sorry – it's Digger, isn't it?'

'You know my name, Luther. By heart! We been talking about fast boats,' I said. 'Is some maths I been trying to work out, yunno – how many engines I going need to get from Venezuela to Camaho in a day. You figure six will do?'

I felt Miss Stanislaus's stiffened finger in the small of my back. I put on my best pretend-English. 'Of course, bossman, if you'd rather we, uh, make ourselves scarce . . . '

His eyes glazed over for a moment. Then, 'No-no-no. You're welcome, honestly. Grab a drink. I'm afraid we've already eaten.'

'A drink will do, thank you. A shandy perhaps?'

'And for the lady?'

Miss Stanislaus bent a wrist. 'Mango juice, think you.'

Luther Caine's face relaxed in what looked like a real smile. 'Would passion fruit suffice, Miss . . . uhm?'

'K. Stanislaus. Passion fruit awright, think you.'

'Scuse me, then. Got to mix a bit. Stay as long as you wish.'

'We will,' I said.

A bow-tied youth came over with the drinks.

'You got a toilet, youngfella?' Miss Stanislaus handed me her glass. She walked across the room leaving in her wake a ripple of cocked, assessing female heads, and a choreography of underhand male gazes.

'And who are you?' a voice asked.

I swung round to face a white gown, a row of smoker's teeth and a tall slim glass, encircled by blood-red nails and a tired-looking, jowly face.

'Michael Digson,' I said.

'Can't be,' she said. 'Didn't he die from something?' She held out a hand. 'Merna, Luther's sister. Eldest. You work for him?'

'No, why?'

'Well,' she waved a tipsy arm at the room, 'all the new faces I meet these days work for him. Quite distasteful, some of them, if I may say so.'

319

'Sorry to lower the tone.'

'Not you. Not at all, Mister Michael,' she burped, 'Jackson.'

'Digson.'

I was barely hearing Merna. My eyes had caught the back of a woman, the cropped black hair, slipping through one of the side doors, her movement so fluid she looked like an apparition. It was the suddenness with which she'd risen that caught my attention. My mind switched to Malan. I wondered where he was – and if he knew his woman was here.

I was tempted to go after her but thought better of it. I turned back to Merna.

'Yor! If Luther employs more like you, my luck might improve – who knows.' She laughed out loud. A few heads turned.

'You said "distasteful",' I said. 'They all look fine to me.'

'Not theeem.' She flopped a wrist, licked the spilled drink off her hand. 'Those ... are ... fuuriends. Our fuuriends. I meant the workmen.' She fanned her face with a limp wrist. 'Duhffrent. Not like ... '

She leaned back, batting her lashes as if she wanted to get a clearer view of my face. 'Theyyy're like, like—' She stopped abruptly.

Luther Caine was at her side, smiling with his mouth. 'Come on, Merns, the gentleman's with someone. Let's get some fresh air. Sorry, Digger.' He steered her towards the veranda at the back, the tendons of his hand taut with the grip on his sister's arm.

Miss Stanislaus returned, edged up close to me. She retrieved her glass from my hand and brought it to her mouth; kept the rim against her lips. 'Yuh girlfriend – Miss Dressy, she here?' She looked around at the crowd.

'She's not, Miss Stanislaus.'

'You sure?'

320

'Definitely – why you ask?'

'Jus been wonderin.' She lifted her chin at the crowd again. 'Missa Digger, what you bring me here for?'

I took her hand. 'I might need your memory. Come, let's take some breeze.' I led Miss Stanislaus to the back of the house. There were people out there on easy chairs with bottles on small tables and glasses in their hands. A swimming pool, blue like a white man's eye, glittered under a row of daylight lamps. A concrete road, with cars parked on either side, wound up the hill from Temple Valley to a clearing under a giant poinsettia on my left. A leisure boat – the type used for skiing – sat dry-docked on a trailer, an aluminium ladder against its side. On the far right, under an open shed, a large grey sheet of canvas partly covered with what looked like hunks of rusted machinery. An assortment of ropes and pulleys.

'Miss Stanislaus, you think you could enjoy this life?'

'Yes, Missa Digger, but with different people.' Miss Stanislaus raised her face at the sky. 'So much light up here, Missa Digger, you could hardly see the moon. You sure you didn come here to show off?'

'I ask you to trust me, so why you harassing me?'

I stepped off the concrete with her in a slow stroll towards the swimming pool. Footsteps behind us. Miss Stanislaus nudged me with an elbow.

Luther Caine approached with Passiflores at his side.

The woman was all smiles. 'I didn't get a chance to welcome you, Mister Digson. Is this your—'

'Partner,' I said.

Passiflores offered Miss Stanislaus her hand, casting a quick shy glance at her face. 'Lovely,' she said.

'You too,' Miss Stanislaus replied. 'How you know Mistuh, uh, Digson?'

321

'He used to be a client at the bank. And you – you . . . ?'

'We togedder.' Miss Stanislaus sipped her juice.

The conversation dried up. Passiflores's eyes kept wandering to Luther's face. He'd stuffed his hands down his pockets, preoccupied it seemed with the dim, jagged rise of the Grand Etang mountains ahead of us.

'We leavin now,' Miss Stanislaus said and squeezed my arm very hard. She rested her glass on the nearby table, took mine from me and did the same. 'Fanks for invitin us.'

I waved a leisurely goodbye and allowed her to drag me out of the house.

We were beside the car when she cocked her head at me. 'What you went up there for, Missa Digger? That man don like you and you don like him. Why you want to go to the house of a fella who' wife you got business with?'

'Dessie tell me they divorced, Miss Stanislaus.'

'Divorce is a piece o paper, Missa Digger. You don't see the kinda man he is? He'll never give up what he think belong to him. He dangerous. Behind your back he watchin you like if he want to rip the flesh off your face.'

'Let him try, I wish he try . . . '

'You talkin like a man, Missa Digger.'

'I *am* a man! What the hell you expect?'

'Right now I tryin to put some sense inside your head. So don gimme no stupid man-talk. That's why you take me up there with you? To show you kin come to his place wiv—'

'Nice woman? Real woman? Like you? No!' I looked her in the eyes. 'I been running through the case in my head. I know now that it was from Luther Caine's account that the money to Dora Wilkinson came. Then it hit me that all this is about boats – fast boats with big engines. Boats that need fixing and maintaining sometimes. Only two people on the island deal in them kinda boats – a whitefella in Easterhall who got a charter and ski business, and Luther Caine who run his boat-fixing business from his house. I went to his house to check it out.'

She fell quiet for a long while, her eyes never leaving my face. 'And what you find?'

'A very jumpy fella, especially when me'n'you went to the back of his house, and when I call him "bossman".'

She nodded. 'That's all you see?'

I shrugged. 'Nuh!'

She looked at me intently. 'What else you see?'

'I see a woman I didn expect to be there, and that start me thinking—'

'It didn look as if you see her, Missa Digger. And you awright wiv that?'

'You not making sense, Miss Stanislaus—'

'You wuz a different pusson with Missa Loofer Came,' she said. 'You walk'n'talk like them, you even look like dem when you stannup mongst them.'

'I grow up suckin salt same like you.'

'Mebbe is in your blood, then?'

'Miss Stanislaus! Why you so flippin hard on me tonight? I done you something?'

She looked away. 'Sorry, Missa Digger, I s'pose I upsettin you becuz I upset too.'

'What I done to upset you?'

'You didn. I not talkin about it no more.'

On the way home, I left her with her thoughts.

At her little gate, my elbows on the steering wheel, I glanced at her. 'Miss Stanislaus, 'spite of everything, I enjoy tonight.'

She dabbed at her face with a tissue, her features softly contoured by the blue glow from the dashboard clock. The road ahead was pale grey and glistening under a bright last-quarter moon.

'Missa Digger, I fink is better for me and you if you go home right now, and I go inside my house.'

'Sure,' I said.

I leaned across to open her door. I didn't know why I did that. I'd never done it before – some impulse perhaps to fill my head with her fragrance that had been intriguing me all night.

I was straightening up when something struck the car. The vehicle convulsed, and it felt as if the night exploded in my head. Miss Stanislaus flung up her arms to shield her face. I lurched backward, my shoulder blades grinding against the edge of the backrest. I felt the sting of glass against my neck and arm. The windscreen had bellied inward.

I threw my weight against Miss Stanislaus.

'Stay low! Run!' I shouted.

I reached out, grabbing at her bag and tugging. Miss Stanislaus shrugged it off her shoulder, lurched forward and was up and running, her body bent almost double.

A thunderclap rocked the vehicle and this time the windscreen gave way. Another crash, followed by the hissing protest of what must have been the busted radiator.

Crouched low, I threw myself out of the vehicle, hit the asphalt and sprang to my feet. Then I launched myself forward. I counted five strides, scooped the Ruger from Miss Stanislaus's bag and spun around to face Shadowman about ten yards ahead of me, a hefty stone in his hand. A long sack hung from his shoulder almost to his knee. He did not throw the stone but rolled it along the road towards me and of course I moved to dodge it. It was then I heard Miss Stanislaus's voice from somewhere behind me, cutting through the dark. 'He got a fishgun, Missa Digger.'

Shadowman swung the bag in front of him and with a swift shrug of his shoulder it dropped at his feet. He'd already armed the weapon when I shot him.

He staggered back. I shot him again, watched him do the animated dance of death before he hit the road and stayed there.

And then there came the quiet, disturbed only by the hiss and click of my wrecked car, the screech of an owl somewhere in the hills above us, and the very faint chuckle of seagulls over the waters of Kalivini Island.

Miss Stanislaus appeared beside me. She rested a hand in the small of my back. 'First time?' she said.

I nodded.

'Is not a nice feelin'.' She prised the weapon from my hand. 'You got your phone?'

Miss Stanislaus stepped away and picked up her bag from where I'd dropped it on the road. She took out her phone and dialled Recovery. 'Hulloo, Miss K. Stanislaus here. Criminal man just get shoot down. Kin we have a dead-body bag, please?'

I glanced at my flattened car. 'I going be needing a vehicle,' I told her. 'Mine gone through.'

Miss Stanislaus repeated my words, gave our coordinates and cut off.

She pointed at something on the grass verge – my phone. I retrieved it and sat by the roadside with my shoulder against hers. She kept her eyes on her feet. I gazed at the fallen man, my mind reeling back to Miss Stanislaus taking down Juba. I thought of the readiness with which Malan would point his Sig Sauer at a man and pull the trigger. I wondered if I'd ever get used to it and was terrified by the thought.

Miss Stanislaus gestured at the dead man. 'Missa Digger, I ask you this before and you never answer me. You an' me – you think we wicked?'

'S'not what I been thinking, Miss Stanislaus.'

'Is de same answer you give me last time.'

325

I glanced at my watch, my ears tuned to the night for the sound of engines.

'I want to walk,' she said, turning up her head at the moon.

She stepped onto the road, lifting each heel in turn to slip on her shoes.

'Where you going?' I said.

'Anywhere,' she said.

I gestured at the shadow on the road. 'When Recovery get here, I come with you.'

'Nuh!' she said.

I listened to the click of her heels on the road until it faded into the night.

I did not go after Miss Stanislaus. A woman walking on her own in the small hours of a moonlit night in Camaho might prompt a bad-minded fella to approach her with his forwardness. But once he got that look from her, he would change his mind. And if he didn't – well – good luck to him.

54

I parked the Department's vehicle on the grass verge of the public road and walked up the concrete driveway to my house. I stood at my door not wanting to go in. I dropped myself on the step and watched the morning light above the Mardi Gras mountains nibble away at the darkness until the shapes of houses and trees emerged out of the foreday gloom.

My mind turned to Dessie, her breath on my face, her love-sighs, my mouth never having enough of her. And it came to me that sometimes love is not enough. There are other things – awful things – that could bind one person to another.

My phone buzzed. I took the call.

'Missa Digger.'

'Miss Stanislaus! You been walking all this time?'

'Eh-heh.'

I listened to the tapping of her heels. 'You walking on concrete?'

'Eh-heh. Missa Digger, we got to talk.'

'Where you now? I come and pick you up.'

The tapping of her heels stopped. I heard her draw breath. 'Not nerecerry, Missa Digger.'

She cut off the phone and for a moment I had the odd sensation of still hearing her. I narrowed my eyes at my concrete drive. Through the stripped leaves of the banana plants that overhung the path, I glimpsed her shifting figure. I stood up and unlocked my door.

Miss Stanislaus halted at the foot of my step and raised her face at me, her shoulders heaving slightly with the effort of the climb.

I raised my eyes towards the Mardi Gras mountains, the sky above them already lightening with the first brushstrokes of morning.

'Come inside, Miss Stanislaus.'

She stepped in after me. I switched on the light, glanced down at her and saw the tiredness in her face and the numbness in her eyes.

'How far you walk?' I said.

She shrugged.

'You decide to walk around the island to get to my place? Don't make no sense.'

'Missa Digger.'

'It could wait till later? You look half-dead, and me, I could hardly stand up. My bedroom is yours for the time being. No charge. I'll take my chances out here.' I swung my arm at the sofa. I kicked off my shoes dropped myself on the cushions.

Somewhere between semi-consciousness and sleep, I heard the shower running then the hefty thuk of my bedroom door. I remembered – before dropping off – sketching the outlines of my report in my head.

I slept through most of the day, woke up to the fuss of the neighbours' chickens settling down to roost. The bang of buckets and the crackle of burning firewood. Already, there came the chittering of the bats preparing for a moonlit night of marauding.

When I raised myself off the sofa, Miss Stanislaus was at

my kitchen table. She'd perched a plate on each of two red bowls. A pair of cups sat on saucers beside them.

The woman looked bright and fresh and alert. Her clothing sat on her as if they had been freshly ironed.

She must have read my mind. 'Missa Digger, I wash all my clothes and dry them.' Miss Stanislaus stood up as if to show me, then levelled those eyes at me. 'You going to have a bath, not so?'

By the time I'd showered and dressed, and returned to the kitchen, she'd boiled sweet potatoes, pum–pum yams and half-ripe plantains, dropped a cocoa stick in a pot of boiling water and flavoured it with cinnamon. She'd raided my tomato plants outside for ripe fruit, diced and peppered them, made finely soused saltfish, stirred them in, and blessed the whole damn thing with coconut oil.

It reminded me of my grandmother's cooking. And for the memory and the sensation, I felt a rush of warmth towards her.

We ate in silence. I observed the thoughtfulness with which Miss Stanislaus spooned the food and brought it to her mouth – the delicacy with which she held the instrument. A foolish person would think that butter would not melt in this lovely woman's mouth.

A small smile creased her lips. 'Missa Digger, why you lookin at me like dat?'

She was dangling the spoon between thumb and index, her chin raised at the ceiling. 'You – you think killin criminal people is wickedness? Not so?'

I shook my head. 'Nuh.'

Now she was looking at me, unblinking. 'What you thinkin?'

I stood up. Her eyes followed my hands as I cleared the table.

'I thinking that I know why y'was so upset with me after we left Luther Caine' place, and why you didn't want to tell me.'

'I come here for one thing, Missa Digger – to find out if you see me different after what I done to Juba. Dat – dat matter to me. A lot.'

'Juba happened weeks ago, why you asking now?'

'Becuz of tonight. I see de way it make you sick. Like you wuz hatin yourself.'

'Miss Stanislaus, you save my life and yours that time. I save yours and mine tonight.'

'That's not what I asking.'

'Lemme finish my words, Miss Stanislaus. What I saying is, it ain't got no Digger or Miss Stanislaus in those circumstances. We not two people: we one.'

She shook her head. 'I'z my own pusson. I always been my own pusson.'

'No, you not. In this job, we not.'

She shook her head again.

I sat back, fizzing with irritation. 'Is so,' I said. 'Nuffing you say kin change that.'

I saw the change come over her, the deadening in her face, then the sudden flaring of her eyes. I followed the swing of her arm, angled my head so that her open palm glanced off my jaw.

'Missa Digger, O God, I – I—' Miss Stanislaus leaned towards me, the offending hand outstretched. I eased back, lifted a finger at the picture on the wall. 'Apart from my granny, you the only pusson to ever get away with that. You ready to go home?'

'You drivin me away?'

'You ready?'

*

330

We drove through Old Hope under a cool white moon, past little roadside shops spilling fluorescent light onto the road. Occasionally, one of the young men perched on a crate outside the door shouted my name or waved. I tapped my horn and drove on.

'You let me hit you,' she said. The woman was pouting with accusation.

'Is what a child would say, Miss Stanislaus. Blame the victim.'

'I know how quick you move, you could've stop me.'

'That's why you take the chance?'

She tapped her bag. 'So why you let me hit you?'

'I shouldn've said what I said.'

I pulled over at her gate.

Her house stood in darkness behind its tall hibiscus fence. Ahead of us, the road gleamed bare and empty. No sign of my wrecked car, or last night's confrontation with Shadowman – apart from the boulders by the roadside.

I angled my chin at her house. 'You goin be alright on your own in there?'

'You goin be awright in yours?' She turned to look at me. 'Missa Digger, h'was waiting for us.'

'I know,' I said. 'Shadowman was following instructions.'

'You work it out?'

'I'll tell you when I sure. Not long from now.'

She slid out of the car, closed the door and poked her head through the rolled-down window. I kept my head straight. Picked up her agitation in her breathing.

'Missa Digger, I want you to know is not a habit.'

'What's not a habit?'

'I never hit a fella before for upsettin me. You believe me?'

'Yes, Miss Stanislaus – all you do is shoot them.'

'Missa Digger, I serious.'

'Me too.'

'And I decide I never goin strike you again. No matter the provocation.'

'That's very kind of you. Thanks.'

'G'night, Missa Digger.'

'G'night, Miss Stanislaus.'

55

My watch said 2.14am – the kind of hour that Dessie and I
escaped to some secluded beach where we sat in the car facing
the ocean, made love or I listened to her talk about the future
she imagined for both of us.

Tonight I would not sleep so I mixed myself an eye-opener
cocktail because it felt right: egg yolk, crème de noyaux,
aniseed-flavoured alcohol, a splash of Martiniquan rhum
agricole. Ice. Stir.

Stirred.

Stirred up.

Raging.

Dessie!

I felt as if a stone had lodged in my throat. In one of the
houses down the hill someone was running their speakers at
full blast, the brassy discordance gnawing at my nerves. I took
a few breaths, returned to the kitchen and sat at the worktop
with the drink, a notepad and pencil in my hand. I sat back
a while and stilled my hands.

I made notes, drew diagrams, reviewed the soundscape of the
party on Lavender Hill the night before, my brief time in Luther
Caine's house with Miss Stanislaus, the magic of the woman's
presence in that cocktail party of chattering people. Sarona.

I felt hollowed-out and feverish when I finished the drink,
picked up my phone and texted Dessie.

1 2 c u.

She pinged me back promptly. *Me 2. U cum? :)*

Yh.

I picked her up at the high gates of her parents' house. She'd chosen a flimsy dress of some fabric that shivered at the slightest twitch of her limbs.

'New place,' I said. 'Up north.'

'Don't care.' She shrugged and leaned into me, dropped a hand on my lap and kept it there.

We drove through Temple Valley, swung onto the Centre Main, cruised past sleeping villages, on lightless solitary roads hunched over by ancient forest trees. Dessie and I could have been the only humans on earth, cocooned by the night outside and the steady hum of the car.

I turned into the road that would take us to the ocean – and already I could hear its thunder against the precipice ahead. 'Dessie, I want to talk about the case we chasing now,' I said. 'You in a mood for that?'

She stirred as if I'd roused her from sleep.

'I ever tell you about the rape riots and what happen to my mother?'

'A thousand times, Digger. You not going to talk about that now?'

'The man that rape the schoolgirl, that make my mother and a whole heap of other women riot, that led to policemen shooting her up so bad – that man who was Justice Minister before the present fool took over. He was your husband's father.'

'He's not my husband any more.'

I braked the car at the top of the rise in the face of a shuddering headwind. Directly ahead, past the narrow headland, the metallic glint of breakers, and above it all, a weak moon.

'Lemme put it another way, then. I want to know what Luther Caine got on you that you can't break away from him.'

She took her hand off my lap. 'Jesus Christ, Digger. You got no reason to be jealous.'

'Jealous! That's not the word, Dessie. A couple of nights ago, a man came out of the night to kill me and Miss Stanislaus. He almost succeeded. He knew exactly where to find us and when. That was directly after we came from your husband's party. Now, only two people knew I was going to that party – Miss Stanislaus and me. So, that makes me paranoid. Y'was up there in Luther's house that night, not so? Miss Stanislaus knew it. She didn't tell me how she knew, but she asked me if I invited you. She didn't look too pleased. Kept doing that nose-pointing thing she does. She asked me twice and I told her, no way, you weren't up there.

'It started me thinking back, Dessie. Dora Wilkinson's account. I asked you where she got all that money from, you said it was a deposit not an electronic transfer. In other words, you lied. I know now that it was an electronic transfer and I happen to know you still manage his money.'

I pressed my head against the headrest and closed my eyes. 'Okay, so you didn't want me to know that you still tied up so tight to the fella after all the hate you say you hate him. And you know my next move would've been to find out who the transfer came from.' I turned to look at her in the face. 'Luther ever told you where the money comes from?'

Dessie was quiet for a long while. Out there, with the car facing the ocean, and the wind pushing against the vehicle, it felt as if we'd be lifted any moment and deposited into the water.

'Dessie, I happen to know that a go-fast boat full of drugs will be leaving this island some time soon. We can't find it here on Camaho but we know it's here. We been looking for the two fellas we believe are the drivers and we can't find them either. I convinced now that Luther Caine knows all about that boat – at least! I suspect that he been asked to fix a couple of engines – at least! There would've been money transactions between him and the people concerned. If you don't gimme the information I ask for, I'll get it still, but I want it from you.'

I thought she was going to tell me she didn't know what I was talking about. Instead I saw the old fear there – the one that made her look small and pinched and timid when, in the early days, she spoke of what Luther Caine would do to her if he ever found her sitting in a car with me. I remembered it, and resented it.

She was muttering to herself, her hands folding and unfolding around each other. 'He'll kill me, Digger; you don't know Luther. He will.'

'He can't! Believe! What you know about the boat?'

'End of next week – I overheard – it's all – Digger . . .'

'That's when the boat leave?'

She shook her head. 'It's when they make the last payment. That's all I heard. That's—'

'Who's they?'

I switched on the roof light, reached for her hand, lifted her chin so she could look me in the eyes. 'Dessima Caine, in all the months we been intimate, I ever deceive you? Is not the fuckin truth I always tell you all the time – regardless of whether you like it or not? Three people dead already becuz ov all this, including Jana Ray – the lil fella you met and liked so much. So why you trying to protect your husband?'

'Digger, Luther's got all my savings tied up in his business. I was married to him and I trusted him. I was stupid. And I need my money because I want my independence. He won't give it back unless I—' She drew breath.

I dropped my arm across her shoulders, sat in silence while she pulled herself together. She slid wet, wide eyes at me. 'The payments usually come in from Venezuela.'

'How often?'

'Months in-between. The last one was, erm, couple of weeks ago.'

'No other payments?'

'One more transaction and that's it, I think. Digger – I—'

'End of next week, you say?'

She nodded.

'What day?'

'Dunno.'

'And the boat, Dessie; where they hiding it?'

She shook her head. 'It's only the money I know about – no boat. Digger, I want you to believe me.'

'Okay,' I said. 'Dessie, this is what I need from you. Please.'

She nodded.

'The last payment – you sure it will be the last payment?'

She nodded again.

'As soon as that money reaches Luther Caine's account, I want you to message me. Please!'

On the way back she leaned away from me, her head against the door of the car. When I pulled up at Dessie's gates, she remained in the car, her eyes searching my face. 'You hating me now, not so?'

'I can't do that, Dessie. Call me stupid if you want. Is just that you don't always have a solid relationship with the truth and right now that's putting me on shaky ground. You do what you have to do to protect yourself and mebbe to hold onto what you got or value – that makes a certain kinda sense. I dunno. Sometimes I ride with it.' I turned to look at her. 'Like you telling me you divorced when you not. You don fink I'd know that? Is easy! All I got to do is check the

337

registry.' I smiled at her. 'And yunno, I start making meself believe it too?'

I sat back and took her hand. 'Now, tell me about Sarona.'

'What makes you think I know anything about that woman?' She cocked her chin at me. She'd gone sour-faced, aggressive.

'I thought I glimpsed her up at Luther's cocktail party. Y'was up there too. It crossed my mind you know her well enough. In fact, you told me you know her on Dog Island – remember when Malan shot that goat? I wasn't listening at the time but you told me.'

'I didn't—'

'"I can't like her. I never liked—" I don't think you finished the sentence or p'raps I didn't hear the rest of it. Was an odd way to talk about somebody you meet for the first time, not so? *I never liked* . . . What you never liked about Sarona, Dessie?'

'Well, it's true. I don't like her.'

'What she got with Luther?'

'They've been off and on for a couple of years. He's even gone to Venezuela to see her.' Dessie sounded bitter. 'She sleeps with him.'

'S'far as I know, Sarona is with Malan Greaves,' I said.

Dessie twisted her mouth. 'He *thinks*.'

'Sarona shouldn't mess with Malan. He's a dangerous fella, even to himself.'

Dessie soured her face again, her voice gone sibilant with the venom. 'Sarona my arse! Her name's Sandra Fernandez. She's Luther's woman and she's been with him while we married.'

'How you know she sleeps with him?'

'I'm a woman, Digger. I know these things.' She rested bright unblinking eyes on my face. 'I think you should tell your friend.'

I shook my head. 'Nuh. But he'll find out. For sure.'

'And then?'

'Your husband will have another man who got it in for him.'

Back home, I threw myself on my sofa, waited through DS Chilman's sputtering outrage.

'Digson, what time-a-morning you think this is?'

'Five past four, Sir, a.m.!'

'You better have a blaastid good reason.'

'I have. I want you to have Luther Caine arrested. I requesting a raid of his premises today. I got good reasons to believe he's connected with the boat we after and may still have the engines we been talking about. And I not ruling out the murder of Lazar Wilkinson.'

'You got the evidence?'

'That's the point of the raid, Sir.'

'Let's talk later, Digson. I will have to make a call.'

'Call who?'

'Your father,' he said.

'The Commissioner? I could ask for what reason? With due respect, Sir, we handle this matter same like we handle every other criminal matter in Camaho.'

'That's not the point, Digson.'

'I taking Luther Caine down. After that, y'all kin fire me if y'all want.'

'I'll get y'arse fired right now, Digson! You want to bet me?'

'Regardless, Sir. I going to finish this.' I put down the phone.

Chilman called back. 'Digson, where your brain gone? You stop using it? You with the man wife. Now you want to arrest him.'

'What's that got to do with it?'

'You even went to the fella house with your other woman to harass him.'

339

'Jeezas Christ, Sir!'

'Digson, if you go after Luther Caine today, or any time, and you don't have the evidence, a good defence lawyer will tear y'arse to pieces in court about your personal vendetta, and put my department under scrutiny. Learn this: sometimes it take a long stick to catch a snake.'

'And is like *people* waiting for the tree to grow before they cut the stick to catch the snake,' I threw back.

56

A dream woke me – a posse of Camaho youths on Ninja bikes – the expensive type that middle-class youngfellas bought, climbed onto in baking leather suits and rode to a hill above the international airport to look down longingly at the only decent stretch of tarmac on the island. My grandmother taught me never to dismiss dreams: they were about all the things that threaten us or frighten us. 'Is the inside-self givin us the answers to all them questions we been askin.'

Engines. I looked at my watch, 3.00am. I dialled Spiderface – our boatman was as crazy about boats and engines as the frustrated bikers of Camaho. A racket assaulted my ears when he picked up. No doubt a beach lime somewhere, full of women, throat-scorching rum and man-food – mainly flour dumplings the size and length of a plump baby's arm, salt-meat, breadfruit, and any living thing the sea delivered at this time of night. I wished I was there.

'Missa Digger, come! We in Levera.'

'Who's we?'

'All of us! Even Missa Malan here with his Princess Lady! I bring them here by boat. Better ride than a car, yunno.'

'What y'all cooking?'

'Dumplins, saltfish, sea-cat—'

'Find a quiet place to talk.'

'Missa Digger, you have to do that to me? Is a whole hill I got to climb to find some quiet.'

'Climb the hill then. I waiting.'

I listened to him gasping and muttering to himself until I could barely hear the racket.

'You could stop now, Spider. Noise gone.'

'Is on top the hill that I reach now.'

I'd taken photos of Jana Ray's drawing, printed them on A4 paper to carry around with me. I reached for those oddly drawn propellers with the same number written above each one.

'Spiderface, if I say 7-557 – that mean anything to you?'

'Seven dash 557? Nuh. What that is, Missa Digger?'

'I talkin to you about boat, right?'

'Nuh – ooh, yuh mean 7557?'

'Same thing, not so?'

'You say seven dash! 7557 different! Is de alien.'

'The?'

'Alien, Missa Digger. V8 powerhead, double exhaust, aluminium block engine, close loop cooling, 557 horsepower, 1.8 pounds per horsepower, ZF transmission, octane scaler, multipoint injection exhaust selector, hydraulic power steering. Weight 1000 pounds. And it cost a lotta money!'

'I still dunno what that is.'

'Outboard engine, Missa Digger. Is boat engine you asking me about, not so?'

'What kinda boat you going put six of them on?'

'Them is the six engines you been talking about, last meeting?'

'Yes.'

'Nuh!'

'Nuh what?'

'Who goin want to do that?'

'You not answering my question, Spider.'

'Six 557s on a boat! Dat's not a boat, Missa Digger, dat's a plane.'

'I asking if is possible, Spiderface.'

Spiderface hummed and hawed as if he were in agony. 'Yes, with a strong enough transom assembly at the back. Definitely not a small boat, becuz all dat power at de back goin somersault it. Boat got to be strong an' heavy enough to hold onto de water.'

He went quiet for a while. 'Department planning to fit one up? Becuz I more than glad to help. In fact, I know a cheaper way — just one engine, yunno. Department don't even need to buy no boat. One engine on my boat and is seventy-five miles an hour we talkin there. Or get a Mercury Verado Pro 300. Put it on my boat and y'all use it for de work.' He sounded desperate.

'Let's say we have one of them boats and we want to keep it outta sight — how you suppose we do that, Spider?'

'Ain got nowhere we kin hide a boat like dat, Missa Digger, even if you cover it up, somebody going to know. Is in Camaho we livin. So when we getting the engine?'

'Enjoy your party, Spiderface. And thanks.'

'Missa Digger, let's talk, nuh.'

'That what we been doing, not so? Thanks again.'

57

I trekked the five miles to the Commissioner's house – a steep uphill walk from my place on narrow mud tracks, then down the other side, and up again to Morne Bijoux and the clusters of sprawling, whitewashed mansions that crowned his end of the hill. I'd received a message through Chilman that my father wanted to see me. *Go easy on him, Digson. He got feelings too.*

He was in the veranda, The Wife behind his chair, her arms draped over his shoulders. She retreated when she saw me.

I'd told Miss Stanislaus about this woman, who, when my grandmother sent me begging at my father's gates, would not look at me. Would send the money with the servant, rather than have him come near me. I used to leave that gate with my hands full of coins and my guts hollow with humiliation, and a longing that I'd learned to replace with rage.

'And how De Wife is with you now?' Miss Stanislaus wanted to know.

'She doesn't stick around.'

Miss Stanislaus smacked her lips. 'Mebbe is shame she carrying now? Mebbe she was finkin that two girlchildren don't stand no chance of gettin love from the father if boy-child there to take all of it? Mebbe she know is what a father do in Camaho?'

I opened the gate and let myself in. Their gardener was putting the polish to what I knew now as The Wife's blue Daihatsu.

'You walked!' He rose from the chair and held out his hand. I barely heard him after that. I was peering through the window looking for my sisters.

A different look from him this time – narrow-eyed and smiling.

'What!' I said.

'They're hiding,' he muttered. Grinning, he raised his voice. 'Michael wants a drink.'

Squawks and giggles and shuffling somewhere in the house. A fridge door banged. A series of shrieks. The chiding voice of The Wife, and then they were racing across the living room, each with a glass of juice in her hand. Lucia and Nevis held out their glass to me. I took both, placed their rims against my lips and tried to drink.

I rested the glasses on the veranda wall and braced myself. They jostled each other for a while, each vying to get a death-grip on my body.

'Enough,' their father said.

They retreated into the house as abruptly as they came.

'Now, I have something for you.'

He went into the house and returned with a bunch of keys. He nodded at the car the gardener had been polishing.

'You lending it—'

'You don't have a car, I'm giving it to you.'

'I can't take it, Sir. I'll make arrangements with the bank to—'

'Take it, Michael.'

'Is your wife' car, Sir.'

'She agreed to let you have it. It was her idea.'

I shook my head.

345

The girls must have been behind the door. Lucia shoved past him. She was already as tall as he.

'Dad, Michael doesn't want the car from you. Give the car to me.' The old man's brows bunched together. Nevis squeezed past him too, threw a quick look at her sister then turned to him. 'Let Lucia have it.'

The Commissioner looked confused, almost boyish in his uncertainty. I saw something shift in him, caught a glimpse of his softness for these two girlchildren. He loosened his fingers and the keys dropped into Lucia's hand.

'Thanks, Dad; it's my car now.' She held out the keys to me. 'I'm the one giving it to you now, Michael.'

She leaned forward, brought her lips to my ear. 'Behave yourself. You hurting him.'

I felt the weight of the keys in my shirt pocket.

I stood there feeling stupid. The old man shrugged and turned his gaze past the high white walls of his house to the Coburn hills ahead, his lower lip pulled in.

Lucia flipped a wrist at Nevis, and with fingers digging into my arm, she steered me down the steps.

''Scuse us, folks. Michael taking us for a ride. Okay, Nevis?'

Behind us, the old man made a sound – something between a chuckle and a cough.

'Where y'all going?' I said.

'Anywhere,' Lucia said.

'I'll take y'all to anywhere, then.'

We got onto the Western Main.

One of those evenings when the fading sun threw a yellow afterglow on everything. The birds were still out making a racket. Somewhere along, Lucia did something with her hand and the roof slid open. There was a blanket of stillness over everything. Sounds travelled clear and sharp. My sisters

346

pressed their heads against the glass to stare at Camahoan women strolling along the roadside with infants on their shoulders.

'Giving the baby breeze,' I said. 'Is how the love affair with Camaho begins. Wherever in the world they go, they will never forget this island.'

'Miss Merry said so too.'

'Who's Miss Merry?'

'Mum's helper. She cooks for us.'

'Helper's the new name for servant girl now? How old?'

'Don't know.'

'What you know about Miss Merry?'

'She's our helper, Michael.'

'That's all you know? Where she lives?'

'Somewhere on the coast, I think.'

'Kanvi,' Nevis said.

'Want to see how she lives? Is time y'all meet the neighbours. Besides, is Fish Friday. Going to be a nice lime in Kanvi.'

On the way, I stopped at roadside stalls, put money in their hands and sent them out the car. I watched them eat roast corn and barbecued fish with bare hands, their shyness replaced with a don't-give-a-damn abandon as they dug into the food, licked their fingers and bared their perfect teeth at vendors. I sat them on seaside boulders with their bare feet in the water while they bit into mangoes and licked at the juices trailing down their arms.

Then I drove to Kanvi – the town that never slept. The air was sizzling with fried fish and conversation. I emptied my little bag of coins in their hands and challenged them to buy whatever they fancied but return with half the money.

They walked through the rows of stalls with smiles and nods and gestures, tossing back their thick plaits and haggling as if their lives depended on it. They were breathless when they got back, hands packed with food trays, with more than half the money in their pockets.

'Ready for home?'

'What's the hurry?'

I drove to the edge of the beach, sat with them facing the sea.

'That's how you live, Michael?'

'Yup! Merry too – in fact, most people here on Camaho.'

We watched the night come over the town. A group of men strolled onto the beach and tossed a net in the waters of the foreshore. Suddenly the whole place began to swarm with children and adults with bottle-torches in their hands. The sand grew warm and yellow, the torches throwing their shadows half the length of the beach. I wondered if they would have done this if Shadowman was still around.

A young man poked his head into the car, waved to another further down the beach.

'Ay, Man! Gimme one of them nice likkle woman you got in there, nah!'

'Hold on,' I said. 'I got something even better.'

I reached into my glove compartment, pulled out my revolver and pushed the muzzle under his nose.

He backed away as if he'd been stung on the arse, spun on his heels and shot off.

The girls were rocking with laughter. I raised my brows, twisted my lips gangster-style and glowered at them. That set them off again.

Out to sea, the lights of fishing boats stippled the darkness. Beyond them, the barely visible bulk of a giant boat, most likely Chinese or South Korean. And as usual, I felt the unease, watching these people on the beach hauling in an almost empty net because of the fish-killing factory out there.

Fireflies were out by the time we got to Beau Séjour – a

mist of blinking lights, the black flag that Lazar Wilkinson's mother had planted by the roadside still standing.

On Morne Bijoux Road, Nevis started a memory game. She covered Lucia's eyes with her hands and challenged her to guess where they were. Lucia never got it right. Nevis always did.

The outside lights of the house bathed the lawn – the shape of The Wife in the veranda, my father beside her. Waiting.

I told myself that someday I'd have to find a way to make peace with the woman. I'd have to reach into myself and offer something that she had never given me, my father's outside child. But right now, I wasn't in the mood.

'Michael, we'd like to go with you again,' Lucia said.

Nevis threw me a sidelong glance and nodded.

'Anytime,' I said.

I waited till they climbed the steps, tapped the horn and drove off.

58

Miss Stanislaus and I were sitting in the shade of a giant almond tree on Grand Beach facing the sea. Teenagers rushed past us in the yellow evening light, kicking up white sand. They hit the water and became silhouettes against the blazing sunset. Boys and girls paired off, sank to their necks in the water and began the old surreptitious game of lovemaking, heads a foot or so apart and still as statues. Their torsos – no doubt angled forward – would be busy underneath. And they thought they were being smart! A saintly soul like Miss Stanislaus would never have a clue.

'Miss Stanislaus,' I said, 'yunno, what's the best contraceptive in the world – that don't cost nothing.'

'The sea, Missa Digger.' She rolled those bright brown eyes at me. 'That's why you an Miss Dressy always in de sea?'

I decided to drop the conversation.

She pulled off her sandals, laid them preciously beside her and cleared her throat. 'Missa Digger, I been thinking about my daughter. I never tell Daphne how I come by her. She used to ask all the time. *What's my father name, Mam? Where he live?* Yunno!' Miss Stanislaus cleared her throat again. 'I kin never find it in me to tell her. One day, she stop asking me, jusso, but I see the question all the time in 'er face. What answer I kin give her now if I *got* to tell her? That Juba Hurs' was her father and I was force' to kill him?'

'I would find a way to tell her, Miss Stanislaus.'

She said nothing for a while, then her voice dropped low. 'Missa Digger, ain got nothing else in the world that frighten me except that. I 'fraid I going to spoil it. Is like all the feelins I got for my girlchild get wash' clean after I clear Juba outta my life, and I want to keep it clean.'

'That's just what I think, Miss Stanislaus – that's all. Is up to you.'

'Missa Digger, I been finkin about you and Miss Dressy too.'

'What about Dessie?'

'I want to know why you holdin onto her. Becuz in your head, you done with Miss Dressy, specially after her father put you down, and she been lying boldface to you to protect her husband name.'

'You not making sense, Miss Stanislaus.'

'I *is* makin sense and y'unnerstan me perfik!' Her voice had risen an octave.

'Okay, so you don like her—'

'For what she *is*, Missa Digger. And she don like you for what you *is*. No matter what she tell you, she'll never want to have your chil'ren. So why you holdin on to her? You not her servant-boy! Open your hand and let her go. Is de same fing you doing to Miss Pet.'

'I *not* doin anything to Pet! I never had no relationship with Pet.'

'So why you encourage her with your sweet-talk? I hear you all de time. Tell Miss Pet you don't want nuffing with her that way. Make it clear to her. Let her live her life.'

She was distracted by a fast boat pulling a skier. It was a beautiful thing to watch. The skier was good, the water butter-yellow beneath the skis – as if she were gliding on a lake of molten gold. The boat slowed and swerved a hundred yards or so further down the beach. The driver leapt into the water with a swift fluid movement of his body. He attached a rope to the stern of the craft and guided it shoreward the way one would do a horse.

'Luther Caine,' I said.

'I know,' Miss Stanislaus said. 'Yunno the woman?'

'Uh-huh.'

Her eyes settled on my face as if alerted to something.

'Tell me,' she said.

'She call herself Sarona and I have to tell you I think you right. I don't think Tamara had anything to do with what happened to Lazar Wilkinson. I believe this is the woman them youngfellas said they saw. Small problem, though – she's the woman Malan believe is his.'

Her lips twitched. 'And you saying we can't touch her because of Malan and Loofer Came?'

'We will, Miss Stanislaus, we got to.'

Miss Stanislaus remained silent for a while. 'Missa Digger, mebbe I the only pusson who don't believe is not just a man-over-woman fight you got with Loofer Came.'

'You change your mind?'

'Uh-huh.'

'When?'

'After I see him lookin at you and killin you in his mind. The man look like a murderer, Missa Digger. You keep sayin you want to pull him down but you going about it like a crazy-fella drivin a bulldozer.'

'All I need is the evidence.'

'From what you arready tell me, it right there in front ov you. It been there in front ov you from time.'

'Dunno what you mean.'

'Miss Dressy, Missa Digger.'

'I already talk to Dessie.'

She held out her hand. 'Gimme the evidence then. Put it in my hand.'

Miss Stanislaus sniffed and cast an eye down the beach. 'That's the point I making, Missa Digger. You don't want the woman to *tell* you de evidence. You want her to give it to you!'

She got up, fished her sandals off the sand. 'Missa Digger, the evenin wastin. Let's take a lil breeze.' Miss Stanislaus lifted a hand at the beach that had become a mile-long curve of glowing amber in the last of the evening sun. 'And,' she dropped a hand on my arm, 'we still got to find Miss Tamara.'

It felt like a long time since we'd been chasing Tamara. I couldn't get my head around the fact that she'd disappeared so suddenly along with two men. The young woman had managed to stay out of sight with the whole Police Force on the island looking for her. It was an embarrassment.

Dead or hostage? Or just a young girl prostituting herself with two fellas who didn't seem to have a problem with killing anybody? My heart sank at the thought of another murder. I was close to certain that they were the drivers of the boat which I now knew existed. That boat would be loaded and ready to go; would have left a long time ago had it not been for two damaged propellers. And why weren't four engines enough to get them out of Camaho at speed? In fact, flying! I'd researched those outboard engines that Spiderface called 'De Alien'.

V8 powerhead, double exhaust, 557 horsepower – it sounded like the kind of thing that could propel you to the moon, just one of them. Six! I'd Googled around until I found the makers of those engines: Seven Marine, based in Germantown, Wisconsin, USA. The 7557 – *The most advanced outboard motor on the planet.* I'd contacted them through their website and enquired how long it would take between ordering a spare part and having it arrive in Camaho. Four weeks they'd said, via Bermuda.

I made a rough calculation, factoring in the time it would take for the replacement to arrive, the two weeks to process the cocaine – based on Caran's estimate – and load the stuff onto the boat plus a couple of days to fit the propellers. In total, just over six weeks. My heart sank with the conclusion. We were the second day into the seventh week. Anytime soon, they'll be gone.

And yes, Miss Stanislaus was right, regardless of her part in all of this, we also needed to find Tamara.

59

Dessie's mother was on their front lawn decorating a long white wicker chair with her person, her dancer's feet daintily planted on a flowered cushion. I parked in the middle of their driveway behind Raymond Manille's Hyundai Genesis.

Mrs Shona Manille nudged her sunglasses up her forehead and looked up, then rose to her feet with an easy, flowing movement. She tilted her chin at the big bay window overlooking us.

'Dessima – he's here.' Her tone was tight with accusation, and I thought I heard in it a warning to her daughter.

I raised my voice. 'I not here to see Dessie, Mrs Manille. I'd like to have a serious conversation with you about your daughter.'

The skin on the woman's forehead tightened.

I heard a tumble of footsteps on the stairs inside. Dessie appeared, dressed in a light blue tracksuit and matching top – Armani, of course.

'Digger,' she called, 'you here to see me?'

I smiled at her mother. 'Sorry, I mistook you for Dessie.'

The woman laughed – a high bright sound. 'At least he's clever,' she said, and lapsed back on the chair.

I followed Dessie to the back of the house where the lawn swept down and ended in a tangle of briar and love vines.

'Dessie, you have to tell your mother all your business?'

'I told her you were pressuring me.'

'I here to talk.'

'Digger, I don't want to talk about Luther.'

'I just trying to limit the damage, Dessie.'

'Damage to?'

'Yourself. I intend to finish what I start. I need a printed statement of all Luther Caine's transactions for the past two years.'

'I can't.'

'Then I'll have to get a court order, and that will mean . . . ' I didn't say the rest.

'He will know I authorised it.'

'He'll be informed that the Commissioner of Police ordered it.'

'I can't.' Dessie didn't sound frightened, just tired. 'Digger, I want to be out of here. I want my own place. I want my money from him, and the money he made me borrow from my father to lend him. If you people do what you're supposed to do with him, I can't get my money back. You think I like—' She stopped short, began chewing on her lower lip.

I could have told her that I didn't think that she'd ever get back her money from Luther Caine. Instead, I showed her my palms and said, 'All I asking now is that you think about it. Another thing: I want a photo of the back of the house facing the swimming pool, with the shed in the picture.'

She shook her head. 'You *asking* me to go up there again? I thought you had a problem with that!'

'And you know why – okay, okay. Up to you, Dessie.' I turned to leave. 'Either way, if that fucker touch a strand of hair on you, I will, I'll—'

'You will what?'

I said nothing more.

'Say it, Digger.' She stood in the hot evening light with

356

a smile I'd never seen on her before, her eyes sweeping my face and pausing at my mouth. And for some reason Miss Stanislaus came to mind.

'Digger,' she said, very, very softly, 'you strong, but you weak too. It's hot out here, you want to come inside?'

I shook my head. 'Is better if I don't, Dessie Manille.'

The next morning at the office I received forty-three screenshots of Luther Caine's account, forwarded from a new Gmail account that Dessie had the good sense to set up.

Thnx. Pls delete Gmail acc.

M not stupid, she replied.

Later that evening the photo arrived. *Cook took it.*

I studied the photo of the shed with what looked like two big squares of tarpaulin heaped at the entrance. Whatever had been covered up there the night Miss Stanislaus and I were at Luther Caine's cocktail party was now gone.

I sat back in my chair in the office and looked at Miss Stanislaus quietly sipping her cup of chamomile tea.

'You somefing else,' I muttered.

60

I was at the Commissioner's house at 6pm.

He took me out on the lawn. The place was ablaze with the last of the evening sun. He rested deep enquiring eyes on my face. 'I'm assuming you're not getting your way with Chilly, so you're trying to go above his head?'

'Is not about people getting in my way, Sir. Is a difficulty I have with progressing my work.'

'So, you *are* going above his head. Okay, Michael, I'll hear it, but I'm warning you if you expect me to override Chilly, I won't.'

'It's about Luther Caine.'

Something shifted in his face. 'Okay, tell me about Luther.'

'We looking for a boat about to leave here any time soon. We looking for the people who will take it out of here with a load of purified cocaine with a street value of anything between twenty-two and forty-six million dollars. US! That's based on Caran's estimate of the quantity that the set-up in the hills was able to produce.'

'I know all that. Heard it a hundred times. What's that got to do with—'

'I coming to that, Sir. What I certain of is that the boat got an engine problem—'

'I've been told that already, Michael!'

'Which Luther Caine was fixing.'

That got his attention. He was frowning now. 'You not suggesting—'

'He's connected to the shipment and to a couple of others before that. I have the proof. I also know for sure that Luther Caine was paid to fix two engines for the boat. The transfer was made in US dollars from an account in Venezuela. I also have evidence of a payment he made through his company to Lazar Wilkinson's mother. Lazar Wilkinson was the victim of the necktie killing.

'I have a photograph of the back of Luther's house where he got a boat shed. Me and Miss Stanislaus paid him a visit. He had what looked like covered-up machinery in that shed. That space is empty now.'

'Michael, are you suggesting—'

'I not suggesting, Sir. I stating! Is state that I stating! I have the evidence here, and I want to know why nobody listening to me. That is what it means to own this island? Money and family name exempt y'all? That's what you telling me?'

'Michael!' His eyes were flaming. 'You're in my place – show me some respect.'

'Okay.' I stood up. 'So I can haul my arse outta your place.'

His hand shot out and grabbed my arm. 'Sit down, young man. Sit!'

I sat.

He'd dropped his voice, seemed as calm as ever. 'Finish what you're saying.'

I could barely look him in the face. 'I have reasons to believe the boat is still here. It's running on six of the most powerful outboard engines ever built. Spiderface in the Department knows all about them. By his estimate they can easily reach a hundred miles an hour, so even if we see them shooting outta here we can't stop them. Basically, they know they can outrun us – or anything in the region, for that matter.'

359

'You sound sure these people still here. You haven't explained why.'

'I'm waiting for notification of a final payment to Luther Caine's account. I'm assuming that would indicate they satisfied with the job. That's when they'll leave.'

'You sure Luther Caine's involved?'

'Yes.'

He looked stunned, as if he were only just beginning to absorb my words. 'I knew Luther from the time he was a boy. He was always in my house. His mother is my cousin, a few times removed.'

'In a small island like this, everybody's family.' I felt exhausted.

'Luther won't do anything without covering himself. I know him well enough. He could claim that he was doing the business he is set up to do: fix boats.'

'He can't! I can prove it.'

'And that he was following a client's instructions. You need to give us something that pins him to this whole affair without the shadow of a doubt, Michael.'

'I got it right here!'

'Besides, you've been consorting with Dessima. Luther will claim it's personal. A Camaho jury can be swayed by that, you know.'

'Specially if they come from this high up on the hill, right?'

He brushed aside my remark. 'Seriously, Michael, you think that you can pull this off?'

'We got to get the drivers of the boat.'

'Reality is, you haven't been able to do that.' He sat back, staring past my head. 'I'm going to talk to Chilly. To digress a bit, Raymond Manille is not on good terms with me these days. He called me recently about a young upstart who came to his place chasing after his daughter. Apparently the upstart in question had no family to speak of, no decent job and little means. He said the young man should find his level. I took that personally. You told him something about arriving on a boat?'

I shrugged. 'I told his wife.'

'That's what really upset him. I suggested to him that the officer had a point.' He chuckled in his throat. 'You didn't get that pepper from me! How's the car?'

'Thanks.' I shrugged.

He said nothing for a long while. 'When you finish this case Chilly wants you to leave. He said he's wasting you and that lovely woman. You two should further your education. I agree. I'll leave you to your sisters.'

They promptly popped out from behind a tall hibiscus bush a little way behind us, their smiles broad and shameless.

'Y'all wuz listening!' I said.

'We always listen,' Lucia said.

'Why d'you think I don't hold meetings here?' The Commissioner chuckled.

I opened my arms and braced myself as they threw themselves at me.

61

Malan arrested Tamara the morning Miss Blackwood sent
me confirmation that a payment had been made to Luther
Caine's account. Ten thousand US dollars. The first payment
that Dessie told me about, under mild duress, amounted to
twelve thousand US dollars. The first amount would have
been for the purchase of the two replacement propellers from
the suppliers in the USA.

An hour later, Dessie pinged me. *Money in.*

My heart stepped up pace. I'd reached for the phone to call
Chilman. It rang before I touched it.

'Digger, I got the whore.' Malan.

'Where she is?'

'Central. De woman is a bitch! She spit in my face,' he
snapped and cut off.

An off-duty officer had spotted Tamara entering the road to
her mother's house and attempted to arrest her. She punched
him in the eye and directed a couple of kicks between his legs
which doubled him over and had him squirming in the road.
He called for back-up. A jeep full of officers arrived and, short
of shooting the young woman 'to calm her down', they were
forced to back off. The news reached Malan in his chill-out
place on the Carenage. He finished his drink, excused himself, dropped Sarona at his house and headed for the village.

Tamara fought him too, but Malan traded punches for slaps until she crumpled at his feet.

There were a couple of holding cells in San Andrews Central station. Pit was for the drunks, low-lifes, absconders, and a stopover for Camahoans in transition to the prison on Edmund Hill. It was a six-foot by four-foot cell, never cleaned and smelling of every imaginable human secretion. House was for the occasionally errant citizen of San Andrews. It reeked of Iodoform and had a thin, fibre-stuffed mattress and pillow laid out on a bench. No sheet. Malan locked up Tamara in Pit.

It was then that Malan called me.

'They got Tamara,' I told Miss Stanislaus.

'Where, Missa Digger?'

'Central,' I told her. 'C'mon.'

'Nuh,' Miss Stanislaus said.

'You not coming wiv me?'

'You not going wiv *me*,' she replied. 'Is me to handle it.'

I knew that tone. I glared at her and sat back at my desk.

Miss Stanislaus looked close to tears when she returned to the office. She could not soften the woman, she said. If Tamara chose to speak at all, it was to deny everything. She knew nothing about no drugs boat, so how people expect her to tell them where boat is and when boat leaving? So what if she had bizness with Lazar Wilkinson, dat didn mean she knew what happened to him.

She didn know where the two men took her becuz they put a towel over her head and didn tell her where she was. She couldn see no surroundings becuz the two fellas never let her out of the room they put her in, unless they threw a towel over her head.

Chilman, who'd walked in earlier and demanded to know

363

'what go on', addressed Miss Stanislaus through me. He fixed me with a yellow-eyed stare.

'You tell the young woman that we not letting her go until she cough-up the information?' Chilman grated. 'You inform her that she's a suspected accomplice to murder and what that means for her? You explained to her that if she continues playing the arse she is not going to see her child?'

'I don fink she lying, Missa Digger. If I wrong about that, I wrong about everyfing.' Miss Stanislaus replied to Chilman through me.

'She not telling the truth either, Miss Stanislaus, and time passing,' I said.

Pet rested a hand on Miss Stanislaus's arm. 'We got to get her to talk, Miss Stanislaus.'

'Mebbe if people start believin what she say, mebbe they get what they want.'

Late evening, we were still at the office when a lawyer named Peter Sandiford called, said he was asked by a concerned party to represent Miss Tamara Crawford, and not only did he have a right to visit and advise her, but tomorrow afternoon he will be serving a writ of Habeas Corpus. Did San Andrews CID appreciate the implications of a Habeas Corpus? Should he have a sample sent over by messenger, first thing tomorrow?'

'Is I ask the lawyer,' Miss Stanislaus said.

Chilman looked sick.

I left my desk and went outside.

Miss Stanislaus came out after me. 'Missa Digger—'

'Why!'

'She got a baby.'

'That she left with her mother and disappear for months!'

'Mebbe she will talk to you, Missa Digger.'

'She won't.'

'Mebbe Miss Tamara dunno what she know. Mebbe you kin—'

'Miss Stanislaus, I tired and fed up. I getting outta here.'

I drove back to my yard, shivering with frustration. Spent the next couple of hours trying not to think about the case.

Mebbe if people start believin what she say. When I looked at my watch it was 11.03pm. I messaged Miss Stanislaus.

1 2 c Tamara. Pick u up 30mins.

Miss Stanislaus was waiting by the road. 'What you goin do to her?'

'I not using no force, Miss Stanislaus.'

'It got different kinda force, Missa Digger.'

'Is an idea I got from my two lil sisters, yunno. Is sixteen hours gone since Luther Caine got his last payment. The way I see it, boat leaving this foreday morning or next foreday morning. We need the woman to talk.'

'Why foreday morning?'

'Just enough light to see where they going, not enough to be spotted easily. Besides, they can't do Blackwater in darkness.'

'How you know is Blackwater they going?'

'They not going back to Venezuela with the drugs – that don't make no sense. They continuing on like Mibo said. To "continue on" to *anywhere* by boat, you got to go through Blackwater, even to Europe, which don't make no blaastid sense to me.'

When we got to Central, an officer in uniform had his shoulder against the grille-work of the cell.

He straightened up when he saw us. 'I trying to get something outta she,' he loud-whispered, unlocked the door and eased past us.

'I sure is not no information he tryin to get outta she,' Miss Stanislaus muttered.

It was the first time I'd come this close to Tamara. Looking at her, I had a sensation of heat and rage. What struck me also was her muscularity, then her eyes – cat-bright, fierce and unafraid, just like her child.

I leaned towards Miss Stanislaus. 'Don look like she going talk to nobody.'

'You try?'

'That's a fighter-woman there.'

'Go get me a cuppa water, Missa Digger. Bring it when I call you.' Miss Stanislaus stepped inside the cell.

I strolled over to the cooler, filled a plastic cup with slow spurts, my ear cocked towards the holding room. Miss Stanislaus's musical chirping went on for a while. After some time I heard the woman's husky monotone. Miss Stanislaus began chuckling at something, a series of short coughs came from the woman, followed by a stream of words.

'Missa Digger, you got the water?'

I walked into the room. Miss Stanislaus pointed at Tamara. I handed the woman the cup.

'Missa Digger, Miss Tamara willing to c'operate, but she want me to stay with her while you 'terrogate her. She say Missa Malan was very rude – he call her a, erm ...' Miss Stanislaus blinked, turned her eyes down at her hands.

'Whore,' Tamara said.

Miss Stanislaus nodded. 'I tell her that she was right to insist. I tell her that you, Missa Digger, goin be very, very respeckful.' That came with a threatening glance from Miss Stanislaus.

'Course,' I said. 'I born respectful. Miss Tamara, I want you think back to the night they pick you up from San Andrews. Miss Stanislaus say they asked you to lie down on the seat so you couldn't see where they taking you?'

She nodded.

'I could ask you to close your eyes? Is good for remembering sometimes. I even bring a handkerchief just in case you
prefer that. It clean.' I held out the blue square of cloth.

She shook her head.

Miss Stanislaus didn't look convinced either, but she must
have seen the desperation on my face. She plucked the ker-
chief from my hand and held it out to Tamara. Tamara took
it and kept it balled up in her fist.

'How long you lay low in the car?'

'Dunno.' She shrugged.

'Okay, you ever travel by bus to Leapers' Town?' It was the
furthest north that any vehicle could go.

'It was longer.'

'Longer!'

She nodded.

'Any difference in the way the road felt at any point?'

'Road is road,' she said.

'I serious, Miss Tamara.' I repeated the question.

She went still, brows clenched, eyes turned inward. 'The
last part was rough.' She looked up – not at me, but at Miss
Stanislaus.

'Rough how?' I said.

'Car dip-an-bounce a lot.'

'No sharp turn before that happen?'

'Nuh! Just the car bouncin me about, all the way up.'

'Up? How you know was up?'

She rolled her eyes.

'And then?'

'And then the car level off and stop. Like I been saying,
them two pyul fellas throw a towel over my head and take
me inside some place.'

'What's pyul?' Miss Stanislaus wanted to know.

'Nickname for South Americans,' I said.

367

'Dey talk Spanish,' Tamara told Miss Stanislaus, her tone almost apologetic.

'Long or short walk to the door?' I said.

'Not long.'

'What shoes you wuz wearing?'

She pointed at her feet.

'Miss Tamara, you mind standing? I want you to cover your eyes now. I going to walk you across the room. That alright?'

Miss Stanislaus touched Tamara's elbow. Tamara stood up, pressed the heels of her hands into her eyes.

I placed a finger on her shoulder. 'When you feel you walk far enough to the door in that place, tell me.' I guided her across the floor. 'What you walkin on – gravel, grass or—'

'Rough stone.'

'Right up to the door?'

'Uh-huh.'

'Any steps?'

'Concrete. Steps wuz wide.'

'How you know?'

'A fella was on either side of me.'

'And once you inside, you on a concrete floor, not so?'

'Nuh, it feel like wood.'

'Wood! You sure?'

She dropped her hands and glared at me.

I left her there and strolled towards the window. I could feel the tension in my shoulders. When I turned around, Miss Stanislaus's face was tight with concentration, her lower lip pulled in.

'And I guessing that when you got inside that house, they didn walk you in a straight line, right?'

She gave me a quick interested look. 'How you know?'

'Just guessin,' I said. 'When they lift the towel, what you see?'

'A small room. One rickety ole bed dat smell of man. Was dark in dere.'

'Warm or cool?'

'The whole place cold.'

'How outside sound?'

She frowned at me.

'Y'ever walk through Sendall Tunnel?'

That quick frown and look again. 'A lil bit like that. How you . . . ?'

I pointed at the window. 'What you hearing out there?'

She shrugged and pulled down the corners of her mouth. 'Traffic.'

'And what y'was hearing in that place?'

'Oh! The sea. Rough sea.'

'You sure?'

'I sure.'

'What they bring you there for?'

'What you think?'

'I not thinking now. Tell me.'

She did not answer me.

'Talk to me about Lazar Wilkinson – you been with him, not so?'

She shrugged and twisted her mouth. 'Lazar was too rough and controllin. I couldn deal with that.'

'And the two fellas?'

'Was Lazar who introduce me. I needed money for my child. Lazar make them pay me upfront.'

'Tell me about the murder.'

Everything about her changed. 'What you trying to say? Same thing dat nasty man who call himself police come here hittin me and tryin to force me to sign paper and confess.'

Miss Stanislaus calmed her down.

'I got one more question, Miss Tamara.'

369

She squared up like a boxer prepared to deflect a punch. 'Ask, I don have to answer.'

'How you get out of that place?'

'They drop me in the big crossroad near Seven Falls. I walk till I get a ride.'

'That's the middle of the island. And at a crossroad. They smart. Harder to tell which direction you come from. Thanks,' I said. 'You kin go home. I'll do the formalities.'

She looked at me, surprised. Miss Stanislaus blessed me with a lovely smile.

'Don't even try to leave the island, though. I got an alert on you. And you see what Malan is like. I don't want him coming after you again.'

At the door Tamara swung back her head, flopped a wrist at Miss Stanislaus. I received a fleeting glance from her. 'You weird,' she muttered. I flopped a wrist at her.

Long, crisp strides across the courtyard, gun-barrel mouth, the head – hair now cropped close – held upright.

Miss Stanislaus was watching me watch Tamara. 'I see you like her, Missa Digger.'

'She got balls, I mean, uhm, spirit.'

'Tell me what you find.'

'Old building on a hill or slope, at the end of a mud road, with a yard big enough to take at least one vehicle. Steps – I believe is stone – wide enough for at least three people to walk. Wide steps suggest big door. Cool inside – remember the Sendall Tunnel question? They dig that tunnel outta stone so I thinkin is a stone building. Wooden floor not safe to walk on, yunno, but the two fellas know it well enough to avoid the bad part. That suggest to me that the building is most likely in disuse. I thinking big old church, Miss Stanislaus – Anglican or Catholic – becuz it ain got no other buildings on Camaho that got those features. What don't make no sense

370

is how close to the sea it is. Ain got no church like that apart from the Catholic cathedral on Leapers' Hill. And that one get used all the time.' I turned to Miss Stanislaus. 'Look to me like she was lying.'

'She wasn.'

'Why you sticking up for somebody you only meet once?' I said.

'Why you putting down somebody you only meet once, Missa Digger? Becuz you can't find a place like that in your head don't mean it ain't got one out there.' She directed her chin at the window. 'Mebbe you fink you know too much, Missa Digger.'

'And mebbe you think you always right!' I threw back.

Back in the car, she sniffed and slid a sideways glance at me. 'Perhaps me'n'you upset becuz we not makin no headway. Missa Digger, you cook for me dis evenin?'

'You comin to my place?'

'Where else?'

'You didn't ask if I expecting people.'

'You not expectin people. Miss Dressy not friends with you right now.'

My phone buzzed. 'Digger, any luck with de whore?'

I gave Malan a description of the place I'd got from Tamara. 'You know any place like that?'

He was silent for a while. 'Nuh – don't have no place like dat. Else I would know it.' He mumbled something and hung up.

That night, Miss Stanislaus and I spent a couple of hours trawling through the biggest survey map of the island we could find.

I finally gave up. 'We wrong, Miss Stanislaus. We been wrong all along. Ain got no place like that. Tamara was lying. Ain got no—' A thought popped into my head.

371

'Hold on,' I said and stepped out of the house. I stared at my phone for a long while. I took a breath and called.

Malan's response was a growl.

'Quick question, Malan: Sarona there with you?'

'Of course, Sarona here! Digger, what the—'

'Malan, I got to tell you something about that fuckin woman. I want you to hear me out.'

'How you call she?'

'Okay, okay. Sorry, mebbe I had a lil too much to, erm, drink, yunno.'

He was bawling down the phone now. 'You drunk! And is my woman you callin and askin for?'

'Sorry, man!' I cut off, my ears hot with embarrassment. I strolled back inside, dropped onto the sofa and sat there staring at the ceiling.

I perched on my step, a chill wind tugging on my shirt. I'd been swinging between hopelessness and what felt like serious fits of depression until Miss Stanislaus got so fed up with my moods she demanded that I take her home. That left me feeling worse.

I could hear bats zipping in the air above my head, their calls so piercing sometimes, it felt like they were driving needles through my eardrums and, not for the first time, I cursed the sensitivity of my hearing. Why was Miss Stanislaus so certain that Tamara was being truthful about a place that didn't exist? Miss Stanislaus even had less faith in the survey map. 'Is only road and hill them print on it. Ain't got nuffing here bout sea and bush! I sure is not no Camaho people who make this map.' That was when she decided to leave me to my fretting and go home.

I glanced at my watch – just past one. I picked up my phone and called Caran.

'Caran, you up?'

'I up now, Digger. Tell me.'

'Caran, I looking for a big ole stone house near rough sea. Big yard, wide doorway, wood floor, on a hill—'

'Hell House,' he said.

Hellon House. I didn't correct him.

'Jeezas!' I said. 'That Bush Ranger job don't deserve you, Caran!'

'What's going down?'

I filled him in. 'Call it logic, instinct, common sense – whatever you want, Caran, but everything telling me that boat ready to go. They got no more reason for staying here. They let go Tamara this morning. She gave us a description of the place the drivers been keeping her.'

'Okay, Digger, instruct me.' I heard the rustle of clothing.

'Is one fifteen. We meet up at the beginning of the road that lead to the place. Let's get there for three fifteen.'

'Hell House make sense,' he said.

'A lot,' I said. 'It never cross my mind. Tell Mary I sorry to call you out this time-a-night. I got to pick up Miss Stanislaus and make some calls.'

62

Hellon House was on the far north-eastern tip of Camaho, facing the raw force of the Atlantic. In front of it, a dripping rock-rise, its crevices and ledges infested with crabs and resting seabirds. In bad weather the house became loud. Gale-force winds rattled the roof and made whirlwinds in the wide stone veranda that faced the raging waters.

After two centuries of hurricanes and the unending assault of the worst seas, Hellon House still stood its ground. The sea had carved out a small circular lagoon – fenced by thick mangroves – to the right of the edifice. To get to it from the sea, you had to know it was there. The stone beach that it led to could not be seen from the ocean or the building.

An Englishfella used to own it – same name as the house. Rumour had it that Hellon, the son of a plantation owner, read a book named *King Lear* and decided to be like that king-fella. Built the big ole house on the rocks, so the gulls became his audience. The fella went crazy. Went stupid. Went the way ov all flesh.

But then, I told Miss Stanislaus, maybe the story wasn't exactly so, because we Camahoans treated history like food: we flavoured it to suit our tastes, and the spicier the better.

Eleven of us: Caran and his three Rangers, Malan, Miss Stanislaus and I; eight hundred yards out on the bucking waters were four coast guard men in a Guardian Class patrol boat, wrestling to keep their 12.7 mm machine guns trained on the exit from the lagoon. I'd called Malan because he had friends in the coast guard. By the time he called me back, the coast guard was on the way.

We raced up the hill with regulation torches in our hands. The front yard and door were more or less as I'd visualised them. Malan and I zig-zagged across the rotting floorboards and found the dirty little bedroom as Tamara had described it. I walked into the room. The only window was about eight feet above me – a big square cut into the stone wall and sloppily boarded over. An old spring bed, covered with a lumpy fibre mattress, was directly under it. A heap of shredded braids with a broken circular comb entangled in it, on the far end of the bed. A toothpaste tube squeezed flat lying on a makeshift stool in one corner by the entrance. Behind the stool, four condom wrappers with Manana printed on the box into which they'd been stuffed. I grabbed the condom wrappers and shoved them in my pocket.

Caran and his crew were out there shouting words at each other. I heard him calling my name and made my way to them through a tangle of young mangroves.

They were on the sharply sloping beach. Toya was pacing the pebbles. She'd taped a large LED torch to the helmet on her head.

She directed the muzzle of her rifle at two trenches that led from the lower part of the beach up to the foreshore. 'Catamaran,' she said. She moved around the indentations and again directed the muzzle at a tapering patch of dryness. 'V-hulls – each bow is about twelve-foot long. Whole boat about forty feet.'

She flicked a booted foot at twelve lengths of coconut trunk. 'They roll it back on these.'

She saw me observing her, did something subtle with her

eyes and head – an underhand don't-even-think-ov-it-fuck-off expression.

'You say V-hull, what's special about that?' I said.

'For speed. Faster in rough water too.'

'When you think they move out of here?'

'Not more than one hour ago – two for the most.' She pointed at some tufts of salt-grass that fringed the beach. 'Bruise still fresh on dem. They don't fix themself back yet.'

I shook my head at her.

'Toya know what she talking about. Eastward Island woman you looking at there, Digger. Sea people, yunno. De real thing.'

We combed the area, pushing southward through half an acre of mangroves because Caran said he thought there was another lagoon further down. There was and it was empty.

Morning had arrived by the time we returned. Malan was on the beach waving off the coast guard. The whole place was flooded with early light, yet the sense of desolation clung to it. I wondered how Tamara had survived it.

Malan stood watching the boat till it swung south for San Andrews. He sucked his teeth and shook his head. 'So you fink we lose them?' He'd fallen into a nasty mood, was glaring at me as if I was the one who'd taken off with the boat.

'Not yet. They won't be leaving daytime. I thinking fore-day morning – a lil while before the sun come up. They need enough light to navigate the rough waters.'

Toya nodded. 'Crosstide too – and Boko Reef, if is really north they headin.'

'Is north,' I said. 'They come up from Venezuela.'

Malan cased his Sig Sauer, his mouth a sour knot. 'I not wasting time here, I shooting ahead. Call me if y'all want me.'

Miss Stanislaus watched me watching Malan's retreating back. 'What you finking?' she said.

'If I right, Sarona won't be here tomorrow. She'll be leaving with the boat she come with. Or she'll try to. I don't believe he knows that.'

'And you not tellin him?'

'Last night I tried to.'

'So, what you got in mind?'

'Dunno yet, Miss Stanislaus.'

Chilman sounded subdued on the phone. Malan had already informed him.

'Who' idea it was to use the coast guard?'

'I asked Malan to handle it,' I said. 'Made sense to me.'

'Well, Minister of Justice know now. He been harassing me with calls. I not answering. I shut down the office and I instruct Malan Greaves to avoid him. You sure that boat leaving tomorrow?'

'I strongly believe so, Sir.'

He cleared his throat. 'What chance we got, Digson?'

'Dunno, Sir.'

'Digson, I want to ask you a pussnal question. The Luther Caine fella – you say he might be involved in this too?'

'Yes, is what I been telling y'all from time.'

'And he been communicating with his wife?'

'Uh-huh?'

'How much you talk to the man' wife about your work?'

'Not much.'

'How much is not much?'

'She knows what I do, Sir. If a case gets on the news, she would want to know whether I was involved in it. Is normal! But I don't discuss my work with Dessie. If that's what you getting at.'

'It *is* what I getting at because what's plain as day to me, Digson, is that the boat-people knew y'all wuz coming. From what Malan tell me, they leave Hell House in a rush.'

377

'I don't think—'

'You don't think, but you don't *know* what she did or didn tell her husband.'

DS Chilman cut me off.

'What happen, Missa Digger?'

'That was Chilman on the phone. He's upset. We let him down.'

'We do we best, Missa Digger, and we best is the best that we kin do,' Miss Stanislaus retorted.

I raised my eyes past the procession of breakers and the dim receding shapes of rock-islands in the far distance – a curving necklace at the end of which lay Kara Island. It made sense that the boatmen had chosen this place – it was the shortest distance between Camaho and Kara Island. After Kara Island, the open ocean. Blackwater was the only obstacle.

I felt a hand in the small of my back.

'Missa Digger, yunno what I been finkin?'

'Tell me.'

'We got one last chance. You finkin de same ting too?'

'Uh-huh – you think the others going want to try it?'

'Missa Digger, they'll go along with whatever you want them to do.'

I turned to face the group. 'Okay! Me and Miss Stanislaus think we got one last window. Listen to what I have to say.'

63

Chilman stayed silent on the other end of the line when I called again.

'Sir, we need transport. I wondering if we kin make use of the coast guard.'

'What you up to?'

I explained our idea to him.

'It not going to work.'

'We dunno unless we try. Mebbe we get lucky. I asking you to use your powers, your contacts, or whatever, to get us a coast guard boat. We want the biggest one they got. Is six of us that going.'

'No other boat going to do?'

'We ain have no time to go looking for no other boat.'

'I'll see what I can do.'

'Don't see, Sir. I asking you to do it. We depending on you. They got to pick us up at Leapers' Bay no later than five this evening.'

When we arrived at Leapers' Bay, the morning sun was just hitting the peaks of Saint Catherine Mountain. Caran left us huddled under a seagrape tree, a hard wind grabbing at our clothing. He returned a couple of hours later with a bundle of waterproof ponchos, a big pot of steaming food, four flasks of hot chocolate, six aluminium cups and two loaves of bread the size of logs. Caran said something to his crew. They followed him and helped him drag a bag from his jeep. They formed a tight circle around it as he knelt in the sand and unzipped the canvas bag.

Guns: AK47s, and another wicked-looking weapon, four times the size of the others with a flat, skeletal stock and a long snout.

'PKM,' he said, looking up at me. 'When them Americans invade Camaho, they make the government they force on us to get rid of them – communist weapons they call them, yunno. Better to get kill with American gun, at least you get a chance to go to heaven. A communist bullet hit you and is straight to hell you going. No argument!'

I cracked up, was laughing so hard Miss Stanislaus thumped me on the back. Caran threw me a wink and set me off again.

'Now, these is real guns, Digger! Fellas like my father save a few. Bury them, yunno.' He rested a big brown hand on the PKM. 'Gas operation, belt-feed, open bolt. Two hundred and fifty rounds a minute. Accurate up to eight hundred metres. It stay alive in any weather.'

'What about them patrol shooters y'all got?'

'They not for war, Digger, they just for public viewing. Okay, y'all! Tidy up and catch a nap. Sand soft. I make arrangements with that shop across the road to use their facilities.' He turned a polite smile on Miss Stanislaus. 'I bring a sleepin bag for De Lady.'

'Think you,' Miss Stanislaus said. I threw her a mock-envy glare. She pretended she didn't notice.

My phone buzzed.

'Six thirty,' Chilman coughed. 'Best I could do. I tell him he's at y'all mercy.' The DS hung up. He called again. 'Good luck to y'all, Digson.'

'What *he* say?' Miss Stanislaus said.

'How you know is him?'

'Your face tell me, Missa Digger.'

'He say good luck.'

'Uh-huh.'

One last chance . . . 'Miss Stanislaus, I leaving you with Caran for a couple of hours. I got to go back to San Andrews. Is important.'

'What you thinkin, Missa Digger?'

'I thinking Sarona and Luther Caine.'

I checked the time: 7.01am. I hurried to my car.

I drove at a steady forty miles per hour. My heartbeat had stepped up pace.

I sat at Pet's desk, slotted in my USB stick and navigated to my Luther Caine folder. I printed out the documents I'd received from Dessie, then spent another twenty minutes highlighting and underlining figures with a marker. I slotted the documents into an envelope.

I drove south to Grand Beach. Dessie had told me that Luther was always down there early setting up in advance for the youngfella he employed.

Of course the skiing job was a cover for what Luther Caine really did – coordinating the cocaine trafficking operations in the Lesser Antilles, as well as fixer and tuner of those high-performance engines for the last critical lap up north. His house on Lavender Hill was a pit stop. Any fool could have seen that the fella could not pay for his lifestyle with the money he earned teaching people to glide on water. But we were accustomed to not looking. Money was as much a part of what he was as the clothes he wore, the paleness of his skin, the squared shoulders and straight-ahead gaze. In Camahoan eyes, Luther Caine didn't need to have money to be wealthy. He would never go to jail, never have to stand inside a court house – like his father, who in his teens had desecrated a schoolgirl and murdered her. And what happm? He got posted off the island to America, returned with an expensive education that made him Governor General in the end.

I found that hard to swallow. Make it worse, my father was one of them.

His white speedboat with a blue dolphin painted at the side nodded on the waters of the foreshore. In the far background, the buildings of San Andrews town − heaped around the edges of a peninsula. It was as if I were looking at another place in some other country. Lone figures speckled the mile-long beach, jogging or walking along the shoreline.

It was 8.47.

Luther was bending over a ski. I pretended to be fiddling with my phone, about to make a call. He must have sensed my presence. His head shot up. I pressed the shutter release. Grey-green eyes settled on my face. I took him in: a nest of wiry hairs spread across his chest and shoulders, blackfella's legs − muscular with prominent calves, and arse that curved like the head of a question mark. Those marks along his shoulder and down his arm were still visible.

The hostility that he had been good at hiding at his cocktail party was there now in every movement of his body.

He was expecting me to say something. I let him wait.

'What you want?'

'You,' I said.

He chuckled. 'I'm not that way inclined.'

He straightened up, raised both arms above his head, clasped his hands and curved his body from side to side. 'Tired of my wife?'

He dropped his arms, a big smile across his face. I was smiling too.

'You here for advice? Don't know how to handle her?' He began busying himself with another ski. 'Dessima is like a pretty mango. But I suppose by now, Saga Boy, you know that. Problem is, when you bite, it's full of worms.'

'You didn't know that before you married her?'

'We're all entitled to one mistake. Still, she's not yours. She'll never be yours. Won't divorce me if I beg her.'

'Still thinking y'all kin own people? Those days over, Luther. They gone for good.'

'I'll tell you what you don't have.' He pointed at his temple. 'This!'

'A big red Negro head like yours?'

'Brains,' he snapped. I'd riled him now. 'Detective, my arse!'

He dropped the ski he was holding. 'I heard she took you to see Raymond Manille? Bet he hated the sight of you. Take this from me for free: Raymond's not protecting Dessima, he's guarding her ovaries. Raymond knows that when a pothound breeds a Dobermann, it makes a thoroughbred of neither the pothound or the offspring.'

'Nor,' I teased. 'Neither nor, Luther, not neither or. Get your grammar straight!'

His hand froze. He straightened up, his face twitching with rage.

'A couple nights ago, a fella named Shadowman came out of the dark, mash-up my car and almost killed Miss Stanislaus and me before I shot him. That was a mistake you made.'

He lifted his shoulders and dropped them. 'Comes with the job, I suppose.'

'Including killing Lazar Wilkinson? Them marks across your shoulder and down your arm, he give you them? Strong fella, Lazar. Not so? The mash-up ground on the beach where y'all kill him tell me he gave you one helluva fight! And if your Venezuelan woman – what's 'er name, Sarona? Sandra Fernandez? If she didn't put him at a disadvantage he'd've cut y'arse. He didn't want no fee. He wanted part of the business. A percentage. And if you didn't do it he was going to sell you out to the police. And yunno Lazar Wilkinson meant it. So you set him up and kill im. You couldn't trust Shadowman to do it the way you wanted, so you done it yourself. Tell me what it feels like to strangle a fella and cut his throat, Colombia gangster style! Like you forgot this is not no fuckin US or Kingston ghetto! This is Camaho, and Camaho got stupid people like me and Miss Kathleen Stanislaus.'

'You've clearly been hallucinating.'

'I got samples of skin that Lazar Wilkinson tore off you. I cleaned his nails. They sitting in my fridge. I got a phial in my car, come spit in it for me so I can run a test and clear your name. Or if that's too lowclass for you, come spit on me, please!'

Once, Dessie had described the way Luther's anger boiled in him until it exploded and spilled over. The way it would heat him up and redden him. I watched the transformation and his struggle to control it.

'And what about Jonathon Rayburn? You think I going to let that pass?'

'I had nothing to do with any of what you're talking about. I don't even know what you're on about.'

'Nothing to do with Juba Hurst either?'

'Who's Juba Hurst?' He pulled back his head and showed me his teeth. 'You trying to catch me out? I know no one by that name.'

'If you say so, bossman.'

I hefted the big A4 envelope in my hand and tossed it at his feet.

'Read this soon as you can, Luther. Is a record of all your transactions for the past fourteen months. I mean all: transfers from a couple of accounts in Colombia, Bermuda and

Venezuela. Transfer to Dora Wilkinson's account to buy her mouth after you murdered her boychild – the last two payments, directly from one account in Venezuela in the name of one Sandra Fernandez alias Sarona – or the other way around.'

What I said next was a lie. 'Before you blow up, I didn't get it from Dessie. Is from the US Drugs Monitor, Bureau of International Narcotics and Law Enforcement Affairs in Florida. They on your case. They want to lose you in jail.'

He didn't touch the envelope. But he'd gone quiet, forgetting which of the skis he was working on. Switching from one to the other, then back again.

'Talking about pothound, Luther, you know what a throw-back is? Is what you and Juba Hurst got in common. You ever wonder where he got his size from?'

I offered him a smile. 'Coupla hundred years ago, they used to breed fellas like him, for the muscles and the size. Like mules, to carry heavy loads. I hear they still got some of them in Cuba.'

I pointed at my head. 'Stupid me! I figure that you from the line of the breeders – I know what you used to do to Dessie. You inherited their cruelty.'

I left him with that and strolled up the western end of the beach. I stopped in the shade of a seagrape tree. Luther Caine rushed the envelope, tore it open and became a living picture of panic.

Run, Luther. I want you to run.

I had my reasons for not mentioning the boat.

Pothound! Who de arse he callin pothound? Hm!

I gave it half an hour, then called Dessie. 'Luther Caine been phoning you, not so?'

'And so early! I'm ignoring him. He's not giving up!'

'Stay clear of him. For all of today, at least.'

'What's happened?'

'He used to try to kill you. Now I sure he will.'

'Why, Digger? I don't understand.'

'Dessie, you swear you dunno exactly when that boat leaving?'

'I don't! Why you said Luther wants to kill me?'

'Just stay clear of him. What's your father' number?'

'Why d'you want it?'

'I won't be around to protect you. Somebody got to let your father know.'

'No!' She cut off.

I rushed back to the office. At 9.30 I called Manille's Hardware Emporium and left a message with Raymond Manille's PA.

In a couple of minutes, he called back. I didn't take the call. He was obviously concerned.

I spent the next half-hour uploading a photo of my ID and the picture I'd taken of Luther Caine to twelve email addresses.

Then I called Spiderface. I figured if he'd been taking Sarona around, he'd have an idea where she might be. 'You with Malan' woman?'

'Nuuh, Missa Digger. De princess gone shopping. I drop 'er off on de Carenage. I got to pick 'er up later.'

'What time is later?'

'Around one, Missa Digger.' He sounded uncomfortable. 'I, erm, could tell Missa Malan you askin for her?'

'Is not what you think, Spiderface. Coupla questions I got to ask her. I not stopping you from telling Malan, though.'

I made a round of the town on foot. Half an hour later, I spotted Sarona in the marketplace. She was bending over a mound of sugar apples, a beige cloth bag hanging off her shoulder. Wide-brimmed straw hat, cream billowy shirt. Green, pleated skirt that reached her sandals.

'Hi, Digger,' she said without raising her head.

Sarona dropped some coins in the vendor's hand, straightened up and smiled – generous, effortless, convincing. I'd seen her turn that smile on and off like a light switch.

My mind returned to Dog Island when Malan shot that goat. For days after, I'd carried Sarona's face in my mind, her staring at me, interested it seemed in what effect the sight of a murdered animal had on me. Dessie had seen that look and misread the dilated eyes, the flared nostrils, the parted lips. It was not attraction, it was arousal – and I wasn't fooling myself. That look had nothing to do with me.

'What's on your mind?' she purred. 'Are you thinking what I'm thinking?'

'What you think I'm thinking?' I said.

'That I should have met you first?'

'I'm already taken – I was when I met you, and I still am.'

'You know you're not,' she chuckled.

The vendor's eyes were switching between our faces, the woman looked entranced. I was sure she couldn't hear our words.

'Malan taking you serious, and in Malan's book serious is dangerous,' I said.

'And you wouldn't have taken me seriously?'

'When you leaving here?'

'Here?' She gestured at the market. The corners of her mouth had tightened. Steady, steady eyes.

'Don't bullshit me,' I said. 'I not Malan. You tell him your name is Sandra Fernandez? You tell him you in business and in bed with Luther Caine? He know Luther plant you inside Camaho police Force to monitor what go on? You warn him that you running out on him soon in that drugs-boat y'all

387

been hiding? You think people on this island chupid? You think we comic-book people, not so?'

She dropped her eyes on the bag, raised her head at me, her brows pulled together in a tight knot. 'So many questions and we're not saying much.'

'What I have to say will start a war between Malan Greaves and me. He don't see you like I see you.' A chuckle escaped her, a quick lift of her head. 'You want to sit somewhere and talk?'

'Nuh.'

Something in her attitude had changed. I looked behind and there was Malan, his mouth twisted into a hateful sneer. 'What's your beef, Digger? You fink you kin break me with my woman? You fuckin can't!'

'Is not what you thinking, Malan Greaves, but you can't see it any other way. Woman made for one thing in your mind – that's all you know.'

'You don leave she alone . . . ' He'd slipped his hand behind his back. Sarona looked interested and alert – that same look I saw on her face on Dog Island.

'Impossible,' I said, gesturing at his gun hand. 'You raise that gun at me, you better use it. Either way, you'll be a dead man before nightfall. I guarantee that.' I looked him in the eyes. 'Just so you know, we been looking for the wrong woman.' I raised my chin at Sarona. 'Tamara got nothing to do with this case.'

'Digger, fuck off.'

'Not because you say so, Malan, but because I got a boat to catch. My advice – keep an eye on your woman.'

I left them there and strolled back to the office.

Sarona said something to Malan. Then that soft laugh came from her.

Fuckin La Diablesse, I muttered. Just wait!

64

I was back in Leapers' Town by late afternoon. Caran handed over to Toya. She called ahead to Kara Island, spoke to someone about a twenty-footer – V-hull if they had one – with the best outboard engine they could find. She wanted it fitted and ready by the time we got to Kara Island.

She cleared an area in the sand, drew what looked like a giant question mark. The tail, she said, was half a mile wide with rock-islands on either side. It was the entrance to Blackwater – nasty water, yes, but no sensible boat avoided it, else it meant a three-hour journey further out to avoid the acres of reefs and 'rock-heads'.

If we placed ourselves on Goat Island, we'd have a full-frontal view of the approaching boat – that was, if our guess was right.

We left Leapers' Bay under a menacing sky with clouds stacked in brooding formations overhead.

'It going to take some time,' the captain said. The fella was so neatly dressed, he looked like an office worker.

With a sea gone black and resentful under us, we entered Blackwater channel an hour later, the engine of the ancient Boston whaler barely managing to push the boat, the craft hardly righting itself before another wave struck it.

'Current,' the captain said.

'Goat Island.' Toya pointed straight ahead. In the gloom,

about half a mile in front, the low, loaf-like shape from which multi-jointed cacti rose in towers. Between Goat Island and our boat were the dreadful seething waters of Devil Tooth.

Miss Stanislaus sat cross-legged, ponchoed and at peace, tending her nails, a plastic cap – elasticated around the edges – protecting her hair.

The captain swung hard left, the boat wallowed and righted itself. Directly ahead was Kara Island.

Toya moved forward, said something in the captain's ear. She looked back at me and straightened an arm at the stretch of water north-east of Kara Island – the wide open Atlantic.

When we docked, Caran camped us down at the entrance to the jetty. The world had gone opaque with rain.

The twenty-footer that had been prepared for us was a fibreglass affair with Mercury Verado EFI 200 imprinted on the engine.

Miss Stanislaus said she would stay behind. Caran pretended he did not hear her protests when he ordered his two men to remain with her. She came forward, gave me one of those wordless face-searches, then backed away, her gaze never leaving my face.

At 3.30am., Toya Furore aimed the boat at the darkness with Caran and I sitting on the plank of wood that served as a seat. Her LED torch once again taped to her helmet. She'd fitted a long rod to the steering, which allowed her to be almost at the front of the craft. I looked at Caran, then at the back of the woman, her body curved forward, her rifle slung over her shoulder. He nodded at me and smiled, and I thought I saw a man who would go to the ends of the earth with his crew and, without a worry, place his life in their hands.

Toya took us to the back of Goat Island, the engine tut-tutting as she eased us through the waterways between the reef that half-girdled the island. She cut the engine, held out a steadying hand to me as I stepped onto a stone beach. We helped her lodge the keel of the boat in the space between two boulders.

She took us on foot up the side of the island through cactus and bramble that seemed intent on plucking out our eyes.

Then we were down the other side, drenched to the bone, facing the storming waters. We spread out on a low rock-shelf, settled down and waited.

The rain let up, enough for us to glimpse the darkly glinting waters at the entrance of the channel. I took deep breaths to settle my nerves and bypass the feeling of futility.

Through the curtain of rain, I noticed the first trace of morning in the direction where I imagined Camaho would be. Then a hint of colour on the water below us.

I'd probably got it wrong. Maybe the boat was going somewhere else. We should have handed this job over to the US coast guard fellas as the Commissioner suggested. Chilman! Stubborn ole goat – full of fuckin demons, making a fool of himself. And us!

I looked at my watch. 4.30.

At 4.36, I felt the throbbing in the air.

I raised a hand at Caran and Toya, heard the *thack* of metal, saw Caran settling the big gun against his shoulder, his cheek fused against the barrel. Toya sat between a fork in the rock, legs folded under her, the stock of the rifle jammed against her shoulders. I released the catch of the AK47 and took a breath.

It emerged out of the dawn sky, wraithlike in the mist. I felt a quiver of disbelief and awe as the thing took shape. Black, sleek, creating its own tide behind it – a high white arch of spume, bristling silver against the pale sky. The sound that came from the speeding boat shredded the morning air.

And then it was upon us. Caran's shoulders were convulsing with the kick of the PKM. I'd braced myself against the rock and leaned on the trigger. Toya sat calm as a Buddha, her rifle dipping and swerving as she tried to follow the trajectory of the boat. We might as well have pointed the gun at the sky and hoped to hit it.

I glimpsed four figures. Black puffer jackets. Cowled. The curved windscreen angled over them. A black-gloved hand shot out, aimed at the stretch of water west of Kara Island.

We'd decided to shoot at the engines in case they got past us. A boiling plume of water hid them.

And I thought, To hell with it, I might as well allow myself to marvel at the fuckin thing. Watch it run – something to talk about to the fellas afterward: a demon boat with hydra-headed engines that moved on water like a plane.

It had finished the turn and was straightening out for the big sprint to the ocean, the thunder of the engines upping several octaves, the bow of the craft tilting further upward.

I stood up, wiped the sweat from my face, saw the extended arm jerk sideways, and then what sounded like a scream – pitched high and bright and terrible.

The owner of the outstretched arm stumbled back as if pulled by some abrupt invisible hand. Then the driver's head switched back, and it became all white water and confusion. The craft banked on a wave, bucked sharply upwards and for a couple of seconds took flight in a backward somersault. The engines wound down like a landing aircraft. The crosstides began a heaving, spitting dogfight over it. The catamaran dipped and tossed until it canted over, washed by great hillocks of water. Then it began the fast southward drift on the tide.

Caran was on his feet. 'Digger, what happen deh? You score?'

I shook my head.

He turned querying eyes on Toya. She too shook her head. 'Could've been you, Chief.' She pointed at the big gun.

392

He pulled in his lips, blinked at the dipping carcass of the boat. 'Not me!'

'Pilot make a mistake, then. Mebbe,' I said. It was all I felt like saying.

'Venezuela,' Toya muttered. 'Tide take it right back there. If coast guard don't long-stop it.'

She jerked her head at the rocks overhead.

We packed up and followed her.

There was a small crowd on the jetty – people who looked more interested in the guns in our hands than in us.

Miss Stanislaus was smiling at me as if to say, 'Missa Digger, we done good.'

'We done good,' I said.

A chuckle burst out of her. 'How you know what I was finkin?'

'Your face,' I said. 'But I not satisfied, Miss Stanislaus.'

She went still as if she were listening to me with her body. Then she dropped a hand on my arm and squeezed.

65

The Justice Minister lined us up behind him, with our hands behind our backs like we were schoolkids in his choir, while Camaho's press corps aimed their cameras at the man. It was because of his policy, his vision, his efforts to create a police force to rival any in the region that the nation was celebrating this victory today – which was why, on 13 March next year, citizens of Camaho could not jeopardise the nation's security by voting for the opposition.

A foolish person would have thought the MJ had been out there on Blackwater himself, chasing after the boat.

I wouldn't have turned up for the press meeting had Chilman not accused me of threatening the future of the Department again.

At the end, the minister summoned us to his office. A yellow hunk of a man, more fat than muscle, who had to squeeze himself sideways through his office door in order to get through it. The air condition was on full blast as usual, his poor secretary sat padded in layers.

Chilman pushed himself past me and poked my hip. 'Digson, watch yourself!'

The MJ mopped his brow, rested jaundiced, fat-cushioned eyes on us and asked us what happened. We assumed the question was rhetorical. We said nothing.

Who the hell did we think we were?

Rhetorical again.

Had we forgotten that we were supposed to inform him through the appropriate channels . . .

For a fuckin change.

. . . of any important exercise such as the one we'd so recklessly embarked on? All the more, because we were ignorant of the bigger picture. Weren't we aware that the war on drugs was a regional concern? American funding came with it, which Camaho could not do without. And – a fat finger in our faces – the last thing anyone wanted was to let our friends in North America even *think* that we could do this on our own. We couldn't!

'We just did,' I said.

Miss Stanislaus, who had chosen to sit directly behind me, kicked my leg.

So, by those parameters, the MJ said, San Andrews CID would be foolish to call the operation a success.

'It was, Sir.'

Miss Stanislaus kicked me again.

Chilman cleared his throat. 'Mister Minister, the fact is we stop them. I don't even want to think what that would've meant for your personal reputation and your ministry if we didn't. I don't even want to imagine how the opposition was going to twist the facts and make it look like the Minister of Justice himself was hampering the investigation by getting in the way of justice.' Chilman coughed, pulled out a wrinkled handkerchief and patted his cheek. 'With aaall the respect I should owe you, Sir, I feel the Justice Minister is cussin San Andrews CID for doing cardinal work.' Chilman coughed again. 'What worrying me now, Sir, is what the Prime Minister will think when he get to hear—'

'DS Chilman!' The MJ stuck a finger in the air. 'I was

referring to third-party perceptions. Not the commendable job you people did. Didn't I make that sufficiently clear to the press out there?'

I shook my head. 'Nuh, Sir, you didn't. How, if I may ask, Sir, do third-party perceptions invalidate the fact that San Andrews CID verifiably and effectively implemented the job that we have been employed to do in accordance with Camaho's policing and government objectives? And why, if I may ask again, Sir, you already using it to promote your electioneering goals when you label it as a failure?'

He stiffened at my words, swung his head towards Chilman. 'That's the quality of staff you see fit to employ in your department? What does he know about government objectives? Was he listening to what I just said? Did he understand anything? And is he still in my office?'

I took his cue, got up, excused myself and walked out.

I hung around till they came out. Chilman marched over, manoeuvred me out on the grass and stuck a finger in my face. I took the cussing, even the manhandling, as he backed me against his car, his finger now under my nose. He threw a quick glance up at the window on the third floor, dropped himself in his car and banged the door.

I glanced up at the window too. The MJ was no longer there. 'He gone now,' I said.

The old DS had his head on the steering wheel, his body heaving with laughter.

Miss Stanislaus was tinkling like a Christmas tree.

Chilman poked out his head. 'Digson, where you get them words from? You went to England for one blaastid year, and they send you back to colonise we arse again. Meet me at the office!'

'Missa Digger, I ever tell you, you not a bad fella at all?'

'Once or twice, Miss Stanislaus, with caveats.'

'Well, you not. Shall we persevere?'
'Persevere we shall, Miss Stanislaus.'
'Missa Digger, somefing on your mind, not so?'
'Mebbe.'
'I sure.'

66

Chilman chose to have us unpack the case at San Andrews Central police station. He invited the area chiefs from around the island, the fellas from the coast guard and a couple of big-wigs from our tiny army. A long, low-ceilinged room, no windows, fluorescent lights. The low-level hum of the air-conditioning.

'Is of national importance,' Chilman told us.

'Is to show off,' Miss Stanislaus mumbled in my ear.

As if to confirm her point, DS Chilman sidled up to me. 'Digson, I want you to go technical on their arse, but don't lose them. No politics either. Okay?' He covered his grin with a cough and sat in front.

I detailed the incidents of the case. Then pulled the narrative together. Pet sat in the aisle, a notepad on her lap.

'For the purposes of this case we got nine deaths – three murders, two deaths by police, and the presumed drowning of four people – three males and a female.

'Let's start with Lazar Wilkinson. Lazar used to pick up the marijuana that Juba brought from Vincen Island on a boat named *Retribution*. Lazar Wilkinson ferried the weed back to Camaho. That was his relationship with Juba Hurst until, three months ago, Juba Hurst moved his cocaine-cooking operation from Kara Island to Camaho for reasons that I'll go into later.

'To help with the processing, Lazar Wilkinson put forward Jonathon Rayburn – I'll refer to him as Jana Ray from now on. Jana Ray was a gifted eighteen-year-old schoolboy, useful to them for his knowledge of chemistry. Purifying cocaine paste involves the use of sulphuric acid, ammonia and potassium permanganate and the extraction of a range of impurities. Jana Ray learned the process quickly.

'I have strong reasons to believe that Lazar Wilkinson died at the hands of the man in Camaho who ran the whole operation. Lazar Wilkinson recruited the boys who cooked and purified the paste that came with the boat from Venezuela. He also recruited Jonathon Rayburn. Lazar Wilkinson was offered a fee for his part of the job but he rejected it on the grounds that Beau Séjour was his village, his territory and rather than be paid a fee they should give him a percentage of the worth of the cocaine. That would've meant a lot more money, of course. He threatened to report the operation to the police in the middle of the refining process if they didn't agree to his demands. The man who oversaw the operation wanted to plant the fear of God in anybody who thought of dictating those kinda terms or spilling to the police. That, I think, accounts for the slit throat and the pulled-out tongue.'

'Who's the man in question?' That was the coast guard.

'Luther Caine.'

I waited through the silence and quick exchange of looks.

'You sure is Luther Caine?'

'I have the evidence.'

'Where's he right now?' South Region sounded uneasy.

'Presumed dead. He was one of the four on the boat.'

'Not that Luther Caine from—'

'Camaho got only one Luther Caine.' I enjoyed their consternation; waited for the mumbles to subside.

'You find out who the woman was?'

399

'One Sandra Fernandez, she called herself Sarona. Venezuelan, I believe. Lazar Wilkinson's weakness was women. I believe the manner in which he was killed came from the Venezuelan woman who used her body as bait to catch him off guard. Her job was to keep an eye on things, including the police, and ensure that the shipment got to its destination.'

'Where Juba Hurst fit into all of this?' Manus Maine – from what he claimed – was the original CID of Camaho until we stole their jobs. They wished us dead.

'Up to three months ago, Juba had his own cocaine-cooking operation on the east side of Kara Island. He murdered an old man named Koku Stanislaus to acquire his property for his operations. When the cocaine base arrived, Juba refined it and sent it on. That's been going on for some time. Three months ago, some senior citizens of Kara Island – all females over sixty – started a guerilla campaign against him by burning down his operation every time he left for Vincen Island.

The room rumbled with chuckles.

'Is funny till y'all experience them,' I said. 'We could even say that it was the old wimmen of Kara Island who drove the operation to Camaho. Operation was already set up when Juba met his, erm, demise.

'It also looks to me that Luther Caine and the woman were running against some sort of deadline, the boat wasn't meant to be in Camaho that long. Two broken engines held them back.

'I sure of one thing: if the shipment didn't come from Venezuela – keep in mind that Colombia, Peru and Bolivia produce the stuff, and Colombia just next door to Venezuela – it came through Venezuela and was handled by Venezuelan nationals. Right now, Venezuela is a jumping-off point for smuggling through the Caribbean to the east coast of the USA and across the Atlantic to West Africa and Europe.

'Miss Tamara, who did some part-time work for the drivers, confirmed the two fellas who controlled the boat spoke Spanish. Besides, I picked up four condom wrappers, branded Manana, at Hellon House. The sticker on the packet was from a store in Caracas named Dia Dia.'

'How you know that?' somebody asked.

'Google,' I said.

'Wozzat?' another voice asked.

'Google it and find out,' I said.

Pet laughed out loud.

'The boat,' Chilman coughed.

'What didn't make sense to me was the destination. A forty-foot catamaran with no more than a windshield to protect the occupants from the weather can't reach Europe.'

Manus Maine raised a hand. I ignored it.

The Head of the Drugs Squad looked confused. 'So you work out where they going?'

'Yes.'

'And it wasn't Europe, so . . . '

I decided to confuse him even more. 'It was, Sir.'

'Then they had a ship waiting?'

'No, Sir.'

I left him with that and went to fetch a cup of water. Chilman looked relaxed and blissful; Pet, as if she wanted to kill me.

'DC Digson, you going stop the head-game and explain what you saying?' Manus Maine was jutting a chin at me.

'Technically, if you dunno it yet, Missa Manus, Martinique is part of Europe. Once you in Martinique or Guadeloupe, you in France. Don't ask me about the logic, but is so.

Martinique is a hundred and fifty miles from Camaho. Why Europe? As a matter of interest they got around five million people across there using up thirty per cent of all the cocaine in the world. And they willing to pay more than twice the price that Americans pay.'

'Back to the woman, Digger.' Manus Maine again. 'You say the boat capsize in Blackwater, foreday morning, so was not bright outside. You say it was raining and it got a lotta rough water all about. How you so sure was a woman you see?'

'I saw her arm, outstretched, and I made a calculation.'

Manus Maine laughed. Chilman raised a brow at me.

'Is called osteometry.'

'Wozzat?' he said.

'Google it,' I said.

'That's all?' Gill wanted to know.

'Yessir, till we find the bodies. I mean, if we lucky. Anything else? Because I tired.'

Malan left the back of the room, came up to me and dropped a hand on my shoulder. 'Nice one, Digger.'

'Same to you,' I said, and drifted over to Caran's unit.

'You two not bad,' Toya said, nodding at Miss Stanislaus and I.

'You amazing,' I said.

'I know,' Toya replied, and the fellas beside her nodded as if they were the only true words they'd heard all day.

'Missa Digger, where you off to now?' Miss Stanislaus was at my elbow.

Caran's group stood at ease, looking down at Miss Stanislaus with something close to adoration. She offered a hand to each. The fellas leaned forward with tiny bows and took it. Toya opened her arms, Miss Stanislaus stepped into them and they hugged like they'd been living in the same house for centuries.

Miss Stanislaus nudged me away from the group. 'We take some breeze this evenin?'

'I need sleep, Miss Stanislaus. I going home.'

'So early?'

'Uh-huh.'

'You sure?'

I pretended I didn't hear her.

67

Like I told Miss Stanislaus, I wasn't satisfied.

I let myself into the office at midnight and went to the storeroom. I switched on the light and hung there a while, studying the shelf of cartridges and the floor. The last time I came in here at some odd hour in the morning was when Miss Stanislaus had armed herself to shoot down the man who'd usurped her as a child. She had good reason, I decided. I relaid the SWS rifle exactly as I met it – in its usual place. I went to the kitchen area, dried my hands and left.

By 1am I was two-thirds of the way up the western coast. I swerved into the rough dirt road that led to Maran Bay. The sea glittered under a flat white moon. The leaves of the dead seagrape trees that bordered the beach were chattering in a high wind. I approached the little building from the beach – more hut than house, built with rough sea wood. A canvas tarpaulin for a roof, anchored by heavy stones to keep the wind from tearing it off. A row of oil drums along one side of the shack, the curved stem of a standpipe above a galvanised enclosure. On the right side of the construction, partly covered with tarpaulin, the sanded hull of the cigarette boat that Spiderface had been building for as long as I had known him.

I slipped the latch of the rickety door, navigated past an old table and, with the light of my cellphone, side-stepped a few half-broken chairs. Stacks of sagging crocus bags and fishing tackle against the wall.

I didn't have to search for the bedroom, I followed the sound of Spider's breathing. I entered and pulled the string that led to a light bulb directly over the pallet he used as a bed.

He'd turned his face to the wall, his breathing deep and regular. I'd seen Spiderface napping on the job many times, always with his mouth open. Now it was closed, the trapezoid muscles along his back so tense they pushed against his flimsy vest. I slipped off my belt, stepped back and kicked the bed.

He sprang up from the old mattress, sliding his hand in one slick motion under the pillow. It emerged with a vicious-looking machete. The buckle of my belt shot out and struck the blade just above his fingers. The weapon leapt from his hand and clattered to the floor.

He staggered back, spun around to face me and blinked.

'Is me, Spiderface. Sit down.'

He dropped his hands, looked back at the bed. 'Missa Digger, what I do? I-I didn do nothing . . .'

'That's for me to decide, Spider-Man. I told you to sit down.'

He perched on the edge of the bed.

I looped the heavy leather around my wrist, lowered my shoulders and pushed my face close to his. 'How long I know you, Spiderface?' I pushed a stiffened finger against his fore-head. 'Two years – give or take a coupla months? That's how long we been rolling together, not so?'

He brought his hands together. 'Missa Digger . . .'

I looked around the room. His walls were covered with cut-out pictures of boats – all kinds and shapes – on the high seas and on shore.

'I see you finish the boat,' I said. 'And you got a chance to test it!'

405

He wiped his mouth with the back of his hand and would not look at me.

'Come,' I said, dropping a hand in his shoulder. 'Put on some clothes. We got to talk, so I taking you for a walk.'

'The DS . . . erm, Missa Chilman . . . He know?'

'Depending on what you tell me, he may never need to know.'

68

I stayed at home all day. When I returned from seeing Spiderface, I found Dessie on my sofa. She shed her clothing and slid into bed beside me. I let her have her way. At the end of it, she got up, dressed and told me she was done with me, she wanted to move on.

'Fine,' I said.

'That's all?' she snapped.

'No is not, but that will do for now. Anyway, your life sorted now!'

'Meaning?' She hung at the door, eyes sullen on my face.

'You have your own house, big enough to live like Dessie wants to live. With your husband gone, is all yours.'

'Digger, what're you talking about?'

'Go safe, Dessie. Look after yourself.'

'Digger, why you talking to me like that?'

'You tell me you want to move on. I accept. What's wrong with that? If you expect me to crawl, I not going to!'

She wasn't looking at me now. She was rubbing the heel of her shoe against the sofa leg as if she were scraping something off it.

Dessie straightened up and threw me a furious look. 'Arrogant!' she snapped.

'Unreasonable!' I threw back.

As she was leaving, she kicked at the glass of my cabinet and told me I wasn't the Digger she used to know, then slammed the door behind her.

In the afternoon, Miss Stanislaus called and asked was I ready to take some breeze with her?

I told her I had to go out later.

She wanted to know when and where. I didn't answer.

'Jus checkin,' she said and hung up.

Late evening, I showered and dressed in a plain white cotton shirt and a pair of close-fitting jeans. I slipped on my pair of Convos, took my belt off its nail then mixed myself a Camaho cocktail. I put on some music – Nancy Sinatra's 'Bang Bang My Baby Shot Me Down' – magical and dreamy and so full of wistfulness it brought a tightness to my throat.

I shut down the player and took to the road.

Through the fast-advancing night, I headed for the yacht marina in San Andrews. I slowed the car just before the round-about in Canteen and looked over at the marina, bristling with masts. Camaho's first capital, abandoned when the British realised they'd built it around the crater of a sleeping volcano that the sea had made into a lagoon. On the hill above the shivering water stood the carcass of a bombed-out house Camahoans called Dread House because a man the nation used to love ruled the island from up there. It was in the big hall of that crumbling mansion that his party comrades summoned him and made him know that if he did not do as he was told they would destroy him. Five days later he was dead.

I pulled up on the grass verge facing a restaurant and bar that sat on the waters of the marina. I ducked into a narrow concrete alleyway, past small dim rooms lit up by giant flatscreen televisions and fridge freezers half the size of each room. The air about me was rattling with dub-step bass and soca music.

Beaumont, Camaho's underbelly: houses stacked ten rows deep with a mesh of shoulder-width alleyways between them. The inhabitants here were neither poor nor rich. They could get whatever took a person's fancy. They supplied the best weed on the island, could pick out an agent of the law blindfolded. A special breed of Camahoans who thrived in the shadowy space just outside the law.

I'd heard enough to know that women ruled this place, repulsing the aggression of their nomadic men with their own brand of tight-faced, don't-fuck-with-me ferocity. Anybody who had no business here was an intruder or an enemy.

Women sat on the walls of narrow concrete verandas staring me down with frank, assessing eyes. One of them, in a buttercup-yellow dress, hair flaring from her head, leaned over and curled a finger. 'Ay, Sweetman, you want some sugar?' She shifted a hip sideways and began bouncing on the wall.

I opened my palms and smiled. 'Thanks for the offer, Miss. I'd've really liked that, yunno, but I got diabetes.' Their brassy laughter beat against my ears.

I had no doubt that Malan liked it here, the way I liked Old Hope. I imagined him as a boy scrapping his way through all this shit with quick fists and a fast mouth until the dangerousness he carried now became as natural to him as breathing. He'd mentioned his mother once, told me that a tree would have done a better job of raising him. Then he'd laughed that hissing, dark-eyed laugh of his. I wondered where his wife and girlchild were now. I decided it was none of my business.

I climbed the steps.

Before I raised my hand to tap the door, his voice reached me. 'Digger, come in.'

Quick dark eyes scanned my body, halted at my waist then settled on my face.

409

He was dressed in knee-length shorts, green khaki, a black T-shirt with a button opened at the front. Rubber slippers a size too large for his feet.

His Sig Sauer was on the table in front of him, its muzzle aimed at the door.

'Offer me a seat, Malan.'

'Take one,' he said. He was staring into my face with a look that I could not work out, but there was no challenge there. He lifted the gun and slipped it into his waistband.

'Digger, what you want dis time o' night?'

'Offer me a drink, Malan. Is the polite thing to do.'

He rose abruptly and strolled to the kitchen.

I pulled a seat and sat down. Malan returned and placed an opened bottle of Malta and a glass in front of me.

'What's up?' he said.

'You mind sitting down?'

'Digger, stop fuckin with my head. Else I throw you outta my place, right now, y'unnerstan?'

I felt my heart quicken, my mouth go dry. I'd seen young men on the streets step away from him at the slightest frown. Bartenders grew nervous when he placed an elbow on their counter and leaned in close. I'd even seen a couple of them drop a brimming glass. I'd also observed how that same attitude attracted a certain kind of woman to him. The only person in the world I knew who would happily take the fight to Malan Greaves was Miss Stanislaus. Secretly, I envied her.

I allowed my eyes to skim the walls – bare except for a picture of a bull fighter, thin and stiff as a matchstick, side-stepping a wounded beast.

'You made a mistake,' I said.

'What you talkin bout, Digger?'

'Only one person in the world I know could shoot like that. Remember I see you do it before – take out two Vincen

Island fellas in a speeding boat from Top Hill on Kara Island after they robbed the bank in the Drylands. I saw you do it to make Sarona love you more – yunno, mix the love with the violence and the fear – when you shot that ramgoat on Dog Island. I even went to the storeroom to make sure I wasn't guessing. You did your best to dry the SWS, but the canvas bag was still wet.

'Digger, I don' have no time for—'

I pushed the drink aside and looked him in the eyes. 'I prefer you shut your mouth and hear me out, rather than gimme a set of lies. I fed up of lies right now.'

He pushed himself back abruptly, threw me a quick dry smile. 'Go on – shoot your crap.'

'I think it hit you when we ruled out Tamara from the investigation. And when them boat-fellas knew in advance that we were coming for them. And you no fool, Malan, you thought about what I told you in the marketplace. It strike you that the woman we been after had to be Sarona. Then when she told you that she was taking a trip – mebbe out of some kind of feelings for you because she could've up and leave. Mebbe she think that it hurt worse if she just break and disappear. Mebbe she—'

Malan shot up from the chair. He'd pushed a finger in my face and was breathing hard. 'Talk your talk, Digger. But don't fuck with my head, y'unnerstan. I not takin that from you . . . '

I rose to face him. 'Take your finger from my face, Malan.'

'And if I don't, what you goin do about it?'

'If you don't drop that fuckin finger from my face, right now – I break it, y'unnerstan? Then shoot me if you want to, like you shot your woman.'

He dropped his hand, began circling the room, his eyes on me like a boxer.

411

'What I saying is that the woman was a plant. Me and Miss Stanislaus been chasing after Tamara becuz of the description I got from lil Eric and his friends in Beau Séjour. Fool me too cuz if you pull off the braids, cut the hair and dye it black, you could confuse one of them for the other. Sarona' job was to keep her finger on the pulse of the police. Coming to think of it, she might've had something to do with Shadowman killing Jana Ray too. She saw Jana Ray with us – the police – and she must've made the connection that he knew enough to blow the whole operation. I believe Sarona done this before. She's too good at it.

'You realise how she used you, and you wanted to hit back. So what you do? You make Spiderface risk his life and yours, middle of the night, and take you to Kara Island. You make him swear to keep it secret. You nearly got away with it, except for the one mistake you made. You shot Sarona first when you should've shot the driver. But you had to make sure you take her out for the arse she made of you. In other words, your feelings override your training.'

He'd gone still. The black eyes on my mouth.

'You shot the woman,' I said. I pointed at my ear. 'Through all that rain and ruction at Blackwater, believe it or not, Malan, I heard Sarona scream when your bullet hit her.'

He'd rested his back against the glass window, his head tilted at the ceiling.

I sat back, the sweat prickling my neck, the night suddenly suffocating.

A tight, red-eyed smile tensed his face. 'People can't make no case against me. I not admittin to nothing. But let's say people decide to point dem finger at me. In a court of law, the evidence will show that I do my job. De job was to stop the boat. Nobody could prove different. So I dunno what you come here for.'

412

'To let you know I not your fool.'

'You think I dunno that? Digger, you an De Woman, y'all the real thing. You fink I don't envy y'all sometimes – watchin the way y'all does flex your brains togedder? You think it don't upset me becuz me'n'you start off working good together and soon as she come, you give over yourself to 'er? Me! From de time I little so!' He lowered a hand a couple of inches above the tabletop. 'Me, Malan Greaves, I decide I come first. Everything else come after me. I follow the rules as far as I could, but Malan Greaves come first. Nothing I can do bout that.'

He threw me a fierce sideways look. 'You ever ask yourself why Chilman choose us?'

'In the early days, yes—'

'Not no more? You still don't work it out? He's not no talent spotter, he's a fuckin demon-hunter becuz he's a demon himself.'

'I dunno where you goin with that, Malan.'

He jabbed a finger at his head. 'What me, you an De Woman got in common, Digger? Use your brain!' He'd raised his voice, his face screwed up as if he were in pain. 'De hole! Dat's what we got. De hole inside we head – your mother gone, you dunno where she gone; you know you'll never find 'er, but you still lookin for your mother. De Stanislaus Woman got 'er soul cut out by a fella and every man she kill is him.'

'And you?'

'You don want to know bout me.'

'I want to know bout you.'

'I not tellin you, Digger. Fuck outta my house and go do what you have to do.'

He blinked, swung his head away from me, but not before I saw the tears.

413

I left him staring past his reflection in the window into the night.

Malan, hard-nut, badjohn. Crying! Malan Greaves – the little fella his mother left with the man she ran away from. The man didn't go looking for another woman to replace his mother because little Malan Greaves would serve him just as well – that was, until Malan stuck a knife in the fella's throat and walked.

Malan Greaves, trying so hard to prove to himself that he wasn't what that fella made of him. Still not sure if he was a man because of all that.

And he thought I didn't know. Pet did – Admin Pet who knew everything.

Is hard to hate a pusson when you know that much about them. Because you've found the string to pull, to unravel the big hard ball they pretend to be. You either leave it alone or pull the string and run, and hope to God you get away. It was what I'd been trying to tell Sarona when I met her in the marketplace that one last time.

Back on the road, I cleared my throat and spat at the dark, became aware of a woman-shape on the grass verge on my right, just outside the pool of brightness thrown by the streetlight. My heart flipped over. Miss Stanislaus, her hair held down by a black headwrap. Dark, loose-fitting trousers and a top to match. Dressed for the night and concealment.

'What you doing here?' I said.

I heard the rattle of Chilman's car just around the corner, driving off. 'Same thing you doing here, Missa Digger.' She raised a finger at Malan's house. 'I have to say I reach here a lil while before you.' She sidled a glance at the restaurant over the water; answered the question I was about to ask. 'Is only Malan does sour up your face like that. I see the way you keep looking at him. And twice in the office you open the drawer with them han'cuff and twice you close it back. I don't even think you realise it. Besides you didn want to go nowhere with me no matter how I ask. So I figure! Besides, t'was not nice at all the way y'was lookin at him.'

'I don't see the logic, Miss Stanislaus.'

'Well, I was right, not so? What I want to know is why you have to go to Malan house half-naked!'

'I not half-naked.'

'Might as well be. You don't do it again, Missa Digger.' Her eyes were fierce on my face, her voice sibilant with irritation. 'Not with him. I keep tellin you, sometimes you behave stupid.'

She swung her small handbag in front of her and dropped in her Ruger. 'Come, Missa Digger, is hifalutin dining for us tonight. I done book a table.' Miss Stanislaus planted a hand on my arm and steered me across the road.

My phone buzzed. I picked up.

'Digson, I never finish the story about the Englishman and de tiger-puppy. You want to hear the rest?'

He'd stopped the car somewhere because I could no longer hear it.

'I listening, Sir.'

'Tiger feeding on Englishfella blood all de while, and he know that soon the tiger going want a lot more. He tell the servant to bring the pistol. Servant was out there long time looking for the gun. You could s'pose the servant hate the master who been running his life; or you could suppose the servant 'fraid to go back in that room. Anyway, servant bring the gun, and guess what happen?'

'Tiger eat them both.'

'Nuh, Englishman shoot de tiger. What you learn from that, Digson?'

415

'Dunno! Sometimes to save yourself, you got to destroy the thing you love?'

He said nothing for a while. 'I never see it like that.'

'How you see it?'

'What born to kill will kill. One day it will try to kill you for sure. You might have to kill it first.'

'You got your piece?' I said.

'Of course I got my piece.' He coughed into the handset and cut off. Then I heard the clatter of his engine. Chilman hadn't sounded drunk at all.

Miss Stanislaus and I turned into the marina. Ahead of us a row of dining places. The air was thick with the smell of seafood – roasted, fried and stewed and god-knew-what-else.

I followed Miss Stanislaus into Silvio's, a restaurant that was all burnished wood and tinkling cutlery, constructed on a small jetty.

At the table, Miss Stanislaus leaned into me, dropped her voice. 'What happen between you and Malan?'

'I had to make tiger-puppy know I got my eyes on him.'

'You not tellin me?'

'Another time. I hungry, let's eat.'

She smacked her lips, then narrowed her eyes. 'Missa Digger, y'ever wonder why Missa Malan stay clear of me?'

'Tell me, Miss Stanislaus.'

'You not goin to get upset?'

'Depends on what you say. Go ahead.'

She rested a hand on the white tablecloth. 'Well. Missa Malan know that before you shoot him down, you goin be countin aaall your fingers and aaall your toes first. By that time – pook! You dead! With me!' She raised her eyes at the room, suffused with soft candlelight and packed with the bobbing heads of rich locals and tourists. She brought

416

the white napkin to her lips and with the most delicate of movements, began patting them. 'He ain't got no doubt that I going to pull the trigger.'

Miss Stanislaus dropped the napkin on her lap. Her expression was strange when she looked at me again. 'Your face, Missa Digger, when you lef to kill that Shadowman fella.'

'What about it?'

'You wearin the same face now. Is Loofer Came you finkin bout?' Her smile was mocking.

'Luther Caine went down with the boat because of me, Miss Stanislaus. They wouldn't let me touch him here in Camaho, so I frightened him with the evidence I showed him. I frightened him onto the boat.'

'How?'

'I convinced him I knew all his dealings, and the US people were after him.'

'But you didn know the boat was going to drown.'

'Nuh, I alerted the French Islands, just in case. They would've been waiting.'

'An' Miss Dressy?'

'Dessie alright. She told me she done with me. I told her, fine, and she broke my expensive glass cabinet.'

'When she tell you she finish?'

'Well, uhm, right after our farewell get-together. Miss Stanislaus, I could tell you something?'

'Tell me.'

'You not going to get upset?'

'It depend, Missa Digger.'

'I prefer to destroy myself than to destroy the thing I love, or allow anybody to destroy it. And I not just thinking about Dessie. Don't get me wrong, Miss Stanislaus.'

She nodded, dropped her eyes on her hands and nodded again.

'Missa Digger, Miss Dressy will come back to you. That what you want?'

'Like you say to Pet – mebbe I dunno what I want. Or mebbe I know and I dunno that I know.'

She frowned, shook her head and soured her mouth. That made me laugh.

Miss Stanislaus offered me a sudden, bright smile. 'I talk to Daphne like you 'commend. I tell 'er everyfing. Before I halfway finish, she want to borrow Betsy and go shoot Juba Hurs' herself. I tell her he done gone already. She say she still want to find im and shoot im.' Miss Stanislaus shook with chuckles. 'Missa Digger, how chil'ren so silly?'

'Food in front of us, Miss Stanislaus. Shall we persevere?'

'Persevere we shall, Missa Digger.'

Jacob Ross was born in Grenada and now lives in Britain. A fellow of the Royal Society of Literature, he is the author of two acclaimed collections of short stories – *A Way to Catch the Dust* and *Song for Simone* – and *Tell No-One About This*, which was nominated by the 2018 Bocas Literary Festival as one of the three best works of Caribbean fiction published in 2017. His first novel, *Pynter Bender*, was shortlisted for the Commonwealth Writers' Regional Prize, and his debut crime novel, *The Bone Readers*, won the inaugural Jhalak Prize.